*Lin Carter's
Flashing Swords! #6*

SOME OTHER BOOKS OF INTEREST, AVAILABLE
FROM TIMAIOS PRESS:

Robert M. Price: *Reinterpreting the New Testament* — S.T. Joshi: *21st-Century Horror* — Bertil Falk: *A Mouthful of Eternity* — Abrigo & Hagström: *Veils Woven in Silence* — G.K.Chesterton: *The Wholeness of Father Brown* — Richard Marsh: *The Beetle* — Edgar Allan Poe: *The Journal of Julius Rodman* — Marie Belloc Lowndes: *The Lodger* — Lady Cavendish: *The Description of a New World, Called the Blazing-World* — Erasmus Darwin: *The Temple of Nature* — Camille Flammarion: *Lumen* — *Memorials of Andrew Crosse, the Electrician* — Lucretius: *On the Nature of Things* — J.M. Rymer & T.P. Prest: *The String of Pearls* — G.K. Chesterton: *Eugenics and Other Evils* — George MacDonald: *Phantastes* — And more.

Visit
www.timaiospress.com
Fact, Fiction and History of
Science and Ideas

Lin Carter's
FLASHING SWORDS!
#6

A Sword & Sorcery Anthology
Edited by Robert M. Price

TIMAIOS PRESS

EDITOR:
Robert McNair Price (b. 1954)
A former Baptist minister, today a well-known theologian and atheist debater, as well as a leading H.P. Lovecraft and weird fiction scholar. Before his death, the fantasy and science fiction author Lin Carter appointed Mr. Price as his literary executor.

COVER:
Art by Régis Moulun
Design by Nicolas Krizan

Timaios Press, Sweden
www.timaiospress.com
Imprint of Aleph Bokförlag

Copyright © 2020 by Timaios Press

All rights reserved
Printed and distributed worldwide by
Ingram Content Group LLC in La Vergne, TN, USA

First edition (paperback) from Pulp Hero Press, July 2020 (retracted)
Second edition (hardcover) from Timaios Press, January 2021
This is the third edition (paperback), January 2021

ISBN 978-91-87611-38-4

CONTENTS

Flashing Words ... 7
Introduction by Robert M. Price

❧

«A Prince of Mars» ... 13
Lin Carter & Robert M. Price

«Curse of the White Witch» ... 37
Wayne Judge

«Bellico and the Tower of Mouths» ... 72
Richard Toogood

«Immortals of Lemuria» ... 84
Robert M. Price

«The Vanishing Conjurer» ... 97
Glynn Owen Barrass

«World of the Black Sun» ... 111
Pierre V. Comtois

«Boscastle and the Swamp Enchantress» ... 136
Jason Ross Cummings

«Varla and the Mad Magician» ... 165
Steve Lines & Glen M. Usher

«Hercules versus the Cyclops» ... 182
Santiago del Dardano Turann

«Tonga of Lemuria» ... 195
Clayton L. Hinkle

FLASHING WORDS

Introduction

It could not be more timely to revive Lin Carter's highly regarded, well-remembered anthology series *Flashing Swords*. Its five volumes offered the best of new and old sword-and-sorcery tales. These books were fine successors to L. Sprague de Camp's many heroic fantasy collections (e.g., *Swords & Sorcery, Warlocks and Warriors*) as well as precursors to Andrew J. Offutt's excellent anthology series *Swords Against Darkness*. Yes, we might have resorted to cute rip-off titles like Clashing Swords or Clanging Swords, but why not just boldly return to Lin's original? Herewith: *Lin Carter's Flashing Swords #6*.

Lin's reputation as an anthologist (cf, his monumental Ballantine Adult Fantasy Series) has eclipsed his legacy as a writer of Fantasy and Science Fiction. Some readers would rather ignore his fiction, as if its very existence must take away from the fame he deserves as an editor. His chief sin in their eyes was the derivative character of much of his work. Certainly he loved to write pastiches of Edgar Rice Burroughs, Leigh Brackett, Robert E. Howard and others. But his goal in penning pastiche was essentially the same as in his editorial enterprise: in both he was trying to perpetuate the literary magic of previous generations for new readers. And there could never be enough of it, so he took it upon himself to add more to the canon, more in the old style(s). Did he succeed? You know he did. He had plenty of readers and fans in his lifetime. And today we find more than one website devoted to Lin Carter and to his greatest creation, Thongor of Lemuria. I find myself wishing he could have lived to see it. Lin was my good friend and designated me his literary executor. And I have in many ways tried my best to perpetuate his legacy. The book you are holding is my latest attempt.

Let me first explain why I regard this book as far more than an exercise in frivolous escapism. Skip my Intro if you want, but in case you are willing to consider larger issues, read on. I think you will find a deeper enrichment in our stories.

* * *

Many of today's social difficulties seem to me to boil down to what author

Ann Douglas called «the feminization of American culture.»[1] I guess I do not qualify as a «feminist» by the current definition, because those who think they own the term seem to think that, in order to qualify, you have to be pro-abortion and march lock-step to the Democratic Party line. You have to be a liberal. And that doesn't describe me. No, I don't qualify because all I believe is that women are at least the equals of men[2] and should be treated and paid as such. But that's not good enough for some people.

Women have endured a long history of oppression by men. Who can doubt that? The long night of male chauvinism is passing, but the pendulum is not settling down in the middle. I guess it never does. I think we are seeing powerful women trying to even the score. It is a doctrine of academic and radical feminism that maleness is a destructive poison that has ruined the world for so long and must now be «cured,» even exorcised. This trend has been evident for some years.[3] Ever notice how fathers are portrayed in sitcoms and TV commercials? As clueless, blundering fools. I see this as propaganda. But someone will say, «Yeah, but look how awfully women were portrayed in movies, comics, TV shows, for so long!» Right you are! But this is just what I'm talking about: two wrongs making a right is the ideology of revenge, not justice.

The «zero tolerance» policy for schools that leads to children being sent home for pointing fingers at each other and playing «Bang-bang!»[4] is part of an ultra-liberal ethos that wants to promote a Unisex model, and that one sex is *female*. Boys must have their budding masculinity «educated» out of

---

1 Ann Douglas, *The Feminization of American Culture* (New York: Avon Books, 1983). See also Edmond Hamilton's story «He That Hath Wings,» in Leigh Brackett, ed., *The Best of Edmond Hamilton* (New York: Ballantine Books / A Del Rey Book, 1977). Charles Hoffman calls it «a moving allegory about the domestication and emasculation of the modern American male.»
2 Ashley Montagu, *The Natural Superiority of Women* (Alta Mira Press / Sage Publications; 5th Edition, 1999).
3 Caroline Hennessey, *I, B.I.T.C.H., Have Had it: A Manifesto of Female Liberation* (New York: Lancer Books, 1970); Shulamith Firestone, *The Dialectic of Sex: The Case for Feminist Revolution* (New York: Bantam Books, 1972).
4 Alec Torres, «Ten-Year-Old Boy Suspended for Pointing Finger Like a Gun.» https://www.nationalreview.com/corner/ten-year-old-boy-suspended-pointing-finger-gun-alec-torres/ ; Andy Campbell, «6-Year-Old Suspended for Pointing Fingers in the Shape of a Gun.» https://www.huffpost.com/entry/6-year-old-fingers-shape-of-gun-suspended_n_6813864

them.¹ Sports and games must no longer be based on competition, lest someone feel dejected because of his mediocrity.² Poor little flowers! This, in case you hadn't noticed, is no way to prepare young men (or women!) for adult life in a Free Market economy and in a world full of powerful national enemies.

The continuous false rape accusations³ serve the same end, seeking to make masculinity, even the natural male interest in women, into a «rape culture.» Of course, such wolf-crying works *against* women because soon it will become habitual to dismiss every rape accusation as the shrill lying of yet another Lena Dunham.⁴ (Am I thus suggesting we ease up on rapists? No; you don't want to *know* what I think ought to be done with those bastards.) Nor is it only the self-defeating futility of crying «Wolf!» There's more at work here. It smacks of an ideology of man-hating.

I have long been puzzled at the feminist hatred of pornography.⁵ «It re-

---

1 Liz Plank, *For the Love of Men: From Toxic to a More Mindful Masculinity* (New York: St. Martin's Press, 2019); Jared Yates Sexton, *The Man They Wanted Me to Be: Toxic Masculinity and a Crisis of Our Own Making* (Counterpoint, 2020); Lisa Wade and Myra Marx Ferree, *Gender: Ideas, Interactions, Institutions* (New York: W.W. Norton, 2nd ed., 2018), Christina Hoff Sommers, *The War Against Boys: How Misguided Policies Are Harming our Young Men* (New York: Simon & Schuster, 2015); Leonard Sax, *Boys Adrift: The Five Factors Driving the Growing Epidemic of Unmotivated Boys and Underachieving Young Men* (New York: Basic Books, 2016); Warren Farrell and John Gray, *The Boy Crisis: Why our Boys Are Struggling and What We Can Do about it* (New York: BenBella Books, 2019).
2 T. Marice Huggins, «Negatives of Competitive Sports.» https://www.sportsrec.com/5027609/what-are-the-benefits-of-competitive-sports-for-youth). Nevin Martel, «Giving Kids Participation Awards Is Robbing Them of a Vital Lesson: How to Lose.» *Washingtonian* August 7, 2017. https://www.washingtonian.com/2017/08/07/giving-kids-participation-awards-is-robbing-them-of-a-vital-lesson-how-to-lose/
3 https://healthresearchfunding.org/8-false-rape-accusation-statistics/; Larry Kummer, «Hidden knowledge: false rape accusations are common»; https://fabiusmaximus.com/2018/09/23/false-rape-accusations-are-common/. «Duke lacrosse case» https://en.wikipella Books, 20enBdia.org/wiki/Duke_lacrosse_case.
4 Selwyn Duke, «Lena Dunham, UVA, and False Rape Accusations.» https://www.thenewamerican.com/usnews/crime/item/19679-lena-dunham-uva-and-false-rape-accusations.)
5 Andrea Dworkin, *Pornography: Men Possessing Women* (Baltimore: Penguin Books, 1974). I trust it is evident that I am concerned here only with this one aspect of

duces women to sex objects!» Absurd. It is simply a highlighting of a particular aspect of beautiful women. It is no different from fashion modeling. Does that reduce fashion models to animated mannequins? If I were a sports fan, it would not occur to me to think of the athletes as no more than exploited cattle. There is much more to all such public people. But what we do not see of their lives is none of our business. This is why our society's voyeuristic curiosity about the private lives and scandals of celebrities is so pathetically sick. So then I have to wonder, «Are these feminists really protesting male sexual interest in women *per se*?» A woman may be a «sex object,» if that's what you want to call it, without being a «mere» sex object. But when feminists refuse to draw such a line, I start thinking of Jill Johnson's book *Lesbian Nation*,[1] in which she argues that all feminism is at bottom Lesbianism.

In some schools boys are encouraged to play with dolls, girls with trucks. Many «Progressives» want to replace «he,» «she,» «his,» «her,» «him,» with «gender-neutral» language[2] so as to promote the illusion that gender is a matter of «social construction.» (Remember the scene in *Monty Python's The Meaning of Life* when the mother asks the doctor if her newborn is a boy or a girl? «Now, I think it's a little early to start imposing roles on it, don't you?») What they are really doing is trying to *make* gender the product of social construction.

No wonder we are observing a sudden epidemic of transgendered youth. They are responding to the propaganda which suffuses our society like clouds of mosquito poison pumped out of trucks coming down the street. What a surprise that a large number of post-surgery converts wind up committing suicide.[3] They are like the fellow in Catullus's ancient poem «Attis»: a convert

---

pornography. There are sordid, abusive aspects of the porn industry, and of course I condemn them.

1 Jill Johnson, *Lesbian Nation: The Feminist Solution* (New York: Simon & Schuster, 1973).
2 Rachel N. Levin, «The Problem of Pronouns.» https://www.insidehighered.com/views/2018/09/19/why-asking-students-their-preferred-pronoun-not-good-idea-opinion; Madison MacWatters, «The Controversy over Gender Pronouns.» https://lshsvalhalla.com/2482/features/the-controversy-over-gender-pronouns/
3 Ryan T. Anderson, *When Harry Became Sally: Responding to the Transgender Movement* (Encounter Books, 2019); Walt Heyer, *Trans Life Survivors* (Bowker Identifier Services, 2018); Melissa Jenco, «Studies: Suicide attempts high among transgender teens, increasing among black teens.» https://www.aappublications.org/

to the ancient Attis cult, who wakes up one morning woefully without his genitals, sacrificed the night before to the god, all of this anticipating the old Ronald Reagan flick, «Where's the Rest of Me?»

The rapid erosion of the family structure ties in with all this because it leaves boys without fathers to mentor them in becoming a man. They have awakening male instincts and energies, and if there is no guidance on what to do with them, maleness will come out in a primitive and violent form. Look at Chicago. And take a look at Robert Bly's once chic but never more timely book, *Iron John*.[1] He employs myth and fairy tale to demonstrate what anthropological field studies have shown about the necessity of male initiation.

Maleness is not everything, not even for males. I think there is a proper psychological androgyny such as Carl Jung and June Singer[2] describe. But it will not be the result of making men feminine. Remember, to make the Tao, you have to have a Yin *and* a Yang.

In conclusion, I have a suggestion. I urge parents to turn their boys on to Robert E. Howard's tales of Conan, Lester Dent's Doc Savage novels, and Edgar Rice Burroughs's John Carter of Mars books, at least for starters. Some will cringe at this: «Oh, but those books are filled with blood and violence! I don't want little Lyle exposed to *that!*» But it's not just books that have stuff like that. There's a rough and threatening world out there from which you ultimately cannot shield your little lambs. Better to introduce these hard realities in a context where the righteous man stands up to deadly wickedness and learns to defeat it using not merely swords and fists, but ingenuity, resourcefulness, integrity, and intelligence. Apron strings don't make very good weapons. But books do. Is the pen mightier than the sword? The pen *is* a sword.

And the stories compiled in the present collection are sufficient proof of that. Here you will thrill to new adventures of familiar and beloved fantasy heroes such as Elak of Atlantis (created by the great Henry Kuttner; continued by Adrian Cole, and now Pierre Comtois) and Thongor of Valkarth, the creation of the Wizard of Lemuria himself, Lin Carter. Nor is Thongor our only Lemurian. We offer the exploits of three powerful warrior women: Varla of Valkarth appears in «Varla and the Mad Magician» by Steve Lines and Glen Usher, while Tonga of Lost Lemuria is the brain child of talented comic

---

news/2019/10/14/suicide101419

[1] Robert Bly, *Iron John: A Book About Men* (Addison-Wesley, 1990).
[2] June Singer, *Androgyny: Toward a New Approach to Sexuality* (Garden City: Doubleday, 1977).

artist Clayton Hinkle. Clayton once posted a drawing of this character online, where I chanced upon it, then contacted the artist, suggesting he create a graphic tale of the buxom Tonga. You see the result! A third warrior woman appears in Glynn Owen Barrass's «The Vanishing Conjurer,» set in H.P. Lovecraft's Dream Lands. Wayne Judge has revived the jungle superhero Ki-Gor, while Jason Ross Cummings introduces his analogue to Howard's Puritan adventurer Solomon Kane: Boscastle the Huegenot. Richard Toogood's «Bellico and the Tower of Mouths» is an altogether fresh venture in Sword & Sorcery, of which you will want to see more. And then there's Lin Carter's «A Prince of Mars,»[1] a substantial fragment of Burroughsian Barsoomianism completed by your humble editor.

* * *

One closing note to underline my point. Originally, *Lin Carter's Flashing Swords #6* was to be published by Pulp Hero Press. In fact, they *did* publish it, at least for a few minutes. The book was listed on Amazon.com, and their «Look Inside» feature posted an earlier version of my introduction. Upon seeing it, fully half of my authors demanded that the publisher withdraw their stories, lest their reputations be sullied by association with my politically incorrect rantings. Then the publisher began to receive hate mail from «offended» souls who threatened to buy no more of the publisher's books. The publisher caved and cancelled the book. A few folks had already ordered copies and received them, but the publisher refused to send me one. No matter, since I at once resolved to replace the retracted stories with better ones, which you see in the present collection. My pal S.T. Joshi once quipped that «the wrong people are reading Lovecraft.» Well, I guess it's equally true that the wrong people are *writing* Sword & Sorcery! Ostensible authors of heroic fantasy are the last people on earth I would have expected to lament «toxic» masculinity, much less to practice the despicable and cowardly «Cancel Culture» censorship. Perhaps one of them will write *Conan the Snowflake* or possibly *Conan the Hermaphrodite*. But not me, by Crom!

Robert M. Price
September 29, 2020

---

1 «A Prince of Mars» originally appeared in *Planets of Peril #1* (Rainfall Books, 2020).

A PRINCE OF MARS

By Lin Carter & Robert M. Price

I.

ON ANOTHER WORLD

My name is Jad Tedron, *dator* or prince, of Zorad on the planet you call Mars but we who roam its dying surface know by the name of Barsoom. But I was not born Jad Tedron and neither is Zorad the city of my birth. My story is a strange one and may indeed be unique in the annals of human experience for all I know. There have been many mysterious elements in the story of my life which no one can readily explain, and I least of all. But I shall narrate here the tale of my adventures as best I can, aware that no one can do any better than is his best...

To begin, then: I was born in a town called Logansville in the Texas panhandle. My father, Matthew Dexter, was a physician who moved to this town after graduating from a small medical school in St. Louis. Here he met and came to love the woman who, in time, became my mother. She was a lovely, gracious woman, the daughter of the town banker, but as she died in introducing me into this world, I am afraid that all of my memories of her are second-hand, at best.

My father's practice ranged over a hundred square miles of arid, sun-baked prairie, and very often I did not see him from dawn to dusk, and in lieu of any other playmate I was forced to amuse myself not only by inventing my own games but also a host of imaginary playmates to enjoy them with.

These were lonely years, as you can imagine, but they were happy years as well. We were not poor, since my mother had inherited a comfortable income from my banker-grandfather. Just before my high school graduation, however, there came upon us that phenomenon known as the Great Depression, and the doors of the Logansville bank closed forever upon the stocks and bonds my grandfather had so assiduously gathered for all those years. At one stroke my father was made penniless, and gone were all his dreams of sending me through college and on to medical school, so that I might carry on in his footsteps in the practice of that profession which has always seemed to me the noblest and most useful of any known to man, the healing of sickness, the comforting of the ill.

I found a job as a roustabout with a small, rundown travelling circus which carried me, in the years which followed, the length and breadth of Texas and into Oklahoma and even to Kansas. This unseemly profession was not one of my choosing, but I soon came to love the cheap, garish, carefree life of the circus, and with my strapping inches and rugged physique, it was a profession for which nature, if not inclination, had ably prepared me.

My father never quite recovered from the loss of his fortune, and although I sent home weekly what few dollars I could spare from my meagre earnings, he began to fail. It was not so much a matter of bodily health, for he had always been robust and hearty, with the stamina of two men, as it was the results of the black mood of melancholy and the feeling that life had defeated him. He died soon after my twenty-first birthday. I made my last trip home to the small town which had nurtured me in my boyhood, to bury him. He sleeps forever under the green sod of the small country church beside my mother. God bless them both, and may their eternal sleep be filled with bright and joyful dreams.

The demise of my father having severed my last remaining link with the town of my birth, I resolved to travel and to see as much of the world as a man of slender means may do. I soon joined Caulfield's Flying Circus, a travelling air show which barnstormed the prairies of the great south-west, first as a mechanic and later as a stunt pilot. For I discovered I had a natural inclination to tinker with machinery and an utter fearlessness of flying, both of which talents go into the makeup of a born flyer.

But it is not my intention to relate here the fairly exciting but uneventful life of Thad Dexter, daredevil stunt flyer, barnstorming aviator and vagabond. For that life was cut cruelly short before I was thirty during a stunt flight at a country fair in the fields outside of Baxter, Wyoming, when my parachute failed to open until it was too late to do more than barely break my fall.

That I survived that disaster, even for half an hour, is probably due to the rugged strength and tireless stamina I inherited from my pioneer forebears. But I did not survive for long, for too many bones were broken and my flesh too terribly torn and mangled for nature or medicine to knit. My last sight was the worn, tired, kindly face of a country doctor whose name I shall never know, bending over me, murmuring quiet words of comfort. That and a strangely prophetic glimpse through a window in the crude little one-room surgery to which the townsfolk had borne me. For just as the odor of chloroform filled my lungs and blotted out the consciousness of Thad Dexter forever, I saw beckoning like a great beacon through the night skies that arched above the dusty plains of Wyoming that distant spark that was the Red Planet, Mars, the planet of mystery. For some reason, that red star caught and held my fading consciousness and I clung to the sight of it, blazing like an eternal enigma through the dark skies, until my consciousness ebbed and went out like a candle blown in the wind. I died there on the operating table; I know this beyond all doubt or question. But I was reborn to live again in another life on another world... and that is the first of the mysterious happenings in my story which I shall not even attempt to explain, for there is no explanation. I was raised in the simple faith of my mother, but my father instilled in me from my earliest years a healthy skepticism against all who pretend to be able to interpret the unknown mysteries of life and death and the world beyond. It was my father's opinion, which I later came to share, that no man can honestly claim to know for certain anything of heaven or the afterlife or the Will of God, and that all church doctrines and dogmas are shallow and ultimately vain and futile attempts to persuade the gullible otherwise.

And if I took my simple childhood faith with a large grain of salt, you can imagine how little credence I placed in the foreign religions of far-off lands. Such wild, outlandish notions as reincarnation and metempsychosis and the Pythagorean concept of the transmigration of souls I deemed little more than fanciful whimsies born of the fertile imagination of the East. There was, therefore, no means by which I could rationalize or explain, even to my own satisfaction, the incredible rebirth upon another planet which followed my death upon that operating table of which my last memories are so clear and unquestionable.

Do the dead of our world go into their graves in the Earth, to rise reborn upon the dead sea bottoms of ancient and dying Mars? If so, in all the span of my second life upon the Red Planet, I have never met another man or woman who could recall their first life on Earth (or Jasoom, as they call it) as can I. Do I truly live upon this strange world, forty-three million miles from my native Earth, or is this second life nothing more than an indefinitely prolonged and amazingly vivid dream born in the dying brain of an earthly aviator, clinging desperately to the guttering spark of life? Or was my former life on Earth the dream, and this strange life upon Barsoom the true and only reality? I can give you the answers to none of these questions, I fear. Nor can any priest or mystic or philosopher, I somehow feel certain. But following the rude termination of my earthly life, I was born again on distant Mars, in the city of Zorad which lies in the northern hemisphere of the Red Planet, on a forested plateau which was once, untold millions of years ago, an island in the midst of Xanthus, the smallest of the five oceans of ancient Mars. These oceans, the greatest of which was the mighty Throxeus in the southern hemisphere of the planet, have long since dwindled away over the inexorable march of many ages, and by the time of my advent upon this world all of the five oceans had vanished, leaving behind only the dead sea bottoms carpeted with ochre moss, where once the pounding billows drove a million years before. All had gradually receded, their waters evaporating into the atmosphere as the old planet aged and began to die, save perhaps for the legendary Lost Sea of Korus which the Martians suppose to exist in the regions of the South Pole, and which may or may not exist in actuality.

The inhabitants of Mars are human in every respect save in their remarkable longevity and in their possession of the mysterious power of telepathy which enables them to read the thoughts of others, even over a considerable distance, and to communicate to some degree with the minds of the strange and curious beasts with which they share their dying world. As for this matter of longevity, a life span of a thousand years is considered the normal life-expectancy of the average inhabitant of the Red Planet.

The city of Zorad in which I was born is ancient beyond the dreams of Babylon or Nineveh or Tyre. Here once flourished a magnificent civilization before those splendid and imperial cities of earthly antiquity were so much as a cluster of crude mud huts built beside the Tigris or Euphrates by primitive men barely emerged as yet from the red murk of savagery. Indeed, from the evidence of the crumbling and long-deserted quays in the oldest, abandoned quarter of my city, where once the stately galleons rode at anchor on the restless waves when Mars was young and fertile, it may be assumed that the city of Zorad was young and newly-built a million years ago. Into this city I was born and the name of Jad Tedron was bestowed upon me by my proud parents. My station in life in this second existence was considerably more fortunate than in my first, for I was the only child of Jugundus Jad, the Jeddak, or king, of Zorad, and his presumed and eventual heir.

As the Prince of Zorad and heir to the throne I was raised in surroundings of the most luxurious splendor, my every need or whim tended to by a host of servants and slaves. My tutors were the wisest and most learned sages and savants of which the kingdom could boast, and they instilled in my young brain all that they knew of the arts and sciences of our ancient civilization, until I was almost as conversant as they in the practice of each subject or skill.

But Barsoom, as I have said, is an aged and dying world whose resources are dwindling away, year by year, century by century, age by age. Few are the remnants which survive of that splendid and glorious civilization which once, in the planet's youth, spanned the globe, and those few city-states and kingdoms which linger on must struggle ceaselessly against one another for the necessities by which to continue their survival. Thus it is that Mars, which by an odd coincidence was named on my native world for the God of War, is a planet of unceasing war, where every realm is at eternal and unending enmity with every other, and each of these cities of the dominant red race into which I was born are constantly at war against the ferocious and indomitable hordes of savage and pitiless green men who roam the dead sea bottoms in titanic numbers and pose a constant threat to the lingering remnants of the more advanced and civilized red race.

Thus I was tutored in the arts of war as well as in the arts of peace, for someday when my royal father, Jugundus Jad, could no longer sustain his place and must embark upon that last, melancholy pilgrimage down the River Iss to that mysterious paradise the priests of Mars believe to lie in the Valley Dor on the fabled shores of the Lost Sea of Korus, I must be prepared to take his place at the head of the fighting-men of Zorad, and be ready to defend our homeland against its nest of enemies. In preparation for the day when I would become Jad Tedron, Jeddak of Zorad, I was trained from the cradle in the use of longsword and rapier, in the skills of marksmanship with the terrible radium rifles and pistols which have come down to us from earlier ages and the secret of whose manufacture has eons since been lost, at least in those neighboring cities which stand on the isles and headlands of the dead sea of Xanthus, and in the use of many another weapon whose descriptions I shall not bore him who reads this story.

I became proficient, as well, in the piloting and navigation of the wonderful and remarkable aircraft employed by the dominant red peoples of Barsoom. These curious vessels, which are known by a word in the universal language spoken across the length and breadth of the Red Planet which translates into English as «flyers,» are the most surprising and impressive of the few relics of the lost scientific achievements of the race which preceded our own. In brief, these machines, which vary in size from tiny, two-man scouts to gigantic aerial dreadnoughts as huge as earthly battleships, are propelled through the thin atmosphere of Mars by powerful radium engines. But the thing which renders them truly astonishing, especially to a former aviator accustomed to rickety, flimsy aircraft little stronger than paper kites, is that they are fabricated entirely from a light, durable metal. It is difficult to imagine any engine built strong enough to lift an airship of solid metal, even one powered by radium, but in this the Martians are assisted by their possession of an advanced scientific discovery yet denied to the savants and inventors of my native world.

This discovery is concerned with the properties of light. The scientists of the Red Planet have learned that any beam of light, whether emanating from the sun or any other source, is divisible into individual «rays,» each of which has different properties. Nine such divisions of light are at this time known to the savants of Mars—in fact, it is due to the remarkable properties of the ninth ray itself that the Martians are able to sustain and replenish their dwindling atmosphere. But it is due to the unique properties of the eighth ray that the Martians navigate the skies of their planet in complicated and ingenious contrivances of solid metal, which would otherwise weigh many tons. For their science is able to produce and store the radiation derived from this eighth solar ray in buoyancy tanks which have the amazing inherent power to reduce the metal flyers to a degree of weightlessness only achieved on my native world by dirigibles and balloons filled with hydrogen or helium gas. A slight variation in their use of the eighth ray of light enables them to use it for the propulsion of such vehicles, by which astonishing velocities are attained. And thus it was that my second youth was spent in acquiring a knowledge of the arts and sciences of peace, and in training with weapons and instruments of warfare. In both departments of life I attained a degree of proficiency which was considered highly admirable by my tutors, if I may safely acknowledge the fact without being accused of the sin of vanity.

Having narrated this cursory account of my birth and youth and schooling, it is not my intention to burden these pages with a more fully detailed description of the education of a Prince of Mars. Suffice it to say that my youth was spent in surroundings of palatial elegance and that I enjoyed every civilized luxury that the condition of royalty might afford, and that I gained considerable competence in the use of weapons.

I cannot recall a time when I was not fully aware of my former life on the planet Earth. The knowledge of this first life was with me from earliest infancy, and, in my ignorance, I supposed my acquaintance with this former incarnation of mine to be the general rule. Often, as a child, I must have occasioned severe alarm and consternation in my parents and tutors by my innocent, childish prattle of the details of a strange life upon another world, which must indeed have caused them to fear for my sanity. Gradually I learned to keep silent on these matters, for it was borne home to me by a thousand curious questions and puzzled glances that my knowledge of the experiences of a prior life on a remote and alien planet was unique to the experience of those around me. At length I learned to guard my tongue, and spoke no more of animals who went about on four legs, rather than six or eight as is common with the beasts of Mars, and on fields of unlikely emerald green, rather than the scarlet sward of the rare Barsoomian forests or the ochre moss which clothes the dead sea bottoms of Mars. Doubtless, as I ceased troubling them with unguarded reminiscences of another life, my elders were vastly relieved and anxious to assign these uncanny «memories» of mine to an over-active imagination rather than to an unstable grip on sanity. But never did I permit myself to forget the weird enigma of my former life, and when as a youth I peered through the mighty telescopes employed by the Martian astronomers, and saw the green fields and blue hills and shining seas of the distant planet whereon I had first been born, it was with a sensation of nostalgia which no words of mine are skillful enough to describe. And there lived ever in the mind of Jad Tedron, Prince of Zorad, as there lives to this day, the mind and memory of Thad Dexter the vagabond pilot who had dreamed of travelling and seeing strange, far-off lands. Well, those dreams had certainly come true, for unto Thad Dexter it had been given by a mysterious and inscrutable Fate to travel further, by some forty-three million miles, than any explorer or adventurer Earth had ever borne, and to visit stranger lands and peoples than any Columbus or Pizarro ever knew!

It was in the spirit of this that I surreptitiously experimented with and trained my innate telepathic abilities, and I believe that I have developed the power to project my thoughts through space to a degree enormously superior to any denizen of the Red Planet in all its interminable history. In the thought that it behooves me to impart some knowledge of my discoveries upon the planet Mars for the edification of my fellow Earthmen, I have striven to the very limits of my telepathic gifts to transmit to the distant world of my birth this very narrative of my adventures.

I cannot know, perhaps I shall never know, whether my thought waves have survived intact across the gulf of so many millions of miles of space, or whether they have been received by a terrestrial intelligence receptive to their wavelength. Nor, for that matter, having been received, if they have even been recorded or preserved in some manner. For it is easy for me to imagine how natural it would be for an earthly mind to dismiss this narrative of incredible marvels upon a weird and alien world as the hysteric phantasies of a disordered brain, or the feverish inventions of sheer imagination, or the incomprehensible fruit of nightmare, or the ravings of a madman.

Perhaps these telepathic communications which I now, with infinite concentration, project into the void are lost between the planets, to disperse in the depths of interstellar space. But it pleases me to dream that my thought waves have impinged upon an intelligence capable of their reception and not hostile to their nature; an intelligence, it may be, willing to recognize the transcendent significance of the discovery that human life dwells among the age-old cities and dead sea bottoms of a distant world, and that humanity is not alone in the breathtaking immensity of infinite and unknown space. Only you, who read these words, if indeed you read them at all, can ever know the truth, of this, my dream.

II.
THE PALACE OF PERFECTION

As I have stated, I do not mean to bore my reader with a lengthy account of my birth and youth and education. This is, in part, because, from my way of thinking, my life on Mars up to my twenty-first year was only a prelude to the mighty adventures into which Fate soon thrust me, and all that I had experienced before that fateful day was merely a preparation for what was to come.

The date whereof I speak was the thirteenth day of the month of Thaad, which was the third month of the Martian calendar. It has lingered in my mind for so long primarily for two reasons, the second and lesser of which is that, as this day fell on the last day of one of the Martian weeks, it was thus virtually identical to «Friday the thirteenth,» a date popularly supposed by Earth superstition to be unlucky. For me, however, it proved an occasion of supreme good luck. For it was upon that day that I first beheld the incomparable loveliness of Xana of Kanator. And that day I count as the real beginning of my life.

A Prince of Mars must fulfill many social duties and must often attend ceremonies or social functions he would otherwise have no cause at which to be present. It is much the same with the members of the royal family of Great Britain, whose official duties obligate them to attend the laying of cornerstones or the launching of battleships, which are not the general run of social events at which a Duke or a Princess might, by natural inclination, desire to observe. As a Prince of the ancient and royal house of Jad, I was, therefore, frequently called upon to visit many public functions in a ceremonial manner. One of these obligations which either I or my father the Jeddak were by custom and tradition expected to fulfill, was to attend to the opening to the public of what the Zoradians call the Palace of Perfection. This edifice is much in the nature of a museum or an art gallery, and serves a purpose very similar to that of such establishments in the life of earthly cities. Therein are preserved all those artifacts from the hands of our ancestors which are considered to have attained artistic perfection. Sometimes the artworks housed therein are the productions of antiquity, statues or tapestries or frescoes salvaged from the oblivion that has overtaken so many of the great Barsoomian cities over the ages. And sometimes, which is extraordinarily rare, the productions of a living artist or sculptor are esteemed so highly as to merit the supreme accolade of being placed in the spacious halls of the Palace of Perfection, among the sublime achievements of ancient genius.

During the first months of the Barsoomian year, it was the immemorial custom in Zorad to close this museum of the arts and to forbid public entry while the many exhibits and displays were cleansed and refurbished with exquisite care by senior artisans employed in these skills. It was during this interval that those contemporary works of art which had survived the scrutiny of a panel of judges composed of connoisseurs of the arts, and had been deemed worthy of comparison with the masterpieces of the past, were installed in the halls and rotundas of the immense edifice. At the termination of this period the Palace was thrown open to the public in a formal ceremony, which, as I have just explained, either I or my father was expected to preside.

On this particular occasion, as chance would have it, my royal father was otherwise occupied with a council on military affairs. The savage green horde of Zarkol, which roamed the dead sea bottoms of the mighty Xanthus, amidst which our city rose, were reported by an air scout in the navy of Zorad to be on the move. This matter, which might portend a serious danger to the realm, precluded the Jeddak from his merely formal attendance at the opening ceremonies, and I was dispatched from the Palace of a Thousand Jeddaks to take his place.

I recall that it was just before the noon hour of the Martian day that I rode forth from the palace of my ancestors by the Gate of the Banths, attended by the officers and gentlemen of my retinue, and their equerries. So precisely are the events of that portentous day engraven upon the tablets of my memory, that I can even report the exact moment of our departure, which was the thirtieth *xat* of the third *zode*, these being the names by which the Martians call those divisions of time which we Earthmen would call «minute» and «hour.»

Crossing the vast plaza upon which the Palace of a Thousand Jeddaks fronts, we clattered down a broad, stone-paved boulevard, lined to either side with immense, flowering *pimalia* trees, known as the Avenue of Victories from the monuments erected at intervals along this way in commemoration of ancient battles wherefrom the legions of Zorad had emerged to bear away the laurels. It was a gay and splendid sight, the broad boulevard thronged with handsome men and women who waved at us as we cantered by on our restless, high-spirited *thoats*. To either side the immense, flowering *pimalias* which bordered the avenue were bright with blossoms. Carpets or awnings in a variety of brilliant hues adorned the carven facades of the various noble mansions or palaces of the aristocratic houses which lined the street. From rooftop and spire heraldic banners fluttered in the breeze, charged with the proud blazonry of royal Zorad.

Arriving at the Square of the Monuments, upon which the museum gallery faced, we dismounted, left our steeds in the hands of the equerries, and entered the vast structure through gates carven in a remote epoch with the frowning visages of Jeddaks and Jeddaras whose very names were forgotten ages ago. We were greeted within the central rotunda by a respectable crowd of Zoradian citizens, led by the officials and curators of the museum in their ceremonial finery.

The rituals were soon concluded and I believe I played my part therein in a manner befitting the solemnity of the occasion. It would have been needlessly rude for me to leave at the moment my official duties were finished; thus politeness decreed that I should stroll about and view the various artworks on exhibition for at least a few minutes before taking my departure. I thank whatever gods may be that I did so! For, hardly had I begun my perfunctory circuit of the central rotunda, where the choicest of the most recent acquisitions were displayed, than I paused in front of a painting as one thunderstruck.

The involuntary gasp of amazement this masterpiece wrung from my lips must have been clearly audible to all who stood within the great, domed chamber. Aware that I had drawn all eyes to me, I laughed lightly, dissembling my awe behind a pretense of aesthetic pleasure. It was a portrait of a young woman of such incomparable beauty as I had never heretofore imagined the human features could attain, nor the brush of an artist express upon his canvass. Her face was an exquisite oval cameo, poised upon a proud and graceful and slender neck, her features delicately chiseled, her great eyes lustrous as black jewels. Her abundant masses of glistening hair, black as a raven's wing, were confined by a gemmed tiara of bizarre design which encircled her brows, and from the starry crest of this coronet there arose a single curved plume, shimmering with the peacock hues of bronze and emerald and metallic azure.

Her complexion was clear and flawless, the warm tint of ruddy copper, glowing with rich carmine in her adorable dimpled cheeks, and her full, perfect lips were the color of rubies. Her raiment consisted of a silken scarf of lucent gossamer, which crossed over one shoulder and then wrapped itself about her slender, rounded upper body, baring her superb breasts which were, however, partially veiled by chains of precious metals and many necklaces of glittering gems. It was the expression in that exquisite face which rendered this portrait something more than merely an admirable technical achievement. For the hand of the painter had caught the living spirit of his unknown model—the roguish humor of her voluptuous smile, the fresh, exciting vigor and zest for life visible in her vivacious, laughing eyes—and rendered them immortal, preserved by the brush of genius for all the ages to come. I stood as one entranced before this miracle of art, devouring with my eyes the laughing, vivid beauty of this young and delicious creature. Rapt as I was, and all but unconscious of my surroundings, I was aware that my fixed attention to this one painting was drawing curious stares in my direction, and that amused whispers were rising from my audience.

A tactful young lieutenant in my retinue, Tas Komis by name, aware that my peculiar behavior was attracting attention, cleared his throat behind me. «An admirable work, is it not, my Prince?»

«Oh, admirable, admirable,» I said in what I hoped was an off-hand manner. «Whose work is this?»

Tas Komis consulted a leaflet in which the new exhibits were listed. «An artist called Quindus Varro. I have heard of him; a genius, but something of an eccentric. He lives in a half-ruined villa beyond the city, eschewing the companionship of his fellow men. The painting itself is entitled ‹Xana of Kanator.›»

«Kanator! Indeed?» I said, pretending polite indifference. «Excellent skill. Let us pass on to observe the other artworks.» But upon the tablets of my memory I engraved the name of the artist and that of his incomparable subject.

Early that evening after a light supper in my suite I repaired to the airship hangar atop the roof of the palace, cast off the mooring lines, and took to the skies in my private yacht. The villa in which the eccentric Quindus

Varro made his abode lay directly north of Zorad, beyond those waterfront precincts of the city which had become abandoned with the shrinking of the populace over many ages. Silent and swift as a hovering shadow, my flyer skimmed above the spires of crumbling palaces and deserted piles of ruined masonry long given over to the stealthy creatures of the forest which mantled the hills to the north and east of Zorad. The night was clear and brilliant, for both of the moons of Mars were aloft at this hour, their doubled moonlight transforming the nocturnal landscape to a scene of weird and romantic grandeur.

The Martians call the lesser of the two moons, which Earthmen know as Deimos, by the name of Cluros; while it is much closer to the surface of Mars than is the satellite of my native world, it revolves so slowly that it requires thirty hours and a trifle more to make one complete circuit of the planet. The greater of the two moons, which we call Phobos, the Martians know as Thuria. It soars at a height of only some five thousand miles above the surface of the planet, and completes one circumnavigation of Mars every seven and one-half hours, presenting to the eye the semblance of an immense, luminous meteor hurtling across the heavens from horizon to horizon two or three times each night.

The villa of Quindus Varro was one of the numerous edifices of antiquity which survive virtually intact due to the remarkable preservative qualities of the Martian atmosphere. The facade of this imposing structure was a colonnade composed of marble pillars, of which two were fallen; the remainder served to support a grand architrave whereon were sculptured with deathless skill the noble and graceful forms of men and women. The upper works presented a rich surface of ornament, heavy with carven faces and allegorical figures, some adorned with noble metals or precious stones. Only the east wing of this palatial edifice was slumped into crumbling decay; the rest of the structure displayed a remarkable degree of preservation.

I brought my flyer down to the courtyard before the colonnade, where slabs of marble lay tumbled about and overgrown with quantities of crimson sward. Tethering the mooring line to the capital of a fallen column, which lay moldering amidst the rank and untamed growth, I strode up a flight of broken stone steps to discover the towering doors of the portal widely ajar. Within I found a great rotunda whose marble floor was littered with crisp leaves and matted with indescribable filth. Colored moonlight fell in glorious shafts through broken clerestory windows to illuminate walls of gleaming alabaster, hung with tattered, faded tapestries, and to gleam along the cobwebbed rail of a graceful stair which coiled to the second level.

A cracked, peevish voice hailed me from the darkness above. «What noisome intruder disturbs the solitude of Quindus Varro? Can it be that my rivals fear the genius of Quindus Varro to such an absurd extent, that they have secured the services of an assassin to forever extinguish that spark of divine fire?»

Another than an inhabitant of the Red Planet might have first suspected an uninvited intruder to be a burglar, but on Barsoom, for some strange reason, thievery is so exceptionally rare as to be virtually unknown, and I have not the slightest reason why. It is another of the many mysteries which I cannot explain to my reader (if any shall ever peruse these words). It is almost as if stealing had never been invented by the dwellers on the Red Planet; if so, I greatly fear thievery to be the only crime or vice unique to the peoples of Earth, for the Martian civilization enjoys, if that is the word I want, every other criminal tendency known to my former planet.

Thus addressed, I stepped forth into a pool of moonlight which fell through a broken roof so that my interrogator could clearly see me from his place above the stair, and announced my name in a firm voice, although for no particular reason neglecting to state my rank in society.

«Jad Tedron, Jad Tedron,» the old man repeated testily. «I know of no such person, by my ancestors! What do you wish of me, sir, that you intrude your unwanted presence upon my meditations?»

I announced myself an admirer of his art, come to view such masterpieces as the portrait called «Xana of Kanator,» which I had but recently seen for the first time, and I inquired whether a live model had posed for him for that painting.

«Of course, you young fool! Otherwise it would hardly be a ‹portrait,› now *would* it? And, before you ask, Kanator is a real *place*, too!» Withal, he hastened me out the door, insisting that he must return to his easel before he lost his inspiration.

III.
GLADIATORS OF KANATOR

The knowledge that the divinely beautiful Xana was a living woman and not, as I had immediately and naturally supposed, a representation of an abstract ideal of beauty, propelled me into a mission I could not have suspected was my destiny. So I at once made ready for a secret flight, in an unmarked skyboat, to Xana's city, the stronghold of Zorad's enemies. I was not such a fool as to enter the lair of my born foes openly. The well-guarded city gate was closely monitored by rotating shifts of hawk-eyed sentinels. The ancient estrangement between our states meant that my face would be familiar to virtually no one in Kanator, unless of course, Kanatorian spies had successfully infiltrated Zorad—as I was about to do in Kanator! My best opportunity to conceal my identity seemed to lie in masquerade. I had donned the plain leather trappings of a wandering *panthan*, or unemployed warrior, whose swordly skills are for hire.

My entry to Kanator was uneventful. When asked, I was ready with a false name. Here I must become Kar Navas, the name of a boyhood comrade who died in a flying accident. In this way I thought to honor him. And if my gambit were successful, he should have saved my life once more, as he did long years before, when he called to warn me of the impending collision that claimed his young life.

The crowds milling about in the central marketplace were abuzz with talk of the annual gladiatorial games, soon to commence. This news could hardly have been more suitable to my purpose. I would, I resolved, enter the games, ostensibly, to put my expertise with the longsword on display in order to attract potential clients who might seek to commission my services.

As I waited my turn to enter the open-air arena, I first had thoughts, fond memories, of earlier years when I received gladiatorial training from my father's elite warriors, to prepare me for the military responsibilities I must one day assume. But these ruminations quickly faded, to be replaced by thoughts of the ravishing visage of Xana, which had been indelibly engraved upon my mind. I hoped that perhaps she might be in attendance at this exhibition, sitting in the crowded stands. I should have no difficulty recognizing her, but, once in the arena, I could not spare a second to scan the wide panorama of the audience. My first opponent came trotting out onto the blood-soaked sand mere seconds following me.

My foe appeared to be a soldier from the great city of Helium, no doubt a slave taken as a prisoner of war some time earlier. I knew how this worked: his Kanatorian masters must have promised him freedom for victory, for the sake of inspiring a genuine battle, a fight to the death. This took me by surprise, as I had understood our clash to be more in the nature of an exhibition match, a competing display of each contestant's skills, in short, a sporting event. But clearly the Heliumite did not view it that way. His furious onslaught was driven by a bloodthirsty frenzy, nor, given the conditions I surmised, could I blame him. Perhaps I would have done the same. Indeed, I was now *forced* to do the same. My life was at stake, so I quickly shifted into the requisite mode and began looking for an opening for the death blow I hoped to strike. Great was his forcefulness, but it was matched by my own resourcefulness. As the Prince of the royal family of Zorad, I had enjoyed the benefit of elite combat training, far in excess of that accorded to the common soldiery even of a great city like Helium. It was not really a fair fight, but what choice had I? Respect for my opponent required me to meet him in battle with my best effort, and I did. My agility, combined with my well-learned evasive tactics, afforded me ample advantage. I regretted rendering the fatal sword blow much as I always regretted the inevitable slaying in the hunt. As he lay prone, covered in his own freely flowing blood, I clicked my boot heels together and touched my blade to my forehead in salute. I had given him freedom from the slavery imposed by the Kanatorians, but he was past appreciating it.

Moments later, a second rival appeared, advancing rapidly upon me. For some reason, I assumed I would be allowed a few moments' respite, but no. This time I must test my skills against a towering green-skinned Thark. He must have spent many years in the arena, judging from his scars and injuries. He even lacked one of his four arms, though he seemed not to miss it, as he deftly wielded a scimitar with each of his remaining fists. His rain of blows spurred me to a spinning, ducking dance such as I had never before performed! I lacked any time to strategize, instead obeying split-second instinct. I imagine the cheering multitude could see but a tornadic blur of green and red from our largely bare flesh. From the heightening reactions of the onlookers, I gathered they had never witnessed such a spectacle as we were providing.

Why were the Kanatorians sending murderous adversaries against me, one after another? I finally deduced that the Jeddak of the city must be present and had recognized my true identity. In eliminating me, the only son and heir of my own Jeddak, he hoped thus to strike a blow against Zorad, provoking a succession dispute and thereby fomenting unrest and instability. In such an inchoate state of affairs, he might take the advantage and attack our city. All this I could see in my mind's eye as clearly as if it were the memory of accomplished events in the recent past.

I forced myself to ignore the rising fatigue and redoubled my efforts to dispatch my giant foe. At once I realized that I had been thinking of the present contest as something of a fencing match, which is what we were supposedly having. The goal in that case would have been to display superior swordplay, the victory blow equivalent to a checkmate in our Barsoomian chess. I had been carrying on a sword fight. Now I must simply bear in on the Thark's death, however unorthodox the means. My limbs felt heavy, but I lifted my sword high and cast it like a javelin straight for the scarred head of the green Martian.

The Thark dropped to the ground, his brains spilling out like lava from a miniature volcano, his three arms falling limp, his nicked swords scattering and bouncing across the ground. I looked back to the opening of the gladiator stable, squinting for the sight of more opponents.

There was one.

I braced myself for renewed combat, pessimistic about the outcome, exhausted as I was. I assessed my foe, noticing his stature, a head shorter than my own. His body was entirely concealed by plate armor, odd for an arena match, where leather battle harness, such as I wore, was the rule. But the figure moved easily despite the obvious weight of the amour. That bespoke great strength. Our swords clashed ringingly. It was as if the swords themselves were dueling, not we who held them. This was closer to what I had initially expected. The warrior did not seem urgent to take my life. Even so, I thought it not unlikely that my end might be near, since I was slowing down and was less easily able either to meet or to evade blows.

But all at once my adversary stood still before me, lowered his weapon, and held out a mailed but open hand toward me. Gratefully, I, too, lowered my sword, a considerable relief to my aching arm.

The crowd fell silent, as the metal-encased figure opened his helmet and let it fall to the sand below us. Then they began to cheer again. What did this mean? What could be afoot here? Finally I stepped closer to my erstwhile foe to get a look at his now-revealed face.

It was not a «he,» but a «she»!

Her hair was plastered to her forehead with sweat, but that did not prevent my recognizing the mesmerizing countenance of my *beloved Xana!*

I was paralyzed with shock. I could barely grasp her words as she addressed the royal box above us in the arena's bleachers. Yes, that must be the Jeddak, Gogus Voth. Xana was speaking to him...

«Your Majesty! My father! This man, though he belongs to Zorad, has acquitted himself in battle this day! He has done nothing to any man of Kanator, slaying only an outlander slave and a subhuman Thark! Who knows but that he is here as an emissary of peace? I beg you, do not execute him!»

The Jeddak now stood and carefully chose his words. He knew he must do or say nothing to bring dishonor upon himself, with so many, including all the nobility of Kanator, on the edge of their seats, listening for whatever he might say.

«You are wise, my daughter! We shall welcome this champion of Zorad with open arms. I am eager to hear of his mission. Guards, accompany the Prince of Zorad to our guest quarters! Welcome among us, Jad Tedron!»

A half-dozen armed retainers appeared and circled me. I was thrilled to see Xana penetrate that phalanx to accompany me to wherever the men might take me. Perhaps she had suspicions about her father's uncharacteristic clemency.

IV.
ROYAL RUNAWAYS

So she was the Princess of the city-state! Varro had not told me this!

I was escorted to a sumptuous chamber, where I treated myself to a hot shower to dispel the sweat, grime, and spattered blood I had accumulated in the Kanatorian arena. After this, I sank into the feather-stuffed mattress, nearly as luxurious as the one in my bed chamber in our palace back home. I fell asleep at once and dreamed pleasantly of the Princess Xana. When might I see her again?

I thought I still dreamed when I seemed to hear the noise of violence out in the hall. But this was no dream! My chamber door burst open, spilling out a miniature avalanche of armed figures, struggling together, knives and shortswords flashing. Xana, well-armed, was among them. I reached for the wrist of one of the men, snapping it and relieving him of his weapon. My fleecy robe made for poor armor, but my superior agility served me well. Well-placed kicks at the guards Xana was battling aided her. Besides, their efforts were half-hearted, since, while having to defend themselves, they knew they dared not injure their Princess. Thus it took no great span of time to gain their submission. Xana had brought a coil of rope in case she and I needed to escape out of a window. We tied up the dejected soldiers, who knew they faced execution for allowing us to escape, just as surely as if they had wounded Princess Xana. I had «borrowed» one of the men's uniforms and weapons. This way Xana and I could probably walk boldly down the halls and out of the building unopposed, her identity acknowledged, mine concealed. Once we reached the broad avenue, the Princess looked around and proceeded to whisper to me in urgent tones.

«My father lied. He is no lover of peace, especially peace with Zorad. He would have slain you on the spot. The gods know, he and his stooges were trying hard enough in the arena! But I hoped to save you as I did. I knew he would not risk the outrage of his subjects, who, heartened by your pair of triumphs, were coming to regard you as a hero. And you *are* a hero, Jad Tedron! A hero to me!»

Here, as I gaped at her in wonderment, I sputtered, «How did you know me? And my name? Did you royal father tell you of me?»

«Not at all, Jad Tedron. He knew that I should oppose his scheme, as I have done from time to time in the past. I know he loves me, and that love makes him indulge me, protect me, even from his own wrath.»

«Then how?»

At this she blushed, her native red skin turning a deeper crimson.

«I have seen your face many times, enough times to fall in love with the man I saw.»

Of course, it was the Martian telepathic ability! Normally, such contact is possible only between individuals already acquainted. Perhaps in this case Lady Destiny was truly involved. I could no longer think otherwise. Love overcame, and I dared to hold her and to kiss her perfect lips. To my great relief, she did not draw away. I knew we were in grave danger, but I cared nothing for it. If some assassin's arrow were to spear my beating heart, I could not complain, for in this moment I had known complete ecstasy.

Luckily, my beloved Xana had more presence of mind than I did.

«The tied-up guards must have been discovered by now. My father has surely dispatched a larger force, and this time I fear I cannot count on his protection. We must flee the city and take our chances outside!»

«If we can make it to my airship, we should be home free.»

«Alas, my Prince, that avenue is closed to us. The Jeddak's troops have discovered it, and it is now guarded by troops bearing deadly radium rifles.»

I quickly shifted into planning mode. As we set out for the city gate, I calculated our narrow range of options. Getting through the portal turned out to present no challenge, since, miraculously, it seemed no one had warned the sentries to detain us on sight.

The guards saluted as Xana smiled up at them. One of the men called down, «Your Highness, is one single guard sufficient?»

«Oh yes, thank you, for he is a mighty champion indeed!» Withal, we proceeded at a relaxed pace, pretending we knew where we were headed.

We walked till we were far enough from Kanator that we felt it was safe to make camp. We found concealment in a dry gully on the rim of the Xanthus Sea bed. Both of us had brought cloaks with which to cover ourselves. We refrained from making a fire for fearing it might attract the unwelcome attention of enemies human and inhuman. But sometimes one doesn't need fire for that.

v.

ATTACK OF THE MOSS MONSTER

Sometime in the deepest part of the night, when neither moon was visible in the sky, a vaguely humanoid figure rose slowly from the thick blanket of ochre moss on the parched sea bottom. Though there was no sound loud enough to wake a sleeper, some instinct prodded me to wakefulness, and I remained statue-still to watch the weedy hulk emerge from the dry morass. Xana had not awakened, even when it commenced to shamble erratically in her direction. I knew I must move quickly to defend her. Yes, she had proven her mettle in combat only yesterday. But I feared she might not have enough time to react should the beast fall upon her before she could come to full consciousness.

I made it to the shaggy colossus in a single springing leap, then brought down my knife with all the force I could muster. I was more than a little startled when the blow had no visible effect at all! But perhaps that is not entirely correct, for I saw, as my eyes adjusted, that my blade had in fact sheared off a quantity of the hay-like substance that covered the thing. I thought that at least I should get a glimpse of its true form, hitherto hidden beneath its ochre pelt. But as Xana woke up and rolled out of the monster's path, I saw that there *was* nothing beneath the covering straw. Xana quickly struck sparks with her flint knife on a convenient stone. It was easy enough to dodge the shambling creature, so I distracted it while Xana fanned the flame, then pitched it at our attacker. It burst into a flaming conflagration. For an instant we both felt relief—until we remembered why we had not lit a campfire in the first place. Thrumming sounds in the distance warned us that our victory pyre had not gone unnoticed. Since the approaching hoof beats, for such they must be, implied a mounted party of some size, we did not bother to flee, knowing there would be no outrunning them. Of course, we had been discovered by a roaming patrol of Tharks.

VI.
AMONG THE THARKS

I believe I do not lack courage. I know that my beloved Xana does not. But we offered the Tharks no resistance. And this because we also are not fools. If we were to overcome the odds facing us, we must wait. Patience grants time for planning. The grunting of the green titans told us little. They must have had some use for us, and the only thing I could think of was that they recognized Xana and hoped to use her as a hostage to gain some advantage, though, as far as I knew, this was not the way of the Tharks. Our captors, members of the fierce Zarkol Horde, did not abuse us, but I suspected this was because they dared not preempt the harm intended by their superiors. At any rate, they took us on a long march to a deserted citadel where they had established a temporary base of operations for whatever mischief they were planning in the area. The place had once been characterized by real grandeur, but the builders and whatever nation they had belonged to must have been centuries extinct, and the structure was now more like a mummy than a living body. Judging by the height of the doorways, the building must have been erected by Red Martians, not towering Tharks like those who had now occupied it. We were led to some rude cell, likely an empty storage room, with guards posted at the door. Of course our weapons were confiscated. We sat and waited, speculating, wondering what our families, and our cities, made of our disappearance and what they might be thinking to do about it. I knew full well that they would not be communicating with each other about it. As I subsequently learned, the Jeddaks of both Zorad and Kanator had concluded that the other had abducted their royal heirs either as hostages or as the first strike in a planned war. But the Tharks had no knowledge of this. Whatever they had in mind, it had nothing to do with the larger crisis at hand. But we, too, were innocent of these facts at the time.

Mercifully, we had not long to wait. Even if that meant only less time before our execution, it was preferable to a limbo of suspension. We were led, in chains, to what must have passed for the throne room of this colony of the tusked savages. Seated on a makeshift dais constructed from a couple of crude blocks draped by what looked like a torn-off section of a faded tapestry, was the chieftain, one Barnok Bol. He cut a mighty figure, as would be expected among a people who respect only combat prowess and the total of one's kills. He had no doubt attained his present position by unimaginable cruelty and blood-lust. One tusk was broken off, and one eye, on the opposite side of his ugly face, had been gouged out. No doubt these wounds were medals of valor in their eyes, souvenirs of celebrated triumphs. He stared at us, mainly at me, for some reason yet to be disclosed, though *about* to be disclosed.

There were no preliminaries. I could not help flinching as Barnok Bol bellowed his rebuke.

«You, puny man, face justice today! You know what you have done!» Frankly, I was mystified.

«Great one! I swear I know not my crime! Are you sure I am the one you sought? I know all Red Martians must look alike to you, as you do to us.» At these hasty words, Xana rolled her eyes.

«Only cowards lie!» quoth he, with a roar so loud it fairly drowned out the impact of his calloused fist on a wooden side table.

Armed Tharks hefted their axes in an ominous manner. They started to inch closer.

«I am no coward, my lord, as you shall see if you will give me the means to defend myself. I have dispatched Tharks before!»

«So you confess your ill deeds!» This was the last thing I expected from the blustering buffoon.

«Of all people, you cannot possibly deem killing in battle a crime!»

Withal, the Thark chieftain rose from his seat as if it had suddenly burst into flame underneath him.

«You slew my father!»

«*What?* By all the gods of Mars, I did no such thing! You have the wrong man, I say!»

But simultaneously, an odd thought occurred to me, very likely an inadvertent thought transmission from the force of Barnok's fury. The Thark I had defeated in the Kanatorian arena—could *that* have been this one's father? That three-armed mass of scarred green flesh? But then I realized it seemed outlandish to me only because I was thinking of a former king on the pattern of any civilized monarch. But the Tharks rose to power by assassination and challenge. The Thark before me now was simply a fortunate brute; his father could well have been an unfortunate one. This Thark Jeddak must have known of his father's death, not by some sophisticated surveillance but rather by his telepathic apprehension of his father's death agony.

«Oh… I suppose I *did* perhaps slay him, but given the circumstances, I could hardly have done otherwise.»

«I care not for your nonsense!» He reached for his sword. Its edge was nicked but otherwise keen. I thought fast but knew that I could hardly win a fight with dodging and sidestepping as my only weapons.

«*There is no honor in this!*» It was one of the throne guards. «We have endured your insufferable tyranny long enough! We are your servants, not your slaves!» Withal, the soldier tossed his war axe to me. The gray shadow of fear descended upon the chieftain's awful face. Clearly, he was unprepared for a challenge, whether from a two-armed or a four-armed Martian. He hopped down off the dais and crouched in a defensive posture, as did I. I could see his prowess had rusted, his career of slaughter well behind him. We circled. I had no fear in me. I cannot say the same for my opponent. «Like father, like son,» I thought, as I prepared to send him to the same hell to which I had consigned his sire.

He looked resigned, without hope of victory. Obviously he had sustained his dominance for years on the strength of his thunderous bluffing. All his attendants were now chanting and jeering, now that their tyrant's bluff had been called. A few were actually cheering for me!

The green Jeddak was already winded. Even with four stout arms he seemed capable of only random and ineffectual blows and swipes. There was little honor in the blow I had necessarily to deal. My foe stood still, awaiting a fate he had somehow managed to stave off for years. My axe did not disappoint him. I stooped and bathed my hands in the fountain of blood gushing from the stump of my fallen enemy. I smeared his blood on my arms and torso while my new friends cheered and waved their weapons in the air. Xana regarded me with the strange mixture of pride and wincing revulsion. At this I could not help laughing. Nor could I *stop* laughing. And in a moment the Tharks joined me. I had not even known their race was capable of laughter. And there was much more I was to learn about them, for they proclaimed me their new Jeddak by acclamation!

VII.

THE BRINK OF BATTLE

I soon learned that tensions between my native Zorad and the patrimony of my beloved Xana had swiftly accelerated, each accusing the other of kidnapping or killing the other's royal heir. The Kanatorians had managed to mobilize first and soon stood in force, mounted on their armored, snorting, six-legged thoats, outside our city walls. The tension was thick as ozone before a storm.

It looked as if the Kanatorian army was about to attack, wheeling their siege towers into place near the Zoradian walls, while the Zoradian archers prepared to unleash a shower of death upon their foes. Suddenly a trumpet sounded down below, distant but swiftly growing closer. The head of the Kanatorian host lifted a mailed arm to signal his troops to wait.

After a few tense moments, a Kanatorian scout pulled up before the general, his thoat lathered from fatigue, and exclaimed, «A Thark army, my lord! From their battle standards I should judge them to be the Zarkol Horde. They are headed this way!»

His superior mused, «What can they want? What business have they here? They are not the largest tribe of Tharks, though quite skilled in combat.»

The rider replied, «I reckon them to have perhaps a third of our force, but it is easily sufficient to sway the balance of the battle to come. What shall we do, sir?»

«If only we knew whose side they mean to take! There is as little love lost between us and the Tharks as between our city and Zorad!»

By this time, the news, as confusing as it was to all, had reached the Jeddaks of both almost-clashing city-states. Jugundus Jad, my noble father, and the Jeddak Gogus Voth, Xana's father, came to the fore. Jugundus found a place along the city wall, while Gogus, astride his gold-caparisoned thoat, advanced to the front lines of his company. Would the approaching Thark army attack? And, if so, which enemy? Or would the Thark warlord first address the two groups of Red Martians?

All eyes widened as they beheld the sight of a Thark commander with a meager single pair of arms and an alien red hide. They blinked when I doffed my helmet and revealed a countenance all too familiar to them. They hardly noticed when another helmeted rider, smaller of stature, trotted up front.

«I am Jad Tedron, Jeddak of the Zarkol Horde, and this is my queen-to-be, Xana of Kanator. We are amply prepared for battle with both your noble hosts if you do not accept my demands.»

«And what may *they* be, usurper?» quoth the Jeddak of Kanator, adding, «I should have slain you in the arena, now that I see your and my daughter's treacherous designs!»

«Keep a civil tongue if you know what's good for you, Jeddak!» This from my own sire, who naturally had more sympathy for me, as dumbfounded as he was. I spoke next.

«Our cities have been enemies for longer than memory reaches. No one can even say what lay at the root of our grudges. It is surely time for intelligent men to put all that aside and to inaugurate a new age of peace. Is it not so, men of Kanator and Zorad?»

Great murmuring ensued among both hosts. Xana and I waited, stroking our impatient steeds and remarking on our joy at seeing our royal fathers again. We had not been away from them for long, but much had transpired in the meantime. My hearing is good, so it was not difficult to catch various bits of conversations. It soon became clear to me that sentiment among the Kanatorians was distinctly unenthusiastic about the prospect of war. I directed my telepathic «hearing» up to the parapets of Zorad, where my father could be seen intensely conferring with his closest advisers. Several times he looked down at us. I believe I even caught him smiling.

I had a brief foreboding when I saw Xana's father dismount to approach us. I tried to read his expression, then sought to penetrate his thoughts, but to no avail, implying he did not yet know his own mind. But all became clear when Gogus Voth, passing me by, took her hand and motioned for her to dismount. She smiled tentatively and then tearfully embraced him. I felt our troubles were now at an end.

VIII.
TRIUMVIRATE

A great day dawned not long afterward. It was our wedding day. The ceremony was held in Kanator, in the royal palace. The nobles of both cities were present in their best finery. So were several of the lords of the Zarkol Horde, my own retainers. In fact Xana and I were united by the Zarkol shaman according to the tribe's ancient rite. In conjunction with this ceremony, the two Jeddaks, and I as the third, signed a peace treaty and formed an alliance between blood brothers. It was decided and officially proclaimed that, upon the deaths of the sovereigns of Zorad and Kanator, their heirs should of course take their thrones, and Xana and I should preside over a small empire of the two cities and the Zarkol tribe.

And the best part of the celebration was the unveiling of a new work of Quindus Varro, lured out of retirement: a portrait of the royal bride and groom.

CURSE OF THE WHITE WITCH

By Wayne Judge

I.

A PERILOUS HUNT

Tembu George leapt back, narrowly dodging the plummeting body that fell from the treetops overhead. It crashed to the ground with a dull thud, just missing him by inches! The corpse was that of one of the Du'Ani Tribe, a headhunter. His face was streaked in white paint in a fearsome pattern that mimicked a skull. He was adorned in necklaces of bone and teeth, most of which were human. An animal hide belt around his loincloth played host to two grotesque trophies, shrunken heads of slain victims. It was clear to the big Masai warrior Tembu George, though, that this particular man would not be able to add any more trophies to his belt, as his own neck had been twisted and snapped like kindling. On the ground around the corpse were six other dead bodies from his evil tribe. Two of them the big Masai himself had slain with his heavy spear.

At that same moment in the rustling and thrashing of the jungle canopy above, a terrific battle was taking place. Two more of the fearsome Du'Ani walked among the thick branches as sure-footed as tree lizards. One of the savages held a crude, long knife and was locked in combat with the man who had thrown his slain brother to the ground. The other was backing away from the fight, holding a struggling, white-skinned beauty in his strong arms. She was bound in ropes made of vines, and her long red hair thrashed as she struggled against her captor. She screamed as she kicked in vain at the headhunter.

«Ki-Gor! Help!»

The slayer of the Du'Ani was a blonde-haired, bronze-skinned giant, clad only in a leopard skin loin cloth. His face was a mask of savage intensity, nostrils flared wide and eyes narrow and focused. Whipcord sinews flexed as he held the knife-wielding hand of the jungle killer at bay. At the same time his determined foe was likewise struggling against Ki-Gor's own knife.

At the sound of Helene, his mate, calling for help the jungle lord bared his teeth like a lion as his strength swelled with righteous fury. His tough, bare foot came up in a vicious kick to the groin of the Du'Ani and struck like a piledriver! All strength crumbled from the headhunter as the shock of the blow caused his eyes to nearly bulge from their sockets and his knees buckled. The unchecked knife of the bronze giant plunged down and pierced the throat of the Du'Ani, sending him into Death's cold, unforgiving embrace as he toppled from the thick branches, a trail of crimson life flowing behind him like a strand from a spiders web.

This second dispatched foe thudded to the ground close to Tembu George, but he paid it no mind. Retrieving his bow from the ground where it fell when the trio was first ambushed, he was busy aiming an arrow at the sole remaining villain, the one who held Helene captive. He noticed his close friend, the white jungle lord, crouched and tensed to pounce like a leopard. The blood-streaked knife in his right hand poised to dole out deadly justice.

«Catch her, Ki-Gor!» the mighty Masai yelled as he let fly his stone-tipped shaft.

The white warrior did not hesitate or waste another second even looking at the man who held his woman captive. His senses were as keen as any lion's and his reflexes as quick. He heard the twang of the bowstring from below and leapt from his perch just as the arrow pierced the skull of the Du'Ani with instant, deadly effect. As the headhunter's body went limp and he dropped to the ground to join his brethren in hell, the bound Helene fell also!

Ki-Gor had timed his leap expertly. His strong hands found purchase on a sturdy, hanging vine that swung him directly into the path of the red-headed beauty. Helene screamed as the ground rushed up to meet her, but suddenly a strong and sinewy pair of legs wrapped around her delicate waist, and her descent was brought to an abrupt stop.

She looked at the familiar limbs that held her, held her like an ape does its young when climbing, and with a sigh of relief she smiled at her husband. Ki-Gor lowered himself to the ground where Tembu George took Helene and gently laid her on the ground. The bronze giant dropped from the vine and cut the ropes that bound his shaken wife. He smiled at Tembu George clapping him on the shoulder.

«A good shot my friend!» Then, lovingly helping his wife to her feet, he brushed her hair back from her face and kissed her inviting, red lips, more desirable than the sweetest fruit the jungle could offer.

«You're safe now, my love. Your charms drew those Du'Ani away from that boy they were chasing, but our blades and arrows taught them the error of their ways!»

With the fighting over, Ki-Gor seemed to gather an air of civilization about him. He had learned this from his wife, who was from the outside world. Though, when need be, as savage and deadly as any beast of the primeval world that spawned him, the jungle lord could also be a gentle soul when at peace.

The white king of the jungle and his bride had come a full two days north from their home, a tree house that sat near a waterfall in an idyllic open glen. Leaving his good friend N'Geeso, chieftain of the pygmies whose tribe was their closest neighbor, to watch over the magnificent dwelling which Ki-Gor had built with his own hands. They had traveled on the back of Marmo, the great grey elephant to join Tembu George in a hunt. Hunting was a favorite and often necessary pastime for Ki-Gor, and the big Masai was his closest friend and favorite hunting partner.

When first they arrived in the appointed meeting area, the shallow bend of the great river, their approach on the mighty Marmo was easily heard. Tembu George had left two of his tribesmen behind with his long war canoe and hurried to greet his friends. As they exchanged a warm greeting, a great commotion had come from where the Masai Chief had left his canoe. Running to see what was the matter, the trio came upon a grisly scene. The two tribesmen of Tembu George lay dead at the feet of a Du'Ani head-hunting party and a frightened young man was scrambling away as fast as possible!

Where they had come from no one could say at that moment, but it was clear they were after the boy. As the savage jungle killers began to give chase they turned their attention to the startled and gasping beauty that had come running with the two strangers. Helene must have looked like a far better and easier prize than the scared boy who was already deep in the green and running.

Seeing the intention of the men, Ki-Gor and Tembu George poised for battle only to hear the scream of the jungle lord's wife as she was lassoed and yanked into the treetops above. This was not at all the pleasant hunting trip the two friends had planned.

Now that the danger had been dealt with, the two warriors decided they wanted some answers from the young man the Du'Ani had originally been after. The hunt was on once again, only this time it was for a scared and lost boy.

The trail was easy enough to follow. In a panic one does not tend to tread stealthily. Knowing that the mysterious native's path would be no problem to pick out and that he had a several minute running lead, Ki-Gor shot into the broken branches and twisting vines like a jungle cat. Tembu George was quick to take to the tree route above and follow his friend on the chase, leaving Helene by the big war canoe with naught but a stone tipped spear, and the company of the dead.

With a look of mock disapproval the shapely red head cast a sarcastic eye at the great elephant Marmo, who was lazily grazing on the tall reeds near the river's edge.

«Well, at least there's one gentleman who doesn't run off on a lady in this jungle!»

The great grey pachyderm took in a trunk of cool river water and playfully trumpeted as he sprayed the astonished jungle maiden, drenching her shapely form from head to toe.

«Ohhh!.. Men!» Helene sputtered, flabbergasted.

Meanwhile the bronze giant and the Masai warrior were closing in on their prey. If the crashing branches and ferns only a hundred yards or so in front of them were any indication, the two would overtake the boy in mere seconds. Suddenly from his vantage point in the high, broad branches of the trees Tembu George spied their target. He also spied something else.

«Brother, wait!» He called to Ki-Gor who was several yards ahead of him on the ground. The fleet-footed Man Mountain stopped and cast a questioning glance up and back at his friend.

«Se'Tha Gomba,» he stated gravely, pointing about to the spot where the runner should have been. The dread native words described the rare giant snakes sometimes seen in the marshy areas near the rivers. A westerner would have called the serpent an anaconda.

Like the child of the forest he was, Ki-Gor climbed up the tree to stand next to his friend as easily as a normal man climbs a ladder. Dropping to one knee he surveyed the area in question with eagle-sharp eyes. There was the running man, clearly visible now and not much more than a boy of fourteen or fifteen summers in age. He was no longer running or moving at all but being very, very still as, rising from the marshy reeds directly in front of him, was the dreaded «Se'Tha Gomba»!

The boy had enough sense at least not to make any sudden moves, but regardless the gigantic serpent would soon strike. Ki-Gor said nothing as he kept his gaze riveted to the scene. He stretched out his strong left hand to Tembu George and beckoned for the big Masai to hand over his bow and an arrow. The anaconda swayed its melon-sized head hypnotically and fluidly from side to side as its forked tongue darted out to within a foot of the boy's terrified face, testing the air for fear. Fear would make its meal taste just that much better.

As Tembu George handed one of his arrows to the white jungle lord he was met with a dismissing hand gesture. Ki-Gor then, still trained on his target, pointed to a specific arrow in Tembu George's quiver. It was a special shaft, fletched with red bird feathers to distinguish it from the others. It was a gift from the old pygmy Chief N'geeso. This arrow was coated in the deadly poison the pygmies used which could drop a charging leopard instantly. It only took a scratch and there was no known antidote.

With the poison arrow notched and drawn to his cheek, Ki-Gor took careful aim. From this angle he could easily hit the boy with only the slightest error. The black-scaled monster opened its massive jaws, revealing its dagger-like fangs in a primeval hiss! Ki-Gor sent forth his deadly missile with grim intent. As the poison shaft streaked unerringly through the jungle air, the boy, in the face of certain death, attempted to dive to one side. This caused Se'Tha Gomba to strike and change its position. The two warrior friends cursed in unison.

Their disdain was premature, however, for, though the arrow did not hit its intended mark, it did still hit. The snake reared back and thrashed its colossal body as the poison entered its cold, cold blood. The large whipping coils, as big around as a sturdy tree, slapped into the young man's ankle which snapped with a wet cracking sound. The native went down with a howl of pain as simultaneously the hissing serpent crashed to the muddy, marshy floor quite dead. Now the two brave men would get what they were after, answers.

2.
BOY OUT OF TIME

His name was Mabuku and he was very surprised to feel the warmth of a fire and a reassuring hand caressing his brow. As his heavy, sore eyelids opened, vision returned in a hazy cloud. He was even more surprised that the woman who attended him had hair the color of a midsummer's sunset and skin as light as his was dark!

In surprise Mabuku sat up in a start immediately feeling the fatigue and stiffness of his limbs and the excruciating pain in his ankle. He winced and saw that two men were nearby as well. One was a large, muscled warrior with a clean-shaven head who wore the markings of a tribe that he recognized from stories his elders told, the Masai. The other was bigger but had skin that was bronzed by the sun and hair the color of spun gold. He wore a loincloth of leopard skin and his build was that of the mightiest of warriors.

Mabaku's mouth was agape and his eyes wide. He had heard legends of a white jungle lord who was good and righteous, a hero with the strength of a lion, the speed of a snake and the cunning of a monkey. Men spoke with great respect of the man called...

«Ki-Gor,» cautioned Helena, «You're frightening him!» The auburn-haired beauty looked at the nervous young man with a calming smile. «Shhh It's okay, we're friends.»

Mabuku did not understand the words but he understood the intent: he was safe now. The young native returned a disarming yet cautious smile of his own and pointed questioningly at the bronze giant.

«Ki-Gor?»

With a raised eyebrow upon hearing the youth speak his name, the lord of the jungle answered, thumping his chest authoritatively with a strong right fist as he did so.

«I am Ki-Gor. What are you called?»

He could see the youth knew his name but not necessarily the tongue in which it was spoken. He repeated himself in several different tribal dialects and finally the boy's eyes shone with the light of recognition.

«I owe you my life, great jungle lord! My name is Mabuku of the Jwahla.»

Ki-Gor smiled and clasped forearms with the boy in the traditional friendly way. Tembu George also exchanged a greeting but eyed the boy with suspicion. He looked at his friend and motioned for him to step aside where he could speak with him in private.

«My brother, this boy cannot be of the Jwahla. That tribe disappeared many years before even my grandfather's grandfather was born. How a youth even knows the name I cannot say.»

The jungle lord watched as Mabuku graciously accepted a gourd cup of water from Helene. He seemed harmless enough. With a nod to the big Masai Ki-Gor went back to the boy's side.

«Why were the man eaters chasing you?»

Gulping down a second cup of cool water, he wiped his mouth on his arm, regarding the bronze-skinned warrior with sad eyes.

«I came across the tribe of head collectors a day north of here. I had no time to waste and so I stole one of their canoes. I have been running from them for over a day now and would surely be dead if not for you! Since I left to find help for my people I have heard many legends told of the great Ki-Gor! The fates have brought me to you!»

The young man smiled broadly. It was a smile of desperation and hope.

«You will help me, wont you? I offer my life to free my people from the cruel slavery of Sirin Tal.»

Both of the men stood back in shock at the sound of the strange name. Their eyes met each other's in a look of impossibility. Helene was confused by the men's reaction.

«What's the matter with you two? If there are slavers in the jungle, you've dealt with their kind before.»

The jungle maiden looked from face to face and finally settled on the downcast stare of Mabuku.

«Who is Sirin Tal? Why does he cause such a reaction?»

Ki-Gor motioned for everyone to sit down as he took Helene's hand comfortingly.

«She,» he corrected her.

Here Ki-Gor interposed: «Sirin Tal is a woman, a legend told to make children go to sleep and not wander far into the wild. She was supposed to be...»

«NO!» interrupted the boy. «The JuJu Queen is real! She keeps my people and others, too! No one can leave ‚only come! The City of Tal Anori is real, jungle lord, real! My scars are real!»

With that statement Mabuku, who had been wearing a simple vest of burlap, tore the garment from himself to reveal the tell-tale signs of a taskmaster's whip. Helene turned away in disgust at the scars which covered the youth's back and sides. Ki-Gor stood with fists clenched in anger.

«Only a coward tortures another man so! Tell us your story, then, Mabuku.»

The scarred boy regained his calm demeanor and smiled apologetically for his outburst.

«I will tell you the tale as my father told it to me, my friends, and as his father told it to him:

«Long long ago a great king from the desert came from his lands to see the wonders of our vast green jungle. He was a kind man but very old. While on his journeys he came to the mouth of the great river, nestled in a valley by a shining lake and hidden from the outside world by a mist that rose up around it.

«Here at the source waters was a peaceful tribe called the Anori. The desert king fell in love with a beautiful princess of the tribe and took her as a bride. As was the custom in his land he sought to build a monument to her in a gesture of undying love.

«From his kingdom in the Arabic lands he brought the finest artisans and builders, and a wondrous city was constructed! Towers of gold and ivory, statues of fine marble and spires that gleamed like torches! It was a monument like nothing anyone had ever seen, and many tribes and many more women of stature became bitterly jealous.

«The bride could not leave her beautiful city because of the petty envy of her own people. She became despised by her own sisters and the only one save her husband and servants who would hold council with her was the old witchdoctor Sirin-Golta. Sirin-Golta was as feared as the new Queen was despised. He taught her the secrets of voodoo and black sorcery and she became very powerful in its practice. She weaved a spell that made her skin as white as ivory in the hope that if her own people would no longer accept her, then perhaps her husband's people would.

«But the desert peoples rejected her as little more than a trophy from a conquered land. A plaything for the old king. Rejected once more, she returned to her golden city in the jungle, depressed and feeling very much alone. Upon her return she discovered that her husband was very ill, and soon the man who took her from her tribe and built a monument to her that became more a prison than a symbol of love... died.

«Grief-stricken, the queen grew more and more embittered as the days dragged on. The old witch doctor had strangely disappeared also, leaving her without a single friend. Her heart became twisted and cruel and she turned herself to the dark arts completely. In an act of revenge she called for a great festival and feast to be held in the city and invited all the tribes and peoples as far as she could send messengers to reach. Many came, the Jwahla, the Kotongo, the seven councils of Bukta-Ngo, and hundreds flocked to the great golden city of Tal Anori. They did not know that they would never leave again!

«Her real name has been forgotten, but all who gathered that day came to know of the evil Queen Sirin Tal!, named after her teacher of voodoo and the city that had become her unwanted home. The festival was a ruse and Sirin Tal worked a spell with a horrible price! If she could not freely leave her city and if her people would not take her back, then she would take THEM into her city and keep them forever! The spell she wove would not allow anyone to leave. Like an invisible wall a man may walk into but never out of!

«The people are forced to work and serve, to fight and die and love at a whim, all for the twisted amusement of the cruel witch! For every one that dies she lives longer, and then the dead rise to do her bidding! They are the Zuvembi, the dead who walk! They are the guards and taskmasters. Imagine it, great jungle lord, forced to work at the end of a lash wielded by your own dead and rotting mother! Most have gone mad, and the few who are not, no longer have the spirit to resist. This is the fate of our people. This is the story of the Dread Curse of Sirin Tal. What was born of love was twisted into the cruelest of evil. Please, mighty Ki-Gor, the story must have an end... it must have an end.»

With the last sentence Mabuku looked at Ki-Gor with imploring eyes. He had told the story with such feeling in his young yet wise voice that Helene had turned away with tears in her eyes. A love story that went terribly wrong. The spitfire wife of the jungle lord never even gave the two men a chance to speak.

«You said no one can leave, Mabuku. How is it that you did?»

The simple question hit the bronzed giant with a start. How indeed? His hand reflexively drifted to the hilt of his knife as he awaited an answer from the boy.

«It is strange.» Mabuku began. «I was born in Tal Anori. Most of the people are the original prisoners you see; the bad juju keeps them from growing old, but those of us who are born within the city age as any normal man. Most of those like me are sacrificed to the Queen at birth but some of us are kept hidden until we can work and not be noticed as ‹new.› Very few of those born within the city live to my age and the spell does not affect us. I was sent by the elders to find help as many before me had been. No one ever returns with help. The jungle is dangerous for a lone man as I well know now.» He rubbed his injured ankle as if emphasizing his statement.

Tembu George gripped the shaft of his spear as he sat listening and watching the boy. He remembered his own father warning him when he was young that if he wandered off too far the white witch Sirin Tal would gobble him up. He shuddered at the thought of the tale having even a grain of truth to it. Snapping his mind from his unpleasant thoughts, the big Masai warrior spoke.

«Surely the witch is powerful and has an army. How is it you think we can end this curse? Convincing enough men of the truth of this tale to gather a large force is unlikely, young Mabuku. The name of Sirin Tal is feared throughout the jungle as a terrifying myth.»

The boy's shoulders sank in defeat.

«You are right, mighty warrior. Perhaps this is why no one who was sent out ever returned with help. The Queen has no army, but the Zuvembi are fierce and already dead. How do you kill a dead man? They say that only her heart can end the curse, but that too has been dead for centuries.»

Ki-Gor stood to his full, impressive height. With a glance at his mate he held up his hands in a reassuring gesture to Mabuku.

«The heart can conquer many things, young friend. It can turn savagery into nobility and hatred into remorse. A man with heart is a man without fear!» The jungle lord took the hand of Tembu George and with a smile pulled him to his feet.

«A man without fear is invincible even should he die, for his heart will embolden others! Go, my brother. Gather your boldest and we will travel to this city of gold and wonder. Where our brave young friend has sought hope for his people let us show him that he has found it!»

Mabuku smiled and let forth a whoop! Helene stood by the side of her man admiringly. Tembu George nodded in agreement and clasped forearms with his white brother.

«Truth and wisdom, my brother. Your heart is that of a lion.»

3.
QUEST TO TAL ANORI

Ki-Gor and Helene made camp while Tembu George set off in his long war canoe for his home village. Not only was he the bravest and strongest warrior of all the Masai, he was also their beloved and admired chieftain. The trip would take him a full day and a half before he would return.

As the trio waited, Ki-Gor spent his time constructing a new bow and fashioning arrows. Helene, meanwhile, told a wide-eyed Mabuku of the wonders of the modern world that lay outside the jungle. The boy was incredulous.

«Metal boats that fly? Aer-o-planes you call them? Ha ha ha! Please, Miss Helene! You are having fun with me, aren't you?»

Ki-Gor smiled to himself hearing Mabuku laugh. He knew the young man had probably never had much to smile about in his harsh life. The jungle lord leaned against his bow and stared long and whimsically at his wife. She was beautiful. Just as she now entertained the injured youth with her stories and her unbridled passion for life itself he remembered how her infectious joy had changed him, too, made him stronger. Love, he thought, the right kind of love can do that.

Night fell and the next day passed. Ki-Gor and Mabuku spent time practicing archery and Helene gathered provisions for the journey: sweet licorice roots and plump red berries. She also smoked several large fish that her husband had caught. It was clear from talking with Mabuku that their trek would take several days by river; he himself had been on foot for over three weeks before he stole the canoe from the headhunters.

The midday sun glinted from the water of the great river. Helene called out to Ki-Gor as the rhythmic splash of oars could be heard drawing closer.

«Ki-Gor! Tembu George has returned!»

With his keen sight the white lord of the jungle looked southward down the waterway. Rounding the bend came the prow of a Masai war canoe, followed by a second. Ki-Gor counted only six men with his friend who wore a weary look on his face.

«Well met, brother! Is this all or are more not far behind?» He helped beach the long black boat as the men disembarked.

Tembu George looked dismayed.

«There are raiders, my brother. They come to make war with my village and I cannot leave it unprotected in my absence. These are all I dare spare unless I wish to lose my lands. The raiders are few but tenacious. The women and children must be assured of protection.»

Ki-Gor dismissed his friend's worried look.

«You are a chieftain first, my brother! A smaller group may be able to enter this city more effectively than a large war party anyway.»

Four of the Masai killed a stag in a nearby glen and the group feasted and told stories of bravery and heroics that night. All listened intently as Mabuku retold the tale of Sirin Tal, and more than one mighty warrior shivered at the mention of her name. Bellies full, the group rested well and arose at dawn's light to begin their long trek north. North to the mouth of the great river, to the mists where no man dared go through.

They traveled for days with no trouble, stopping when they grew tired to make camp and hunt. Sometimes they paused for a brief and friendly bit of trading with tribes seldom seen. Some of the tribes had been encountered by Mabuku on his quest. It was from them he had heard of the great Ki-Gor. They journeyed far, farther than any of them ever had to the north, through Karamziliand, the empire ruled by the fierce yet just lDingazi, a man who owed Ki-Gor his life. The jungle lord and the Masai had never traveled more than a day's full journey past the northern borders of Karamziliand until now.

It was dusk of the eighteenth day of travel that Ki-Gor heard the birds and insects grow strangely quiet behind them. The creatures of the jungle could sense hostility, and someone or something had begun to follow the group. Using the hand language that N'Geeso had taught him, a way of silent communication the pygmies used when hunting, the jungle lord alerted the group to the unseen danger that lurked behind them. Whether it was in the water or along the banks he could not tell but he ventured a guess that they would find out when they made camp that night.

Beaching the war canoes, the group immediately gathered stones to arrange and lit a fire. Normally two to four of them would go off to hunt for meat, but this night they did not. Something or someone was following them and it was safer to stay together.

Helene and Mabuku each made a bed in one of the long canoes so as not to be out in the open. Ki-Gor, Tembu George and the six Masai took turns standing guard four at a time while the others slept. Anticipation ran high, but the men did their best to act normal so as not to give away to the unseen enemy the fact that they were onto them.

A light mist crept into the party's camp as the last hours of darkness began. The fire burned low and the sounds of the river lazily lapping portrayed a deceptive calm. Ki-Gor's keen senses, honed by a life in the dangerous jungle, snapped him from sleep with a start. He made no sudden moves but turned his head to find that Tembu George was also awake and looking to him knowingly. They eyed the Masai who stood watch. Good and true men, they manned their posts alertly yet seemingly unaware of the impending sense of danger which had jarred the two men from sleep.

With a sudden and startling snap of branches and an unfamiliar yell the quiet was broken! As they made camp earlier Ki-Gor had set several snares concealed along the treeline. Someone had just tripped one. The men sprang to action! Ki-Gor leapt to his feet with an arrow notched in his bow, and the Masai formed a circle to protect the boy and Helene. There in the treeline was the silouhette of a man, upside down and thrashing wildly as he hung by one ankle and bobbed helplessly from the snare he had tripped. As eyes adjusted to the misty night several more shadowy forms could be seen among the trees. Ki-Gor rallied the men with a mighty war cry and signaled the attack!

One shadowy form pitched backwards as two stout shafts sprouted from his chest. Another found his arm pinned to a tree but had little time to feel the excruciating pain as a second arrow pierced his skull through the left eye, killing him instantly. Several more rushed from the trees into the camp. Crude long blades of black iron swinging over their heads with faces and bodies painted in a skeletal pattern of chalk white. Ki-Gor's eyes grew wide in recognition as his knife sprang into his strong right hand.

«Du'Ani! The headhunters seek revenge!»

In the chaos of battle one of the Masai blocked a viscious attack from the hacking blade of one of the man-eaters and countered by bringing the shaft of his spear up, slamming into the chin of the Du'Ani and knocking him backwards off his feet. Where his head struck the ground a second snare was triggered and the vine rope closed around the neck of the surprised headhunter, yanking him skyward with a sharp snap! As the brave warrior stared at the hanged man in surprise a second Du'Ani's blade bit deep into his spine with a meaty—THWACK!—sending the unfortunate warrior to an agonizing death.

As the evil, grinning killer wrenched his blood-slicked chopping blade from his victim's back he shuddered involuntarily, and with a wet cough of a grunt looked down to see a stone spearhead erupt from his abdomen in a spray of gore! At the other end of the weapon stood Tembu George, teeth clenched in anger at the sight of his tribesman being cut down. There was no time for hesitation. He wrenched the spear from the Du'Ani corpse and wheeled around in time to see mighty Ki-Gor slam a rock-hard fist backwards across the mouth of one headhunter, sending him reeling away, while at the same time plunging his knife into the heart of a second.

Tembu George both admired and feared the savage battle prowess of his white-skinned brother. Though heroic in spirit he was a feral beast in a fight! The headhunters saw this as well and drew back hesitantly from the jungle lord.

Ki-Gor crouched and pointed commandingly at the three remaining assassins with the blade of his fearsome knife, dripping with blood. His mouth was an animal snarl and his mighty sinews flexed with the anticipation of a kill. The sound of bowstrings drawing tight met his keen ears as the Masai circled the dreaded cannibalistic killers. Tembu George snapped a single word in his native tongue and the twang of the bows sounded the final breath of the Du'Ani.

In the aftermath of the battle a second Masai was found to have been slain and a third was assigned to return with their bodies to the village. The men would be given a hero's funeral and their women would be given the opportunity to bid them farewell as was custom. This left only three warriors to accompany Ki-Gor, Tembu George, Helene, and Mabuku to the city of Tal Anori. Only one of the long war canoes would be needed; the second would be used to return the fallen home.

The ensnared Du'Ani was cut down, fully bound and left by the banks of the river. Ki-Gor noted the tell-tale signs of crocodile footprints in the mud as he regarded the killer coldly.

«The jungle will decide your fate.»

With Helene and Mabuku accounted for and unharmed the group set off once more on their way. As the morning mists cleared, the group spoke not a word. Trailing his gaze along the passing banks of the river, the jungle lord pushed the blood lust from his mind and sighed deeply. The gentle and understanding touch of his wife anchored him back from savagery. It always did.

Eight days more of travel brought them to where the current pushed strong against them. The river was no longer lazy, it was defiant. Small wakes made paddling more and more difficult. The canoe had to be turned to shore and stowed as they realized the rest of the journey would be on foot.

The forest here in this unfamiliar area where the group disembarked was shrouded in white mist. A mist that grew denser the further the group walked. No animal sounds were heard here. All was still and silent. Staying within earshot of the river, they used the sound of the rushing waters as a guide through the haunting shroud of fog. The unnatural quiet made Helene anxious and she held Ki-Gor's arm closely.

«Mabuku, you had to have come through here. However did you manage?»

The red-headed beauty's words were met with a look of absolute fear from the young man. His response was a furtive hushing as he motioned for all to gather near. In as low a voice as he could manage the boy spoke:

«Please Miss Helene, this is the domain of the Kanango! The Ghost Men! We must be quiet as we pass through the forbidden mists or risk drawing their attention.»

Ki-Gor calmed Mabuku by patting his shoulder and just as quietly responded.

«Ghost Men or not, this area has a very bad feel. It would not hurt to remain vigilant and quiet.» All agreed with a nod as the jungle lord said one last thing:

«Stay close together; the fog grows thicker and it would be easy to become lost from one another.»

Something felt very wrong indeed to the bronze-skinned giant, but he heard and smelled nothing but the dampness of the mist and the river to his left. Staying close the group set off again, eager to break out of the maddening white. As they left the area where they had spoken a pair of eyes seemed to open in the fog itself! Eyes that followed the group with curiosity as they disappeared in the distance. Eyes that seemed to float by themselves in the rolling cloudy whiteness.

Tembu George watched as his men grew more and more uneasy. They were brave warriors, but the fog made it impossible to tell where they were or how far they had gone. Dutifully they followed Ki-Gor who himself was merely keeping an ear trained on the flowing river as a guide. As weariness and monotony set, in one of the Masai let out a start and crouched down as if awaiting an attack.

«AIYEE! Bwana, there are ghosts!»

Weapons were drawn and readied instantly in reaction to the cry. Ki-Gor scanned the white nothingness to no avail.

«I hear nothing. I see nothing.» He smiled disarmingly at the spooked Masai. «We are all tired; perhaps we should rest. A fire may warm our courage if we can manage any dry wood.» The jungle lord was also feeling on edge in the strangely silent whiteness but he believed a weary mind would play tricks long before any ghosts menaced them.

Staying as close as possible, the group scouted up stones and wood to build a fire. Most of the rocks were covered in lichens and moss, as was any fallen wood. The damp of the area seemed to permeate everything. Tembu George threw a moss covered stone in frustration.

«We cannot build a fire in this cursed place!»

Where the Masai chieftain had thrown the fist-sized stone a dull thump was distinctly heard, accompanied by a yelp of pain!

«ARRHH!!»

The group turned towards the sound, which had not come from any of them, with a start! Weapons reflexively readied, the six men and Helene formed a back-to-back circle, all eyes staring in vain at the constant fog that surrounded them.

«Ki-Gor!» Helene gasped. She pointed to a distinct red-veined pair of eyes that seemed to float in the mist.

Suddenly a second pair popped open and then a third! The hairs on the back of Tembu George's neck stood on end as he looked up and saw more eyes peering down from fog-hidden branches! More and more, from every angle the very fog itself seemed to come alive with dozens of eyes. Mabuku fell to his knees in fear.

«Kanango! Kanango! It is them! The Ghost Men!»

Ki-Gor still could not smell the familiar scent of man, but if a stone could make one cry out in pain then these were no ghosts! He locked eyes with a pair in front of him, red-rimmed, sleep-deprived bloodshot orbs. Slowly and deliberately he sheathed his knife and turned both empty palms towards the blinking watcher in the white. If these unseen stalkers had wanted to kill them they could have easily done so long ago. The jungle lord felt no hostility yet; he wondered if he could trust his instincts in this place where his senses had already failed him. His answer came in the form of a voice.

«Why do you venture into our mists, travelers? You would do well to return from whence you came. Past our home lies only sorrow.»

Closer now stepped several pairs of the eyes. It was still hard to discern in the shifting white, but the eyes most definitely belonged to men. Men who were covered from head to toe in a thin alabaster mud which clung dried to their skin and meager clothing. The bizarre mud men were unarmed and stared quizzically moreso than threateningly. Helene gasped at the sight. The strange men made for a startling image. It was quite easy to see how legends of ghosts abounded when men spoke of the forbidden mists near the mouth of the great river.

Ki-Gor motioned for the others to lower their weapons.

«We travel in peace. We seek the lost city of Tal Anori which lies just beyond your land of vexing whiteness.»

The mud man who had spoken arched an eyebrow at the jungle lord;

«You would go into the city of the witch queen voluntarily?» He harumphed sarcastically. «Be you fools or madmen?»

Tembu George's temper flared at the insult. He drew in a breath sharply and began to speak but was stopped by the sudden voice of Mabuku as the boy rose to his feet with a newfound pride.

«I am Mabuku of the Jwahla, slave of Sirin Tal. These brave warriors come to free my people from the cursed city. You will either leave us in peace or stand aside, Kanango!»

The mud men laughed at the sound of that name. Their spokesman turned his gaze to the young man.

«Ghost Men? Boy, we are no spirits, only men. Men who have for centuries been forced to pay tribute to the evil Sirin Tal! If your mission is as you say, then we will help you.» The obvious leader inclined his head in a respectful bow to Ki-Gor.

«You are close warrior. Very close indeed to the city of death and sorrow that you seek. Had you continued on your path you would have fallen into an inescapable bog of quicksand. We will show you the path, warriors. Come and we will take you to the gates of Tal Anori!»

From all around and even dropping from the mossy branches above, the mud men made their presence known. Cautiously the group followed the strange tribe into the mists as the leader continued to speak.

«It was three hundred years ago that the desert king died. Three hundred years since Sirin Tal's heart turned black with hate. Since that time we, the Wakizi, have acted as guardians here in the forbidden mists. We keep the lost and travelers away from the city of Tal Anori to spare them a horrible fate.»

Torches could be seen burning through the fog ahead, small huts and fires that burned away the ever-present white. It was a relief to see the village as they entered it even if it was filled with the strange tribe covered in the ghostly mud.

The Wakizi proved very kind indeed. Food and drink were freely given to Ki-Gor and his group, and a warm place to rest their weary bones. As they ate their fill they learned that the leader of the tribe was named B'Alu and it was he alone that spoke with them.

«We Wakizi are required to bring two of our young each season to the city gates as an offering to the Witch Queen. We are not warriors, we have little skill with which to resist. The times we have she has sent her Zuvembi into our village to spread terror and death, for only the dead may walk from the gates of that cursed place! Be assured, warriors, that you are not the first to come in hopes of ending her reign. We always help any willing to try, but no one has ever come back.»

Ki-Gor wiped his mouth with the back of his hand and swallowed the roasted meat he was eating.

«There is always hope, B'Alu. We must try. This evil has caused too much pain for too long. Come the dawn we move on to Tal Anori.»

The chieftain of the mud men sighed in resignation. It was clear he held little faith of the group ever being heard from again.

«Very well, hero. Rest yourselves and I will take you to where the mists end when you are ready.»

4.
BEHOLD THE CITY OF SORROW

Hours passed in welcome yet somewhat anxious slumber. As the adventuring group stirred themselves they were greeted by the ever-present white fog. Though the torches and fires burned it away within the small compound it still crept and crawled in ghostly tendrils throughout the village of the mud men. The village was like an oasis within the mists and Ki-Gor and his companions could not be sure if beyond the vaporous wall it was night or day.

B'Alu and one of the Wakizi men waited patiently until their guests seemed ready to continue. With Helene and the men fed and prepared for travel he signaled for them to follow.

«It is not far, heroes. I will take you to where the mists end and no further.»

Ki-Gor took the lead and Tembu George guarded the rear as they padded off into the blinding white. B'Alu had taken a thin, crude rope and, grasping one end, passed it down for each member of the party to take hold of. This would ensure that no one strayed or was lost while trekking through the thick shroud.

Gradually the fog grew less dense, from a solid cloud to a thinner veil within an hour's walking. The chieftain of the mud men stopped suddenly, as did his tribesman. Turning to face the explorers he seemed noticeably nervous.

«Two hundred paces, jungle lord.» He pointed in the direction they would have still been walking had he not stopped. «I will go no further, but I will pray for the gods to watch over you.»

The bronzed giant inclined his head to B'Alu in a respectful bow.

«Thank you for your kindness, good chieftain.» He hesitated then. Ki-Gor wanted to say something, anything that would give the dour and resigned man a glimmer of hope. A word that might bolster his crushed spirit. Instead he smiled and placed his right palm to his heart, a commonly recognized gesture throughout the jungle lands that meant «friend.» The Wakizi chieftain returned the gesture in kind with a sad smile. What more could be said? The strange tribe of the mud men had existed on the mist-strewn borders of the cursed city of Tal Anori under the oppression of its ruler for generations before B'Alu was born. Despair was something the Wakizi were born into.

The troupe continued on. Some fifty paces away Tembu George looked back and saw how the clever camouflage caused all but the eyes of their two guides to disappear. With a sudden blink the men were gone! Vanished back into the fog as if they had never really been there to begin with.

Soon faint sounds of birds met Ki-Gor's ears once more. Smells and sounds returned to his jungle-trained senses lifting the weird silence of the white from his shoulders. Indeed the mood of the entire group seemed to strangely lift in a sudden moment. As if emerging from a stationary cloud, the group entered one after another back into the bright day of a green paradise!

It was a small, grassy hill they stood on. The strange mist somehow stopped as if against some invisible wall behind them. Reaching back in amazement Helene ran her hand through the barrier of fog which now stood behind them. Cautiously they crested the hill and gasped at the wonder they beheld.

A vast walled city, gold and ivory spires lancing towards the heavens and fluttering red flags that flew from the tops of stone towers. Each and every building within sight was a work of art that rivaled the grandest mountain in sheer beauty. The late-day sun glinted off of rooftops which shone with the unmistakable brilliance of pure gold. It was absolutely breathtaking.

«Tal Anori,» stated Mabuku grimly. «Behold the City of Sorrow.»

The two senior warriors scanned the city walls with a look of consternation. Tembu George shrugged as he and Ki-Gor exchanged the same look.

«The gate must be on the other side from us, my brother.»

The young slave shook his head and pointed to where two statues stood.

«Look closer: the gateway is concealed yet still guarded.»

Dropping to his belly, Ki-Gor crawled low and silent in the grass. He moved as swift and agile as any snake, creeping to a spot many yards from the others to where his hawk-like eyes could view the two statues better. What he saw turned his stomach. Slithering back to his companions he rose once more to his feet with a grim countenance.

«I take it, Mabuku, that those are what you called the ‹Zuvembi›?»

The young man nodded with a look of dread resignation.

«They will not move unless obeying orders or if they are attacked. Some will stand as still as stone until they rot into a skeletal husk! They are mindless and all in the city know that they are merely the shells of those we once knew, but…»

His last words were cut off by a catch in his throat. Helene attempted to comfort the boy who was apparently remembering an unpleasant occurrence with the creatures. He cleared his throat and continued.

«The wall itself is a clever illusion of intricate stonework. There is an open gateway between the two guards, yet unless you view it from an exact angle it seems to be a solid wall.»

«There appear to be no more than those two. We should be able to take them out easily,» mused the Jungle Lord.

Mabuku waved in dismissal.

«You will not have to fight them. They allow anyone who approaches to enter. Unless the spell of Sirin Tal is removed, you will not be able to leave. I and others born within the walls seem unaffected which is why we are sought out and killed. Though I am the only one now.»

The group seemed to grasp this fact all at once, and Ki-Gor took his wife in his strong arms and kissed her deeply.

«You will stay behind. I will find a way to signal you within two days. If not, then go, go and call the debt owed me by Dingazi in Karamzililand.»

Helene protested with customary fire: «I go with you! Better to be by your side than lose you forever! I swear, Ki-Gor, you know I'll just follow you anyway and I can handle a spear or knife as good as anyone!»

Her face was a mask of determination. She pulled her husband's knife from its sheath and with a quick turn let the weapon fly! It buried itself in the narrow trunk of a small tree with a SHUNK! By any account it was an excellent throw.

Ki-Gor looked at the red-headed beauty, angrily at first, and took her once again by her soft, white shoulders. Then his stern mouth broke into a grin and he kissed her once more.

«The wise men always say never argue with a lioness!» The jungle lord laughed as he retrieved his knife from the tree it was stuck in. Tembu George and his Masai warriors joined in the merriment.

«My brother, I don't know why you even try!»

Mabuku simply stared down at the guarded portal, not sharing in the others mirth.

«I will walk us in. Any movement I do or replies I give, please follow along. We must get through the gate and inside off of the streets as quickly as possible!» The young man did not wait. He started off down the small hill directly towards the sentries. Ki-Gor and the rest followed quickly behind.

Soon the walls loomed before them and the clever illusion of angular stonework became apparent. There was indeed an open gate in the wall. The intricately fitted stone was actually a wall within a wall, slightly offset and angled so as to appear solid from any direction except dead on. The Zuvembi were now clearly discernible as well. The sight that had made the bronze-skinned warrior's stomach churn did the same to the others now. The ribs of the creatures were starkly visible behind emaciated black skin. Lips were dried and withered back to reveal a hideous rictus grin of clenched teeth. A smell like rotted meat assaulted their senses, and the two unmoving things stared blankly ahead with milky white eyes as flies swarmed about them in a cloud. Each one held an iron-capped cudgel in its bony, leather-skinned hand.

Mabuku walked casually between the two nightmares and through the gate. Ki-Gor gripped Helene by the hand subtly and reassuringly as the woman closed her eyes at the gruesome sight and followed the boy through. Once all were inside they beheld a street of immaculate stone and a handful of workers cleaning and repairing the buildings and the street itself. «Citizens» appeared to be toiling at mundane tasks for no other reason than to appear busy. Upon their entrance the newcomers noticed that the people seemed to be purposely ignoring them. When they did catch the eye of a citizen, he or she would flinch and quickly turn their head.

A sudden sound seemed to agitate everyone around including Mabuku, who shook with panic! The quick-paced slap of booted feet on the stone street could only mean trouble! Mabuku turned towards Ki-Gor and the others with wide eyes.

«Hurry! Follow me! She knows there are new arrivals!»

Bolting into a nearby empty hut the group weaved through stacks of ancient and unused sundries and out a small back entrance into a narrow alleyway. Mabuku seemed to know exactly where he was going and did so at an incredible speed. The others followed down the alley and over a low stone wall. Over the barrier they clambered at a breakneck pace: the boy followed by Helene who was given a boost by Ki-Gor who then followed. Next came Tembu George and Garan, the oldest of his accompanying warriors. Zu'An followed over the wall in a panic as a tremendous crashing sounded behind him! The group stopped in their running as Tembu George looked back to the last man over.

«Where is Dala?»

Zu'An clearly did not want to stop running as he stared into the eyes of his chieftain.

«The dead men! They brought him down! They move with the speed of Leopards!»

«HURRY!» yelled Mabuku.

Frustrated, and with Tembu George swearing an oath of revenge, the group bolted into the back door of a building that was detailed in ivory tusks and gold leaf. Scurrying through a mass of straw pallets on the floor, the young man moved one of the primitive beds aside to reveal a hidden trap door. Yanking it open revealed a stone stair that spiraled deep down into the dark unknown. Mabuku frantically hurried everyone down the steps and then joined them himself, closing the secret door behind him. His fingers found a familiar length of cord fitted through a small hole in the door and he pulled it briskly. The cord was attached to the straw bed in such a way that, when pulled, the pallet slid over the trap door, hiding it from view.

Knowing hands recovered a flint and torch from a niche in the wall, and the young slave soon held a welcome light in his hand illuminating the stone passage.

«This is my daily existence in Tal Anori. Hiding and venturing out only when I must. These tunnels will take us to a safe place: the temple where sits our council of elders. The elders will know how to reach the palace and the white witch herself.»

Ki-Gor cast a grim eye to his Masai friend. «I have fought with voodoo priests before. We will end this curse. It is my experience that the evil spells casts by such beings end with them.»

«Yes, my brother.» Responded Tembu George, «Sirin Tal must die.»

5.
THE WHITE WITCH

In the tallest tower of Tal Anori, in its highest room, stood the white witch Sirin Tal. She was tall and graceful in movement. Her alabaster skin seemed to accentuate the features of her Nubian face, and the gown she wore of black silks and exotic feathers clung to her womanly curves as if the garment itself were making love to her. Her hair was black and hung in braids adorned with beads of solid gold. She was exotically beautiful and if not for one single terrifying feature, any man would have gladly fallen to his knees in worship of her. That feature was her eyes. They were as red as a midsummer sunset. Not in part but in entirety, each orb was a bright and disturbing red. To have those terrible eyes fall upon you was to invite nightmares.

Lithe as a dancer, she walked across the floor of her chamber to a black cauldron that sat in the center of the room upon a bed of red-hot coals. The cauldron bubbled and hissed with a dank and unknown liquid as thick as molasses. Waving her left hand over the steamy surface of the cauldron's contents, she stared deep into the inky substance and smiled. Images that only she could see rippled in the searing hot liquid. Portents of things to come. Sirin Tal had seen an image of a bronze-skinned warrior strapped to the stone altar which sat cold and empty on the opposite side of her chamber. The smile she wore was cruel and short-lived as she turned her blood-red gaze to an undead sentry who stood near her chamber door.

«Bring me the new one who was captured. Go.» She waved a delicate and long-nailed hand towards the creature in a dismissive gesture.

The Zuvembi bowed its head and walked from the room at a surprisingly normal gate. Though the undead things looked like they should move slow and shamble, they in fact were as agile as the living and faster when need be.

Sirin Tal glided to the window of her tower and gazed down upon her city of gold. With eyes closed she concentrated and could see a dozen places throughout the streets at once! With her powers she could see through the eyes of her Zuvembi slaves wherever they were. This power meant that very little escaped her notice within her domain. Not only could she see everything, but the white witch could hear it as well. The voodoo sorceress had seen the group of strangers enter Tal Anori. She had admired the bronze-skinned giant as he passed through the gate. She smiled to herself and softly whispered aloud;

«I have such plans for you, my golden haired warrior…»

The sound of scuffling at her door brought her attention around. Two of the undead guards held the captured Masai warrior, Dala, by his arms in unbreakable vice-like grips. One of his legs was twisted awkwardly and swollen, obviously broken. As the red-eyed alabaster face of Sirin Tal turned to Dala with a wry smile the Masai screamed. The stories he had grown up with were now proving to be horrifyingly true!

The pitiful scream echoed from the tower to the streets below. The slaves who toiled throughout the city shuddered for but a moment. Screams from the tower were unfortunately nothing new to them. Within a small temple-like building wherein Ki-Gor and his group had surfaced from the tunnels however, the scream was heard as well. Faint but unmistakable terror. They exchanged a stern look and turned their attention to a row of twelve chairs that circled the room. In each chair sat the elder of a tribe, and upon each face at hearing the scream was a look of weary sadness.

Ki-Gor grew hot with anger, pointing an accusing finger at the seated elders.

«How can you sit while your people are tortured and whipped? How long have you endured this suffering and just accepted it? Are you not men!? Is it not better to die than to live in eternal servitude?»

Helene took hold of her husband's arm, trying to calm him as he seethed in indignation. The oldest of the twelve chieftains, at least in appearance, raised his head in equal anger and stamped his tribal effigy stick on the stone floor.

«Who are you to accuse us of being cowards, outlander!? Do you think in three hundred years we have not tried to destroy her? You think it better to die when death brings this?»

He stamped his stick twice more on the stones. The staccato rapps signaled two men to push out a tall, wheeled box. Inside it was one of the Zuvembi, bound in chains. It had been a woman once, but now it hissed and its milky white eyes stared hatefully at the strangers who stood among the council. Like a feral beast it thrashed violently. The council leader would not look directly at the creature but instead stared dead at Ki-Gor.

«She was my sister, outlander. Death is no escape here. There is nothing heroic about becoming a mindless monster. Not in cursed Tal Anori.»

Ki-Gor blanched at seeing the creature. He had spoken out of anger and out of turn. Tearing his gaze from the undead woman, he offered an apology.

«Forgive me, elders, I spoke with my heart and not my head. Tell me what must be done to end this nightmare and I pledge my might to your cause.»

«As do I!» rang the voice of Tembu George stepping up to the side of his friend.

The leader sat back in his chair and exchanged nods with the other elders. Smiling, he motioned for Mabuku to come forward.

«You have done well, true young one, to bring us men of courage, heart, and passion! It is emotion and drive that will defeat the cold and heartless.»

The thrashing of the chained Zuvembi abruptly stopped. This sudden cease in the noise of rattling chains caused all eyes in the room to turn in its direction. Its partially decayed head slowly and deliberately rose with a look that never before had been seen on the face of one of the undead creatures, a smile! The teeth parted and a sound that was at first a cracked and hoarse whisper from long dead vocal chords slowly became a horrible, nightmarish voice.

«*Hear me. Hear the words of your Queen Sirin Tal!*»

A collective gasp of shock and horror filled the room. Garan of the Masai warriors began to make tribal symbols and gestures believed to ward off evil. Ki-Gor reflexively stepped in front of Helene protectively, tensed like a lion ready to pounce. Tembu George readied his heavy spear as his skin crawled with superstitious fear born from a lifetime of ghost stories about the white witch. The council elders and Mabuku simply stared in disbelief as the Zuvembi continued in its unearthly voice.

«*Your golden-haired warrior and his companions cannot help you. You will spend eternity in toil as is your sentence! You dare to plot against Sirin Tal? I am sending you back the Masai as a warning. Serve me in life or serve me in death--the choice is yours!*»

A peal of thunderous and terrible laughter burst forth from the creature, echoing in a chilling cacophony throughout the chamber! The eldritch strain on the Zuvembi must have been too much, playing vocal host to its dread master. It decayed at an incredibly rapid rate. Skin and tissue dropped from the skeleton like leaves from a dead and wind-blown tree. As the leathery pieces hit the floor they crumbled to so much dust.

The elder who had once counted the creature as his sister cried out in woe, averting his eyes. As the skeletal remains fell into a slack pile amid the iron chains a great BOOM! was heard against the temple's ancient doors.

«They are here!» cried several of the council in unison.

BOOM!—BOOM!! On the third impact the doors splintered open and half a dozen Zuvembi armed with iron capped cudgels poured through the portal! They scanned the room with their dead eyes but made no move. A seventh undead monster limped through the portal then, dragging a broken leg as it hissed and hobbled directly towards a shocked Tembu George.

«Dala NOOO!!» Cried Helene. It was indeed their Masai friend who had made the journey with them, now a mindless zombie slave of Sirin Tal!

Ki-Gor unslung his bow and notched an arrow.

«Damn you, witch,» he grated through clenched teeth as he let the shaft fly. THUNK! The missile buried itself right between the eyes of their former companion, snapping his now wax-like face around to the side with the impact.

Dala did not fall. Slowly and deliberately he turned back to face the group. Grasping the shaft of the arrow with his now dead hand Dala pulled it from his skull with a wet, sucking noise. Blackish blood dribbled from the wound down his face as the gory arrow clattered to the stones. Ki-Gor lowered his bow with brow furrowed in surprise.

«How do you kill a dead man?!»

As if on some unknown cue the zuvembie rushed in to attack. Mabuku showed a youthful courage unlike his ancient elders, taking up a ceremonial spear from the wall and rushing to Ki-Gor's side. The members of the council ran in two separate directions. Doubtless to more hidden tunnels, thought the jungle lord as he watched them scatter like ants before the rain.

The zuvembi were indeed fast. Iron capped blows brought down three of the slower council members in rapid, bone-crunching succession. The other chieftains scrambled down into the tunnels like rats even as their fallen brethren began to rise to their feet with milky white eyes!

The two remaining Masai, Garan and Zu'An, were at their wits' end. The weapons they wielded bore little effect against the living corpses, and they soon found themselves backed into a corner. With hands thrown over their faces they screamed as the clubs arced up and swung inexorably down with a sharp finality.

Helene, Tembu George and Ki-Gor backed quickly and cautiously towards one of the escape tunnels where the council leader beckoned furtively. Mabuku had become separated from them as he attempted to cover the escape of several others. A zuvembi warrior leapt at Ki-Gor, brandishing his bludgeoning stick overhead. With no hesitation the jungle lord leapt forward to meet him head on. Both his sinewy hands locked onto the cudgel, and instantly the bronze giant could tell that the creature far surpassed even his prodigious strength. But, having wrestled with the mighty man-apes of

Mu'Baka Mountain, Ki-Gor had learned how to throw a stronger opponent by subtle shifts of weight and foot positioning.

With a shout he employed such a technique, and the nightmare was flipped head over heels through the air! The mindless monstrosity toppled into a torchier which sloshed its flaming conflagration over it. The leathery husk that was once a man was quickly incinerated by fiery doom.

«FIRE!» Shouted Ki-Gor. «Fire will destroy them!»

With a triumphant smile Tembu George used his spear to hook another torchier and topple it in front of him. The flaming oil spilled and splattered in front of him and Helene, creating a wall of fire that caused the zuvembi to retreat hastily from them.

Ki-Gor was on the opposite side of the barrier, but with a confident tone he bade his wife and best friend to go.

«Into the tunnels! I will take the second path with Mabuku and be along quickly. Go!» While shouting the command the jungle lord had deftly avoided four of the monsters and snatched two torches from the wall with monkey-like agility. He tossed one of them in a high arc to Mabuku.

«Catch, young one! Together we can make it out of here!»

The smile Ki-Gor gave the young slave filled him with pride. He would return honor to the Jwahla name by fighting alongside the bronze-skinned giant. Helene managed one worried look back through the flames before she was ushered into the tunnel with the door slamming and bolting shut behind her.

The remaining two warriors dashed madly about the flames, using them as a barrier and an obstacle against the zuvembi. Mabuku swung his torch like a club into the face of one of his foes, setting it ablaze. A second grasped at his vest and reared back its terrible cudgel for the kill. The young slave stabbed the fiery weapon into the monster's chest, scorching him but at the same time snuffing out the torch! As he fell from the creature's grasp to the floor two more closed on him swiftly.

From his own battle area Ki-Gor saw the boy's plight. Attempting to reach Mabuku, he nimbly avoided and countered countless blows and grabs in an intricate play of move and countermove. Rolling, blocking and jumping he was soon at the boy's side and, swinging his torch, he kept the undead killers at bay.

«On your feet, young one!» cried the jungle lord as he pulled Mabuku to his feet.

The young slave winced and fell to the stones again. His ankle was swollen and twisted. The wound dealt him by the giant anaconda had been re-broken.

«Go without me Ki-Gor! My job was only to get help here and I have done that!»

«I'll not leave you behind, lad,» said the bronze-skinned giant hefting the young man over one shoulder while keeping the horrors at bay with the torch in his other hand.

As the jungle lord turned to spy the trap door of the escape tunnel, he felt a dull impact against him from behind and, with a spasm, Mabuku went completely limp. Wheeling around, Ki-Gor saw the half-burned form of one of the zuvembi, clutching its cudgel that dripped with fresh new blood. With horrific realization, he let Mabuku's limp form fall to the ground as the remaining monsters circled around him.

«Come on then!» snarled Ki-Gor with teeth bared and nostrils flared. He would not die without giving a good accounting for himself.

The cudgels raised all around him and a hand clutched at his ankle! The grasp turned his attention towards the floor where he looked down into the now milky white eyes of Mabuku! And then the blows fell upon him like iron rain. Blackness claimed him and mighty Ki-Gor met it unafraid, cursing the name of Sirin Tal as darkness overtook him.

6.
CRYPT OF THE KING, TOWER OF THE WITCH

Helene looked at Tembu George with concern. They had run through the tunnel for ages before entering into a grand stone chamber of black marble columns and gold reliefs wherein they collapsed from exhaustion. In the center of the dome-roofed chamber were two rectangular sarcophagi. The graves were detailed in exquisite carvings and ornaments of gold and jewels. An arched stairway came up from two sides of the twin tombs and led up to the ceiling and a circular, well-like opening to a chamber above.

As soon as they had entered this chamber, the remaining council elders stopped cold and began to shake and mutter fearfully to each other.

«The sacred tomb! In our hasty escape we have stumbled through the tunnels to the sacred tomb itself!»

After regaining his breath Tembu George gazed about the splendor of the room in awe even as he caught up one of the trembling men by their many strands of necklaces.

«This is the tomb of the desert king? Why should we fear being here?»

«The Queen is said to visit here often!» stammered the man. «And through the upper chamber is the adjoining tower to her own!»

The big Masai let the cowering, superstitious man fall from his grip.

«Then that suits us well. When Ki-Gor finds us we are in a good place to strike at the witch!»

The council leader shook his head gravely in reply.

«Your friend will not find us here, I am afraid. Only one tunnel leads here, the one we scurried into out of haste and chaos. The tunnel he and the boy were heading to does not connect to this one.»

Helene turned with a start.

«What!? We're separated from Ki-Gor and Mabuku? We have to go back then!»

«Do not worry my sister,» cautioned Tembu George as the jungle maiden started for the tunnels again. «Our goal is the same. Ki-Gor will be heading for the tower of the white witch as well.» He glanced towards the top of the ornate arch of stairs as he spoke.

Curious, Helene approached the sarcophagi with a quiet reverence. Both of the rectangular stone edifices were devoid of any sort of lid. Peering into one casket, she put her hand to her breast as she spied the well-preserved form of a very old and bearded Arabic man, lying in state in a red silk turban and draped in robes of gold-embroidered white. Though he had lain here for at least three centuries, he appeared as though only sleeping.

The second of the stone coffins, meant for the immortal queen, was, surprisingly, not empty. The auburn-haired adventuress was shocked at what she saw within! It was another man, grizzled and short of body. It was garbed in the common accoutrements of a tribal witch doctor. And like the noble king beside him, he looked as though only asleep. In contrast to the long dead king whose face, even in death, looked kind, the witch doctor's frozen expression was one of hate and cruelty. In the left hand of the scowling corpse was a small braid of black hair.

«Who is this that lies in the queen's coffin?»

The council leader looked utterly confused by the question but refused to go near the thing. Tembu George padded over and peered within.

«Houngan. This is the body of a VooDoo Priest.»

Hearing this, the frightened elders grew paler still and more than one uttered a single name: Sirin Golta. The witch doctor who had schooled the white witch in black magic! But why would he be interred in her place? The big Masai was familiar with the ways of voodoo, having fought the black magicians before. Recognizing the braid of hair as a talisman the witch doctors used to hold sway over another, he pulled it from the dry fingers of the corpse. As he did so it immediately crumbled into a fine powder, and a smell like sweet perfume filled the chamber. With a shudder he started up the stairs to the round exit which led to the small tower beside that of Sirin Tal, wiping the residue from his hands. The fiend had died still trying to work magic over another soul.

«Quickly, even now Ki-Gor may need us!»

Helene bit her lip in worry as she ascended behind her stalwart friend leaving the shivering council behind to their prayers.

«I'm sure he made it to the tunnel. I only hope he hasn't fallen into trouble!»

Trouble would be putting it lightly. Consciousness returned slowly to the jungle lord accompanied by throbbing pain in his thick skull and the taste of his own blood in his mouth. How long he had been out he could only guess, but it felt like hours. His back felt cold as if he were lying on the stone floor. Attempting to bring his hand to his aching head, he was surprised to find he could not move it. Nor could he sit up or bend his legs! Shaking the cobwebs from his mind and blinking away the spots before his eyes, Ki-Gor strained his neck to survey his situation. He was less than thrilled with what he discovered.

Chains of heavy, solid gold bound his arms to a raised rectangular marble platform. Likewise his ankles were ensnared. His body was stretched out like a giant «X» across what appeared to be some sort of altar. A voice broke the silence of the room suddenly. Female and pleasant, yet very commanding and cold at the same time.

«*Yesss my golden-haired warrior, awake! I would not have you placid as I work my charms on you.*»

The bronze giant strained against his chains with all his strength and bared his teeth towards the shadowy figure standing over him.

«Remove these chains and I will work my own charms over your corpse, witch!»

The right hand of Sirin Tal slashed out in angry reply and her long red fingernails scratched open a shallow cut across Ki-Gor's muscled chest.

«*SILENCE CUR! Ahhh… Now see what you made me do, my pet?*» Slowly she ran her index finger across the scrapes on his chest and licked the blood from it sensuously.

«*I have plans for this fine body and you made me hurt you.*»

Ki-Gor recoiled in shock as for the first time he beheld the blood-red eyes of the white witch, now fully locked onto his face. Her cold lips kissed his forehead and he shuddered at their icy touch.

Tembu George and Helene had gained the roof of the building they had been in. It was a small round tower that sat nearly touching the much larger and highly ornate tower of the white witch herself. Some hundred yards up was a solitary window that flickered with firelight in the dark of night. The intricate ivory scrollwork and ornamentation made climbing the tower as easy as ascending a ladder. Before the Masai could say a word, the jungle maiden had leapt up, grabbing hold of the tower's ornamentation and climbing towards the window.

«Never argue with a lioness,» he muttered under his breath. «Especially when she is searching for her mate!» Grasping the stonework, Tembu George climbed after her.

The council elders had lost their fear. Something seemed different about the tomb now. Once the sweet smell had washed over the room it was like an intangible heaviness was lifted. The elders walked cautiously, yet without their customary terror, towards the sarcophagus of the Queen. It was as if something drew them to it. As the leader peered over the lip of the stone coffin he spied the ancient body of Sirin Golta, the old Witch doctor. The form which had appeared, according to Helene, to look like a slumbering old man was now beginning to decompose! The chieftains murmured amongst themselves until a voice, a woman's voice, seemed to whisper soft and lilting in each man's ear at the same time.

Memories lost ages ago returned to the men, and with those memories courage was renewed! Chief among the returning thoughts was the single thing the ghostly voice had said. The true name of the Queen was at long last remembered!

Back in the tower of Sirin Tal, Ki-Gor was testing his strength against the golden chains that held him, but to no avail. The white witch walked the length of the altar from his head to his feet, trailing her hand down the length of his sun-bronzed body. When she reached the end she stopped suddenly. A twinge of pain had elicited a small curse from under her breath.

«*Something… is wrong. Yes, I think you have arrived just in time, my little jungle lord. This… body grows weak and I find I am in need of a new vessel. I will begin my spell at once! Soon you will belong to me body and soul!*»

Ki-Gor growled a retort through clenched teeth as he stared at the evilly grinning Queen.

«I will resist you to my dying breath!» With that he spat at her in an act of defiance.

Wiping the spittle from her immaculate cheek, Sirin Tal laughed.

«*You don't understand, my little jungle lord. No* man *can resist my magics! Soon I will… Eh?!*»

The sound of bare feet running fast across the stones of her chamber floor turned the white witch's attention towards the window. With a determined look on her face that would have made the bravest male warrior think twice, Helene had not only made it up the tower but had bounded through the window and was flying at the Queen with her right fist aimed squarely at the witch's jaw! In the time it took for Sirin Tal's head to turn towards the distracting noise the punch landed like a sledgehammer! POW! Her head snapped back from the impact as blood and spittle flew from her mouth. She stumbled back and fell on her posterior, taken completely by surprise. Helene drew a knife from her leopard skins and pointed it at Sirin Tal.

«Two things witch: I'm not a man and that one is *mine!*»

The queen of Tal Anori locked her crimson eyes on the jungle maiden with an intense hatred as she wiped blood from the corner of her mouth.

«*You will pay for that, bitch. ATTEND ME!*»

The command brought forth three of the Zuvembi who crashed in from the doorway. The undead creature first into the room was horrifically familiar.

«Mabuku! Oh no!» gasped Helene. There was no time for tears, however, and she knew it. Between the monsters and her was the bubbling hot cauldron of hissing black gunk. The jungle maiden placed her foot against its lip and felt the hot iron burn her flesh. With a scream and a push she toppled the cauldron towards the zuvembi splashing the boiling muck at them in a sickening black wave.

As she was regaining her feet from the savage indignity visited upon her, the boiling hot substance sloshed over the left hand and foot of Sirin Tal, scalding them and causing her to stumble back against her throne-like chair with an anguished howl. As the stuff sloshed over the legs of the undead it pushed their feet out from under them and laid them face-first into it. The smell of boiled flesh filled the air as the zuvembi writhed about, losing great chunks of themselves as the meat fell from the bones like a chicken in a pot.

Tembu George had clambered in through the window in the chaos and hurried to Ki-Gor where he hastily snatched up an ornate hatchet that lay against the base of the altar and made quick work of the chains that held his friend.

Springing to his feet, the bronze giant shared a quick smile with his she-devil wife.

«To think I wanted you to stay behind!» He grinned as he hefted a length of the gold chain for use as a weapon.

The boiling muck had greatly cooled and seeped into the crevices of the stone floor by now, leaving behind an unrecognizable and bloated mess that had been the three zuvembi, one of which had been poor Mabuku. Tembu

George leapt to the heavy chamber door and closed it even as the sounds of running feet were heard on the outside stair. More undead guards were hastening their way! The door had a heavy iron bolt that the Masai Chieftain threw into place.

«This cannot hold for long! Finish her!»

Sirin Tal leaned heavy against her throne, the flesh of her left hand hideously blistered and steaming. Helene circled at a safe distance with her knife as her husband traveled in the opposite direction with the heavy chain.

Ki-Gor's keen eyes saw the devil woman's lips begin to move quickly and quietly as she attempted to mutter a spell. Lashing out with the heavy chain, he struck her across her face, cracking her jaw and further bloodying her mouth, cutting off the magic words!

The jungle lord stared at the hissing woman accusingly. «You dishonor the love of your husband, your king. You use bitterness and hatred to torture those who slighted you so long ago.» He snarled almost animal-like in contempt for the wicked creature before him, yet, too, he felt sadness for her.

«Mabuku was a brave young man,» snapped Helene with a tremor of rage in her voice. «He was born into your world of despair and torture and yet his heart remained bright! That boy was stronger than you and your magic could ever be!»

It seemed the end was upon the evil queen. Wounded with nowhere to run and no time to weave a spell, she was through. Sirin Tal, however, smiled.

«*I know my time is undone. But you still lose, my little jungle lord. With a mental command I have sent the zuvembi to kill all the remaining people of Tal Anori. I may be dying, but so shall they!*»

The cruel woman laughed maniacally as her statement spread a look of horror over the faces of her executioners. Tembu George looked perplexed.

«Then who is pounding on the door?»

«Let us in, brave heroes! Let us in!» It was the council leader from the other side of the portal.

Hastily opening the heavy door, the Masai moved aside as three of the elders stormed into the chamber with grim purpose. The leader pointed an accusing finger at the white witch.

«Your spell is undone, Sirin Golta! I speak the name of the true Queen of Tal Anori!»

Sirin Tal's weird red eyes grew wide in shock.

«*Speak not the name! I claimed this body! It is mine!*»

The council leader set his jaw firmly and stood his ground with a stately determination.

«Release the queen, Sirin Golta. Release Da'Ajani!»

At the sound of the name Da'Ajani, the white witch screamed! Her body seemed to flicker in and out of view. Ki-Gor stared in disbelief, as the form of the statuesque woman became that of a gnarled old man. Seeing this transformation, Helene and Tembu George both gasped in awe. The jungle maiden looked back at the council elders.

«It's the witch doctor! The one from the queen's sarcophagus! But how..?»

A faint smell of sweet perfume filled the air as the tower began to shake violently. Cracks appeared in the wall and Sirin Golta fell into the throne gasping for breath in his weak and ages-dead body. It seemed impossible, but the pieces fell into place. It must have been the bitter old Sirin Golta who killed the King to cause the Queen to despair. The old witch doctor had then exchanged bodies with the royal widow, condemning her soul to his own dead body even as he became immortal in hers! He was a parasite. Living off of the despair of a lonely woman. The jungle lord had narrowly avoided becoming his next host!

Ki-Gor, with leopard-like speed, fastened the chain he held around the witch doctor and bound him to the throne.

«Everyone out now! The tower is falling apart with his death! The spell is broken!»

The elders raced out the door and down the steps before they could be stopped, while the three adventurers headed for the chamber window. Looking out over the stunning city of gold and ivory they beheld a terrible and wondrous scene. Vines and growth claimed buildings at a fantastic rate! Stones decayed and crumbled and gold roofs became misshapen as the spell that held off age washed away. The zuvembi that could be seen dropped truly dead where they stood and the handful of living screamed and ran for the city gates.

As strong vines grew up the sides of the tower, Ki-Gor sent his wife down one, using it as a rope, and beckoned for Tembu George to quickly follow. The jungle lord was last out the window and, as he spared a look at the old Voo Doo priest chained to the throne, he saw a heavy stone from the chamber's roof fall upon him, crushing the chair and its captive beneath it.

They soon gained the now worn and overgrown streets and along with the few remaining citizens they ran for the gate and safety. The going was hard. Falling stones and rapidly growing vines that lashed out like whips from every side! Entire buildings crumbled into ruins as they bolted past. As the exit loomed closer, the thick tendrils of a heavy fog began to rapidly fill the ruined city behind them until a thick white mist obscured the dead wonder from view.

7.
TRUTH AND LEGENDS

The lost people of Tal Anori gathered around the white jungle lord expectantly outside the ruined walls of the city. There were not many left. Perhaps seventy or so at best. They looked to him with a glimmer of hope in their eyes. One weary, older woman finally spoke to him.

«What do we do now, white god? Where will we go?»

Ki-Gor looked over the crowd with his piercing gaze, rubbing his wrists from where the chains had bit deeply.

«It is time for your chieftains to once again be chieftains.» He gave a stern yet reassuring look to the Council of Elders and continued.

«You are a new tribe now, born from many old ones and for a time I expect you may want to learn what it is to be free once more. Follow your hearts and learn from your past. That is all any man can do.» He drew Helene close with a strong right arm.

The old woman smiled at him.

«We will sing songs and tell the legend of Ki-Gor from this day forth!»

The bronze giant held up his hand as if to halt the statement right there.

«Save your songs for brave Mabuku, warrior true of the Jwahla!» A cheer rose up from the crowd chanting the young man's name.

The chanting ceased abruptly as from the nearby jungle came hundreds of the mud men, the Wakizi. The mist that now enshrouded the lost city was the same that had covered their lands, mystically transposed to cover the ruins. The white-covered men and women made for a startling site as they approached. Upon seeing Ki-Gor, the chieftain of the mud men, B'Alu, placed his hand over his heart and smiled broadly.

«Well met, my brave friends! As we have stood guardians of the fog for centuries so shall we remain.» The two tribes accepted each other in friendship and a great feast was soon being planned in celebration.

Bidding farewell, the heroic trio took their leave. From the top of the low hill that overlooked the dead city Ki-Gor smiled. They had accomplished a good thing. Tembu George returned the smile to his friends and placed a hand on the shoulder of each.

«Mabuku's story, Ki-Gor. He said it needed an ending. I think he would be happy with this one.»

END.

EPILOGUE

Deep beneath the ancient city in the tomb of the King and Queen was a beautiful sarcophagus. It had once been two separate stone coffins but the earthquakes had toppled them together and the marble had crumbled in such a way as to make it appear as one large crypt. On one side lay a noble looking man of Arabic descent. He was dressed in a red turban and white robes embroidered in gold. On the other side lay a beautiful black-skinned woman in a robe of white silks and stylized feathers hammered of gold and silver. The hands of the couple were lovingly clasped together now in eternity. Though they were centuries old, the bodies of the long dead King and Queen looked as though they were merely sleeping and each face looked blissfully at peace.

BELLICO AND THE TOWER OF MOUTHS

By Richard Toogood

I am an old man now.

And with that hubris peculiar to old men I resort to my memoirs in the belief that posterity itself attends upon them with bated breath. I suppose I am no different in this regard from every other ageing fool who belatedly seeks to justify an innocuous life with a record of their thoughts and opinions. For what is retrospection if not a defence of inconsequence?

I spent the first eighteen years of my life closeted amid the academies and scriptoria of Varsity City. If nothing else this did at least equip me with the tools needed to carve a monument out of my own past. Which only makes it all the more of a pity that a scholar's life should provide such poor material out of which to construct anything worthwhile.

So it was a day of singular good fortune for you, dear reader—though I myself considered it anything but at the time—when I found myself engaged as publicist, amanuensis and confidant by an individual of an altogether more colourful character than my own. By recounting his adventures as he confided them to me, and in supplementing them with those episodes to which I was the principal witness, it may be that something of my own facile story is preserved even so just as the paint of the portrait preserves the mean canvas to which it is applied.

The man of whom I write answered to many names. To some he was known as Slaughtermeister. Among others he was referred to, in fearful whispers, as Woe-Sower or Hammerhand. While between the Hippocamorphs of Kankreedy he was called *Maalgovor*: literally, the Factotum of Death. But to most of the peoples and species of this world of Vitracolee he was simply Bellico—the Bastard.

He was an intimidating brute of a man, and I do not believe I ever succeeded in feeling fully at ease in his company. He had a volatile and mercurial temperament, capable both of studied ruthlessness and of flying off the handle at the most trivial provocation. The end result in either instance was invariably the same: splintered bones and pulverised organs.

He was not a tall man by any means, being scarcely more than my own average height, but possessed of a far stockier build. His arms and legs were like fossilised roots, while his torso was as square and solid as a ceremonial plinth. His usual costume was a kilt of cured hide bound about by a thick iron-buckled belt, and hob-nailed boots. Sometimes he adopted a loose sleeveless shirt, but in all the time we travelled together I never knew him to wear armour of any description. He always favoured speed and freedom of movement in his fighting style over the hindrances of protection. In any event I doubt whether any armour ever forged could have served a man better than did the hirsute cocoon of Bellico's own weather-beaten flesh.

His features were those of a grim primitive effigy hammered into the contours of a crudely carved head. His eyes were angry embers glimmering at the bottom of deep dark wells. His mouth was an ugly gash gouged into the jutting promontory of his jaw. For reasons best known to itself this mouth favoured the curve of a sinister smile over any other expression. And it made for a grisly spectacle, being so clearly at odds with the character of the face that wore it.

A great many years have now elapsed since the following events took place, but I can still see clearly the special relish that tightened like a tourniquet upon that mouth on the day that Bellico the Bastard abdicated his duties to go loafing about on a beach instead.

The occasion was the Feast of Groth. This, so Bellico solemnly informed me, was a day of total idleness where he came from. I was in no position to dispute it, having scant knowledge of the quaint customs of tribal religions, and lacked courage to express the doubts I might have had in any case. But I was still something of a gormless youth at the time and I suppose I must have unwisely allowed something dubious to seep into my expression.

Even now my resolve fails me at the memory of the murderous glower I was delivered as a consequence. We were still in the process of getting to know each other in those early days, but already I knew better than to challenge him even tacitly. I had seen him hand out several vicious beatings for the mildest injuries to his pride. Fortunately I was quick witted enough to remind him that he had previously expressed the view that *all* faiths and beliefs were superstitious claptrap and that he had nothing but contempt for any being who practiced them. With that a gleam of sardonic amusement returned to his gaze and a sigh of relief escaped me, although from which end of my body it would be improper to specify.

«Aye, that's true enough, scrivener,» he acknowledged with a scornful grunt.

«A man does better to piss into the air than grovel to any god to send him rain.»

And yet there we were, the two of us, skiving, on account of the birthday of a deity which one of us had never heard of and the other didn't believe in. By rights we should have been hightailing it back to Clenched Fist Keep and to the Constable of Vorbolos who resided there to report to him the war readiness of his frontier forts.

When I asked Bellico why this was he laughed uproariously. «Did you ever hear tell of *any* atheist who demanded to work on a holy day?»

And so we steered our mounts off of the military road and picked a cautious path down a wind-wracked headland until we came to a bleak bay which fringed a foaming sea. It was no sort of a day for sunbathing. Even with Protillo Maximus and Minimus both riding high in the morning sky there was precious little warmth in the day. The daylight was a bilious shade of green and the water seethed with hostility as it fizzed upon the shingle. But that is where we dismounted regardless, and while I lounged upon a rock and addressed myself to my lunch, Bellico struck a strangely defiant stance at the water's edge.

In his right fist was gripped the haft of the great mace called Morguemonger. In all the time we travelled together I can barely recall an instance when it wasn't, and more often than not, dripping with blood and brains. Try as I might, I could never purge myself of the sense of sick dread with which the sight of that grim weapon afflicted me. Absurd as it may sound, I have never known anything to exude such a dreadful sense of malice.

Bellico's own attitude to the thing, naturally, was altogether different. He had a habit of bracing the shaft against his hip so that the ugly spiked head rested conspiratorially close to his own, bending his ear—so I came to think—like some poisonous crony.

«Did you ever hear tell of a place called Nekrosestus?» he asked me arbitrarily.

I shook my head. One consequence of receiving the best of educations, as I had, is that one invariably graduates from it knowing next to nothing practical. In my experience it is usually those who were denied any proper schooling that most value learning for its own sake. Despite his crude manner, Bellico often astounded me with the breadth of his own knowledge.

«Well well,» he remarked with a disdainful snort. «Even the memory of the mightiest cannot survive the vacuum of modern education, it seems. It was a city of sorcerers, scrivener, back in the old times before magic was eradicated from the world.»

I watched his fingers drum thoughtfully upon the haft of the mace. After a few moments of considered silence he added:

«Do you know it had a reputation for evil so profound that it came to be known as Horroropolis? It is said that its rulers dealt in dooms and deviltries and that it demanded tributes in flesh of every race and breed it came into contact with.»

«To what end?» I asked him as I fumbled in my satchel for my writing impedimenta, belatedly conscious of the fact that this was precisely the sort of rumination that I was being employed to record.

The broad slabs of his shoulders lifted and sank in a careless shrug.

«No one knows. Some say that the people who were trafficked there went to feed the monsters which it was rumoured were bred behind its walls. Others maintain that they were sacrificed instead to the dark patrons of the city. But then again their fates may have been more mundane. For is it not the lot of the vanquished always to serve as drudges and bedfellows to the conqueror? The truth will never be discovered now in any case.»

«I presume some form of poetic retribution befell the place, then,» I prompted him after he had lapsed into a reflective silence.

«You could call it that, I suppose,» he grinned with savage relish.

This is the gist of the tale which Bellico then related to me, while the clouds appeared to cluster within earshot and the cold wind supplied a doleful accompaniment...

* * *

The emissaries and ambassadors of Nekrosestus ranged far and wide in their search for new lands and peoples to fetter in thrall to their city's authority. Whatever dark appetite it was that the Nekrosestrians needed to cater to with foreign flesh, it was a voracious and insatiable one. Eventually they came across a tribe of nomads roaming the frozen wastes of Tondramark. It had become their custom at such first contacts to orchestrate some spectacular magical gesture in order to demonstrate their power. This usually involved the summoning up of a monstrous metaphysical entity or the turning inside out of some luckless wretch. Over time these practices seeped into the commonwealth of knowledge, creating a wave of dread and terror that the Nekrosestrians displaced by the simple act of their ferrying forth. Such was their foul reputation that when they came upon these nomads of Tondramark they found them already fully cowed in advance of their arrival.

But power is a thoroughbred, and like all such beasts, without constant exercise it becomes flabby and feckless. Even if these savages no longer warranted a display of sorcery, the Nekrosestrian ambassador still judged it prudent to hammer home the message of his people's might. And so he formulated the idea of leading an embassy of tribal elders to gaze upon the wonders of the great city from afar. As anticipated, the sight thunderstruck the frightened chiefs and sent them to their knees agog with terror.

So gratified was the ambassador by the response to this prudent initiative of his that he failed to observe that the climate of awe did not extend itself to the shamans of the tribe. He did not notice the sly conspiratorial glances that these bent old men shared between them. For their shrewd eyes, rheumy with age and craftiness, did not see the domes of glass and gold, or the soaring silver towers wreathed in clouds of incense. Their degenerate vision flittered disinterestedly over the spurting fountains of mercury and missed entirely the reptilian texture to the tessellated roofs. If it lingered at all on the regiments of lewd gargoyles that crouched atop the quoins and cornices of the city then it found no response in their inscrutable faces.

It was something else entirely which captured these men's interest and caused their toothless mouths to purse with savoured glee. For unremarked by the ambassador's arrogant eyes was their delight in the depth of the river valley in which the city stood and the sparkle of the suns' light on the ring of distant glaciers. When the shamans had joined their chiefs in grovelling convincingly before the ambassador's boots they were all given leave to depart, with the promise that twenty of the tribe's most robust young men and women would be delivered to the city's gates in short order. As the embassy disbanded so the shamans slipped away from their companions and journeyed north, as fast as their wizened limbs could carry them, into the icy wastelands that hunkered upriver of the city's imperious black walls.

They had understood at once that it was futile for them to attempt to attack the city directly. Their rustic magic was feeble in comparison with the powers which the sorcerers of Nekrosestus had at their disposal. But deeds of surprising magnitude were not beyond them when they pooled their resources and worked in unison. During the course of the interminable feuds which the tribe engaged in with rival clans they had more than once obliterated an advancing war band by snatching a meteor out of the night-time sky and cratering it at a place of their choosing. It was not an endeavour to be undertaken lightly as the effort involved was usually fatal. But on this occasion such qualms were irrelevant to them because the spot upon which the shamans chose to land their hammer blow from space was the very one on which they themselves were stood.

As a consequence they were denied the satisfaction of hearing the crack of the hurricane winds that decapitated the proud turrets and towers of the city. Nor did they observe the hungry abysses that opened up ravenously beneath its tumbling walls. They did not witness the flare of the fireball that cremated the citizens where they stood. And they were deprived of the sight of the vaporised glaciers which drowned the city's ruins forever at the bottom of a boiling sea.

* * *

«And that is where they lie to this day,» Bellico concluded with an expansive gesture at the truculent waters which lapped warily around his toecaps. For a while he stood lost in thought, and it seemed to me as if his interest in the subject evaporated along with his voice. I was not in the least surprised when he suddenly stalked off without any further word of explanation. I watched him search for a suitable spot beyond the high water mark and then throw himself carelessly upon his back, demonstrably committing himself to that bout of protracted inactivity which would surely have commended him to Groth if only he had been able to benefit from a belief in that indolent deity.

I busied myself for a time annotating my short-hand notes with some additional thoughts and observations. Then, feeling the nip of the sea breeze, I took myself off for a stroll along the beach in order to warm myself up. I did not reflect too deeply upon the tale I had just been told. In a world purged of all sorcery, such as was my naive belief at the time, it seemed absurd even to afford it a second thought.

It was a bleak and barren shore to which Bellico's sudden whim had brought the both of us. The headland lay exposed to the full force of winds sheared off from the distant polar cyclones and the cliffs had a mauled and dismembered look to them. The beach was strewn with the flotsam and jetsam of forgotten shipwrecks; shredded webs of rigging, busted barrels and corroded ironmongery lay everywhere. So when I came across a vaguely man-like shape jutting out of the eroded cliff-face I presumed it to be the figurehead of some long lost vessel and experienced a morbid curiosity to have a look at it.

It was crusty with the shells of all manner of marine life, but I was so absorbed in the task of stripping it of its costume of blanketing seaweed that I did not register until afterwards how carcinogenically malformed these all were. My scrabbling hands had almost succeeded in revealing the thing when I snagged my finger painfully on something sharp. Bellico would have laughed derisively to see the fuss I made of such a paltry injury. His whole body was a plaid quilt of gruesome scar tissue, every injury an anecdote which would come to occupy my scrivener's stylus for years.

But it was my own wound that was of most concern to me at that moment. I remember that I cussed and bellyached about it something awful. But the fact is that it was not a deep cut, and I doubt if more than two or three drops of blood at the most seeped through the seaweed to moisten the desiccated surface beneath. But whatever foul enchantment it was that invested the thing, that was enough to bring it back to abominable life.

You can imagine my disbelief when, after parting a thick fringe of limp, dry kelp, I found myself confronted not with some serene ship's carving but by the most evil-looking visage I had ever seen in my life. A visage which, even as I blanched in the contemplation of it, I was aware it was likewise contemplating me with malignant intent.

The features of the thing were cartoonish and primitive in execution: slanting eyes, splayed nostrils, and rubbery lips framing a yawning fang-filled mouth. It had a naivety to it that would have been absurd if confined to a static image. But I found no source for amusement in it. All I was aware of was a twisted expression invested with such blistering scorn and rancour that I went sprawling as I stumbled backwards in unapologetic terror.

Suddenly I could not move. I could not even speak. It was as if whatever soporific medium had served to sedate the thing was now transferred to my leaden limbs. My own stolen youthful vigour meanwhile was busy excavating the thing out of the ground under the effort of a number of gnarled and contorted limbs which spontaneously erupted into view from beneath the sand.

I could only lie and look on, moribund and aghast, as the thing stood revealed in the harsh unforgiving light of the double sun. And even as I did so my brain went to war with my eyes over the veracity of what they were witnessing. Each could agree that the thing was artificial. The twisted limbs bore the unmistakable texture of petrified wood. The elaborate stripes and swirls of colour that decorated it boasted the tincture of faded paint. But they could come to no consensus to explain how a thing which, whilst clearly bearing the telltale marks of the craftsman's adze and chisel, could now be twisting this way and that as if exercising long dormant muscles. To exacerbate the woes of my disbelieving brain my ears then reported to it a new and alarming development. Try though my brain did to refute it, the ghastly thing was talking. And not just with one vile voice but in a clamour of different tongues.

«What is it, Spleen, what can you see?»

«Turn around, half-wit, so I can have a look.»

«Aw, shut your trap Gall, you aborted cunnilunger.»

And with that there was traded a torrent of abuse and profanity so rapidly that it blended into an almost incoherent babble. And of such toxic a calibre also that even now I balk at the idea of reproducing what little I understood of it.

As the thing swivelled its long columnar form experimentally, so an array of monstrous faces slowly rotated into my view. Some of them stood proud from the body of the thing, others carved in bas-relief, while the remainder were sunken intaglio fashion into the shaft. A few were recognisably human in aspect, but most were wholly alien. Several displayed a quite disarming realism, while others replicated the primitive crudity of the first. But what united each and every one of them was a glower of such rank malevolence, of such corrosive vitriol, that their scrutiny turned my bowels to water.

«Human livestock!» I heard a high pitched voice shrill with blood-curdling glee as a creature with a single pearl-like eye swept its gaze hungrily over me. This observation was answered with a frenzied chorus of yells and a demand from every yammering face to be shown the discovery for themselves.

«Scrawny runt!» observed a tusked snout with evident disappointment. «All gristle and not much meat.»

«I bag the heart then» shrieked another voice.

«I bag the kidneys!»

«CARVE GALL'S NAME INTO THE BRAIN!»

If anyone wishes to understand the quintessence of pure rectum-emptying fear, then I challenge them to replicate the trauma of having their organs allotted for consumption before their own disbelieving ears. My mind reeled in such extremis of panic that I experienced one of those strange shifts of perception that sometimes accompany instances of profound stress. I remember suddenly looking down upon myself and being aware of a curious equanimity that was completely at odds with the gibbering terror that was so palpably possessing my physical form. With a curious sense of detachment I observed the advancing horror which I could now see was supported by four pairs of bunched and stunted legs. As it moved, the long striving shadows it cast under the patronage of competing suns seemed to menace my body between the closing blades of monstrous scissors.

The shock of being snapped back into my own skull had the effect of an immersion in cold water. Suddenly I was scrambling frantically to my feet, my boots ploughing intractable furrows into the unsupportive shingle.

My breath was coming painfully in a hyperventilated wheeze, but a fleeting backward glance rewarded me with the sight of the lumbering horror being left far behind.

Then something like a heavy wet whip cracked agonisingly around my body, stopping me in my tracks before yanking me violently off my feet. I looked down dumbfounded to find a thick moist ribbon coiled around my torso. Even as I tugged and tore at it in desperation so it began to tighten with asphyxiating force. My furious struggles were quickly stifled as the air was starved from my constricted lungs. I felt the stale blood begin to hammer in my temples, heard the groan of my ribs as they began to break. And yet somehow my bulging eyes still found time to register the ghastly sight of the gelatinous ribbon snaking backwards into the body of the following horror through one of its many masticating mouths.

It is absurd the thoughts that can percolate through one's mind at moments of ultimate peril. I can distinctly remember experiencing a preposterous sense of remorse that posterity was going to be cheated of the great books I was destined to have contributed to it. And then, even as coherent thought began to gallop away from me upon the back of a hallucination, and my eyes blushed red with the imminence of death, there came a sudden rush of air into my body followed by the sensation of flight. The next thing I knew I was floundering in the surf having been contemptuously discarded like a piece of litter.

A thunder-faced Bellico was striding purposefully along the beach towards us. If I took umbrage from the fact that he did not trouble himself to spare a single glance in my direction in inquiry of my welfare then equally I did not fail to marvel at his reckless bravery.

I have heard it suggested that men as cock-sure and self-confident as Bellico was shouldn't be credited with courage. Because courage implies the conquest of one's own fear and such men are too proud to admit to fear or to accept that there is anything capable of imperilling them. This seems a churlish and mean-spirited attitude to me, but then I have long since ceased to be surprised by people's pettiness. At that particular moment Bellico's manner appeared laudable enough to me. My opinion was not one shared by the grotesque pillar of mouths which awaited him.

«What in the name of Crovor do we have here?» shrilled one of the leering faces acidly. «An animated relic? A creaking artefact? Or could it be the god of war's grandfather himself?»

«More likely a half-blind dodderer who mistook a mace for his walking stick» opined another.

The jibe was met with a chorus of cruel and callous laughter which as before immediately escalated into a barrage of voices vying with one another in the vileness of their insults: «baffled dotard,» «toothless bed-wetter» and «cretinous old fart» are about the only ones I can bring myself to preserve from those I heard before individual meaning was again lost in a nonsensical hysterical jabber. The deranged toxic raving of the hate mob. When it finally came to an end an almost hygienic silence settled over the scene, disturbed only by the passage of the wind through our clothes and the whisper of the rising tide.

Throughout it all Bellico had stood silent and unmoved. Now he threw back his head and laughed loudly and contemptuously.

«You must have me confused with someone else. Do I look the sort of fainthearted wanker who runs blubbing and bleating from a declamation of words?»

The contrast between my wretched capitulation to terror and Bellico's disdainful bravado could not have been any more pronounced. But then few scribes ever stand the comparison between their own behaviour and the heroic ideals they pursue with the pen, do they?

I watched Bellico's thick spigot-like fingers flex portentously about the haft of the mace, causing Morguemonger to seem to stir restlessly in response. The gesture was not lost on a squamous scallop-shaped face which directed a fresh spate of caustic invective towards him.

«You shit-smeared geriatric ape. There isn't a weapon forged on this planet which can harm a servitor of Nekrosestus. But chance your arm by all means. *Before we tear it from your body and beat you to death with the bloody end.*»

A jubilant light appeared to flare and flicker briefly in Bellico's eyes as he hefted Morguemonger high above his head. For an instant the universe itself seemed to circulate around us like a fascinated spectator, captivated by the profundity of the moment. Then Morguemonger crashed downwards detonating with the force of a thunderclap.

BOOM!

The rolling echo of the impact was followed by a ghastly shriek. I threw myself to the ground as lethal shards and splinters of wood exploded outwards in all directions. In the clash of conflicting certainties it was Bellico's creedless faith that had been rewarded. The goading visage he had hit had not been merely destroyed but utterly obliterated. A spray of viscous purple pus erupted out of the ugly crater where it had rested raising smoking blisters where it spattered across Bellico's flesh. Whatever pain this inflicted upon him elicited no visible reaction. His arm rose and fell again.

BOOM!
And again.
BOOM!
And yet again.
BOOM!
And with each gargantuan blow so another grotesque mask was crushed, shattered, stove in and demolished.

The monstrous entity did not expire meekly though. Its gnarled limbs bludgeoned Bellico mercilessly. His flesh was ripped and raked and gouged by curling wooden claws. A web of serpentine tongues enmeshed his limbs. But every assault only seemed to feed his appetite for carnage. I watched the muscles of his left arm bunch and bulge with obscene strength and saw the ensnaring tongues wrenched physically from their roots and tossed flopping to the ground. Heedless of the blood that ribboned his body, Bellico pounded Morguemonger over and over and over again into the thing's disintegrating form. His grim features were rapturous with relish as he beat out a staccato overture of destruction.

BOOM! BOOM! BOOM!

When at last silence returned to the scene only a solitary graven face still registered a flicker of malevolent life. By some perverse coincidence it was the same primitive effigy that had first confronted me. Now it might almost have been a mirror for Bellico's savagely exultant expression. My quota of courage has always been very small, but it did not require a very large investment for me to then approach the thing in its crippled state. It brought me near enough anyway to hear the harsh valediction Bellico delivered.

«Morguemonger was not forged in any furnace on this world, you fool. It was wrought out there in the smithy of the stars. It came here long ago in the fireball that obliterated the city of your dark masters. It alone possesses the power to extinguish your magic and it has made me the scourge of your kind.»

And with that he delivered one final murderous stroke and we were alone once again on that desolate shore.

* * *

We made a bonfire out of the shattered debris of the thing and then, while we watched its embers add a thousand stars to the night-time sky, I summoned up the nerve to ask Bellico the obvious question.

«It was a Nekrosestrian spite pole,» he told me with a disinterested shrug. Only after it had become obvious to him that this information had left me none the wiser did he add with an impatient snort;

«A sort of hate battery, I suppose you could call it. They were used in the old days to amplify the potency of curses. I've come across a few of them in my time. The foul things can lie dormant for untold ages until some gormless bastard reactivates them.»

It seemed superfluous to me to admit to anything. And I knew he would have despised any attempt at an apology. So I retained a mortified silence. I fully expected him to be furious with me, but he displayed no sign of being so. If anything he radiated an aura of grim satisfaction. And I found myself wondering whether he hadn't expected something of this sort to occur when he brought us here.

Looking back on it with the cynicism of my advanced years it does not seem as unlikely to me now as it did back then. We had stood adjacent to the ruins of a city of evil sorcerers. Was it so unreasonable to assume that some dark and dangerous relic of the place might still be found in the vicinity? Perhaps if I had taken more note of Bellico's story then I might have concluded something of the sort at the time and thus spared myself a traumatic experience.

And now that the story is finally done and dusted with, and I am able to fully reflect upon it, I suddenly find myself wondering if that was not the entire point of the exercise. An object lesson to intolerant youth about the importance of showing an old man's stories their proper respect. Maybe I had been too glib previously in my attitude towards his recollections, in the way in which young people always are whenever their elders begin to reminisce, and he had contrived a way to demonstrate to me the folly of such conceit.

If that truly was his intention then it certainly reaped dividends as I never repeated the mistake. And even if I didn't always believe everything he told me thereafter, I was never again imprudent enough to give him any reason to doubt it.

IMMORTALS OF LEMURIA

By Robert M. Price

1.
MORE THAN A DREAM

Thongor of Valkarth tossed and turned in the great bed. Night noises such as the distant cries of the Lemurian lizard-hawks and the echoing roars of the leonine *vandars* of the nearby jungle were too familiar to have disturbed him, but something had. And his distress was itself sufficient to disturb his beautiful queen, Sumia, Princess of the Flame City of Patanga where Thongor, its conqueror, ruled as Sark, having years before overthrown the bloodthirsty priesthood of Yamath, Lord of Fire.

Sumia shook him awake, which seemed to calm him somewhat, though his beetling brows still knitted in worry.

«What is it, my lord? A nightmare? An omen?» Experience had taught both Sumia and her husband to take such things very seriously.

«No, my heart, not a dream. Or not *just* a dream.» The bronze-skinned Sark sat up and ran a hand through his disheveled, night-black mane as he stared into the distance. «A true vision, I think. I saw my mentor, Sharajsha, abed, wasting away. He said nothing but seemed to beckon me with a feeble gesture of appeal.»

«Will you go to him? Many kingly duties claim your attention in the day ahead of us. Can you send another to learn of Sharajsha's welfare? Perhaps Ald Turmis?»

«The mage did not appear to him, or to Karm Karvus, or so I assume. It's me he wants, or needs.» Withal, Thongor climbed off the bed and made to prepare for this new mission. «Mayhap it is but an idle phantom of sleep. When I arrive, I may find I have embarked upon a fool's errand, but I have been a fool often enough before. Better safe than sorry.»

At sunrise, the Valkarthan king, mounted on a saddled *kroter*, that slim but muscular and swift-footed reptile, was trotting through the golden gates of the royal city, waving to return the salutes of the guards along the city's fortress wall.

The path to the wizard's manse was familiar and well-trod, and Thongor might as well have taken it blindfolded, so preoccupied was he with pending troubles. He was the Emperor over most of the major cities of the West, and there were seemingly endless outbreaks of crime, disease, and rebellion. He gave these matters serious thought, each in turn, mentally drafting proposals to offer to his council of advisors, something he should be doing today. But he knew that neglecting the summons of the Wizard of Lemuria might lead to a danger to dwarf all these mundane challenges.

His golden eyes surveyed the margins of the road subconsciously, knowing that no hint of approaching danger would go undetected. He rode without bodyguards and retainers, confident both that he was equal to the challenge of possible highwaymen and that armed men, no matter how many or mighty, would likely prove of little use against the kind of peril that might await him. Anything that could reduce Sharajsha to decrepit weakness must be a terrible force to be reckoned with. But the Nineteen Gods had watched over him this far. They had not yet disappointed him, nor he them. And so he rode in silent contemplation.

When at length he arrived at the castle of the mage, the sun had set. The vast walls of the structure gave the appearance, probably illusory, of having been carved from an unimaginably vast single boulder. They were illuminated from no apparent mundane source. The traveler found the great, foot-thick wooden doors standing open in welcome. He tied his *kroter*'s reins to a nearby lotifer tree where there was good grazing, and he proceeded to enter. Given whose domicile it was, Thongor was not in the least surprised when the massive doors closed behind him without the aid of any human hand.

He passed through room after room, distracted by none of the weird treasures scattered everywhere and mounted on the walls, from tapestries depicting events in no known earthly history to mounted heads of beasts either extinct or not yet evolved. Thongor felt his business with Sharajsha was of utmost urgency and he was determined to get right to it. He did not call out, not wanting to make the old man waste his strength in answering him. He quickly located the master bed chamber and strode directly to the bedside of the humbled magician, now bereft of any hint of magical potency.

The rheumy eyes slowly opened to view Thongor. There might have been an effort at a smile, but the younger man could not be sure. The wizened arm rose hesitantly, and the heavily veined hand came to rest on Thongor's ham-like fist. The living ghost of a man managed a halting whisper, as Thongor stooped down to listen.

«I knew you would come, my son...»

Thongor had always known Sharajsha as a man of advanced age but had never guessed how old the wizard might actually be. The very thought caused his nape hairs to prickle. He knew such men had secret means of extending their lives' span, of fending off the assaults of old age. But now it seemed that the stymied years had at last caught up with him, had taken long-sought revenge.

«What has befallen you, my father? And what may I do to restore you? I am at your service.»

The faint voice paused to gather strength. Finally, the ancient form uttered the words, like an echo of unheard speech, «Here, this will be easier, now that you have come so near...» He weakly made to lift Thongor's hand to rest it on his wrinkled forehead. Seeing his mentor's intent, the Valkarthan made the implied motion and placed his calloused palm gently across the aged brow. At once he heard the familiar deep, strong tones of his old friend, but in his mind, not with his ears.

II.
AN UNSUSPECTED WORLD

«I am at last near death, as you can see. You have doubtless thought me undying, and I have truly lived upon this earth longer than you would believe. I dared imagine myself immune to death, a conceit no mortal ought to entertain. Forsooth, having lived so many... years, I finally came to forget the prospect of death. But of late something has rudely reminded me. I must needs tell you things for which the men of this age are not yet strong enough to know. I must, if you are to help me, and if you do not, I must surely perish. So listen.

«You above all men know that the Thousand Year War against earth's primal masters, the Dragon Kings, is no myth, as some today imagine. You know the truth of the victory of Phondath the Firstborn of your race, over the reptilian tyrants, because together you and I reenacted it once we learned of the resurgence of the Dragons. Together we gained access to the Star Stone in Thurdis and cut from it wherewith to fashion a new Sword of Nemedis, the twin of the blade of power used by Phondath to gain that primordial victory. And, if you are willing to accept it, I knew you for the true reincarnation of that same Phondath returned!»

Thongor's golden eyes widened at this impossible revelation, and he struggled to return his attention to the wizard's words. He feared what shocking secrets might pour forth next!

«I had in former times apprenticed myself to an ancient order called the

Golden Druids, only to learn, to my horror, that they secretly worshipped the Dragon Kings. Indeed, it was their blasphemous rites that allowed them to return to our world, which they hoped to make their own again. I fled from their company, filled with self-reproach and vowing to apply the powers I had gained under their tutelage to serve the human race rather than to subvert it. At this time, my boy, I sought you out, with what results you know.

«I found I possessed a vestigial psychic link with my former brethren and so became aware of their flight from Lemuria to a refuge far away. It seems they feared reprisals in case their alliance with the Dragons should become known, I suppose, through me. I owe them my great longevity, now nearing its end. Save for one hope. I bid you undertake a perilous journey, certainly not the first I have asked of you, to seek out the Golden Druids. If anyone can help me, it is they, though I know they may be little inclined to do so.»

«And how may I persuade such men, who must needs deem me a hated foe?»

«Declare amnesty and forgiveness, as only the slayer of their gods may offer. They are still human enough, I hope, to long for their ancestral home, our shared Lemuria. Perhaps they may discard their old hatreds, even as the conquered populations of Patanga, Thurdis, and your other former enemies have done.»

Thongor reminded himself that his true enemies, the corrupt tyrants and druids he had displaced, had by no means come to think kindly of him but surreptitiously continued their efforts at revenge. Their subjects, true, had embraced him, but as their liberator from hated oppressors. The cases were not similar, something that must have escaped the ailing and desperate Sharajsha.

«Tell me, where are these Golden Druids? How far must I travel?»

«I shall entrust to you a secret hidden from the foundation of the world. This earth is much vaster than even the wisest of men believe. There are many land masses upon it, fully as large as Lemuria and even mighty Mu. And more than this, the very earth is not a flat disc, as it appears to the eye, but verily a *round ball*. A great ball hanging unsupported in empty space.»

Thongor found himself staggered, fully as astonished as the first time he had witnessed Sharajsha's feats of sorcery.

«Surely... surely this is madness...!»

«My son, you know this world is filled with monsters and magicks...»

«Aye! But the world itself, by your account, is monstrous!»

Sharajsha's mind gently laughed. «Nay, it is so, Thongor. You need only get used to the notion, as you eventually grew accustomed to the strange sights and bizarre ways of civilization. I tell you these things because of the destination of your journey. For the Golden Druids dwell *on the other side of the world.*»

A dizzy Thongor protested. «How may a man make such a journey? It must take centuries, no? Even by airboat...»

«Nay, nay. There are ways known to me. Look over there.» Thongor knew where the old man meant, as an image appeared to his mind's eye. He turned to a table across the room, where a drawer was found to contain a purple crystal. It was diamond-shaped, like two pyramids joined at the base. It seemed subtly to pulse with life, though it gave off neither heat nor cold. The thing was perhaps five inches from top to bottom. Thongor returned to the bedside and laid his hand again on Sharajsha's brow. Their telepathic link was restored, and the mind behind the now-closed eyes began again to speak.

«The Golden Druids reside in a great cavern within and below a mountain. It is called *Shasta*, though no man knows who named it. The vast expanse contains a double pyramid of purple crystal identical to this bauble save for size, and it possesses great and strange properties, the nature of which even I know not. This small crystal bears a name conjecturally rendered as ‹the Purple Star.› It is made of the same unknown substance as its gigantic counterpart, so that there stretches between the two a link spanning all space and time. It may be that, looking into either, one glimpses a perspective where time and space do not truly exist, and all is One. Or so some say. At any rate, if any of this be so, you need only gaze into the crystal Star for the distance between Lemuria and Shasta to vanish. Ancient scrolls speak of this as ‹the Tunnel of Ubb, Father of Worms,› but the reason is lost.»

«Just look into it, eh? Will my clothing make the journey with me? And Sarkozan? Or will I arrive naked as a babe?»

But there was no answer. Sharajsha, fatigued from the mental effort, had sunk into a deep slumber. Thongor wondered if perhaps the ancient mage had been asleep for the whole interview, if the bizarre revelations he had vouchsafed were no more than fever dreams born of dementia. Well, he would soon find out. He would know if reality could be more outlandish than mad dreams.

III.

INTO THE VOID

Thongor stood at the foot of the bed contemplating the sleeping form of his ailing mentor. Reassuring himself of Sharajsha's even breathing, the royal barbarian paced away from the bed and gazed idly at the strange gem resting in his palm. He wondered how one entered into the proper contemplative state in order to...

And at once he found himself falling with no more carpeted floor under his booted feet. His bare knees felt the impact of landing before his feet did, as he fell against a structure whose four planes converged at an acute angle. Thongor pressed his palms against the planes before him, noticing for the first time their translucent violet hue. He took a quick inventory and was relieved to find he still possessed his tunic and boots, his broadsword and the purple jewel. The violet-tinted light entering the huge glassy expanse above his head had a striking effect on the purple of its miniature twin, deepening its intensity. But Thongor did not dwell on this phenomenon. He saw an audience before him, on the other side of the glass barrier.

In his undignified posture, he felt reluctant to make the opening speech Sharajsha had written for him. So instead he barked, «Release me, damn you! Or, so help me, I'll smash this cursed thing!» Withal he made to draw Sarkozan from its scabbard but smoldered with chagrin as his elbows bumped against his confinement.

There was no room to free the sword. A semicircle of seemingly identical faces registered no amusement. Their silence was broken by not so much as a titter. But one of them made a simple gesture in the air, and Thongor dropped to a level floor some four feet below. His muscle-coiled legs absorbed the impact, and he rose from his crouch with some measure of dignity.

«Behold! I am Thongor of Valkarth, Sark of Lemuria and vanquisher of the Dragon Kings! I am come to announce amnesty and to welcome the Druids home. Your exile is ended! And I bring you greetings from your brother, Sharajsha!» He hoped his imperiousness (or was it pomposity?) would impress them suitably.

One of the sitting, identically robed figures had commenced speaking, but, strangely, Thongor could not tell which one. The hollow voice sounded somehow metallic, as if the product of a mechanism. Thongor's eyes flicked about the shadowed chamber, but in vain.

«We know who you are and why you have come, young man. Little escapes us. We have accordingly given the matter some thought already. And we have a counter-offer to make. We know of this Thongor. Any hulking ruffian may claim to be he, so we shall provide an opportunity for you to prove yourself. Do not decline it if you wish matters to proceed one step further.»

Cold, purple flames engulfed him for an instant until he found himself in a small arena, with a mob of semi-human Beast-men advancing upon him. Thongor had faced such foes before. He was not too surprised to find them here on the far side of the world. Why not? But he had not fought them in recent days, since the chieftain of these apish warriors in Lemuria had sworn fealty to Thongor's empire after a battlefield alliance had smoothed out longstanding hostilities between them. These particular creatures, on the other hand, knew nothing of such matters. In his experience, their kind were typically fierce fighters, effective against one another, but clumsy against true men. If they could not overpower an opponent in short order, they were at a significant disadvantage, a disadvantage Thongor determined to press.

This was the latest of a series of surreal experiences, so much so that Thongor half-suspected it was all a bizarre dream from which Sumia had never awakened him. But that could prove a dangerous supposition. As his stinking, drooling opponents loped toward him, Thongor assumed a fighting stance, sword drawn, legs braced apart, weight balanced on the balls of his feet. Easily dodging the lunging troglodytes, he executed an intricate dance of death, lopping off tongue-lolling heads, ripping open hirsute abdomens, hacking off limbs, all the while receiving nothing but minor nicks.

He knew he could never have defeated so many fully human foes so quickly. These Druids obviously had no sense of real combat or they should have given him steeper odds to beat. It took mere minutes for the Valkarthan to litter the field with random scraps of mangy, bleeding flesh. Satisfied with his victory, cheap though it was, Thongor turned to face his gallery of observers. Little did he suspect that, as far as they were concerned, he had just signed his own death warrant.

«All right, barbarian—you *are* the true Thongor, confidant of our former compatriot. You have proven yourself. And you have won the right to learn that which Sharajsha seeks: the secret of immortality.»

Thongor was amazed how swiftly matters looked to have been resolved. Could his task be completed so easily? Easily for Thongor of Valkarth, that is. A pair of the mute scarecrows broke off from the rest, a group of immobile statues, and indicated the way to a suite in the underground labyrinth. Here he was to relax after his adventures of the day. As they escorted him, then departed, Thongor marveled at the comparative opulence of the accommodations, a sumptuousness glaringly inappropriate to the ascetical mien of these spindle-shanked sorcerers. In any case, he could use the rest. So he stretched out on the bed and instantly fell into a deep slumber. This time Sharajsha sent him no messages, as much as Thongor wished he might. Or if he did, Thongor slept much too soundly to receive them.

IV.
SECRETS OF LIFE AND DEATH

Thongor awakened at the soft tread of the Druid who entered his room in the morning. He said nothing but motioned for Thongor to follow him. The Valkarthan knew any words directed to the man would be wasted so he offered none. He followed his guide to a great hall, albeit one virtually empty of decoration, even of furnishings. But at the far end he saw an exception: a high vaulted throne dwarfing the figure that sat upon it. How odd, Thongor momentarily mused: a throne was usually designed to magnify the stature of its occupant, but this one had the opposite effect, making him that sat upon it look like a doll in the lap of a child. Thongor strode forward and stood before the throne. He waited for his host to speak. And he did.

«Thongor of Valkarth, Thongor of Lemuria. We have promised to reveal to you the secret of immortality and vitality in search of which you have journeyed so far.»

«I understand, my lord. But may I know who is addressing me?»

«Of course. I am the head of this druidic order. My brethren esteem me a god and call me the Ray King because of my mastery of the Seven Rays of life and death.»

Thongor squinted, believing he caught sight of a dim rainbow nimbus over the man's head.

«The means of extending life indefinitely is this: to consume the vitality of lesser mortals. Thus did the Dragon Kings teach. Thus do they teach to this day.»

Thongor was startled. «You mean some yet survive?»

«The Golden Druids did not depart Lemuria alone. They brought with them the greatest of their divine patrons, the Naga King.»

Thongor's golden eyes rose to scrutinize the great canopy of the throne: it was a huge effigy of the nine-headed serpent, the Naga. It was an ancient symbol familiar to all Lemurians. And just as suddenly, the question arose in his mind as to why the speaker referred to the fleeing druids in the third person. Was he not after all one of them?

«In this remote recess of the world the Golden Druids have siphoned off the life force of a dwindling population. But the time comes round too soon for replenishment. We have sought to replace those whom we have consumed. I have applied the rays to primitive hominids, evolving them into the half-intelligent creatures such as you slaughtered. But they proved useless for our purpose. It is only the vitality imbued with the light of reason that imparts such life to superior men.

«Thus have we foraged farther afield. We have battened on poor old Sharajsha through the Purple Star. Without realizing it, he gave himself a reprieve when he passed the gem to you. But still he lies at death's door. Even now it creaks open to receive his mortal shell. Your arrival is most fortuitous, as very great vitality resides within you! It should supply many years of immortality for the Golden Druids. Your combat yesterday demonstrated your great might, hence your great worth to us.»

«But what ‹life› is it if one but continue as a silent puppet such as your lackeys?»

«You are surprisingly observant, mortal man. The eight men you have seen drifting about vacantly are extensions of myself. Once they lived long lives of power and knowledge, like your mentor, until I took their lives into my own. And now I shall take your valiant soul into myself.»

Thongor lost consciousness for a split second as the light in the great chamber changed and a curtain seemed to drop away. What had been a carven throne with nine fanged heads now stood revealed as a living thing, a towering mass of squamous horror with nine waving stalks. The four heads on either side of the central neck were those formerly seen atop the robed figures of the silent Druids. But now for the first time real emotion marked their countenances: each and all writhed in muffled torment, while the middle head, which remained serpentine, hissed and spat with hunger and wrath.

No one had bothered to confiscate Thongor's broadsword, which must mean they did not consider it dangerous, but Thongor knew not what to do but free it from its sheath. Come to think of it, Sarkozan was not his only weapon. He reached into his belt pouch and palmed the Purple Star. He now felt it throbbing with energy. He looked at it, then back at the looming Naga King, last of the Dragon Kings. A sudden inspiration told Thongor that the purple gem might be used to drain life force just as the Naga King did. He realized that Sharajsha had sent him this hint across the etheric abyss, and he hefted the stone and pitched it into the ravening jaws of the monster.

As if the unearthly spectacle were not enough to drive a man mad, what happened next paralyzed the Valkarthan with amazement. He had seen much in his brief years, far more than most men, but he had seen nothing like this. A kaleidoscopic vortex burst forth, and the dragon that swallowed the gem was now swallowed *by* the gem, like a cyclone consuming itself. The air was charged with stinging static. The blade of Sarkozan seemed to gather some of this discharge like a lightning rod, leaping from Thongor's nerveless hand. He himself was thrown backward by the shock but managed not to lose consciousness this time.

Now thankfully alone in the maze of Mount Shasta, Thongor knew he must hasten to find his way to the great double pyramid if he were to have any chance of returning to Lemuria across the seas. He had, remember, been swept up from one location to another by the magic arts of the Golden Druids and so could not retrace his steps. So he perforce explored, wasting time with blind alleys and false leads until at last he chanced upon that which he sought. All the while, the pulsing throb of the violet jewel grew more intense, beginning even to emit a loud, heavy hum. Thongor feared it might explode in his hand, but he knew he dared not discard it.

As soon as he neared the inverted pyramid, into which he could see no opening, the gem in his hand sent forth a searing current, but Thongor, shuddering, somehow retained his grasp. The purple bolt sizzled in the burning air, bridging the distance between the giant gem and the small one. Defying every instinct, Thongor strode into the crackling path of the current. As the violet fire surged painfully through him, he found himself again in a timeless, undimensioned place, not in the spaces known to man but *between* them. He had sensed no motion until he felt it cease. He expected to find himself again in Sharajsha's bed chamber, fearing to find the old man asleep in death. But he did not. He did not go the whole way. Nor was he alone in the tunnel between the worlds.

V.
IN THE TUNNEL OF THE WORM

What had gone wrong? And could it be made right? This would not be a good place to be stranded! The light here was very strange, strobing from positive to negative and back again, faster than the human eye could follow, as if the optic laws presupposed some other type of sight. Thongor could not say whether there was no color at all or if a different color palette prevailed here. But he could see well enough that something was approaching him, and rapidly. It looked like a huge worm with an unstable outline and a slavering maw, obviously intent on devouring him body and soul. He had encountered creatures of the same general type before, and they were never easy to deal with. No walls were visible, but the space was nonetheless confined. Flight was impossible. He had no other choice but to attack, whatever good that might do. As ever, Thongor did not shirk the prospect of death. A man's life must end sometime—unless he were one of the Immortals of Lemuria. And he was determined to make his ancient friend Sharajsha one of them! This mindless vermin must not stand in his way.

He did not hesitate to hack with his sword, but, as he feared, it had no effect: the gelatinous ooze of which the thing was composed merely came together again, the severed portion collapsing seamlessly back into the original loathsome mass. He returned Sarkozan to its scabbard, admitting its futility in the present circumstance. But as he slammed the blade back into its sheath, his eye caught sight of the purplish glow of the object in his belt pouch. It had proven its value as a weapon and might again.

It was nigh impossible to concentrate on the gem while dodging the surprisingly swift dartings of the bulky creature. It could have no real mind, but then instinct was often tactically better than strategy. Sometimes intelligence was a handicap. As a man, Thongor had to *try*; as a brainless slug, his opponent simply *did*. But, luckily, so did the gem: blazing violet rays at once bathed the repulsive slime-beast, frying its undulating mass to a crisped husk. The tunnel vanished along with it, Gorm be praised, and Thongor found himself, without apparent transition, at his destination.

VI.
AN OLD MAN'S FATE

Arriving at Sharajsha's bedside, Thongor had to steady himself, as one resisting the momentum of a headlong plunge. But it took only a moment to produce the crystal. The figure before him lying tangled in the bed sheets began to stir, aware of his friend's sudden presence. Thongor could see at once that the magician began to feel power rushing into him, convulsing, but less passively by the moment until he looked less like a banner snapping in a strong wind and more like a jungle cat stretching and arching its knotted muscles.

The Valkarthan beamed with joy at the sight, though he was half afraid Sharajsha would break brittle bones in the process. But alarm galvanized Thongor as the old man suddenly collapsed back onto the rumpled bedding. From the white-bearded lips emerged the voice of the slain Naga King in all of its irony-dripping disdain.

«You have served me well, foolish savage! I shall now complete the process, and a rejuvenated Sharajsha, formerly traitor and coward, shall be my new vessel. You have my thanks.»

Reflexively, the stunned Thongor loosed Sarkozan, but he knew not what to do with it: he must not be maneuvered into having to slay his old master!

But then things changed. The bed chamber suddenly appeared crowded with half-seen shapes, drifting into and through one another like insubstantial clouds. Thongor instantly surmised who they must be. Somehow the spirits of the eight Druids whom the Ray King had absorbed had become free, no longer imprisoned inside the slain physical form of their reptilian master. As no more than a possessing spirit himself, hovering above others, the Naga god could no longer hold them.

They commenced to attack their former master, fighting a weird ectoplasmic battle half-visible to Thongor in the air above the thrashing form of the unconscious Sharajsha. Thongor again sheathed Sarkozan, frustrating its hungry blood lust and, under a sudden inspiration, he quitted the room to go searching amongst the sorcerous relics festooning Sharajsha's domicile. It seemed a daunting prospect, like seeking one particular coin in a vast treasury, until he saw the door of a hidden vault opening before him by itself. He knew this must be Sharajsha's desperate gesture. Within, Thongor spied the very Sword of Nemedis forged from the Star Stone, the selfsame weapon he had used years before to whelm the Dragon Kings even as Phondath the Firstborn did at the dawn of time.

Still, he could hardly smite Sharajsha with it!

With a few great strides, Thongor regained the bedchamber of Sharajsha and quickly surveyed the scene: the magus's body again lay supine, though twitching with the still-raging battle of the ghosts. Thongor recalled the telepathic link he had not long before established with Sharajsha, and how he had done it. And now he gently laid the glowing, blinding blade of Nemedis across the old man's forehead, fearing to blister the wrinkle-webbed skin. It was a simple gesture that turned the tide. The shrieking Naga evaporated into the void.

The spirits of the eight Golden Druids now stood before him, bobbing as with a breeze and translucent to the light. A collective voice arose from the company.

«Our brother Sharajsha was right and we were wrong all those years ago. The temptation of dark secrets and forbidden powers tempted us astray. He alone saw our error. We shall henceforth attempt to make things right. We shall now return to Shasta, in this undying spirit form. Perhaps we may aid and guide humanity. And who knows? Mayhap one day, a new Ray King, a true Bodhisattva of Light, will appear among us to carry our wisdom to the outer world.»

Like a dream when one awakes, they were gone, obviously requiring no aid from the purple crystal. Sharajsha now sat up, alert and restored, fairly glowing and rejuvenated. And he did not share the wide-eyed astonishment of his brawny protégé. He seemed to understand exactly what had happened. Thongor remained largely mystified but asked him for no clarification. He had learned enough, indeed perhaps too much, in these last days. But one question he had to ask.

«But are you truly immortal, my master?»

«Time or Eternity may tell, Thongor of Valkarth!»

THE VANISHING CONJURER

By Glynn Owen Barrass

The path leading to the castle was filled with potholes. It was not the best of signs; she hadn't noticed them in such proliferation the first time out. The zebra she rode took them with aplomb, probably used to the rough terrain. It was a large, hardy beast, quite unlike the zebras they rode across the continent. Ansell had borrowed it from a nearby farm, the smiling bumpkins wishing her luck on her journey. Did she need luck?

Ansell felt the hesitance in her steed's gait as they entered the courtyard fronting Stein's Castle. Overgrown box hedges, a border wall of sorts, surrounded the courtyard. Inside, between cracked stone slabs, stood trees brimming with bulbous brown fruit. A dead Maga Bird lay rotten on the stones, its multicoloured feathers grey in the twilight.

The zebra neighed, attempted to halt. Ansell hushed the beast and gave it a tap of her heel. Was it the dead bird, the courtyard, or the castle itself that disturbed it?

Castle. The structure they approached was hardly that. Standing three stories high, the ‹castle› was small, built from brown sandstone brick. The east wing had a conical tower at its corner, standing a little higher than the building's red-tiled roof. *More a manse, then, than a castle,* she mused. The evening shadows clung to the manse, forming a veritable cloak that wrapped its eaves and façade. Was Stein's Castle concealing secrets, or was it huddling in fear against the cooling night air?

A small, one-storied stablehouse stood near the east wing. She didn't direct her zebra there. Instead Ansell rode the animal closer to the double doors leading into Stein's Castle. Windows lined the walls above and around the entrance, only one of them illuminated. This was not a good sign. Just the large, stained-glass window above the entrance was lit, multicoloured and bright. Now she was closer, Ansell noted the ivy clinging to the east tower, almost covering it entirely. She could climb that, sneak in through an upstairs window if things came to it. If she thought the element of surprise was necessary.

The zebra had begun shivering beneath the saddle. *This is far enough*, she thought.

Ansell guided the zebra towards the nearest tree, as noisome as it appeared in the deepening shadows. The zebra crushed some festering fruit underhoof: Ansell caught the sickly sweet odour. That smell grew stronger as she brought her steed to a halt. She dismounted it, took the reins, and stepped forward while looking down. There were broken fruits all around the tree. Their innards were yellow, like puss from a diseased wound. Ansell eyed the tree with distaste, reached for one of the lower hanging bows with a leatherclad hand. It creaked, scabs of bark coming off in her fist. The tree was dying; probably they all were. She wrapped the reins around the branch's thicker end, stepped back, and examined the boughs above her head.

What condition were the trees in the last time?

Ansell couldn't recall; she had been too busy saying goodbye to her companion Tamara. An apprentice mage, the girl had come here for further magical training. A lump formed in Ansell's gut. *My girl, what have you gotten yourself into?* She turned from the tree, patted the zebra's flank as she passed. All answers lay in Stein's Castle, and she strode towards it with firm steps and grim intent.

They had spent much time together, Tamara and herself, travelling from the port of Hlanith, across the Cerenarian Sea, then to here, the lands beyond Celephais. After a painful parting, Ansell had decided to stay at a nearby village, to look for adventure, something to take her mind off...

She reached the steps to the entrance, ascended them towards two large wooden doors. Brass knockers, shaped like the heads of strange beasts, stood at the centre of each door. A griffin and a manticore: fabulous creatures. Perhaps not so fabulous, in these lands. *Should I knock? No.* Ansell pushed the doors, watched them slide inwards on well-oiled hinges. The doors opened up to reveal a wide, brightly lit lobby. A clock ticked erratically from somewhere, the only sound within the room.

Ansell stepped forward, placed her hand on the hilt of her sword. Her boots touched a varnished wooden floor. *Wooden panels from floor to ceiling...* This was not what she expected. It was quite a homely place really.

A chandelier hung from the ceiling, beyond which stood a wide staircase, the ornate gold and red banisters leading to a second floor. A balcony looked down, from the west, east and north sides of the lobby.

Appears to be deserted, or else folk are hiding... or dead.

She came forward a few steps and paused, examining her environment. Doors lined the wood-panelled walls, three in the east and the west walls, another two flanking the staircase. The ticking issued from a coffin-shaped clock, stood against the west wall. Light was provided not from the chandelier, but rather four yellow globes hovering at the cardinal points of the ceiling. It was a sorcery Tamara could perform, though the girl needed to concentrate to keep them lit. Whose willpower kept these illuminated?

«Hello?» she asked the empty room.

A sudden sound made Ansell spin on her heels, unsheathe her sword in one deft motion. It was only the doors, creaking closed of their own volition, or perhaps from some hidden mechanism. She released a breath, watched them slide shut and conceal the nighted courtyard.

Ansell turned, headed forward, her sword ready. The answers were ahead, not back there. A day ago, a travelling circus troupe had passed this way. They claimed to have witnessed strange lights, heard screams from the castle. When news reached the tavern Ansell was staying in, she had feared for the wellbeing of her friend.

Halfway to the staircase, something on the floor caught her attention. Ansell crouched to examine it. *Them.* A pair of bloody footprints had been deposited on the floor. They faced the doors behind her, and joined a trail descending from the stairs. They were small, the size of a young woman's or boy's. Ansell reached down, touched the print on her right, smearing the blood a little. *Still fresh... But where? Footprints usually lead somewhere. What the devil happened here?* Ansell stood, looked from the footprints to the chandelier directly above them.

«Hum.» *Did the owner fly away, like a nymph?* With the cobwebbed chandelier holding no answers, Ansell headed for the stairs, staring at the footprints as she ascended.

As such, the man-shaped silhouette near the top of the stairs surprised her. She ducked, crouched into a fighting stance.

Ansell awaited an attack that didn't come. A few moments later she relaxed, stood, and examined her almost foe.

It was a naked satyr-like humanoid, with swarthy features, goat's horns on its brow. The body was thick with fur, especially the legs, which terminated in cloven hoofs. The beast stood static, crouched with its clawed hands raised in a menacing pose. Someone had skinned and stuffed this creature, mounted it upon a circular pedestal covered in small black rocks. Ansell grimaced. She knew the species, this being one of the rapacious and sadistic Men from Leng. Fighting the urge to cut it down on general principles, she sneered back at its cruel, flabby lips. Even in death, the black marble eyes portrayed a cruel animal cunning.

She ascended the last steps, then turned left, leaving the beast at her back as she followed the blood trail. The south ends of each balcony held staircases, ascending to another floor. Doors lined the walls leading that way, three to a side like the lobby.

This place... again Ansell wondered at the construction of Stein's «castle.» It was improper. Wizards lived in damp, stone, echoey places, or noisome huts hidden deep in the wilderness, not—

More blood, she thought, pausing. The footprints ended at a door ahead and to her right. A small pool of congealed blood had leaked out from beneath that door.

This is... «Not a good sign,» she said. *Shouldn't have come alone. Should have brought backup.* Ansell snorted. Who could she have brought? The bumpkins from the village, or the bumpkins from the farm? She continued towards the door, steeled herself and gripped her sword tightly. She gave the door a hard kick, followed it as it flew inwards.

«Oh my gods.»

Ansell gagged at the smell, halted, then staggered back a little.

This was like nothing she had ever witnessed. Placing her hand over her mouth, Ansell breathed between the gaps her fingers made.

The room had wood-panelled walls, a plaster ceiling and floorboards underfoot. A glowing orb shone down from the ceiling's centre. Gore, organs, and scraps of skin carpeted the floor, with more blood spattered across the walls and ceiling. Ansell composed herself, stepped forward across the visceral mess. There was no way to avoid it, not if she wanted to examine the strange object in the corner. Multiple footprints in the gore led that way. She stepped on something that popped, *an eyeball,* she thought, and managed not to gag.

Blood clung to her boots as she approached the object. The stench coated the insides of her mouth. This was still better than breathing through her nostrils.

Why? How? The thing in the corner was a gate most surely, rectangular in shape with a greyish-silver shimmer to its surface. The gate's construction was at least in keeping with the room. Human limbs formed its frame: arms and legs moulded together by some obscene sorcery. They were deathly pale, lined with bulging blue veins. The top section of the frame was centred by a head. Bald, it stared down with eyes as obsidian as the stuffed beast's at the top of the stairs.

From the features, she guessed it was male, human, though it was difficult to tell with all certainty. Did it matter?

«Tamara,» she asked the rank, lifeless room. «What in all the hells of the netherworld happened here?» A crackling sound caught Ansell's attention, and looking down, she saw the tip of her sword had passed through the gate's shimmering surface.

«Oh.» She tugged the sword back, fought a little resistance as she did. Ansell stared from the tip of her sword to the gate. *So, whatever goes in can come out.*

Were there answers beyond the gate, answers to the castle's desertion and this charnel room and… «Whatever *you* are?» she addressed the gate, scrutinized the looming face.

Ansell turned and examined the room behind her. *How many bodies are here? Did whatever left the footprints beyond the door do this, or had a survivor left them?* She took her hand from her mouth, returned her attention to the gate, and stepped forward.

A transition of lights and chaotic sounds followed. One moment she was hovering, prone and defenceless in an abyss of mystifying shapes and cacophonic noise. The next, Ansell was on her knees, dizzy and disoriented, fighting not to retch. Her sword was on the ground beneath her. Thankfully, she hadn't dropped it in that bizarre transdimensional passage.

The ground was formed from cracked, reddish earth. It resembled dried blood. Ansell looked up and stared aghast at the environment surrounding her.

Damn. She retrieved her sword, stood unsteadily. The air was thick, acrid-tasting, not the air of her world but of an alien realm the likes of which she could never have imagined.

The sky was a dark purple in colour. Mountains, jagged and cyclopean, lined the horizon, either formed from purple rock or dyed that colour from the light. The mountains were breath-taking in their magnitude—even those nearest her were so tall they pierced the sky. Below the mountains the world was even more fantastical.

Bright purple mist clung to the foothills, and below the mist, oceans of flowers, scintillating and metallic, smothered the landscape. Groups of tube-like, bone-coloured protrusions stood interspersed between the flowers, spotting the landscape in their hundreds.

Were they plants, fungi, or natural geological formations? Ansell didn't dare guess. On this strange world, all bets were off.

A thought returned Ansell's gaze to the ground. The blood was gone from her heels, the earth completely clear of blood from whomever came before her.

«Huh.»

She turned and found the gate, or at least, that shimmering greyness shaped like a doorway. There was no necrotic frame on this side of the portal. The landscape beyond held more mountains. Their fanged shapes spiked the horizon, some so distant they stood as mere hints against the purple sky.

The sky though!

Three celestial orbs hovered there, all impossibly close and huge. The nearest was white, leprous in hue, the two behind it red and green, though the red planet was mottled with dark spots. They seemed ready to fall and crush the weird landscape at any moment.

A claw-like mountain partially concealed the white orb. If she climbed it, could she touch the planet from the peak? Ansell shook her head, took a deep breath of acrid air. She wasn't here to explore, but to learn the fate of her friend. As such, she scanned the immediate area. She soon found marks of passage in the flowerbeds beyond the gate.

There were seven sets of prints, some overlapping. They tramped the flowers, thus making the trail easy to follow. They took a relatively straight path across the field, heading towards a forest of tubes.

Ansell stepped around the gate and started across the field. The flowers crunched like ice beneath her boots. As big as her palm, the petals were teardrop shaped, metallic violet and blue.

The trail continued in a roughly straight direction, no diversions tempting a stranger to explore. Her lungs began to ache a little, no doubt a symptom of the strange air. Ansell hoped there would be no permanent damage. The silence of the place perturbed her, this uncanny valley of metallic hues. The only sounds were those Ansell brought with her, and things continued this way for a while.

The separate paths converged as she neared the tubes. There were sounds now, so low they were barely perceptible. The noises resembled the sighs of people, or winds issuing from unseen caverns. Yes, that was it, she realized, approaching one of the nearer tubes. The sound issued from its hollow depths, wind from deep below the ground. The tube was taller than her by a few heads, and much wider. Did it grow, or was it some stone or mineral growth native to this world? Whatever the origin, the moans issued incessantly from within, from some underground realm to which the tubes were connected.

Ansell hoped Stein hadn't taken his students down there. She raised her sword, tapped the tube. The hollow sound it produced made her think of stone. *Curious. Could I dare go crawling down into that unknown?*

Ansell entered the forest of tubes, and soon after, the moaning was all around her. It made her feel uncomfortable. On edge. The flowers began to thin, whatever answered for sunlight not reaching them in the shade. The trail continued, however, meandering around the tubes and—
What the? A whimper reached her ears, ahead and to her right. With quick strides, Ansell went forward, readying herself for an encounter with the unknown.

A pair of feet protruded from beyond one of the tubes. Brown cloth boots, matching trousers. Ansell's heart leaping into her chest, she rushed towards the prostrate being. It wasn't Tamara, she saw, but rather a young man leaning against a tube. He wore a dark green robe, the kind an apprentice mage wore. The hood hung over a pale, pain-filled face. A metallic grey spike was embedded in the folds of his robe, the surrounding area wet with blood.

His eyes opened when Ansell paused before him.

«Help me,» he asked in a hoarse voice.

Ansell went to her knees, examined his chest. *His wound, not fatal, bleeding has stopped.*

«Water. Do you have water? Please, I implore you.»

«I can give you that,» she replied. Lowering her sword to the flowers, she shrugged her backpack from her shoulders. «But you have to tell me what happened here.»

The injured man stared back from watery blue eyes. He swallowed loudly, then, «Stein, our master... he was obsessed with... with clay tablets we brought from Sarnath.»

«Sarnath. Don't know it,» Ansell replied absently while digging through her pack. She found her leather water skin and her crossbow, passing the former to the young man without looking up. A weak grip took the water, then a few moments later, there was a gulping sound.

She loaded the crossbow with a bolt from her belt and placed it on the ground beside her sword. There was something Ansell needed to ask, but she was hesitant to do so. She took a deep breath and turned to him.

He had stopped drinking, held the water skin to his chest protectively.

«Continue,» she said, making the word an order.

«We constructed... my gods... we constructed a portal from the dead... there's a graveyard behind the castle... then... something came through... massacred five of us... loose in the castle, last I saw...»

«Wait.» Leaning over, she retrieved the water from his reluctant grip. «Was there a girl with you, Tamara?»

«Tamara? Uh...»

She knelt closer, grabbed his cloak in her fist and pulled his face towards hers. «It's important. Remember!»

The apprentice licked his lips, blinked. His eyes lost focus for a moment before he found her gaze again.

«Stein had us enter the portal with him... she's with him. We encountered some creatures... oh lord, but I barely escaped.»

Idiot wizard.

«Idiots!» Ansell spat the word. She released the young man and worked quickly, tightened the cork on the water bottle, attaching it to her belt. The crossbow came next, clipped onto the opposite hip. She closed her pack and pulled it onto her shoulders.

«You... you're leaving me?»

Ansell retrieved her sword and stood.

«Were they alive when you last saw them?» she asked without looking down. Her eyes were set on the path ahead.

«They were faster than me... please... water?»

«I'll come back for you,» she replied half-heartedly, and ignoring his continued pleas, she continued on the trail.

I should go back, ask him what's ahead of me. Creatures, huh?

Ansell walked with more caution, as the path meandered between and around the tubes. Were the abyssal sounds growing louder? Perhaps, or perhaps her ears were more attuned. Was that a clearing ahead? Were the tubes beginning to thin out?

«Oh!» Ansell halted, looked down. So accustomed was she to stepping on the crinkling flowers, it was a surprise to find her foot landing on something wet. *Blood*, she realized, a large blob congealing upon the flowers. *So where's the source?*

The scenery about her exploded with motion. Chaotic sounds appeared, akin to hellish pipings from a hundred flutes. The source?

Skittering, monstrous things were pouring from the tubes. Metallic grey, each had multiple legs, mirror-like eyes protruding from gangrenous forms. Ansell swung her sword as one leapt. Its piping sounds became a shriek as she severed its limbs, sliced its bulbous torso. When a second horror pounced, she thrust her sword, green with hissing gore, running the thing through. Then one attacked her from behind, its cruel, stabbing claws piercing her armour. Ansell lost her balance, fell backwards with a grunt. Her sword escaped her grip as another horror leapt atop her. Panic wasn't the word for it. The one behind her squirmed and stabbed, the one above sent dagger-like limbs towards her eyes. Ansell blocked the attack with her right forearm, cried out as the points punctured her armour.

I need a weapon! She pulled her knees up, dragged a knife from her left boot. Then, using all her strength, she kicked the horror away. It stumbled back, multiple limbs flailing.

Ansell began stabbing the creature behind her. The fluting screams were disorienting, but with steely determination she put her blade through its pulsing flesh repeatedly. A shadow then appeared, either the attacker she had booted away or one of its companions. Club-like limbs came down on her. She turned her blade, ready to return the attack. If she was to die, she would go down fighting.

Faceted eyes stared down, reflecting Ansell's face a dozen times. And then, the horror was aflame. Immolating and struggling atop her, its limbs shrivelled as she watched. Ansell kicked the dying thing away, scrambled to her feet. What she saw came as an utter surprise.

Three green-clad figures had appeared from between the tubes. Robed like the man she had left behind, two poured flames from their hands, burning the horrors to death. One she recognized: Tamara, raven-haired, her dirt-smeared face determined as she burned a dying horror. Her eyes glowed red, like bright, burning coals. The final apprentice attacked the predators with a staff, though with little effect, as two of the undamaged things cornered her.

Ansell spied her sword, knelt to retrieve it while sticking her knife in her belt. Then she dashed forward, slashing at one of the monsters cornering the girl. Her attack sent limbs and green gore to the ground.

«Hey trouble!» Tamara yelled over the howls and sounds of flame. «You went to this much bother to get rescued by me again?»

«Again?» Ansell laughed. Her foe was a limp, dying thing, and Tamara's enthusiasm was infectious. The cornered girl was jabbing the other attacker, her staff sending crackles of blue electricity through its prone form. Her short blonde hair and delicate features were spattered with green blood.

The creatures' cries were dying out. Ansell thrust her green-slicked sword into the ground and caught some well-needed breaths. The blonde girl was still bludgeoning the dead beast, a snarl on her lips. Ansell looked around, saw the area covered in dead and dying things, their smouldering bodies issuing an acrid stench. The other apprentice, a male with a shaved head, stood staring at the carnage, a ball of flame in each hand. Her friend and former companion was bent forward, her hands on her knees, getting her breath back.

When their eyes met, Tamara rushed towards her, embracing Ansell in a grip surprisingly powerful considering the girl's petite size. Tamara's body was terribly hot, but Ansell returned the embrace regardless, hugging her tightly. Tamara sobbed a little. Their eyes met, Tamara's still holding the glow of magical fire. Her tears hissed and became steam. She blinked and released her hold on Ansell.

Tamara looked her over, her expression one of grim concern. «Those spiky limbs, did any snap off into you?»

Ansell heard the other two apprentices' approach. «No, why?»

Her friend grinned, wiped her brow. «Thank Karakal! They're a killer.»

Tamara raised a hand towards the figures pausing at Ansell's left. «Ansell, this is Bink and Polly,» she said, pointing to the male and female in turn. «Guys, this is the one I told you about, the lady that got me here in one piece.»

«You're the one that faced down the Gug?» Polly asked, her tone one of pure admiration.

«And battled the pirates?» Bink added, his boyish features beaming.

Tamara cleared her throat. «We can talk later.»

Ansell was glad of Tamara's interjection; she was growing a trifle embarrassed.

Polly, gripping her staff two-handed, shook it purposefully. «We need to return for the Master. He was some ways behind when we escaped the spider-things.»

«Stein?» Ansell questioned, and the pair nodded in unison.

She turned to Tamara.

«No, they got him,» her friend said. «I saw him go down.»

«He's a wizard, a powerful conjurer; he can survive that.» Bink was shaking his head.

In denial perhaps? Ansell had no idea of this Stein's capabilities, but considered him a fool regardless, for bringing his apprentices to this foul realm.

She was about to advise the trio to flee with her, when a shape appeared beyond Tamara.

«Oh my.»

Three heads turned as one at her words.

Polly gasped. Ansell took a step back.

«Master Stein...» Tamara said. Whatever else she was about to say faded from her lips.

The wizard moved sluggishly, his breathing laboured. His head was round, bald. A long grey moustache trailed down his chest. He wore voluminous red robes, fringed with gold. It wasn't just the robes that were large,

Ansell realized; the body beneath was huge, bloated. Spikes protruded from his body, resembling the still-smouldering horrors' legs.

Ansell gripped her sword tight as the apprentices, Tamara included, started to back away.

«My pupils,» he said in a weak, croaking voice. Then Stein exploded with a *pop*.

Ansell barely had time to shield her face as gore, flaps of skin, and flying bones scattered in every direction.

There was screaming, male and female; an, «Oh, gross,» from Tamara.

Ansell lowered her glove, and her jaw dropped. She was aghast at the scene before her.

Polly and Bink were crouched on the ground, still shielding their heads. Tamara stared at the cloud of atomized blood hovering in the air, held in suspension by the atmosphere or some dark sorcery.

No, she's not staring at the cloud, Ansell realized, *but the thing floating inside it.*

The being had two heads, two eerily beautiful faces surrounded by long, golden hair. They were elven in shape, with high brows and pointed ears. Outspread wings jutted from its naked shoulders, bearing sharp, sword-like protuberances in place of feathers. The wing-tips were red with Stein's blood. The entity's ivory body was covered in delicate scales and ribbed areas, from its neck down to its petite toes.

Beneath it lay Stein's remains, bent legs, amputated arms and chunks of torso.

Such a magnificent being from such a charnel birth. Ansell looked to its dual faces. The eyes were closed, the lips set in gentle smiles.

«Guys, get up,» Tamara said, backing off towards Ansell.

«Nonterraqueous,» a weak voice said.

Ansell looked down, left, and found Stein's head staring up at her, his bloodied lips moving.

«The word translates to: ‹Not of the earth or sea,›» he said. «A celestial being I hoped to catch. I suggest you flee for you lives.»

She sensed Tamara nearing and raised her hand, bringing the girl to a gentle halt. In the periphery of her vision, she saw the other two standing.

«Tamara,» Ansell said, removing her gaze from Stein.

«Ansell,» her friend replied.

«Run,» Ansell continued, and a moment later spun on her heels. She made her escape across the flowers, through the forest of tubes.

Sounds of singing filled the air, originating from two clear, beautiful voices. The words were alien, hypnotic. Their seductive tug had Ansell biting her lower lip.

«Everyone here?» she shouted, between pants.

«All here,» Tamara replied behind her.

«I got the head,» Bink said, his voice strained from exertion.

«The head?» Polly.

«The head,» Bink repeated.

They tramped flowers as they fled. The alien song grew nearer. The forest of pipes moaned louder, too, in sympathy, in synchronicity with the ethereal voices.

Ansell expected deadly wings to overshadow them at any moment.

Celestial being, she thought, and snorted. *Damned wizard.* The strange air was making breathing quite difficult; from the puffs and pants of her companions, she guessed they were suffering, too.

Upon turning a corner, Ansell found the young man she had encountered earlier. What remained of him, anyway. His limbs were bent and splayed, his torso a bloody crater.

Not another one!

«Keep moving!» she ordered her companions. There were muttered exclamations, a gasp of horror from Polly. Ansell didn't look back. She wanted to but fought the urge.

«Tamara, you all right?»

«Yes… Just this air…,» her friend replied in strained tones.

Soon her group reached the final few tubes. They had begun to roar, drowning out the angelic singing. Beyond their noisome bulks lay the fields of metallic flowers. This sight brought relief to Ansell's harried mind.

A straight dash across the flowers and they would be safe.

Her legs ached more than her lungs now, her knees burning from this flight from horror.

Ansell spied the gate's shimmer ahead. An encouraging sight, it had her speeding her gait despite the leadenness in her legs.

«I see it!» Polly cried. «Thank the gods!»

Ansell felt ready to drop, feared she would slip on the flowers, fall face down at any moment.

With the sounds of the pipes diminishing, the singing inaudible or stopped, freedom was in their grasp.

She stumbled to a stop near the gate, took deep gasps. A moment later, Tamara was by her side. The girl's brow was damp, her usually white cheeks flushed with red.

They made eye contact, and Ansell laughed.
«The things you get me into!»
Tamara's fatigued features broke into a grin.
«I'm going in. Come on, guys!» Polly said.
Ansell looked up, watched the petite apprentice step towards the gate. Her body froze in the static, then she was gone.
Bink appeared to her right, still cradling the wizard's obscenely living head. He turned to her and Tamara.
«Me next?» he asked in anxious tones, and nodded towards the portal.
«Pass me the head,» Ansell ordered.
«The head?» Bink replied, a dumb look on his face.
She nodded, and he reciprocated. Accepting it one-handed, she tucked it under the crook of her sword arm.
Bink headed through the gate.
«You next,» she told her friend. She watched the girl head towards the gate, then hesitate.
Tamara turned to Ansell.
«You'll be right through after me?»
Ansell smiled. Tamara returned it. Moments later, she was one with the static, then gone.
«And you, you old bastard!» She took Stein by the nose, stared at him in distaste. «You can reap what you sowed.»
The sorcerer's eyes blinked open; his mouth yammered. She tossed the head into the air and, as it fell, kicked it with her boot.
Stein howled as his head spun through the air. It ditched and landed some distance away.
Just desserts.
Now it was her turn to leave. Ansell shook the remaining blood from her sword and sheathed it. She took a deep breath and stepped towards the gate. A chaos of noise and lights followed, the latter near-blindingly bright. Fabulous shapes unfurled and throbbed around her, and then she was somewhere else.
The charnel room appeared, as spattered and as gory as before. Ansell stumbled, unsteady on her aching legs. Tamara was there to stabilize her. It was good to breathe real air again, as blood-tainted as it was.
Her companion examined her in concern. She didn't mention the head.
«I'm all right,» Ansell said, taking Tamara's hand a moment. «The others?»
Tamara grinned. «They rushed off. I don't blame them.»
Ansell nodded slowly, unsheathed her sword.

«Now this.» Spinning on her heels, she swung her weapon, sliced into the gate's macabre frame. The limbs bent inwards, leaked black fluid.

The gate flashed, bulged. She withdrew her sword and backed away a few steps.

A loud sucking sound filled the room.

«Should we run?» Tamara asked.

«Wait,» Ansell replied.

A moment later, the frame bent inwards towards the gate. Then the whole thing shrank into oblivion before their eyes.

Damn. Ansell felt Tamara's hand on her shoulder. She continued staring at the place the gate had been. There was nothing there but a swiftly diminishing shimmer.

«One of those celestial things came through the portal before we went in,» Tamara said.

Ansell nodded.

«We'll probably end up hunting it, won't we?»

Ansell turned to her friend. «Most likely,» she agreed. «But let's rest a spell beforehand.

They turned together, headed towards the door.

For the first time in many days, Ansell felt contented, happy. Her fine mood remained even when she stepped on an eyeball.

WORLD OF
THE BLACK SUN
By Pierre V. Comtois

1.
A MISSING HEIRLOOM

Elak rubbed his sore knuckles as he made sure the burly Gunderman was actually unconscious.

Dark and wiry, Elak barely measured up to half the Gunderman's weight, but what he lacked in size he more than made up in experience and skill. He had simply ducked under the man's clumsy swing and drove upward, delivering a blow under the chin that came all the way up from his heels. As a result, the Gunderman fell over as if he were poleaxed, hitting the rough floorboards with a boom that silenced everyone in the bar.

A pair of bouncers took the man by his ankles and dragged him to the door. Inside the tavern, activity slowly returned to normal as Elak made sure there were no more comers. Seeing none, he turned back to the wench with whom he had been speaking when the Gunderman broke in insisting she was with him.

«That must have hurt,» she said, leaning her elbows on the bar and inclining her head to the waiter who knew what drinks to bring without needing to be told.

Elak shrugged. «Not if you hit at the right angle. The worst of it was the roughage growing out of his jaw. It was like sandpaper.»

«I've got some liniment up in my room,» she said. «We'll put some on and see how you feel.»

«Just so long as it isn't too expensive,» replied Elak knowingly.

The drinks arrived and even Elak was surprised to see how the wench guzzled down the strong Singaran whiskey. Feeling no need to show off, he took his time with his own.

Just then, some raucous laughter from the bar's entrance drew his attention. Some street urchin had entered and stopped just inside the swinging doors. He peered through the murk of weed smoke and fire fumes until his eyes rested on Elak's.

Elak left his empty glass on the counter and placed his hand on his chest with a look on his face that seemed to say «You're looking for me?»

Shoving a drunk aside, the boy made his way across the crowded floor and came up to him.

«You Elak of Cyrena?» he asked.

«That's me,» acknowledged Elak offering nothing more.

«Have a message for you,» said the boy, holding out a rumpled piece of paupers' papyrus.

Reading the message, Elak suddenly straightened and became serious.

«You'll take me there?» he asked.

The boy nodded, holding out his hand. «They said you'd pay me two dublais for the job.»

Elak grunted pulling out the money and dropping it in the boy's palm, then threw a few more onto the counter. «Let's go.» To the wench: «Some other time, my sweet.»

The woman barely took notice, already looking out for another mark.

Outside the bar, the night was clear and cold. A few stars shown overhead in the gap where the buildings that formed the alley crowded together. Homeless huddled like bundles of old rags against the foundations and it took some careful maneuvering to avoid them while not stepping into the open sewer that trickled down the middle of the lane. Luckily, however, they did not have far to go as the boy led him around a few corners to a slate-roofed hovel where some weak lamp light managed to filter outside. The boy rapped on the rude door and without waiting, pushed it open.

Out of elementary caution, Elak placed his hand on the rapier at his side and waited until his eyes adjusted to the dim light before entering. He stood in a large room with a hearth at one end and some rude furniture here and there. A doorway led to an alcove or something in the back. On a cot covered in dirty linen lay the chubby form of Lycon, his sometime partner in perdition. Was the fool recovering from another epic drunk?

«Is this the man?» asked an oldster sitting by the hearth fire.

«He answers to the name of Elak,» said the boy and left, banging the flimsy door behind him.

«Do you know this man?» asked the oldster.

«I do. His name is Lycon. A friend of mine.»

«Found him outside my door. Heard a scuffle. When I went out, there he was. Bloody and beaten. It happens here.»

Elak approached his friend and leaned over him. Lycon seemed to sense his presence and opened his eyes.

«Elak. So they found you.»

«What happened, you useless cur,» asked Elak not unkindly. «Were you rolled?»

Lycon nodded. «Had a little too much to drink. A couple bravos followed me from the tavern and jumped me. Handled me pretty rough, I'm afraid.» He tried to move, winced, and fell back. «Broke something, I think.»

Elak looked up at the oldster.

«Ribs,» was all he said.

«Can he stay here till he mends?» asked Elak of the oldster. «I'll pay you.»

The man shrugged. «I'll not refuse payment, but I would have taken care of him regardless.»

Elak figured the old fellow was a Merciful, one of a cult of do-gooders in the city. He did not waste time trying to figure them out. «Good. Here's what I have.» He tossed the man a small pouch of coins. «You owe me Lycon!»

Lycon smiled and froze. Even that effort hurt. «There's something else, Elak.»

«What's that?»

Lycon looked at the oldster.

«Do you mind stepping out for a bit?» Elak asked the old man.

Wordlessly, the man stepped into the alcove.

«I lost something,» said Lycon after the third man was gone. «I think my attackers must have stolen it along with my purse.»

«What?»

«A medallion I wore around my neck...»

«That piece of junk? It was only a bit of raw iron...»

«But it held great sentimental value for me, Elak. It was given to me by my father, a good luck piece handed down from father to son for many generations.»

Elak looked askance at his friend. «A likely story. It sure didn't give you much luck tonight.»

«I still would like it back. Can you try to find those thieves and retrieve it for me?»

The look on Lycon's face was so pitiful and pleading, Elak found himself nodding. Anyway, it would not do for two thieves to be robbed by other thieves. It just was not done.

«Very well. Have any idea what they looked like?»

«One was taller than the other. The shorter one wore a circlet on his head and spoke in a Larangian accent. The other could barely put two words together.»

«Not much to go on, but I'll ask around. Maybe I'll get lucky. In the meantime, work at getting well and mind your keeper.»

With that, Elak was gone into the night.

2.

THE PLOT THICKENS

Outside again, Elak gave the issue some thought. If he were a thief, and he had been, where would he have gone after a job? Well, in the matter of goods, to a fence. He knew of more than one in the city, but he wanted to catch up to the thieves themselves, not arrive after they were long gone.

On the other hand, if the thieves had also acquired some cash as well as goods, they would have kept the cash for themselves. And likely would have gone to spend it before going to the fence with the rest of their booty. That meant either a tavern or a brothel and in the city-state of Mandazar both were the same. The two would also not have wasted any time, so it was likely they went to a tavern that was nearby. Why cross the city if they did not need to and risk a run-in with the gendarmes?

Very well. A tavern in the neighborhood. Elak shrugged. Might as well head for the Evil Tidings where he himself had ended the night. It was the closest.

Not a little while later, Elak found himself again in the tavern where he had skinned his knuckles. The place was still roaring despite the late…or rather, early hour. There were lowlifes, sailors and pirates both, and local workmen aplenty as well as a female clientele who were not exactly the pick of the litter. They had been in the trade a little too long in Elak's estimation. Crossing to the bar, a rough plank thrown across a series of empty wine casks, he signaled the barkeep.

«I'm looking for two men,» said Elak.

The bartender shrugged.

«One is bigger than the other and is dense as a stone, the other has a Larangian accent.»

The barkeep looked bored.

Elak dug into his doublet and produced some coins. He tossed them on the counter.

«Upstairs,» said the barkeep, scooping up the coins. «Third floor. Door triple.»

Elak thumped the bar with a fist, congratulating himself on his luck.

Weaving among the gamblers, drunkards, and blowhards, he found the rickety wooden staircase that led to the upstairs rooms. Finding the third door on the third and topmost floor, he decided to give those inside no warning and kicked the door in.

It slammed back on its leathern hinges smacking against the wall as Elak leapt in, rapier in hand. He had to hand it to the two, they could move fast when properly motivated. And the sudden sight of a man with naked steel in his hand provided plenty of motivation.

In a trice, Elak took in the situation: the smaller man was at the window attempting to crawl his way out. Elak decided to help him while evening the odds. He gave the man the sole of his boot and, as he turned to face the big one, heard the long scream and sudden crunch as the Larangian he had shoved hit the floor of the alley below.

Almost in the same instant as the smaller man moved for the window, the wench they had been prepared to share was scrambling from the dirty bed, her naked figure only a white blur as she darted for the open door. Nevertheless, Elak recognized her as the wench who had come on to him at the bar earlier in the evening. He smiled grimly at her situation but allowed her to leave. His business was with the man that still faced him.

Realizing he was cornered, the man drew a long dagger from his sash. It was the only weapon with which he could counter Elak's blade. The resulting contest was nothing to speak of as Elak's longer reach cut the man's hand forcing him to drop his blade. In a trice, Elak had crowded him into a corner, the tip of his rapier pressed into the flabby skin under the man's neck. Sweat immediately sprang from beneath his scalp and he froze.

«Wha… what's this about, friend?» the man asked, unsure what to do with his hands; leave them at his side or raise them in self-defense.

«Leave your hands down,» hissed Elak. «And talk quickly. You and your partner rolled a drunk earlier tonight. He may have been no good to himself or anyone else, but he was my friend. And Elak of Cyrena always stands by his friends. Do you know the man I'm talking about?»

«Y… yes. Me and Jacker only rolled one drunk tonight. I counted them. There was only one.»

«Yes, yes. Only one. Where's the loot you took from him?»

«Jacker. He kept the loot. We shared the money and bought the wench for tonight. We were going to share her, too…»

«All right, all right,» said Elak, becoming impatient. «What did you do with the items that were not in the money bag?»

«There weren't any pretty things. Uh. Three rings. Uh. A bracelet. Uh…»

«Never mind the itemization! What did you do with them? Where are they? Are they in this room or…?»

«Uh, no. We fenced 'em. Jacker, he said it was too cumbersome to carry the other stuff around and that it was getting late. Better to sell them quick and get a wench before the night was over.»

«Never mind about the damn wench!» Realizing that it would be daylight soon, Elak figured that time was running out if he were to recover any of Lycon's things from a fence. Those in Mandazar were known to move merchandise fast. «Who did you sell the takings to?»

«A feller called Jorpur…»

«Where?»

«The Avenue of the Jewelers. We went in the back way…»

«You're going to take me there. Right now.» Elak took the point of his rapier away from the man's throat and shoved him toward the open doorway. A knot of curious onlookers had gathered on the landing outside, but they gave way as Elak and his prisoner emerged.

«Down the stairs, hurry,» urged Elak, concerned that the gendarmes might be attracted by all the fuss, particularly if anyone noticed Jacker's body in the alley.

«What did Jacker call you when he was alive?» asked Elak of his reluctant companion.

«Jacker called me Bruiser but my real name is Inbo. I hail from the midlands but came to the big city when…»

«All right, all right,» said Elak. «That's enough. I don't need your life story. And do I need to keep my rapier in your back or are you going to cooperate?»

«Oh, you'll have no problem with me, sir. Inbo is friendly. Inbo is everyone's friend.»

«Except for those you steal from.»

«I'm real sorry we stole from your friend. That was Jacker's idea. He said it was easier to roll a drunk than to steal from a man in his right mind.»

«Jacker was a fool and a swine,» said Elak, suddenly happy that he'd ended the thief's career.

When they stepped out of the tavern, dawn was just about to break with the city's many towers and minarets becoming clearer in the growing light. Somewhere, a few miles distant past the urban sprawl, was the sea that separated Atlantis from the eastern mainland and Elak imagined that there was a hint of the ocean in the fresh morning air.

«Pick up the pace, Inbo. We're in a hurry.»

The big man moved faster as they made their way through the rabbit warren that was Mandazar's low rent district, but soon, with the still-empty streets to help them, they reached the market center with its stalls and storefronts. By then, the sun was just peeking breaking over the rooftops. Soon the city would awaken and the streets would be crowded with local farmers and their produce, early morning shoppers, and patrolling gendarmes.

But before Elak could worry too much about that, he spotted the Avenue of Jewelers and steered Inbo in that direction. Soon, the big man had led him to an alley that in turn led to an access space behind a row of shops.

«It's right over here, Mr. Elak,» said Inbo, approaching a non-descript wooden door. «Jacker used a special knock to get in.»

«Go ahead and use it,» instructed Elak.

Inbo proceeded to knock. Three raps then two more with pauses between. Soon Elak heard the sound of latches being undone from inside and when the door began to open, he forced his way in, pushing Inbo in ahead of him.

«See here!» said an indignant voice. «What's the meaning of this?»

Inside, Elak kicked the door shut behind him and pulled out a dirk he kept up his sleeve. He used it the same way he had used his rapier on Inbo earlier in the morning. That is, by shoving its tip up under the man's chin.

«Urk!» Was all the man could muster as he backed against a wall.

«Inbo, is this the man you and Jacker dealt with?»

«It surely is, Mr. Elak.»

«A nice set up,» said Elak looking about. «A perfectly legitimate jewelry store. No doubt a duly tax-paying one, too, with the stray bribe to keep the local gendarmes at bay.»

«What do you want? Who are you?» said the proprietor, finding his voice past the tip of Elak's dirk.

«Only one thing,» said Elak, easing the dirk back a bit. «I want to see all the merchandise you fenced this past evening. Don't worry. I'm not here to steal your take. I'm just looking for a single item and I'll leave you alone.»

«I don't know where you received the idea that I was a law breaker,» wailed the man. «I'm a legitimate businessman...»

«Don't give me any of that!» said Elak, again pressing the tip of his dagger into the man's flesh. «I'll carve you from ear to ear if you lie to me again!»

«All right!» fairly shouted the petrified jeweler. «I am a dealer in stolen goods. I just don't have any of it here. You must believe me!»

«Inbo,» said Elak without any hesitation. «Search the store. Turn it inside out. Make sure he's telling the truth.»

And as Inbo did as he was asked, Elak ignored the sounds of overturning displays and smashing furniture as his eyes remained steady on those of the frightened fence. Having attached himself somewhat to Elak over the past hour, Inbo was proving useful.

When the sounds ceased, Inbo returned and reported that he had found nothing except the store's regular merchandise.

«What did you do with the loot you received last night?» Elak demanded.

«I... I sold it to my buyer...»

«Who?»

«I'm not supposed to say...» Elak pressed the dirk farther into the man's flesh, drawing blood. «No! No, stop! It went to the palace. The palace!»

«The palace? You mean to the king?»

«Yes. An emissary comes each night to collect the takings. They pay in gold.»

«Let me get this straight,» said a disbelieving Elak. «You say someone from the palace, an agent of the king, comes for the stolen goods and pays in gold?»

«Yes.»

«When does this emissary come?»

«Each morning at four bells. After all the thieves have left their takings with me.»

«And this emissary is prompt?»

«Very prompt.»

«Then we'll wait for him. Do you have anything to eat around here?»

3.
MYSTREL

It had been a long day hiding out in the back of the jewelry store. Elak had set Inbo on helping the proprietor, whose name was Obos, to restoring order in the shop. After that, it was only a matter of staying out of sight while Obos dealt with the occasional customer. Eventually, night fell as it always did in Mandazar and the shop closed. But only for ordinary business. After that, there was far more activity at the back door than ever there had been at the front as thieves began dropping by with their loot. Obos paid them in debased coins and gathered the merchandise in a wooden box. Elak, a thief himself at times, was nevertheless impressed with the range of material there was: brass candlesticks, rings and other jewelry, temple goods, silverware, rare books, even gold teeth.

Finally, the string of thieves trailed off and four bells could be heard out in the night as the bells in the temple of Ishtar sounded the hour.

«They will be here soon now,» said Obos, standing by the door.

No sooner had he uttered the words than there was a knock at the back door. Elak signaled Obos to open up and took a position against the wall, his rapier in hand. He motioned Inbo to stay out front in the store.

«Enter, quickly,» said Obos in a husky whisper.

A cloaked figure stepped into the room followed by a second who stood a good ten tobits taller than the first. Elak judged he was the one to put out of business first and brought down the pommel of his rapier on the man's head. He fell unconscious to the floor.

Immediately, the first man spun about just as Elak slammed the door shut. The tip of his blade hovered menacingly over the other's breast, freezing him in place.

«What goes on here, Obos?» demanded the cloaked figure. But the voice gave the game away and with a flick of his rapier Elak uncovered the emissary.

«A woman!» he declared with some surprise. «Since when do the men of the palace send a wench to do their dirty work?»

«'Ware, stranger,» said the woman. «I don't take kindly to insults.»

Elak chose to hold his tongue for the moment and instead studied the figure before him. And figure it had by the looks of her hourglass shape. She wore a man's trousers and loose blouse but they did a poor job of hiding the curves underneath. Glaring at him from under arced brows and burnished bronze hair to match, was a face that could have belonged to someone barely older than a teen. Woman indeed! Girl was more like it. And a mighty handsome one at that or he was no judge of females.

«None intended,» Elak finally elected to say. «Who are you?»

The girl said nothing.

Elak pointed his rapier at her fallen companion as if to stick him.

«Mystrel,» said the girl hurriedly. «Don't hurt him. He's just a guard from the palace.»

«And what do you here, Mystrel,» asked Elak, removing his rapier from over the fallen man.

«I came to collect certain items from Obos here.»

«Stolen goods, is that right?»

Mystrel nodded.

«For whom? Where do you take them?»

The girl hesitated, but finally decided to answer. «I take them to my father, the king's treasurer.»

Elak could not control a gasp. The king's treasurer! What goes on here?

«Why? What does the king's treasurer want or need with this assortment of junk? Because that's what they all add up to compared Mandazar's treasury.»

The girl shrugged. «I don't know. I just do my father's bidding as he does the king's.»

«And once collected, where do you go with the loot?»

«I go back to the palace and give it to my father of course.»

Elak thought quickly. Was it worth the risk to continue to pursue the quest for Lycon's trinket? After all, the search had already gone far beyond his early expectations. It was all bordering on affairs of state at this point. Very dangerous ground as he had ample experience to judge. But then, Mystrel was a pretty bundle and to spend some more time with her was worth the risk. He realized that women had been his downfall more than once in the past, but he had emerged from those scrapes relatively unscathed, had he not?

Stooping, Elak dragged the cape from about the body of the fallen guard and threw it about his own shoulders. Once he had adjusted the hood, it was difficult for the others in the room to tell whose visage lay within its shadows.

«Inbo, tie up the guard and keep him here until I return. Obos, too.»

«Yes, Mr. Elak. But where are you going?»

«To the palace with the lady here. If I'm not back in a day or so, make yourself scarce. In fact, you should leave the city. Hand me the loot, Obos.» Turning to Mystrel. «What now?»

«Place the merchandise in the satchels that hang on either side of my horse.»

Elak did that and the covers over the leather satchels were secured. After that, he mounted the guard's horse and held the reins of the other.

«Get up,» he said to the girl. «And watch yourself. I won't hesitate to stick you with this sword if you try and betray me. We're going up to the palace and you behave as you normally would just as if I were your bodyguard.»

«What is it that you're after?» asked Mystrel, unable to contain her curiousity. «If it's the merchandise, then why don't you just take it?»

«Because I'm not interested in these useless baubles. I'm after only one thing and it's not among these trinkets.»

«Only one thing? What? Your mother's wedding ring? A sweetheart's anklet perhaps?»

«Something that was stolen from a friend, if you have to know. I promised I'd get it back for him.»

«It must be worth plenty for you to go to this much trouble for it. Assaulting a member of the king's household guard and kidnapping the daughter of one of his trusted servants.»

«Kidnapping? Is that what you call this?»

«Isn't it?»

«No, it isn't. One kidnaps in expectation of payment. There's nothing of that here.»

«Oh, then I'm free to go?»

«Don't be foolish. Just lead on and keep a civil tongue in your head.»

Elak did not want to admit it, but the girl's spirit was softening his attitude toward her. That, and her physical charms. He steeled himself against falling for her wiles.

Saying nothing more, Mystrel urged her mount forward and Elak, staying within rapier range, followed.

4.
A PALACE MEETING

It was still dark when they reached the palace gates.

Made of heavy iron and oakwood, the gates were well footed in a sancrete reinforced stone wall that encircled the palace complex; a vast collection of hidden gardens, statuary halls, towers, and crenallations. Somewhere in that darkened pile lay King Mirdates himself, no doubt swaddled in lotus dreams of virgins and honey-dipped pomegranates.

Outside the walls, the rest of Mandazar still slept. Or at least its law abiding citizens did. The rest, a substantial number, were just getting off drugged jags or drunken revelries, puking in back alleys or falling unconscious in darkened plazas to await rough treatment from impatient gendarmes.

The palace itself was located on high ground, above the miasma of the city, as were Mandazar's other major landmarks. Crowning the other six hills upon which the city had been built, were temples dedicated to the many gods of Atlantis, chief among them Poseidon and Ishtar whose magnificent domes Elak could begin to make out against the eastern dawn light.

«Ho, the guard,» called out Mystrel, drawing Elak's attention back to the business at hand.

There was movement from the darkness and as a guard approached, Elak tightened the grip on his rapier, now sheathed beneath the cloak he wore.

«Who goes there?» asked the guard.

«The Lady Mystrel and her bodyguard.»

Recognizing the girl's voice, the guard moved to unlatch the gate. «Welcome back, my lady.»

One leaf of the gate swung back, allowing Mystrel and Elak to enter. This was the moment of maximum peril. Should the girl choose to betray him… but she did not and they proceeded into the inner court. Elak wondered at that, however. Why did the girl not warn the guard? She could have spurred her mount and escaped, leaving him to perhaps slay the guard but there would have been others quickly on his tail. He chose to remain wary. The girl might be up to something, and he resolved not to be taken by surprise.

What followed was a leisurely but circuitous ride among side gardens and bridle paths leading to the stables. There, the girl left the horses in the charge of a wrangler and signed for Elak to take the leathern satchels. He did so, throwing them over his left shoulder, leaving his sword arm free.

They entered the palace through a rear door and passed along a maze of corridors and winding stairs obviously used by servants to come and go without being seen by the highborn. Finally, after going up many flights, Mystrel exited the back corridors into the palace proper. Now Elak was met with wider spaces and vast, vaulted ceilings that threw back the sounds of their passage. Stained glass windows towered in the walls and richly carved furniture dotted the hall. But even with all of that, Elak knew from experience of such places that it was yet far from the inner rooms of the complex.

Finally, Mystrel drew up to a heavy oaken door and knocked. At first, Elak heard nothing, then there was the sound of someone fumbling with a lock on the inside. A tumbler gave and the door was pulled open. Mystrel led the way inside, Elak following.

Behind him, a middle-aged man, tall and graying at the temples, closed the door again and relocked it with a heavy key. Mystrel's father, the king's treasurer, no doubt.

«You're late tonight, daughter,» said the man and stopped, staring.

Elak had deposited the leathern pouches on the flagstone floor and tossed aside his concealing cloak. What was revealed was not the familiar guardsman but a lean, dark haired man with a rapier at his side.

«I don't understand,» said the man. «Who is this?»

«Father, meet Elak. A thief.»

There was sarcasm in her voice, but amusement, too.

«A thief? Then why did he come here? Why didn't he simply run off with the valuables?»

«Your daughter is only slightly correct, sir,» said Elak. «I have been a thief in the past but this time, I'm looking for a particular trinket belonging to a friend. It was stolen last night and I've learned that it was brought here with other stolen items.»

«If you're speaking the truth, then you had better forget all about it. If the item is here it belongs to the king now.»

«And why is that, by the way? What interest does the king have in dealing in stolen merchandise?»

«I don't think that's any business of a common thief…»

Whipping his rapier from its scabbard, Elak used it the way he'd used it more an a few times that night; by pressing its tip to the man's throat, forcing him back against the door.

«I'm making it my business,» said Elak, dead serious. «Now where's last night's take? You're the king's treasurer, I hear, so I know you can answer all my questions. And what's your name, by the way?»

«Sanjarome,» said Mystrel suddenly. She had disappeared for a time but now her return was heralded by one of the most pleasant scents Elak had ever smelled. He turned his head to look and was taken aback at what he saw.

Mystrel had taken the occasion of his interview with her father to slip away and now had returned in new apparel. Gone was the ensemble she had worn to the jewelry shop. It was replaced by the latest fashion in elite circles: a breezy mauve chiffon designed to hide nothing but the essentials with the sheer folds arranged in such a way that men often imagined that those essentials were also on view. Elak had heard that such garments were equipped with a minor enchantment that ensured no vitals were inadvertantly exposed and seeing how impossible it would be for any woman to move about without such safeguards, he believed it.

Suddenly finding his heart thumping in his chest and his loins tightening, it was an effort for Elak to suppress his emotions and concentrate on the business at hand. Still, there was also an aromatic scent emanating from the girlish figure before him, an exotic scent that he'd never encountered before but that was obviously intended to enflame the senses.

«What is that scent you're wearing?» he finally demanded by way of covering up how Mystrel had so thoroughly rattled him.

«It's called Midnight Conjuring,» explained Mystrel, not fooled at all by Elak's strategem. «It's derived from the petals of the Black Lotus. It was a gift from the king himself.»

«That so?»

«Hmpf,» Mystrel sniffed, padding barefoot across the cool stones to settle in a cushioned armchair by her father's desk.

Managing to drag his eyes from the girl, Elak turned again to Sanjarome.

«As I was saying, what's the king's interest in all this stolen loot?»

Since Elak's rapier point still pricked his throat, Sanjarome had little problem answering. «It's part of the king's tax collection apparatus.»

«Tax collecting? In what way?»

«The taxes charged by the city-state of Mandazar are already the highest in Atlantis. So high that any more demands made on its citizens would surely result in an uprising, something the king would not like to see for a myriad of reasons. But the question remained: how to raise more money without possible revolution? The answer came one day when the administration received an offer from a wizard across the gulf, on the mainland. He offered to pay in gold for all the valuables Mandazar could collect. It was decided to contact all of the businessmen in the city...»

«You mean fences?»

Sanjarome nodded. «They were offered gold direct from the treasury in exchange for all that their clients brought in. It was a fraction of the gold the wizard was willing to pay the king for the merchandise, however, so the profit for the city was still substantial. In effect, the scheme created a new income stream for the administration, a kind of hidden tax...»

«Clever. So the law-abiding citizens of the city are being fleeced coming and going.»

Sanjarome shrugged.

Sensing that a point had been reached when force would not be needed to keep Sanjarome talking, Elak removed the blade from his throat and pointed it to the floor.

«And this wizard, why is he so keen on collecting what amounts mostly to junk?»

Sanjarome shrugged again. «Who knows? It doesn't matter to the king or to me. Just so long as the account books are kept in balance...»

«Well, enough of that. If you'll just point me to last night's haul so I can search it for the item I'm looking for, I'll take it and be on my way.»

Elak was in a hurry to get out of the palace and on safer ground back in the tavern district but would regret taking leave of the alluring Mystrel...

Sanjarome cleared his throat, holding his hand up to where the point of Elak's rapier had pricked the flesh. «Unfortunately, shipments are made nightly. Last night's collection is already gone, sent by boat across the gulf to the mainland.»

«What?» Elak was seeing red now. All night he had been on the trail of Lycon's useless trinket and every time he was close to retrieving it, it slipped farther away. Now it was clear across the gulf of Majiz? And likely in the lair of a wizard? The time had now come to question his quest. Was it worth it?

He had experience with wizards and none of it was good. Dangerous, in fact. Was he prepared to risk his life to continue the search? Surprisingly, it did not take much thought. The part of himself that had once spurned the regal trappings that had been his as a prince of Cyrena came once again to the fore. The lure of adventure and the unknown grew stronger than simple caution and good judgment. Very quickly, he found himself looking forward to the new adventure.

«Tell me, Sanjarome,» he said finally. «Do you know the directions to this wizard's lair?»

5.
WATER CROSSING

As he had discovered in his career as a thief, it was easier to leave a building than it was to get in. So it proved with the palace as Elak drifted silently among the elaborate gardens arriving at the wall that surrounded the grounds. With guards looking out rather than in, it was a simple thing to scale the rough stones and drop on the other side. After a dash downhill, making sure the rising sun was at his back, he entered the city below without problem.

His immediate goal was to secure a boat sturdy enough to get him across the gulf from the peninsula upon whose tip lay the city of Mandazar. Thus, he spent the morning down at the city's docks nosing about, asking questions designed not to arouse suspicions of his true intention which was not to go fishing but to cross the gulf of Majiz to the mainland. He succeeded in finding a skiff to rent, convincing the owner that he was of the minor nobility seeking only a pleasure jaunt along the coast. Some coins were exchanged and the boat pointed out to Elak.

He had had some experience in navigation and the principles of boating from teachers in younger days so the operation of the boat's single sail and rudder were no mystery to him. A tiny cabin for protection against the rain filled the boat's midsection. Inside were extra spars and canvas, but Elak did not bother to inspect it before he arrived at the dock late in the day to take possession of the craft.

Intending a night-time crossing so as to avoid detection, Elak boarded the skiff just as dusk was settling over the land. Ahead of him, the gulf waters appeared glassy and smooth and a half moon shone in the sky. Far down on the left, facing the open sea, a dim glow lit the horizon marking the location of Poseidonia, chief port of Atlantis. Immediately to his front, the dim coastline on the opposite shore was visible with a lonely light shining farther to the north. That would be his object: the hold of the wizard Naganos, signaling for the ship from Mandazar bearing the nightly haul from the evening before.

Elak dropped the sail and secured it to the boom, then settled back on the hard bench by the tiller. There, he grasped the lanyard in one hand, the tiller in the other. Immediately, the night breeze filled the sail and pushed the boat out into open water. The same wind that propelled the little boat swiftly to the middle of the gulf, also brought the smells of sea air mingled with those of the approaching land. Those natural scents were a balm to Elak, who thought that perhaps he had been spending too much time amid the stink of the city. After this adventure, it might be good to venture into the countryside for a change. Such bucolic thoughts brought his musings around to Mystrel. It would be pleasant to share her company in the fields and forests outside Mandazar. Elak could even imagine he smelled the girl's so-called Black Lotus perfume wafting on the night air. He sighed heavily in recollection.

With Mystrel on his mind, Elak was grateful for the gentle conditions over the gulf and looked forward to a quick and uneventful crossing.

He was doomed to disapointment.

«Are we across yet?» came a voice from somewhere.

Elak came to immediate attention. Had it been his imagination, or…?

There was movement from the dim interior of the cabin. A sheet of canvas was thrown aside. It was the girl, Mystrel. Not a dream. Not his imagination. Immediately, all previous thoughts of cultivating her company after he returned from the wizard's lair vanished. Instead, they were replaced by surprise and then anger.

«What are you doing here?» he demanded. «How did you…?»

«It was very simple,» the girl explained, unwinding a pair of long legs from where she had curled up beneath the sailing. Elak could not help but notice that she had changed her outfit again. This time, she wore something more suited to an adventurous outing than a palace soiree: a pair of very tight, very short bottoms and a short-waisted jerkin that left her midriff bare. Her bronze hair lay scattered about her head, drooping coquettishly over one eye. Elak found himself softening, thinking the adventure would be much more appealing with her than without, but he couldn't let her know that.

«I went to Obos' shop,» she was saying. «Did you know that Inbo has a job there as bodyguard now? Well, anyway, I asked Inbo if he knew where'd you'd gone. I suspect that Inbo would be putty in a woman's hands.» She winked knowingly. «At least he told me all I wanted to know with hardly my needing to bat an eye in his direction.»

«But why?» Elak wanted to know. «Why did you want to come? You know it's likely to be dangerous. One doesn't tackle a wizard in his lair and expect an easy time of it.»

«Certainly not,» said Mystrel, making as if to climb out of the cabin.

Elak held up a hand. «Stay where you are. There's no room in the boat for a passenger.»

Mystrel made a mouth and settled back the best she could.

«Just as you say. It might be dangerous and I figured you might need some help. Or maybe someone who could plausibly explain our visit. After all, I am part of the king's network for moving the stolen goods.»

«But not the part of it involving crossing the gulf to deliver the loot to the wizard.»

Mystrel chose not to answer that. Instead, she changed tactics. «What I really want is to have an adventure. Most of the time, I'm cooped up in that drafty palace.»

«An adventure… in that rig?» Elak inclined his chin in the direction of Mystrel's revealing outfit.

«What's wrong with it? It allows me freedom of movement in case I have to move fast.»

«You'll need to move fast all right, if the male population of Mandazar ever catches sight of you,» mumbled Elak.

«What was that?»

«Nothing!»

The rest of the trip was made in silence, mostly because Elak had motioned for it as the skiff drew closer to the looming coast. Sound traveled a long distance over water and Elak feared that even the wavelets lapping against the hull were too loud.

Ahead, the solitary light indicating the wizard's lair grew in size and brightness until it seemed to hover several hundred feet from the ground. All around, the sound of the sea washing against a rocky shore filled the night air and, as a precaution, Elak lowered the sail and broke out a pair of oars.

«You want to be useful?» he asked Mystrel. «Come out here and take my place at the tiller.»

The white skin of the girl's legs flashed in the moonlight as she scrambled out of the cabin and plopped her bottom on the wooden bench.

«See that stretch of beach there?» whispered Elak, pointing to a narrow spit of land between boulders. «Keep us headed in that direction.»

With that, he placed a loose board meant for the purpose across the gunwales, sat down, and dipping the oars into the wine-dark waters, he propelled the boat forward with strong, regular strokes. Mystrel did all right at the tiller and they made straight for the shore. Soon, the prow of the skiff was sliding along the pebbly beach and Elak had hopped out to drag the boat up the rest of the way.

Just ahead, about a hundred klotes up shore, loomed the wizard's edifice, a squat, bulky thing silhouetted against the clear, starry sky. There seemed to be other architectural outcroppings about the base, but the tower portion was obviously the main part of the structure. Far up near the top, a light shone from a single window embrasure, showing the way to the edifice for anyone coming by water.

Elak reached into the boat and lifted out a pair of leather satchels like those Mystrel had used to haul the stolen items from Obos' shop.

«You stay here,» he told the girl. «Don't do anything to attract attention. If all goes well, I'll be back within the hour. If not, well, you wanted an adventure. You can find your way back across the gulf to Mandazar.»

«Stay here! I'm going with you!»

«You're doing no such thing,» insisted Elak. «I told you about wizards. They're a temperamental bunch. No telling how I'll be received. And at the very least, I'm not expected. So just stay here and watch the boat.»

«But I tell you, being the daughter of the treasurer, I might be able to…»

«The wizard wouldn't know you from an Atlantean sandworm. Now do as you're told.»

Angered, Mystrel folded her arms about her chest and sat down with a thump. Elak wanted to believe that she would obey him and stay with the boat, but he knew the chances of her doing that were thin. Given enough time to think it over, she would muster the courage to leave the boat and come trailing after him. So the trick was to get his business over with as quickly as possible before the girl had a chance to mess things up.

6.

NAGANOS

Hoisting the satchels onto his shoulder, Elak made his way up the rocky incline to more firm footing above. There he found a rude path leading to the tower's entrance. He had been told the password by Sanjarome, so he expected no initial trouble getting into the building's lower rooms.

The moon was still overhead, but its light revealed little of his surroundings. It appeared to Elak that he stood on a particularly desolate stretch of coastline with nothing but uninterrupted darkness stretching for who knew how far on the landward side of the tower. If there were sounds from out there, they were drowned out by the unceasing lapping of wavelets on the rocky shore below. Hiking the satchel on his shoulder, he moved on, arriving at the tower's entrance soon enough.

A stout wooden door prevented immediate entrance to the dwelling, so Elak made sure to thump the flat of his fist heavily against its timbers the way he had been instructed. He was to count to ten before uttering the password, which he did.

No sooner had the final syllable left his lips than the door swung open on soundless hinges. Elak stepped boldly inside a stone-sided room lit by a few torches hung about. No one was there to meet him. Behind him, the door swung shut on its own. Elak was not surprised. Wizards often employed minor spells for such tasks to impress those unfamiliar with their powers. If it worked, the wizard was spared having to expend more of his energies on stronger enchantments.

Elak let the empty satchels slip to the floor and withdrew his rapier. Now employing more caution than when he had entered, he began to climb the circular stairway that led to the tower's upper reaches. Here, torches were absent and as he climbed, the light thrown by those below dimmed until he stood in virtual darkness. Suddenly, there was a low growl from above and Elak froze.

A guardian? Some wizards held familiars from the netherworld in thrall and used them to protect themselves from enemies. Was this the accustomed welcome for those delivering him his nightly loot?

«Ho! Up above! I am come from the king of Mandazar with his nightly tribute,» called Elak.

But there was no reply. Instead, he heard the growl again and this time there was a definite note of unfriendliness in the sound.

Elak gripped his rapier more tightly and took his dagger in his free hand. Slowly, he began edging himself back down to where there was more light. But his retreat must have been noted by the familiar because it chose that moment of disadvantage to pounce.

Not one to wait on an enemy, Elak retreated the more, preventing the thing from completing its leap onto his shoulders. Instead, it landed on an upper stair, one that allowed Elak's retreat to within the compass of the light thrown by the torches below.

Now he could see what he was up against: a hulking beast all covered in a coarse matting of fur. Its full height was hard to guess as it crouched, its burly fists supporting it from below. It resembled for all the world the ape men of the jungle islands south of Atlantis, but Elak knew there was much more to this creature than mammals spawned on this world.

Quickly, while it gathered itself for its next leap, Elak lunged.

The tip of his rapier struck true, penetrating deeply the creature's broad torso, but when it was withdrawn, not only was there no blood, but the point of entry sealed itself almost instantaneously. Meanwhile, the creature itself seemed to have felt nothing. Its massive sloping head merely lowered as it prepared to spring.

When it did, Elak was no longer where he had been. Instead, he was in the lower vestibule moving backward toward the door. But now, exposed in the light of the torches, the beast appeared in all its menacing glory. Fully twice the size of a man, it reared up, its long, muscular arms waving over its squat head, and it lurched toward its prey.

Elak dodged aside, thrusting inward with his rapier again but with little hope it would do any good. He was right. Circling his slower-moving foe, he tried again with multiple thrusts all over the thing's back, once even piercing its head clean through, but none of his efforts were at all successful against the creature. As a result, concern had begun to well up in his mind as he backed himself within the entranceway to the stairwell. Perhaps the more narrow confines of the stairwell and being above his foe rather than on equal footing would offer some advantage. Now he was swinging wild. Hacking and slashing with his blade, most of the blows useless as his rapier was not an edged weapon. But the wild swings proved to be his salvation.

One of them struck against a sconce holding one of the torches in the ante-room, knocking it loose. It fell against the beast, instantly engulfing the thing in flames. Its dry, furry pelt proved particularly cumbustable and in seconds the familiar became merely a blazing pylon that caromed about the room in mindless pain. Its howls filled the enclosed space such that even Mystrel must have heard them from the boat far down on the beach.

Elak watched as the beast was slowly devoured by the flames and reduced to a heap of ash on the stone floor. Breathing a sigh of relief, he turned and resumed his climb up the tower.

Now his way was open clear to the topmost chamber which encompassed the entire circumference of the tower, which was not inconsiderable. There, he saw three things: a vast pile of treasure, the total haul of thieves from a number of Atlantean cities all gathered in one place; a strange contrivance, large enough to admit a man, that filled the room with a low hum; and a man dressed in the cerements of wizardry whom Elak presumed to be Naganos himself.

«Be at peace,» said the man who, outwardly at least, did not present an aspect of menace.

«It's fine to talk of peace after sending that creature after me,» replied Elak, still holding his rapier against possible deceit.

«Certainly you don't hold it against me that I seek to protect my property from unwanted intruders?»

«I used the password. For all you knew, I was the nightly courier from Mandazar.»

«Well, you have me there,» said Naganos. «Perhaps I should have informed the cities sooner that I no longer required their cooperation.»

Then, changing the subject, he said: «I call myself Naganos. And you?»

«Elak, late a princeling of Cyrena but now a...» He was going to say thief but quickly changed his mind. «A soldier of fortune. Just now, I'm on a mission to find an item stolen from a friend. The trail led me here.»

«Then you are truly a bold adventurer,» said Naganos, whom Elak now noticed spoke with a kind of slur in his voice and even a stiffness of movement about his features.

To cover his discomfort, Elak returned to what they had been talking of before.

«You said your business with the cities is done.» Elak gestured to the small mountain of loot piled at one end of the room. «All this, then, is enough to satisfy your lust for valuables?»

«Lust was not the reason for my arrangement with the cities,» said Naganos. «Through my alchemical skills, I could already provide myself with all the gold I wanted.»

«Then what was it all about?» Despite not trusting the wizard, Elak could not help his curiosity. It never did make any sense that someone with so much gold at his disposal would bother collecting stolen goods with most of it worthless, the pickings of thieves whose eyes for what was valuable were often indiscriminate.

«I made the arrangement for one purpose only,» revealed Naganos. «To acquire one piece of a certain kind of quartz needed to complete the engine you see here beside me.» He waved a hand in the direction of the contrivance that Elak had noticed when he first entered the room. «As you can tell by the sound it makes, I have been successful and have no more need for these useless trinkets.»

«Then you have no objection if I take the item I've come for?»

Naganos laughed, but it sounded more like the gurgling of a drowning man than any mirth Elak had ever heard.

«You are free to rummage about the goods all you choose,» said the wizard. «I am leaving this world, never to return.»

Elak hesitated. «Leave? Are you a Muvian, then? Or from Grondar?»

Naganos laughed that horrid laugh again. «I am from nowhere you can possibly imagine. From so far away, there are no stars in the heavens. A world bereft even of light.»

«I... don't understand,» said a doubtful Elak. He knew that wizards enjoyed creating back stories for themselves intended to impress the gullible.

«You do not believe me,» said Naganos. «And yet, I could make you believe. But what would be the point? What you think or believe is of the least interest to me. Why, if I were to reveal myself as I truly am, you would run screaming to the sea and drown yourself to escape the knowledge.»

With that, the wizard moved toward the device that had stood by all this time, still humming in its hellish way, still emanating waves of force that now seemed to pound at Elak's eardrums.

The sound became so insistent that he was forced to cover his ears with his hands even as he saw Naganos step into the opening in the side of the device, and suddenly he was jerked from Elak's sight into its interior.

It was then that Elak felt the tug himself. He stepped back, to get farther away from the pull, but it was too late. Invisible hands seemed to grip him and pull him toward the still humming device. He struggled against it but discovered it was impossible to resist. He was being drawn into that opening even as Naganos had been!

7.
WORLD OF THE BLACK SUN

Panic and fear were the sensations that filled Elak's mind as he was dragged across the threshold of that infernal machine. And though other functions of his brain had been overwhelmed by the danger he faced, he somehow managed to keep hold of his rapier even as he felt the folds of his clothing pulling him on, his hood disappearing into the yawning opening ahead of him. He had little time to wonder about the hat, however, as he himself was next.

The transition from the familiar Earth of Atlantis was swift and immediate as a bone-chilling cold replaced the dank humidity of the tower chamber. Around him, all was dark, a blackness more impenetrable than could be found in the deepest cave. Suddenly, he found himself standing still. The pull had gone and he felt the crunch of soil beneath his feet. He staggered a bit as his mind returned to its accustomed paths and sanity gradually overtook the blind panic that had temporarily held him.

The first thing that struck him was the cold. A cold that bit deep, deep into his very bones. Quickly, he sheathed his rapier and began slapping his body with his hands and stamping his feet in an attempt to keep warm. He could not see it but was sure his breath was being expelled in clouds of steam that likely froze on the air before settling to the ground as crystals of ice.

Slowly, as his eyes adjusted themselves to his new environment, he discerned that there was light of a sort. Not much, but enough to suggest the outlines of nearer objects. Beyond a few feet however, all was darkness. He looked up then, hoping the stars would help him in figuring out where he was. In his youth at court, he had been taught by astrologers and sky scryers about the heavens and the bodies that inhabited them. There was a theory that they were other worlds like the Earth and other bodies like the sun. Even things that his teachers called «galaxies,» clusters of suns that existed infinitely far away beyond the limits of terrestial observation. Now, as he gazed upon strange heavens, he knew that he was far from home. On another world, as Naganos had said. For above was only empty sky. All black save for a few overly bright specks here and there. Elak guessed they were the galaxies of which his teachers had spoken. One of which, it suddenly dawned on him with utter clarity, must be the home of Earth and Atlantis.

Spinning about, hoping to find familiar stars and failing, he saw for the first time the main object that filled the alien sky of this terrible world: a huge, black sun whose presence was given away only by the dim corona that encircled its cold bulk. It was that weak light that allowed Elak to see at all on the world he found himself inhabiting.

It was then that, for the first time in his life, a feeling of complete despair came over him. His soul resisted and tried to fight back, but his mind overcame resistance, and the facts as he had discovered them in the last few minutes, were undeniable. Unless he could escape this world, he was doomed. And looking around, he knew that escape was impossible. With no indication at all of the method of his transport to this world, his chances of return were nil. And more, the cold would kill him in a few centiles, almost before he could contemplate his regrets.

But even as he despaired of ever escaping back to his Earthly home, his somber thoughts were interrupted by a sense that he was not alone. That there were living presences out in the dark. Not minor or thoughtless things, but enormous presences. And they were all about him in the dark. Perhaps still unaware. Perhaps dreaming the long sleep of cold and isolation. But they were there and conscious but indifferent to his presence. He sensed that, to them, he was but a gnat. Beneath their notice. Was Naganos one of them? What was it he said those long ages ago? That if Elak could but see him as he really was, it would have driven him mad? Suddenly, understanding struck him. This was no longer some theoretical problem. Some wizard's trick to fool the uninitiated. This was living reality. A reality in the form of this cold, dead world, its black sun, and no visible means of escape.

Uncaring of the malign presences that threatened him, Elak collapsed upon the frozen surface of the dark world. On his knees, his arms still about him, he rocked back and forth on his haunches, mumbling long unused prayers to Ishtar, prepared now to die far from his own kind.

Then, when he had reached the end of his endurance, with the cold permeating his entire being, and ready to commend his spirit to the gods of Atlantis, he once again imagined he could smell the sweet scent of the Black Lotus. Pleasant thoughts of Mystrel filled what remained of his conscious mind. But was there not something peculiar about how he imagined smelling it before? It was difficult to get his brain to function again after being slowed down by the cold, but he managed. Yes. That other time, over the waters of the gulf, it turned out that it had not been his imagination. It had been real. And Mystrel was there, on the boat with him! Was it possible that this time was the same?

Lifting his head, he sniffed the cold air and sure enough, there it was again. That scent of the Black Lotus. What was it Mystrel had called it? Midnight Conjuring! That recollection was enough to bring the first smile to Elak's face since he had left the girl in the boat. Dragging himself to his feet, he staggered a moment. Then, gaining his balance, he sniffed the air again and found the scent. Slowly, haltingly, he moved in the direction where it seemed to grow stronger. As he moved, his stiffened muscles began to loosen and hope was an ember deep in his soul.

Forgotten were the looming presences just out of his sight. Now his only thought was to follow the scented trail to Mystrel, who now grew so much larger in sentiments that he had long kept in check. For years during his career of adventuring, he had allowed no woman to take a strong hold on his heart. But now Mystrel had succeeded in doing that. All he wanted was to fall into her arms and never leave.

And suddenly, it happened. The dark world was gone and, all atremble, he was in Mystrel's warm embrace, holding her to him like a drowning man clings to a life preserver.

Later, as he understood it, the quartz Naganos had sought as the final piece that would charge the device to open a portal between Earth and his own native world, had been exhausted by continuous use. With no one on the Earthly plane to stop it, it simply kept on running until out of power. It was only Elak's incredible good luck that Mystrel had decided to leave the boat and venture into the tower when he failed to reappear.

She had arrived in the upper chamber only minutes before the transport device shut down but it was enough time for the scent of her perfume to be drawn into the opening and so out to where Elak crouched nearly dead.

When he had recovered enough, Mystrel helped him down from the tower. Never was he so thankful for the pluck of a female and even more so for her love. So much so, that he had completely forgotten the reason he had ventured into the wizard's lair in the first place. By the time he did remember, they were already back across the gulf to Mandazar. But Elak comforted himself with the realization that he could never have found Lycon's trinket amid the mountain of loot that filled nearly half that tower room.

EPILOGUE

Elak was happy to see that Lycon was now sitting up in bed. His ribs had been tightly wrapped and the oldster had taken good care of him.

«You're back!» cried Lycon upon seeing Elak step into the room.

Outwardly, nothing had changed about the Atlantean but there was a more serious look about his face that had not been there several days before when last he had seen Lycon. But it was one his friend did not notice.

«Now before you ask,» said Elak, heading off any questions by Lycon. «I have to tell you, I couldn't find your medallion. It was impossible because, you see…»

Lycon lifted a hand in signal to silence Elak.

«It's all right, Elak,» he said, reaching inside his nightshirt and pulling out the very medallion. «I found it. Or rather, Mondresor here did. He had it in the nightstand all the time. In fact, if we hadn't asked him to leave the room when we discussed it, he would have been able to tell us that he had removed it for safekeeping.»

Elak was nonplussed. The thought of all that had happened to him in quest for the medallion and his near fatal exile to an unknown world left him speechless. He did not know whether to laugh or cry. He decided to do neither and instead simply bade Lycon goodbye. Whether they would ever see each other again was uncertain, perhaps even doubtful. For surely the lovely creature waiting for him outside was far more agreeable company than the oft-drunken Lycon.

BOSCASTLE AND THE SWAMP ENCHANTRESS

By Jason Ross Cummings

I.

NO HONOUR AMONG THIEVES

Zambokka and his men rode across the baking plain beneath the merciless glare of the African sun which leaned on them without cessation. The plain stretched out in front of them, an endless expanse of grass and vast-boled and misshapen baobab trees. The razor-sharp grass reached up to the stirrups of their horses. In number, they were six, five of them being Zambokka and his men and the other being their prisoner, a young woman who was gagged hands and mouth, now offering pitiable and muffled protestations.

The man riding hindmost took out a spyglass from among his cluttered saddlebag and looked behind him, attempting to make out something now far distant, the thing that was causing them to flee.

«We are being pursued, Zahib!» he called out nervously to his leader, Zambokka.

«What are their numbers?» Zambokka swiftly shot the question to his man, who took another look.

«I cannot tell their numbers. I keep losing sight of them, but they sweep up some dust from time to time.»

«We shall keep heading directly to the north. Soon we cross from Shengaali land into the Caliphate! Those settlers will dare not tangle with us after that lest they risk full-on war!»

The man riding next to Zambokka placed his hand on his shoulder; it was Usmal, his half—brother. «This raid was unsanctioned; we have broken a treaty signed with the settlers as well as the Shengaali tribe, all to satiate your appetites. And the use of explosives! That was entirely unwarranted. You have brought shame on our house, shame on the Caliphate.»

«Those settlers had it coming! They lay claim to the best grazing land; they fill the heads of the Shengaali with stupid ideas! The settlers will not be able to give us any trouble; they have no support from the European powers for their cause. They are alone; we will easily crush them if they chose to make trouble!»

«You broke the treaty we have with them, Zambokka! I am taking you back to the settlers to face their justice.» At this, Zambokka saw that he was facing down the barrel of Usmal's drawn pistol.

Zambokka spat upon the parched ground. «Ha, you fly your true colours, brother, or should I say, traitor!»

«Nay, it is you who have chosen to dishonour our father and betray the settlers. Someone must show true leadership, Zambokka!» He spun around upon the horse and addressed the other men.

«Zambokka is now relieved of his command! All you men shall join me! We head back to Mahimbe, we take him with us and he shall be handed to the settlers to face their justice.»

There were some grumbles, some dispute, but well they knew the hierarchy of the nobles, and they were in no position to oppose Prince Usmal who outranked Zambokka in the scheme of things.

But in addressing the men, Usmal had turned his back, and in that brief moment Zambokka knew it was now or never. His scimitar whipped from its scabbard, the sound drawing Usmal's attention as he veered around on his saddle to face the onslaught of Zambokka. He discharged his musket, the ball deflected upon Zambokka's right shoulder, but all too late, and the scimitar was true in its swift passage. Usmal's head bounced upon the parched ground.

His body remained propped up upon the saddle for a frozen moment, a jet of warm blood fountaining from where the missing head should have capped it. Some of the ample ichor splashed over his unwilling passenger, Esmerelda, who let out a muffled scream from behind her gag.

The body of Usmal slumped awkwardly sideways off the horse, and into the broadening pool of blood upon the red and sandy earth. Esmerelda, seeing a chance, dropped from her horse at the same instant and made as fast as she could for a grove of baobab trees clustered some twenty yards distant, driven by sheer fear of what must soon await her. Though lithe and fleet of foot, she ran awkwardly, hands bound behind her.

«Stop her!» Zambokka cried from his horse, pointing with his bloodied scimitar as if trying to stab the very air.

Alcan, the youngest of the band, had dismounted and was tending his horse whilst all this transpired. As the blood-spattered girl ran past him toward the baobab grove, the quick-witted youth went for a lump of rock he saw embedded in the scruffy grass, swiftly reached for it and expertly lobbed it at the girl. His crude missile produced a hollow thud against her skull. Esmerelda let out a groan as she plunged into the long grass.

«Alcan, you fool, pray that you have not killed her!» cried out one of the other men.

The injury to Zambokka's shoulder was not inconsiderable, but he had survived it and he now drew his steed about and faced his men.

II.
INTO THE PIT WORLD

It seemed like an eternity since the crude band had clambered up the low range of hills that marked the boundary of this strange and perverse crater world. Over many muttered objections they had entered into its clammy, dank mouth. The men knew well that too much of such talk would result in cold steel through their bellies or a swift musket shot to their skulls.

The party of kidnappers made their slow way ever deeper and further down the steep sides of the crater. All was misty, at times green at others some shade of purple. The vegetation in this strange crater world almost defied any reasonable description; it grew in uncanny profusion unlike the arid and burned grasses of the grasslands and near-desert of the lands which surrounded it.

Everywhere there was strangeness and hostility in this strange world, spiders the size of dogs eyed them with their many eyes from the trap-door burrows, insects the size of small birds buzzed hither and thither, Zambokka and his men had their scimitars and muskets at the ready at all times as they plunged ever-deeper into this misty and hellish crater-world.

One of the men, called Khalil, half carried and half dragged poor Esmerelda as they made their way deeper into the steaming and verdant abyss that was the crater of T'Amgura.

Another of the men, Khalik, carried the strange spherical devices in a sack, gingerly attempting not to give them too hard a knock, these devices, inventions of the scientist sorcerer to the court of the Caliph, Mukassa, these were the explosive devices that had wrought such devastation on the Hugenot settlers at Mahimbe.

* * *

Esmerelda worked to loosen the bonds that constrained her hands and feet, as she struggled on the deck at the rear of the strange vessel which floated upon the surface of an equally strange lake. Her head throbbed from where she had been crudely coshed during her abduction by the coarse brutes who had raided the trading post where she made her home in the temperate highlands. Her long skirt was now mere tatters, revealing her long and lithe legs and feet shod in sturdy leather boots made by the best leatherworker in

Goa. The skirt had been torn to shreds by the arduous trek through grassland, swamp and jungle and by the rough hands of her captors.

Up to this point, her life had been the good life, her family having come to West Africa a generation ago, fleeing the impoverishment of arid and drought-stricken southern Europe. A beleaguered family of humble origins, they stoked fire in the belly to carve out a new life in this new land; with its attendant opportunities and dangers. And at length the family's fortunes had improved dramatically in the wilting heat and dust of Africa. She grew up not suffering the travails of her forbears in the old country. Up to now she had lived a charmed life of servants, of living off the fat of the land, but it was a life of reward that had been hard earned by her father and grandfather before him. They had worked hard building their trading post and livelihood, raising hardy cattle resistant to the plagues that prevailed here that killed all but the hardiest of livestock.

How had they accomplished all this? By their skill and know-how, naturally, but also due in no small measure to the traditional knowledge that some would deem witchcraft. Her grandmother, *Tia Fatima*, seemed able to ward off the malarial plague raging far and wide by the use of potions, incantations and rituals. Competition from other settlers was devastated by the dreaded tsetse fly and assorted other pests, to all of which the Da Silva cattle were immune.

Their salted meat earned good acclaim as far afield as Goa and Macau. Her grandmother had been a great beauty with flowing red tresses and green eyes, a trait Esmerelda shared with her grandmother and her late mother. She continued the proud family tradition of keeping the sickness away from the cattle and the people of the highlands, her skill having brought forth admiration in some, condemnation from others (not least from missionaries) who had her for a witch. Now it seems she had attracted the covetous attention of these brigands, as her reputation had spread far and wide.

Her captors were adorned in distinctive and decorative waistcoats and pantaloons, though now much tattered and ragged from the rigours of their descent. Zambokka's men manned the oars of this strange vessel, guiding it along the indented shoreline of this unearthly and stinking lake from which strange mists of purple and green bubbled up. Before them lay a narrow inlet hemmed in by a dense wall of strange and mangled vegetation which was everywhere in evidence in this weird twilight world at the bottom of the forbidden crater. Visibility was limited to about fifty feet in any direction.

The vessel that they had procured had been found unattended by a swampy inlet on the banks of the lake where a small and overgrown stream ran into it. Was it a fishing vessel of some kind left by some natives who fished the waters of this strange lake on the floor of this perverse crater world? Who could say? But it seemed able to float and would see them across this lake to the far side of the crater, and would suffice the purposes of he and his men admirably.

«We shall rest at that spot on the shore for the night. The light ebbs swiftly now, but when it returns to this accursed world we shall proceed out across this lake, climb the far wall of this devil's crater and make our way back home to Dukkar!» Thus declared Zambokka, taking another hefty pull from the large wicker-clad bottle of palm wine.

Zambokka was a minor prince in a household of some twelve sons, not one of them high on the favoured list of his father, The Caliph of Dukkar. Still, he had admirable attributes: he was handsome, he was strong and skilled with the sword and musket. He was also sly and cruel.

As his men jumped ashore, and made preparations to break camp, he turned his attentions to Esmerelda, still lying bound-up.

«You, my red-haired dove, shall know the pleasures of one of the house of Dukkar before your journey east along the trade routes. You'd better have a drink, my sweet dove; I assure you, it will be as parching a journey for you as for us!» He proffered the bottle of palm wine under her nose and she turned away in disgust. He cradled her chin in his manicured hands, each finger adorned with a ring set with a priceless jewel befitting his royal birthright. «You fail to understand the gravity of the situation in which you now find yourself, girl!» This, before cuffing her roughly across the cheek. Esmerelda shrieked and lay back on the floor boards of the strange boat and sobbed.

«Bastard! My father has wealth and authority. My family has standing even amongst the chiefs of the natives along this coast all the way to the Fouta Djalon highlands!»

Zambokka let loose an uproarious laugh. «Try as you may, you'll put no fear into me girl! Your fat kings and rulers hold no sway here in these lands. My kindred and I thrive as brigands and bandits. Ha! Even the great Bonaparte could not bring us to heel. In any case, they could search the world for us until *Al-Malhama* and not find us!»

A look of resignation crossed Esmerelda's beautiful face as this statement hit home. She was all alone in this strange and hostile place so unlike anything or anywhere she had ever before seen.

III.

BOSCASTLE ON THE TRAIL

Boscastle followed the trail that Zambokka's raiding band had left through the baobab-dotted grassland which spread out for a seeming eternity under a trackless blue sky. For some days now he had been hunting Zambokka's band of cutthroats who had abducted the daughter of the Huguenot trader of Mahimbe. A number of the settlers as well as local tribesmen had proffered their assistance in returning the girl to her home, but Boscastle had declined, explaining how they would only impede his progress.

The settlement of Mahimbe had been hard hit by the raid that had come without warning in the stillness of the night. An explosion of loud crashes mimicked thunder, levelling buildings and outhouses which now lay in smouldering ruins. Young Alain Devonne had been found bloodied and crazed. He said the raiders were Moors from Dukkar who rode on horses and thrown some kind of device which produced the thunder flashes and devastation. He knew them of old, but surely there was a treaty with the Caliph! Why did they attack the settlers now?

Some of the throng of musket-armed settlers were baying for blood, but Boscastle had determined he would deal with this brigand alone without the hot-heads in tow.

Boscastle cast his mind back to before he had departed that morning, packing his saddle bags. He had held his betrothed, Emilie Archard, daughter of the settlement head, Francois Archard, in his strong arms. He was content, happy for probably the first time in his fraught life. He'd made her a promise he'd return, and so he would.

The pony upon which he rode was one of Da Silva's, hardly as fleet of hoof as the lithe Arabian stallions upon which served as mounts for Zambokka and his band, but it was rugged and sturdy, Boscastle knew this country well and this stood in his favour as his quarry must be careering blindly and clumsily through the seemingly eternal fields with their razor-sharp grass which went up as high as the horses' stirrups.

Boscastle was long of limb and wiry, these years on the savanna having further accentuated his leanness. His head was covered in tight blond curls and he had deep-set intelligent eyes that burned with determination. He wore tough riding boots and trousers. A wide-brimmed slouch hat kept out the ever-roasting rays of the merciless sun.

The trail led ever on and on through the grass until a low range of hills sprang into sight amidst the baobabs on the very edge of the horizon. He recognized this feature for the boundary of the lip of a crater. The landmark filled his heart with foreboding as he recalled the words Zongoza the Shaman had whispered to him some weeks earlier: «Beware the crater of T'Amgura.» He had been seated before the camp fire across from the wizened old shaman who sucked upon his pipe, inhaling the deep and aromatic magical herb which burned with a sweet pungence and endowed one with mystic insight.

«It is so broad across at its lip you cannot see the far side of it, it is many days journey to travel around it. Foul smokes and mists ever rise up from its choking depths and spread across the sky of the savanna. All the tribes of the plateau give it the widest of berths. They will not hunt there nor take their cattle near there for terror of it. Our tribal legends say it is the hole made by a star which fell to the Earth in the ancient days.»

The sky above underwent an astonishing change in appearance, as it seemed clouds of the strangest hues billowed up from the strange land concealed on the other side of the low range of cliffs. The scent of spilled blood and entrails assailed his nostrils as he came to a clearing. In it, he saw the bloody work of one of the pride of lions that stalked the plateau.

IV.
THE BATTLE BY THE CREEK

As Boscastle stepped out into the clearing, four rogues were making camp on a slightly raised embankment where the mud was drier. A fire had been prepared and some fish kebabs were cooking away above the smouldering embers on a grill, along with brewing coffee.

The Huguenot plainly saw the girl from his place of concealment behind a dense wall of tangled swamp vegetation, answering precisely to the description her father had furnished. Her red tresses flowed. Her garments had been torn to shreds, revealing shapely legs, now scratched and bleeding in many a place.

One of the brutes had her pinned up against the starboard rail of the one masted vessel, he shouted and berated the poor and terrified creature in French, switching on occasion to an Araby dialect, some words of which Boscastle could make out, others not. She screamed as her captor cuffed her with great roughness; at this point it became too much for Boscastle and he stepped out of hiding, his two pistols drawn, one aimed at the man on the deck of the boat, the other at the men upon the embankment scant yards away.

«Release the girl, you devils!» he shouted. «First man that moves shall die! I never miss!» Nor was this an idle boast, for he had served as an officer in the King's navy for a time, and his prowess with both blade and pistol was the stuff of legend

One man who had been crouching by the fire threw something, it whizzed past him harmlessly into the water. Boscastle fired, the shot finding its mark directly in the centre of the knife thrower's head just below the line of his turban. Brains and gore splattered out of the other side of his cloth-bound head as the pistol ball exited. The wretch swayed for a second, then slumped into the earth making a dull and squelching thud in the mud.

The man on the deck who had been throttling the girl, seeing this, drew a pistol from a brace of them stashed in his girdle. He fired, the ball grazing Boscastle's left shoulder. Searing pain shot through him instantly, but Boscastle raised his remaining loaded pistol and aimed at his attacker. He fired, but a dank fizz was all that occurred. Damn! The realisation dawned upon him: the powder had become sodden in the journey through the swamp! The other men were now upon him. The first came at him with great strides but utterly no skill, waving his scimitar and screaming like a banshee. Boscastle ran him through with ease and, lifting his left boot, pressed it into the man's chest, swiftly kicking him away and withdrawing his bloodied cutlass at the same time. The other man had come up on Boscastle's rear flank wielding a long pole that had been part of the dhow's cargo. He swung it savagely at Boscastle, and it struck him square in the centre of his back. The Huguenot went down into the muddy mire, the man standing over him and drawing his scimitar from its scabbard.

With Zambokka's attention diverted, Esmerelda, the bonds on her hands now loosened, leaped onto the rail of the vessel just as Zambokka released the shot at the yellow-haired stranger who had suddenly appeared from the surrounding swamp. Without hesitation she plunged into the swirling and murky waters of the creek. She heard a great commotion on the river bank: cries and shouts. Zambokka screamed behind her; he too had taken a leap from the deck of the vessel in pursuit of the valuable scarlet-tressed booty who now attempted to escape his clutches.

Esmerelda swam as best as she was able through the brackish, brown water of the creek, still clad in her tattered clothing and heavy leather boots. She did the only thing she could think of: she held her breath and submerged, trusting the tidal pull of this strange lake to carry her away to safety, at least temporarily…

* * *

She was safe for now, she judged; it seemed she'd ended up in another channel some distance from the vessel, though distances were impossible to estimate; the channels and dense walls of twisted roots and leaves obscured the view in every direction. Several channels opened up in the wall of swamp growth in front of her; at length she chose one of them at random, as they all seemed similar. Then she saw a figure up ahead, sodden and covered in mud, scimitar in hand, as he trudged gingerly and silently through the water, furtively glancing in every direction. It was Zambokka. That he had not seen her was obvious as he passed out of sight and up into another of the narrow creeks that were everywhere in this swampy maze.

She breathed a sigh of relief. It was then that it happened: something massive fell upon her from the leafy canopy overhead, massive coils wrapping around her in a hellish and crushing embrace. It was a monstrous serpent from out of the worst nightmare of the deepest pit of hell, a serpent with a girth thicker than a corpulent man's waist. The coils tightened; she tried to scream, but only a weak moan escaped her lungs. The monstrous, coffin-shaped head lowered within an inch of hers and the probing tongue flickered over her beautiful and now petrified face...

Esmerelda's vertebra began popping as the grip tightened further still... then it happened: a loud report and the sudden loosening of the grip of the strangling serpent. She shook herself free of the now-limp coils and flailed on the floor of the muddy swamp creek. Standing but a few scant feet before her was no one but Zambokka, his grime-streaked face contorted in a sadistic grin. «Fear not, my dove, you won't escape that easily, but by the time I'm through with you, you will wish the serpent *had* devoured you!» He pulled her roughly to her feet and shoved her in the direction of his boat. Soon they clambered aboard the vessel, Zambokka pushing the girl from behind at the point of his scimitar.

At once, seemingly from thin air, Boscastle's cutlass was at Zambokka's throat. «Your men provided me with but a little sport! I have relieved them of the burden of their Godless lives; they now lie dead in the mud, food for the crabs. It's your turn now, Zambokka!»

The pirate dropped his scimitar, useless given the swiftness of his foe's attack.

Boscastle's hardened face cracked into a wry grin. «Worry not, Esmerelda!» he called to the girl as she made for the other end of the boat, tearing herself free from Zambokka's grip.

«How dare you, scurvy dog! Bastard son of a jackal and a snake!» Zambokka spat onto the deck.

«Say what you will." replied Boscastle. «Reach for your sword and we shall see the outcome!» A look of hatred welled up in his green and deep-set eyes. «You and all your type who thrive on the misery of others shall be held to account. Now, take up your sword, sir, and let's finish this!» The sweat and stress were now beginning to make themselves evident in the bearded visage of the Caliph's son.

«I am Zambokka bin Achmat, son of the Caliph of Dukkar! This outrage shall be avenged!» Boscastle stepped further back from him, proffering his hand in a gesture towards Zambokka's jewel handled scimitar that lay on the boards of the deck.

«Final chance before I just run you through like the rabid coward you so evidently are, Your Highness!» Boscastle offered him a salute in a mocking gesture.

v.
THE COMING OF THE AMPHOIDS

From behind them the girl let out a scream which cut through the thick and syrupy air. «Look out!» she cried as a shadow fell over both Boscastle and Zambokka. In an instant Boscastle realized that they had been netted like a pair of fat fish! The net was of some thick and fibrous rope and heavily weighted along its edges. He and his mortal foe were swiftly wrestled to the deck, and hands grasped at them, but he could see nothing. He was being manhandled by some invisible force. Instantly the thought of geests and phantasmic entities crossed his mind as he did his best to wrestle back against this force unseen!

Once more the girl screamed and it seemed all a sudden that some veil was lifted as blurred figures revealed themselves around him on the deck, shimmering in the fetid, hazy atmosphere.

The emerging sight froze Boscastle's churning blood: at least a score of creatures which had stealthily clambered on board were in form like men in having legs, arms and a head, but that was where the resemblance ended. Their skins were grey and palid, like a corpse in the early stages of putrefaction. The eyes were large and lidless like those of a fish. They were clad only in some form of harness and a colourless breech clout. Each carried serrated knives and spears and wore a green jewel pendent which dangled freely about the necks. In overall appearance a comparison to some kind of frog-like monstrosity would be most apt, both in general appearance and gait. Their feet and what passed for hands had four webbed digits, and many wart-like growths covered their slimy hides. And they reeked. Four or more of them now laid hold of the net in which Boscastle and Zambokka thrashed and smote futile blows at the creatures.

At this point Esmerelda's screams grew louder and more shrill, mixing pain and loathing, for a number of them had her in their clammy grasp at the vessel's stern. Boscastle had managed to draw the dagger he kept concealed in his boot and cut through some of the strands of the net. It was sufficient; in a heartbeat he was free, flinging the net from him. One of his assailants confronted him wielding a spear with a wicked serrated edge, but he brushed it aside and drove his cutlass deep into the creature with such force that it was pinned to the door of the cabin. While it convulsed and thrashed the Huguenot leapt past several others who were similarly armed, as he made straight for Esmerelda. One of the creatures holding her down rose up to meet Boscastle. He had retrieved the spear of his fallen enemy and now plunged the spear through the creature. Taken by the momentum of the spear-thrust, it fell skewered and writhing overboard into the waters of the swamp. Its wide-open mouth revealed triple rows of razor-sharp teeth in a death hiss before vanishing under the brown waters.

By the time the other one released the girl from its grasp and rose to meet him, Boscastle had his dagger drawn and grappled with the creature, attempting to drive home the thrust into his opponent's torso. The misshapen frame of the creature concealed surprising strength as it appeared that it and Boscastle were more or less evenly matched. Esmerelda grasped the heel of the creature's misshapen and webbed equivalent of a foot. The ichthyic devil stumbled upon some clumsily stacked crates and cases Zambokka's men had left on deck, affording the chance Boscastle needed, and the dagger found the heart of his foe. The latter let out a loud hissing shriek before ceasing it's thrashing and lying still on the deck.

Boscastle looked around him. Zambokka having broken free of the net and retrieved his scimitar, engaged the spears of the creatures who poked their spears at him. He had slain two of them, and it seemed all the others had withdrawn to the safety of the tangled roots of the twisted trees that lined the creek. The last two creatures disengaged Zambokka and agilely leapt overboard into the fetid waters to join their comrades.

«Djinns! This is your doing, witch!» Zambokka pointed a well-manicured finger accusingly in the direction of Esmerelda. «It is you who summoned these abominations from the mucous pits of Shaitan!»

Boscastle straightened himself up from his crouched position and spoke. «Djinns, demons—I doubt it; whatever they are, it seems they can be killed. He kicked aside the corpse that lay slain on the deck, its head almost severed by a scimitar swipe, bleeding its vile and sticky ichor over the deck.

Zambokka angrily stormed over to where Boscastle and the girl stood, his blade black, sticky and dripping. Boscastle held only his short dagger but stood to face him all the same. As he adopted the stance to face the onslaught, his boot caught the edge of a precariously positioned sack, it tipped over disgorging its contents onto the timbers of the deck. Metallic spheres thudded loudly upon impact, one of them rolling close to Boscastle's boot, and he bent over to inspect it.

«You're using grenades, I do see! My oh my, just when I thought you could slip no lower in my estimation, you go and surprise me. Doubtless these are the cause of the devastation at Mahimbe. It's almost a pity I don't have to finish you off quickly!»

«Now I shall cleave you in two! You infidel dog!» Zambokka cried, his bearded face contorting in rage. It was then that Boscastle felt a sharp pain in his neck, much like the sting of a wasp, then another in his leg, Zambokka and Esmerelda also convulsed likewise, as a sharp and whizzing sound cut the air. Darts, darts fired from the direction of the creek, loosed by the amphibians whose direct assault had failed. As it turned out, the projectiles were coated not with deadly poison, as might have been expected from their prior use of razored spears, but rather with some numbing potion, and it was fast acting, Zambokka had now dropped his sword and was losing control of his limbs rapidly.

«Quickly, girl! Stay close to me! I'll get us out of this!» Boscastle cried out, but it was useless: his speech was starting to slur and his vision began blurring. In seconds he was soon aware only of the girl's distant whimpering. He had a vague apprehension that the boat was now moving and that a great many of the frog-like creatures now streamed out from among the tangled roots of the mangrove trees.

VI.

THE HIDDEN CITY OF POSIDONA

Boscastle began to regain his senses. His dreams became those of a drowning man, sucked into a dull and abysmal whirlpool. Then he burst into sudden wakefulness. He found himself seated in a cage with iron bars all about him and above him. Rising water half-filled the space, and he had awoken just in time to prevent his head from slipping beneath the foul-smelling water. He was able to stand up to his full height so that his head could protrude through the cris-crossed bars above him and get a good look at his surroundings.

It seemed the cage was one of a great many at the edge of a creek in the vastness of the swamp from which huge and tall trees towered on either edge of the creek. In among them he espied planked boardwalks and what appeared to be human dwellings made from some shining crystalline substance. Figures were moving about, but Boscastle was unable to make out much by way of details as the dense tropic foliage formed a dense cloak of concealment. His observations were rudely interrupted by a harsh hissing sound as one of the now-familiar creatures cuffed his head harshly with the haft of a spear, shooting a bolt of pain through his head. Recoiling, he withdrew to the safety of the cage. The creature issued guttural barks deep in its throat as it shoved its spear tip into the Huguenot's face as a warning not to stick his head out again.

He was all alone in his dank prison; of Zambokka and the girl there was no sign. His brief glimpse above the bars had afforded him the sight of the surrounding area, revealing similar cages to his in close proximity—as crude prison block in this weird lost city of the swamp. Boscastle had but a bare awareness of the passage of time, as little light filtered into these regions. Once a day wooden bowls containing surprisingly clear water, plus some unidentifiable food, were left on top of the bars.

On the third day of his captivity, he heard the clank of a massive key in the lock at the top of the cage. One of his captors lowered a ladder into his cell. Two of the guards spear-prodded him to an oval platform in a clearing just a short distance away. Boscastle cursed as his eyes batted in their adjustment to the light.

In the clearing stood three girls, all exquisitely beautiful, each wearing a figure-hugging red robe. Their features were fine, even elfin, golden eyes set aslant amid flowing tresses of jet-black. Around their necks they wore the same green jewels that all of the guards wore set into pendants. Boscastle found himself standing before them, and felt emboldened to speak, but he was pre-empted in this when a voice reverberated inside his head, perfectly coinciding with the moving but silent lips of the middle girl!

«Welcome, Boscastle! Welcome to the realm of Posidona...,» the voice echoed within his skull.

«What manner of witchery is this? And how is it that you know my name?»

«Of us you need not fear. My name is Lintara, and I am charged with the task of bringing you into the presence of our Queen Druliana. This is Yizilda.» Withal, she indicated the girl on her left with a sweep of her hand. «She is gifted in the design of tools and weapons for us, and our Queen's wisest advisor.» At this introduction Boscastle immediately felt an uneasy stirring in his gut. For all her beauty, Yizilda exuded an air of arrogance and treachery. This lent her a hardness not in evidence in the elfin visages of the others. «If you would be so good as to follow us we shall answer any questions you may have...» At this they began their journey up the ascending causeway. Boscastle had trouble keeping their pace, given his sodden condition and the stiffness of his limbs from days of cramped containment.

The robed women, accompanied by the two subhuman guards, led Boscastle up along the causeway that was built right into to the massive boles of the vast trees. In diametrical contradiction to the crude boardwalks, the causeway shared the crystalline substance of the dwellings he had seen before. All around were similar causeways linking beehive-shaped structures among the forest. A strange luminosity permeated the pleasant and floral-smelling air, certainly less dim and dismal than one would expect in the midst of a forest. The air, too, was utterly incongruous with the close mugginess of the swamplands outside the city. And, to his great relief, this enclave was free of any bothersome insects.

Boscastle called for a break, a pause to enquire as to the nature of this environment. The women did not object but readily responded with their curious mind-song once again. It seemed that this city was protected by an unseen barrier, within which its rulers were able to control the weather. All of the bee-hive house structures, they explained, were fashioned of a resinous balsam derived from the trees themselves. They soon resumed their journey.

The most imposing thing about all that Boscastle's senses now drank in was the huge centrepiece statue of a robed and helmeted female deity dominating the courtyard of what must have been a temple. This was undoubtedly the likeness of Posidona, he thought to himself, but all was moving too quickly for Boscastle to dwell overlong on such musings.

He made other attempts to communicate with the woman Lintara, but she was blocking him, and his attempts were met with a painful spear jab to his backside from one of the amphibian guards. The lethargy induced by the poison sedative was by now fast wearing off.

On a number of occasions one or more of the girls did stop to communicate with the guards. Though the Huguenot heard nothing with either his ears or his mind, he knew the subhumans could receive the transmissions. It must, Boscastle deduced, that they communicated via the green gems that all wore. True, he bore none, but he figured the amphibians must lack sufficient brain power unless aided by these devices.

At the very top of the hill they were climbing, the party reached a structure similar to the other hives, but far larger. The high vantage point afforded a comprehensive perspective on the land in which he now found himself. This city or settlement, however one cared to name it, was situated at the very middle of the lake at the centre of this crater called T'Amgura, cut off from the world outside. Perhaps this race of people had resided here for many thousands of years. Certainly they resembled no race the widely-travelled Boscastle had ever encountered. This, then, was the secret of T'Amgura hinted at by his friend, the shaman Zongoza.

In the busier areas of this tree-top city Boscastle observed many women going about tasks of various kinds. Some were attired in robes of bright red, others in verdant green hue. If the purpose was simple variety, why only these two colours? Boscastle pondered the significance of this as he was led further along the ascending causeway to keep his royal appointment.

VII.
QUEEN DRULIANA

Escorted into a surprisingly Spartan throne room, Boscastle was nonetheless not surprised at the Queen's appearance. She might have been a sister of the three women who accompanied him. Her throne looked purely utilitarian, its arms lined with unfamiliar-looking mechanisms. Her gown was mostly similar to the ones they wore, only green, not red. She also wore a modest metal circlet with one of the green crystals at the centre of her high forehead.

«Welcome, Boscastle, we apologize for the manner in which you have thus far been imprisoned...» Her telepathic voice addressed him. It «sounded» exactly the same as Lintara's communications: neither possessed any human or personal tone.

«Having examined your mind as far as we were able, we have decided to free you. But the girl and the one called Zambokka will stay here...»

«By all means, Your Majesty, keep that cur Zambokka. I was about to kill him anyway... But the girl Esmerelda must accompany me back to the settlement at Mahimbe, whence Zambokka kidnapped her. I am charged with her safe return.»

«Oh, we are well aware of the shortcomings of Zambokka. That is why in the best interests of both our world and yours he will not be allowed to return to it. But his violence and ill-natured traits will be perfect as attributes of the next generation of our soldier-class amphoids...»

«And your Esmerelda, we must have her for the sake of the bloodline we seek. You would not begrudge us that, surely. You will be permitted to go your way as soon as we can wipe clean the slate of your mind and deposit you safely away from the bounderies of our realm with no recollection of how to retrace your steps here.»

«The bloodline you seek?» Boscastle cried out in disbelief. «You mean she's some sort of prize pig for breeding purposes? This is something I cannot allow...»

A flicker of a smile crossed the face of the Queen. «You fail to grasp our predicament here in this hidden realm of ours, Boscastle. We are an ancient people who fled from our world, one of many moons circling a great planet that once orbited the sun between the worlds you know as Mars and Jupiter.

It was formerly a world of forests and verdance. But on the primary planet, Iomat, there erupted a war in which our people had no part. Vast powers were brought into play, drawn from the planet's atmosphere and from its very core. World-shattering cosmic weapons were fashioned as a civilization plunged to its destruction after time untold of peaceful pursuits.

«But our scientists were not altogether helpless. A portion of our moon was transferred, environment and all, into a hollowed—out asteroid, plentiful in the orbit of Iomat. Our wisest mages of old contrived, by some means long lost to us, to propel the asteroid towards your world untold millennia ago.»

Boscastle had little real understanding of all this; still he listened with patience and diligence as Druliana continued with the story.

«The asteroid, Posidona, made landfall here upon your world, causing upheaval on a scale undreamed of, but it remained largely intact, and our forebears were able to go forth into your then-primitive world and impart knowledge.»

She hesitated for a time before continuing. «But over time, things within this sealed asteroidal dome grew stagnant, though its life support systems did continue to function, as now. We lost much of our knowledge, and wisdom was lost through insularity and weakened breeding selection. It is with this in mind that we send the amphoids up into the outside world to procure breeding stock to replenish our depleted bloodline.»

«And so our people arrived on this world, the next world as one travels inwards towards the Sun. We came in ships able to navigate the airless voids between the worlds, vessels able to harness the unseen cosmic energies which pervade the great Void.

«Upon our arrival, we found this a young world. Our forebears founded a great civilization upon the vast continent that straddled the ocean…» Her glance indicated the ocean somewhere out in the darkness. «But, alas, here we did not find peace…»

She paused and took a few languid strides over to where Boscastle stood and began running her hands sensuously over his shoulders and face. Boscastle did not resist. It was by no means unpleasant, but that was moot, as she seemed to be wielding some mesmeric force.

The Queen resumed her wistful narration. «There were other beings here who waged war with us, beings more akin to the serpent than to the simian. They dwelt on another continent situated in the ocean you now name the Pacific. The conflict was catastrophic, both for us and for them. Our continent was inundated by the ocean, lost never again to be found…»

Her hand made a sweeping arc. «What you see here is the remnant of a once great people, a lone off-shoot or colony, if you will, a people now imprisoned and stagnating in dire need of a new infusion of blood: Only one in five is now fertile. The body elements of the girl Esmerelda contain just what it is that we seek, so for this reason she must remain here.»

Boscastle spoke up: «But what of these creatures who serve you?»

«The amphoids you see, they may seem monstrous to you, but they are only our servile class, a mixing of the sacred chemistry of man and that of the swamp amphibians. They carry out tasks of hard and back breaking labour as well as more trivial chores. Things are not all well with them either, it would seem. There are reports of stirrings of sentience amongst their ranks. This would be the cause of great concern should they oppose us in open rebellion. Their rate of spawning would be a catastrophe if kept unchecked. It is fortunate indeed that our handlers maintain such a level of control over the minds of the brutes. Chief among our amphoid handlers is Lintara, whom you know.»

Queen Druliana paused once again. Then: «Lintara and her Red sect, they are the rationalists, they place faith in science. I am Queen by blood so I rule here in Posidona with my priestesses, marked by the green robes. I fear my hereditary grasp on power here grows tenuous. We of the green robes regard ourselves as philosophers and aesthetes, finding the science and methods of the red-robed ones cruel and heartless.» She paused again as if what she was about to utter was in some way a blasphemy. «May the great Goddess forgive me for the saying of it, but I fear we may be witnessing the unfoldment of a schism.»

VIII.
ZAMBOKKA TURNS THE TABLES

Zambokka wrenched at the shackles that restrained him in his dank, dark cell somewhere in the roots of this vast hidden city. He reasoned that, as the shackles seemed to be composed of some flimsy and resinous substance, they would yield to his concerted and repeated efforts. But thus far they seemed every bit as strong as the iron shackles he and his family used to restrain unfortunate slaves and prisoners back in Dukkar. Indeed his accustomed role was that of captor, not of captive, a role for which he was finding himself singularly ill-suited.

For the moment, he resigned himself to leaving off his efforts and slacked back against the mouldy wall of his cell. Yet it was at that moment that he heard the door being opened by one of the amphoid guards, accompanying the radiant figure of the girl Lintara, who now entered the cell.

«It has been decided that Boscastle is to be released after we have wiped clear his memory. You and the girl shall remain here in Posidona, but you are to be converted for use in the next batch of amphoids…»

«You mean I am to be converted into one of those loathsome creatures? Never!»

Without even the scarcest of hints of irony, Lintara continued. «Not exactly; it is just your material bodily constituents, your parts and chemistry, that we shall use. Your attributes have been weighed and considered by the council, and this is their decision. You should consider it an honour.»

Quoth Zambokka: «I know well the look in your face when your Queen addresses you! She treats you with disdain, as an underling. Lady Lintara, I assure you that back in my kingdom, the kingdom of my father, that is, you shall be at my side and we shall rule!

«Join with me, my Lady! We shall consolidate our empires as one! With the occult and secret knowledge you hold we can fashion terrible weapons. We can smite the English, the French…» Zambokka tugged on his shackles once more, futilely, letting loose a gasp of exasperation.

«You know I speak the truth! You could be the rightful ruler here! Once and for all get rid of your queen who misuses you and treads you underfoot. It is you and your priestesses who control the slime creatures, is it not?»

Lintara turned to leave the dingy cell. «Ready yourself for your dissolution, go into oblivion in the knowledge that the sum of your parts is going to good use…» There was the merest hint of a wry smile on the beautiful but strangely and cynically contorted face of the science priestess.

IX.
ESCAPE

«Wake up, Esmerelda, wake up!» Boscastle lightly slapped the face of the girl as she lay curled up in her sleeping silks. He had made his stealthy way past the dim-witted guards into the beehive-shaped house that had been assigned to Esmerelda.

«What…?» She stirred groggily.

«Sshhh,» Boscastle gestured. «I must get you away from here, far away from here, for your sake and for mine. Seems they plan on doing away with my mind, my memories… everything…» His whisper was low and harsh to avoid detection. «Here, take this, it's a little something I stole from their thaumaturgy room while nobody was looking. It should perk you up a little…» Withal, he proffered her a ceramic vial of some green liquid. She drained it. After a few moments her eyes brightened and she began to move.

«Whatever that is, it has potency,» she declared.

«This city is not the paradise it seems. We find ourselves in the midst of some kind of power struggle between the red robes and the green, and I want no part of it. I cannot fight women in any case,» Boscastle remarked.

«I *must* stay, I've been chosen, I'm... what would I do back in Mahimbe? Wait to see if one of the local boys fancies me? Or grow old working for my father? Here I could amount to something.» Esmerelda tried to force the words out of her throat.

«No, girl, the red-robed ones are adepts of some sorcery of the mind. They impart thoughts onto the blank fabric of your mind. much as one would write words upon a blank paper leaf with a quill. We must get out of this place, I must get you back home. I'd sooner face Napoleon's armies than those red witches.

«I think I can manage to find our way to one of the less-used causeways. It's late; far fewer of them are about. If we are able to get to the lower levels of the city, I'm sure I can locate a point of egress from this city, through its permeability shield. Zambokka's ship is down there somewhere, and we can open the gates to the city with one of those green jewels.»

Esmerelda swiftly looked about her, locating and donning her boots and original attire, now partly repaired.

«There's a system of portals, airlocks through the skin of this rock bubble, some sort of vortex which leads up to the outside world. That's how the amphoids make their raids on the upper world, at least from what I've been able to tell.»

The pair stole their way along the causeway. Even in the darkness it seemed lit by some strange and effulgent force that permeated the very air like thousands of fireflies. And it did in truth seem that the conditions of their home world were closely emulated within this bubble-like enclave: their very bodies felt lighter, their movements swifter.

At this late hour proper concealment seemed an impossibility. They had barely gone further than a score of steps into the semi-murk than they were surprised by a flurry of sounds and motion. From out of a recess at least a dozen figures streamed out before them, a number of red-robed women with a small company of the loathsome amphoids. At their head was Lintara. She regarded Boscastle and Esmerelda with disdain. Hands on her hips, she threw her head back and let out a mirthless peal of laughter.

«Going somewhere, Boscastle?» she inquired, her voice dripping with sarcasm. «Are the lodgings not to your taste?»

He and Esmerelda attempted to move backwards along the causeway, but more figures emerged from the darkness behind them. Once again there were Lintara's priestesses with amphoids among them, but it was the figure at the head of them that caused Boscastle's blood to freeze over.

«What's the matter you, worm? Jakyll got your tongue, has it?» bellowed Zambokka. His raiment and weapons had been returned to him. He waved his wicked scimitar threateningly in the direction of the two.

Boscastle turned and faced Lintara. «You make a grave error freeing this one! You don't know what he's like....» Lintara pushed through to the point on the causeway where Boscastle and Esmerelda stood. She stood at Zambokka's side, and he placed his arm around her shoulders. «What the devil is this! What will your queen make of this, Lintara?» She laughed once again.

«What Druliana thinks is no longer of relevance. This night the city of Posidona shall welcome a long overdue change of rule!»

Boscastle's face twisted at the realisation of all that was occurring here. «I'll wager this is something *he* talked you into!» He pointed accusingly in Zambokka's direction. «I care not either way, just allow the girl and me to continue on our way to leave this city. We are not armed. Whatever plans the queen would have had for the girl and me no longer matter.»

Lintara's face hardened. «Enough foolishness. Seize them!» Her beautiful features were now contorted in rage. Two of the priestesses leapt to lay hold of Esmerelda, but she lashed out and, with a mighty kick, one of them went flying clear of the causeway, falling screaming into the darkness somewhere below. Several of the amphoids were upon Boscastle at once, but he laid hold of the haft of one of their spears and wrenched it from the grasp of the amphoid. Wielding it as a club, he leapt for where Zambokka and Lintara stood further along the causeway, screaming savagely as he did so. But he found his way blocked by at least a dozen slimy and bulky amphoid bodies. The impact felt odd, as if against a heap of wet cloth. And more of them came from out of the shadows to assail him.

Esmerelda was fighting furiously against at least a score of Lintara's redrobed women, and a pile of senseless bodies served as proof of her blows' effectiveness. She reckoned she must have broken the noses of at least another three as she lashed out with feet and fists, but the numbers were now overwhelming as her assailants piled on top of her.

«Don't harm them, you fools!» screamed Lintara above all the noise and clamour of the battle that was raging all around.

Boscastle managed to break loose from underneath the pile of foul, cadaver-like bodies of the amphoids. But he felt he'd been darted with the toxin once again as the all-pervading blackness began to envelop him. He staggered towards Lintara and Zambokka, wielding the broken remains of the spear. Zambokka intercepted him with ease and laid him down with a vicious blow.

Zambokka looked down on Boscastle and smirked, «How I've waited for this moment!» He raised his scimitar and made ready to separate his foe's head from his torso.

«No!» Lintara yelled out, almost too late. «He must be preserved so his material may be used to fashion the next generation of superior amphoids. Slay him and you will take his place!»

With a grunt and a sigh, Zambokka let his scimitar fall to his side. Suddenly events took another odd turn. Esmerelda had broken free of the throng of priestesses that had held her. Picking up a wicked-looking dagger she had procured from one of her assailants, she rushed screaming towards where Boscastle lay.

«Esmerelda, escape and warn the queen of this treachery! And be quick about it, girl!» Boscastle screamed. She stopped in mid-motion, looked behind her. The throng of priestesses fast approached from the rear, while some amphoids were closing in on her from the other direction on this narrow causeway. Without a second of hesitation she leapt far clear of the causeway out into the inky blackness…

By this time the paralysis had had overtaken Boscastle's body in its entirety, and he could only open his eyes and make out events around him.

«Quick, get this one taken down to the laboratories at the lower levels. Work must proceed at once in order to extract his vital chemistry if the next batch of amphoids is to be superior. He has slain too many, and they must be replaced—with him!» Lintara barked her orders at a number of the nearby priestesses. Three of them hoisted Boscastle's prone form aloft and proceeded to carry it down towards the lower levels of the city.

«Careful with those!» The Huguenot heard Zambokka's rough voice scream out. Some amphoids were hauling a large, heavy crate, one which Boscastle recognized, the crate which contained the grenades from Zambokka's ship!

It had been the pure rush of the moment and the joy of battle that had spurred Esmerelda's leap off of the causeway and into the dark unknown. She was by no means sure she would survive the leap, or if she would maim herself from the impact. Such were the thoughts that raced through her head in the seconds that she fell through the darkness. Then she landed.

Soft and leafy, almost a disappointment compared to what she had anticipated, one of the larger branches served as a fall-break for her. It was directly beneath another causeway, and she was swiftly able to draw herself down onto it. Examining herself, Esmerelda found nothing untoward besides some cuts and scratches from the fall and one bleeding wound she'd doubtless gotten from the fight at the upper levels. She could even hear the voices and commotions up above: Lintara and Zambokka amid their throng of traitors. This causeway lead upwards, and somewhere up above was the throne room of the Queen Druliana. Time grew short and she and Boscastle and all Druliana's people would be surely doomed if she did not act swiftly.

The wound which she had sustained to the shoulder was bleeding and bothering her more than she had at first thought it would; nonetheless, she continued her climb. It was something she was good at.

At length she reached the throne room. It was unguarded, no doubt because the amphoids were engaged elsewhere with the in-progress coup. As Esmerelda clambered onto the connecting causeway that led into the entrance, she was able to see that Druliana stood in the company of a number of the red-robed priestesses of Lintara's sect. They made no threatening gesture but doubtless they were in on the impending overthrow.

Esmerelda burst into the throne room at a sprint and cried out, «Queen Druliana, beware! These women of Lintara's sect seek power, and they plan to kill you!»

The Queen looked up in blank surprise. One of the red-robed girls was the first to react to this unexpected interruption. «The red-tressed outsider—it is *she* who brings sedition and rebellion!»

Esmerelda retorted, «May you choke on your words and trip over your own lying tongue! It is you and your sect who plot against the Queen!» At this the girl's face turned white and she drew a curved dagger from within the folds of her robe, and lunged at Esmerelda.

She had easily foreseen this unimaginative move and thus dodged the thrust, grabbing the girl's wrist and twisting hard till she felt the bones crack. The dagger clattered to the floor as the girl screamed and attempted to escape Esmerelda's grasp. But she laid hold of the red-robed figure and bodily heaved her over her shoulder and hard against the floor where she impacted with a dull thud and lay motionless.

A sudden look of terror overtook the face of the other priestess standing by Queen Druliana. She, too, drew a concealed dagger and held it threateningly to the throat of the queen. «Not a step further; I warn you: I will slit her throat!» Withal, she roughly pulled the queen off her throne and held the razor edge so close that it drew a small red trickle from the monarch's perfect skin.

Without a moment's hesitation Druliana brought her elbow into play, jerking it backwards harshly into the ribs of the priestess who threatened her. The latter let loose a whoop and staggered backwards, releasing her grip on Druliana.

By this time a number of green-robed girls had been attracted by all the commotion They laid hold of the two would-be assassins, but one broke free and retrieved one of the fallen daggers, plunging it into her own heart.

The throne room was now a hive of activity. Remaining red-clad acolytes of Lintara swiftly made for the various causeways leading out into the night. A stragglers were soon dealt with.

Then they all heard it, ear-splittingly loud crashes. The horrifying realization swept over Esmerelda, who knew this could mean but one thing. «It's the grenades that Zambokka brought with him; he's using them to gain advantage!»

The crude irony of this all showed on the face of the queen. «We are undone by the crude explosive devices of the outside world, a world we've succeeded in shutting out for eons... all for a misbegotten plan to rescue our bloodline. I have destroyed us with my grievous error of judgment. I ought never to have agreed to Lintara and Yizilda's plan which allowed those outsiders into our sanctuary....»

Esmerelda grasped the Queen roughly and shook her, in abandonment of all notions of respect and protocol. «There is no time for recriminations and guilt now! If you and your followers wish to survive this day you'd better gather what you can and head to the lower level docks. We can use Zambokka's ship and several of your own vessels. Or you can stay here and be killed or enslaved by Lintara and her traitors!»

From everywhere came cries of pain and terror as the explosions continued as the swords of the amphoids and the red priestesses dealt out death to the unsuspecting denizens of the lost city of Posidona.

x.

THE VATS OF THE AMPHOIDS

«Hurry and bring him to the vats!» yelled Yizilda at the amphoids who carried Boscastle. The dim-witted brutes had torn his shirt from him and were busy trying to remove his sturdy trousers and boots before tossing him into the smoking vat. Several of them roughly handed him up the ladder leading up to the lip of the huge translucent tube wherein the strange and effulgent liquid bubbled, emitting choking fumes.

Atop a platform area at the lip of the tube Yizilda was barking her orders to the amphoid minions: «You tarry too long! Don't concern yourselves with that!»

Seemingly from thin air a lance transfixed one of the amphoids; it gargled and leaked its foul ichor as it plunged from the platform to the floor of the laboratory far below. And now clambering over onto the platform area was Esmerelda! The remaining amphoid grasped for her, dropping Boscastle to the deck of the platform with a resounding thud. A swift sword thrust from Esmerelda impaled the slow-witted beast and it, too, fell over the parapet to the floor.

«You meddling outsider! The queen may favour you, but there is a new order this night in Posidona, and we don't need you!» At this Yizilda lunged for Esmerelda's throat with great savagery, surprising Esmerelda, who had expected she would submit meekly. The two women collided and grappled on the decking of the platform, often slipping in the slimy amphoid blood. Yizilda was marginally the slighter of the two in terms of physique, but as was the general rule of the Posidona race, her slender frame concealed surprising strength.

Esmerelda was not one to be outdone. Her upbringing had made her no stranger to hard labour when occasion demanded it. Growing up, she had often wrestled with her brothers, and she now fought tooth and nail against her elfin-faced aggressor, whose normally beautiful and soft features were now contorted in a loathsome visage of rage and hatred.

It was with every vestige of her remaining strength that Esmerelda was able to pivot her lithe legs to project the body of the elfin wench into the air. The woman landed against some clumsily stacked crates which fell on top of her with great clatter and crashing.

For some seconds she waited for Yizilda to get up and come at her again, but such an attack never came. She picked up Yizilda's dagger from where it had fallen, then produced a glass vial from a pouch. She went over to Boscastle where he lay, slumped where he had been casually dropped by the amphoids. Tilting his head back, Esmerelda poured the contents of the vial down his throat. He spluttered, bringing up most of it, and she just hoped enough of the stuff had penetrated to counteract the effect of the darts.

«Wake up, Boscastle!» She shook at him. «Time is short! You must come to your senses and be quick about it!»

Boscastle groaned and pulled himself into an upright position, as he tried to focus his eyes upon Esmerelda's face.

«They're using the grenades from Zambokka's ship to destroy Druliana's people. Lintara is murdering all who oppose her! Druliana and the others are now congregating in the lower levels of the city. It's their only hope of escape, for us to open that gate and get out of here. If we stay we will be either enslaved or butchered!»

The restorative effects of the antidote now started to come into play as Boscastle raised himself to his feet.

«Very well...» he mumbled drunkenly. «We shall need to lead them there straight away....» He picked up a sword from one of the amphoid corpses.

«Lead the way...»

«We'd best take the lesser causeways which lead to the vessel docks at the lower levels. The whole city is rife with the amphoids carrying out destruction and murder at Lintara's bidding....»

Hearing the echoes of tumult all around, Boscastle remarked, «I fear we are too late already!» Nonetheless, he and Esmerelda continued along one of the downward leading causeways. The hitherto air of freshness and peace had somehow vanished from the atmosphere all about them.

«Something is amiss here, I can't quite fathom it,» he remarked to Esmerelda once more. «The explosions—they seem to have somehow torn a rift in the fabric of the membrane that shields this city from the outside world. It will bring with it destruction and decay, of that I'm sure.»

They arrived at length at the docks situated at the lower levels. The way was no longer lit up by the glowing air, but the odd braziers at scattered intervals nonetheless allowed them to fumble their way through the otherwise stygian blackness.

XI.
THE TANGLED WEB OF LINTARA

Zambokka's vessel along with several others was immediately in evidence, Druliana supervised as others loaded the vessels with supplies and provisions. Upon seeing Boscastle and Esmerelda, Queen Druliana's face's serious tone lightened somewhat.

«I'd thought you both perished! We now embark upon our escape; it is the only option which lies open to us. Lintara and her followers control the amphoids. If we attempt to stay and resist, there will be just one outcome, our certain destruction!»

A puzzled look crossed Boscastle's face. «Why would Lintara do this? Surely she will destroy herself and her followers in the process! The very membrane of the city is breached and death and decay now leak into it, I can feel it....» Druliana interrupted him at this.

«Lintara and her red sect have long harboured thoughts of sedition against me and the prevailing order here in Posidona. Foolishly, I long believed her better nature would win out. Though I deplored Lintara and her sect's methods, in my mind I thought what they were doing would ensure the long—term survival of Posidona and her people. I was very much mistaken, it seems. She and her followers, commanding a newly created batch of amphoids, should soon manage to reseal the membrane and any other damages done, once my followers and I are dealt with, that is.» She straightened herself up to summon some dignity in the recounting of her failings.

«Well, it seems my presence here, along with that of Esmerelda and that traitorous swine Zambokka, has indeed precipitated some form of crisis in your city. For that I am truly sorry, Your Majesty.»

She waved his words away. «None of that is of any consequence any more, Boscastle. Our immediate challenge is to leave the city before we are overwhelmed and slaughtered.... It appears the airlock allowing access to the outside is blocked. We will have to clear it by hand.»

Up ahead stood two pillars which thrust themselves upwards into the darkness of this dim-litten lower level. The space between them was festooned with what could only be likened to massively thick strands of a web spun by some monstrous arachnid.

«Spiders? Is this the work of spiders?» Boscastle's brow furrowed at the implication of what he was observing. Spiders were not his favourite species.

«No, it is the plasma secreted by the amphoids.»

«I suppose that's better. At any rate, I shall set to work clearing it immediately....» Withal, Boscastle pried his cutlass loose from the wood of the cabin situated at the rear of Zambokka's vessel. The amphoid corpse which it had skewered had now disintergrated into stinking and cloying corruption on the surface of the deck, impregnating it's timbers with foul and clinging ichor.

He made ready to leap from the deck and into the dark and frigid waters and swim the short distance to the blocked portal when he heard Esmerelda's voice behind him. «I'll come with you and assist you, Boscastle!» He turned to face her.

«No, remain with these others and help them. We must be ready to pull away as soon as I've cleared the way up ahead. Gather oars, poles, whatever else you can find and make haste, our time runs short....» With this he leapt over the side and into the inky blackness of the water.

He held one of the light-emitting devices of the Posidonians before him as he made his way through the frigid murk of the water, his unsheathed cutlass clumsily stashed into the girdle of his trousers. He was dimly aware of the voices of Esmerelda and several other of the women on the prow of Zambokka's vessel behind him who held up their own lighting devices to cast as much light upon the task before him as was possible.

He felt slithering, serpent-like forms brush up against him as he made his way towards the columns. With the breech in the protective wall of the city, it seemed the swamp creatures outside could now swim in unhindered.

Boscastle set about severing the strands spanning the two columns. The strands gave way with relative ease, and the task of clearing the way between the columns was soon nearly complete.

«I'm almost done here,» he called back to those on the deck of the vessel. «Make ready to push away.» But fate had other plans. Just at that moment it seemed that the very forces of Hades itself were unleashed.

Screams arose from the women on the deck of the vessel as the horrendous forms of a score or more amphoids emerged from the shadows around the edges of the wharf. The distinctive sound of the compressed air dart weapons of the amphoids could be heard. Several of the women were hit and collapsed as the amphoids bunched up and made ready to storm the deck of the ship.

Something clattered onto the ground and came to rest among the clustered amphoids, their dim and hive-minded intellect not grasping its significance as the fuse on it slithered and hissed. Then came an ear-rending crash as it seemed all the air in the surrounding area was compressed, then instantly released with a mighty whoosh and a deafening crash and flash of light. It seemed as if the entire area of the wharf side was covered in a vile downfall of amphoid body parts and stinking bodily fluids.

A grin wry grin shot across Boscastle's face as the realisation dawned upon him that Esmerelda had made use of the grenade which they had retrieved in Yizilda's laboratory.

«Esmerelda, get the vessels to push forward....» Boscastle's words were cut short as a screaming figure leapt up at him from out of the murky water: Zambokka, his face a mask of snarling hatred and rage. The two men grappled in the water in a frenzy of limbs. Boscastle's sword was lost; he'd dropped it and now it lay somewhere below him in the inky blackness of the waters.

Boscastle now struggled with Zambokka unarmed, whilst the Arab wielded one of the resinous daggers which he had carefully selected and honed to razor sharpness.

«You may have escaped the laboratories, you dog, but you won't escape me again! I care not if you're dead or they use you to breed a new crop of amphoids!» He dove for Boscastle, thinking his opponent must be exhausted by now, but this was a near fatal miscalculation, as the Huguenot averted the dagger and twisted Zambokka's wrist to an almost impossible angle and he mercilessly drove the dagger back into the body of his attacker.

Zambokka's lips parted in a shrill shriek of pain and desperation as the dagger was driven home. Boscastle attempted to sink the dagger as deep as he could, but the frigid water was having a numbing effect upon him. Zambokka's body grew slack, and the triumphant Boscastle released it and the dagger protruding from it.

The women were now propelling the vessel with oars and poles. It was pulling past him, but one of the women extended her pole for Boscastle to grasp, and he clambered aboard. He looked into the smiling face of Esmerlda da Silva who offered him a cloth with which to dry himself.

«Our next business is to get you safely back home, lass.» This he said with a grin touching the corners of his mouth. And in no time Zambokka's captured vessel, along with several others containing the faithful remnant of Queen Druliana's partisans, passed through the portal and into the surrounding swampland.

XII.
THE JUST REWARD OF ZAMBOKKA

Zambokka lived. His head hurt, but the wound in his side was not too severe. The Christian dog Boscastle had failed to kill him. It was his good fortune that he had not lost consciousness and drowned in the shallow waters of the bay. Slowly and painfully he made his way through the murky shallows to clamber up the embankment.

Boscastle and the few green priestesses had made good their escape in his old ship by this time, of this Zambokka was not in any doubt. Still, with his new-found Queen it would be no problem to gather a crew and make the relatively short sea voyage back to the Caliphate of Dukkar; from there he could equip the Caliph's simple navy with the weaponry of destruction that Lintara would furnish him from the long disused arsenal of Posidona. The thought of this enticed a grin to shoot across his deviously handsome face. Revenge on Boscastle and those like him would be satisfying indeed!

A short distance inland, while lost in his reverie, he found himself suddenly confronted by Lintara and a dozen or so of her acolytes. «My Queen! I live!» he cried out, his voice growing slurred. «I will require some tending to my wound....» Lintara gazed unemotionally at the way Zambokka was holding his hand over his bleeding left side.

At a motion of her hand a number of her acolytes departed and returned in short order with a silk-covered pallet. Several of the priestesses attended him, one administering balms and ointments to dress his wound, another fastened his hands and legs in straps with which the pallet had come equipped. Why they should do this last was a cause of some puzzlement to Zambokka.

«Worry not, My Queen, within a short time we will have the upper hand once again. Once I gain access to your weapons stores and can be instructed in the use of them, we can set out to Dukkar, where my father the Caliph will...» She held up her slender hand, signalling him to silence.

«It appears that Queen Druliana has made good her escape along with the bloodline female and that conniving Boscastle. With him gone we are lacking in a human subject to provide the much needed body chemistry for the next spawning of amphoids...»

Zambokka's expression changed as the full ramifications of Lintara's words sank in. Furiously he began to thrash and struggle against his bonds, but try as he might, he could not break them.

You, my love, shall make an admirable substitute! We shall have some rebuilding to do, and you possess the building materials we require. I shall have need of a strong-backed workforce...»

«You treacherous slut!» Zambokka screamed at her, spewing spittle that dabbled his beard. «We had plans of conquest together, the unifying of our kingdoms; why are you doing this to me?»

An ironic smirk crossed the beautiful but now harder face of Lintara. «Oh, you did serve as a distraction for me for a time, but a distraction was all that you were. You proved yourself untrustworthy; of this I've seen ample proof! In the long run, you would have betrayed me.»

As Zambokka was carried away on his pallet to the vats, he cursed and called upon a thousand djinns to smite the city of Posidona, but either they could not hear, or they did not care.

VARLA AND THE MAD MAGICIAN

A Varla of Valkarth story
by Steve Lines & Glen M. Usher

Varla pulled at the reigns of her mount and turned to scan the vast expanse of red sand behind her, narrowing her eyes against the glare of the Lemurian sun. On the far horizon she could just discern the jagged peaks of the Ardath Mountains which stretched from the crashing waves of Yashengzeb Chun, the Southern Sea, to the mountain-girt inner sea of Neol Shendis in the north. Between her and the mountains lay the crimson sands of the desert of Nianga and the cities of Darundabar and Dalakh standing on the mighty river Ilth, which paralleled the course of the mountains as it flowed down into the Southern Sea.

Varla was tough and lean, with firm sinewy limbs and strength far beyond her twenty years. Sun and wind had burnt her skin a clear bronze, and her unruly mane of long, unkept black hair swung loosely about her face, stirring to the touch of the desert breeze. Her sword of Valkarthan steel, sheathed in a worn leather scabbard, was strapped across her back; the hilt rising at her left shoulder. She was clad in vest and breeches and wore high boots of *bouphar* hide. Her handsome face twisted itself into a scowl and her strange golden eyes blazed with sullen fires as they took in the undulating dunes and saw a faint cloud against the sky.

Gorm curse them! Her pursuers were still upon her trail.

All morning the riders; lean, hawk-nosed warrior-priests from the town of Vazrad, had been trailing her across the barren wasteland of the Niangan desert. Her mount was a *kroter*, a slim long-legged reptile built for speed. It ran on its huge, powerfully muscled hind legs and had a long neck and tail with forelimbs hardly larger than a man's.

Varla reached into a sackcloth bag that was slung from her saddle and pulled out a writhing yellow maggot over a hand's-breadth in length and fat as a baby's arm: the last one in the bag—breakfast for her mount. She tossed it in front of the kroter, which snatched it from the air, snapping its great jaws hungrily. It wasn't much of a meal, but it would have to do.

As Varla stared at the approaching dust cloud she could just discern the riders that were its cause. She counted seven in all.

She cursed the tenacity of the priests of Iao-Thaumungazoth and spurred her mount onwards towards the next dune, cursing the series of events that had led her to this sorry pass.

* * *

Varla was an outcast. Her home had been a valley in the land of Valkarth in the Lemurian Northlands, where the frigid waves of the Great Northern Ocean, Zharanga Tethrabaal, crash unceasingly against a desolate, rock-strewn coast. She had been forced to flee her home after slaying her tribe's shaman, the vile Xarthan. For two years she had wandered the bleak frozen plains of the Northlands, making her way slowly southwards. Passing through the Mountains of Mommur, she had eventually made her way into the Dakshina, the fertile Southlands of Lemuria. On entering the jungles of Chush she had been captured by slavers and put in chains. Here she had met the dashing Patangan, Phan Grivas, and the pair had become firm friends. They had been taken to Dalakh, a city in the desert land of Nianga and it was here that they had come up against the vile wizard Xothar Vool and the Black Dawn and foiled their plot to aid the exiled Dragon Kings in returning from the netherworld to subjugate Lemuria.

After their adventure the pair had remained in Dalakh for a two or three months until Phan Grivas had taken up the offer of serving as a bodyguard on a trade ship headed for Tsargol. Varla, who'd had enough of ships and the sea, had decided to ride north-east, skirting the Niangan desert and the Grey Wastes, towards the fertile lands of the Gulf of Patanga by kroter. She had a desire to see more of the places she had hitherto only heard about in tall tales around the fire back in her native Valkarth. So, that morning, as dawn unfurled its banners of crimson and gold, she had bid farewell to the Patangan, and left Dalakh heading north, following the river Ilth.

* * *

Varla had been in the thrice-damned town of Vazrad but moments when she saw a young girl of about six years of age wandering down the main thoroughfare, lost, alone and crying. Passers-by paid the child no heed; indeed most took pains to avoid her, so Varla dismounted, lest her kroter alarm the child with its fearsome countenance, and made her way over to the weeping girl.

«Hello, child, what ails thee?» Varla was a warrior and not used to conversing with children. The girl made no reply but continued to weep. Varla tried again, crouching down low to present a less threatening aspect. This time her voice was softer. «Are you lost?»

The child answered. «My mama, she has gone. I don't know where she is. I want my mama.» The girl began sobbing uncontrollably.

Varla placed her hands upon the shoulders of the girl and gazed into her large, tear-stained eyes. «Don't worry, child; we shall find your mother. She cannot be far.»

At this the girl's weeping subsided somewhat.

Varla looked about her but could see nobody who might be the girl's mother.

«I want my mama!» yelled the girl. She was about to burst into tears again, so the Valkarthan, in a simple act of legerdemain, contrived to pull a small pebble from her left ear. The little one yelped in amazement and took the stone, gazing at it in wonder. Bolstered by this success, Varla then caused another pebble to magically appear from her right ear. Again she squealed in delight. She was about to conjure a third when—

«Blasphemy!»

The shout rang out loud and shrill, and Varla turned her head to see a wild-eyed woman running towards her.

«The outsider blasphemes 'gainst the Black Lord! With sorcery and vile magic she casts spells upon my innocent daughter!»

Varla got to her feet. She had an uneasy feeling things were turning sour. The child saw the woman and screamed «Mama» and ran towards her.

The woman swept the girl up into her arms. She wrenched the pebbles from the child's hand and threw them at Varla. «This witch seeks to entrap my daughter with her magical arts!»

The passers-by were now keenly interested in the scene unfolding.

«Blasphemer!» shouted one in the midst of the swelling crowd.

«Blasphemer!» screamed another.

«None but the high priests may practise sorcery in Vazrad,» roared a third.

Soon the whole crowd was chanting *«Blasphemer! Blasphemer! Blasphemer!»*

Things had turned ugly. Varla thrust her way through the ever-growing crowd and made haste for her kroter.

«Blasphemer! Blasphemer!» The cries of the angry mob followed her.

Then: «The high priests! They come!»

Varla glanced in the direction where all eyes pointed and saw a small group of kroters heading her way. Atop the beasts, the sacred black steeds of Iao-Thaumungazoth, sat Ebon Acolytes, the high priests of the Black Lord of the Abyss. Swiftly they thundered towards her, brandishing their scimitars. It was evident they sought her death. The Valkarthan reached her kroter, dived into the saddle and urged the beast into a run.

Ere long she was far from the streets of Vazrad in the Niangan wasteland with the Ebon Acolytes hot on her tail.

* * *

Aedir the Sun God was climbing high in the sky and already the heat was oppressive. As she rode, Varla wondered why she should be so important to the Ebon Acolytes: why they should trail her so far out onto the baking crimson sands? Mayhap the vile wizard Xothar Vool, who had escaped the destruction of the Dragon Kings in Dalakh, had joined forces with the Ebon Acolytes to wreak his revenge against the barbarian who had thwarted his plans?

She was pulled from her ponderings as the desert floor suddenly erupted in a violent explosion of sand within which Varla could see the roiling coils of a Niangan sandworm.

«*A xorth!*» she cursed.

Her kroter, startled, reared back on its massive hind legs and Varla, equally surprised, was thrown from her saddle.

Her reactions were as swift as a *vandar*, the black lion of ancient Lemuria. She landed on her feet drawing her blade, poised for danger and ready to spring into action

She had learned of the xorth, one of the loathsome sand worms that inhabit the red wastes of Nianga, while in Dalakh. A close cousin to the *xuth*, the fearsome giant worms that inhabit moldering catacombs and caverns deep beneath the earth. The xorth are much smaller, about twice the length of a man, but no less ferocious. Eyeless, they seek their prey by vibration and smell.

Silently she stood and regarded the creature warily as the sightless worm swayed before her. Its wide, circular maw was filled with needle-like teeth and dripped with thick, viscous saliva. Its rank breath filled her lungs, the vile stink causing her to grimace in disgust.

It reminded her, too, of the *slorgs*, the slithering woman-headed monsters she had slain in the temple of the Glimmering Ones back in Dalakh.

The slorgs had fallen to her sword; so would the xorth!

Without warning, the worm lunged, its snaky head lashing toward her, fanged jaws agape.

Had Varla been some pampered civilised female she might have frozen immobile with sheer panic, falling to the xorth's first onslaught. But the women of Varla's people were accustomed to the harsh life of the frozen Northlands and, often as not, fought side-by-side with their men on the bloody battlefield.

Swiftly she moved aside as the xorth's head flashed past her own, her reflexes as fast as the creature she faced, the fetor of its charnel breath rank in her nostrils. Lightning fast it twisted and Varla had to use all her barbarian reflexes to avoid its second lunge.

Awkwardly she aimed a blow with her sword, but with the creature so close it was difficult to get any power behind her attack and it was all she could do to penetrate the creature's tough hide. But her blade was well-honed and its keen edge sliced open the worm's leathery skin. Black ichor spilled from the gaping wound but the xorth seemed unaffected by its injury.

Again and again her savage sword hacked into the worm as it lunged at her, and only Varla's lighting-fast reflexes saved her from its vicious jaws.

Then, without warning, it dived deep into the sand, which parted like the waves of a crimson sea, and moved away from her, the sand undulating with the creature's passing. It swam through the ground like a *poa* in the swamps of Chush. Varla stood, surprised but wary. Maybe she had wounded it more grievously than she had thought.

But no! As she watched, it turned and, faster then she thought possible, clove the sand like an arrow, moving swiftly towards her.

With her lips drawn back baring her teeth in a mirthless grin, she planted her legs firmly in the sand and grasped her sword in both hands, holding it high above her head. She thought she knew what the creature was about. Its method of attack was surprise; it was used to overpowering its prey in one mighty surge.

Well, she had a surprise of her own!

She had to time her attack to perfection. If she was wrong, she was dead!

Anxiously she waited as it swam towards her, then as it erupted once more from the sand, she brought her blade down with all the strength in her steely-muscled flesh. It almost clove the worm in two, biting deep into its vicious maw and continuing on down its body as the xorth's own momentum threw it onto her sword. Entrails and gore splattered messily to the sand to be absorbed greedily by the parched earth. Varla twisted her blade savagely, throwing the carcass away from her.

The doomed creature flopped and writhed in its death throes, trying vainly to bury itself in the sand and escape.

Varla watched as it died.

Wiping her brow with the back of her hand she cleaned and sheathed her blade. Her kroter was standing a few paces away. It, too, had remained immobile at the xorth's attack, out of instinct Varla guessed. She walked over to it, took the reins and patted the creature's flank. As she prepared to remount she looked into its eye and saw its transparent inner eyelid close and remain closed.

She frowned. This could mean only one thing.

She turned and gazed upwards. A darkening of the skies to the west confirmed her fear. A mass of billowing clouds of crimson sand was rising hundreds of feet into the air and sucking up more sand from the dunes as it came towards her.

«By Tiandra's teats! *Sandstorm!*»

She would need to find protection fast! Ripping a length of cloth from her bedroll she tied it about her mouth and nose and wished she had a transparent inner eyelid like her reptilian mount.

In the time that it took her to do this the leading edge of the storm was upon her, the biting sand almost blinding as it lashed her face. She knew if she didn't find some sort of shelter soon she would die, for the sand would shred the skin from her bones. Even the tough reptilian hide of her kroter could not resist the fury of a Niangan sandstorm indefinitely.

It was then, through half-closed eyes, that she saw it, a short distance ahead amid the swirling storm.

A ruined structure protruding from the sand.

«Thank Father Gorm,» she muttered as she made her way towards the ruin leading her kroter, sheltering from the worst of the storm behind its body.

As she drew closer she saw that it was a tremendous dome half-buried in the swirling sands. It looked to Varla like a temple of some sort, but what little of it she could see through the growing sandstorm was of an architectural type unknown to her. Parts of the structure had fallen in, and Varla struggled to lead her kroter towards one of them. The wind pulled at her like the malicious fingers of demons; sand flew into her half-closed eyes and her ears. Eventually she reached a shattered section of the dome at ground level and, with her mount behind her, tumbled inside. Instantly the fierce howling abated to a dull roar and she was able to open her eyes.

She saw that she was on a wide balcony that ran around the edge of the building. She hitched her kroter to the railing and stepped back a pace to get her bearings. There was a loud crack as the floor gave way beneath her and she tumbled into darkness.

* * *

Varla hit the ground heavily, and the wind was knocked out of her. Luckily, she had fallen only about fifteen feet and suffered nothing more than bruising. She swiftly rolled to her side fearing that her kroter might land on top of her, but fortunately it was still on the balcony above, tethered to the railing. She got to her feet and realised she had fallen onto a still lower balcony.

By the dim light seeping down from above she saw that the dome was the vast roof of a colossal building almost completely buried beneath the scarlet sands. Below her a massive chamber sprawled and so huge was it that it faded into the gloom with no end in sight. Occasional shafts of ruddy light illuminated the murk of this eternal twilight, entering where a collapsed minaret, spire, or column had caused sections of the roof to collapse.

Slowly she made her way around the balcony, carefully checking the floor as she went. Ere long she came upon a stairway, lost in the shadows, which led downwards into deeper gloom. She also found a torch in an iron sconce affixed to the wall at the head of the stair. Above, the light was fading with the storm still raging, so the Valkarthan made a closer inspection of the torch and found, to her surprise, that the oil was moist.

Varla wondered who had replenished the torch and if they were still within the city.

She reached into her leather waist pouch for her flint and after several frustrating attempts managed to get the torch to burn. Warily she descended the stairs by the uncertain light it provided. She was aware that if anybody or anything did lurk deep within these ruins she would be easy to spot.

She reached the floor of the chamber and moved left, keeping to the wall. At intervals she found other torches which she lighted as she went so she could see more of her surroundings. She was indeed in a huge circular chamber with one great entranceway. Vast pillars and columns rose up from the rubble on the floor to the dome above. The columns were richly worked with twisting arabesques and leering faces of demons grinning malevolently. Hideous gargoyles and many-headed gods gazed down, wicked and threatening, from portal, arch, and balcony.

The entire chamber was like the nightmare of a mad sculptor. Every wall was covered with thronged figures, clustering faces, fantastic flowers, serpents, beasts and immense hieroglyphs and symbols.

Her torch illuminated rivulets of sand falling through the holes in the roof in a blood-red rain. As she went forward she began to glimpse shapes at intervals in the gloom ahead. Soon she was able to see them clearly. They were crumbling statues grey with dust, shrouded with cobwebs, and gnawed by the teeth of time; most were standing on cracked pedestals, but some had fallen. Statues of long-forgotten kings, she surmised, but the faces of these notables, those that hadn't been ravaged by time, were evil of aspect with thin, sneering lips and sinister countenances. Surely no one would assume such an aspect when posing unless their faces had permanently grown that way through habit.

«This place stinks of desolation and evil,» the barbarian muttered to herself, «and the reek of ancient magic is heavy in the air.»

Then a terrible thought occurred to her.

«Could this be one of the ancient cities of the Grey Magicians, lost these ages past beneath the shifting sands?» In her shock at the realisation she spoke aloud. Her voice echoed sonorously around the great hall. «Is this the ruin of Kuth, or Shandathar, or even grim Sanjan itself?»

She shivered with the barbarian's superstitious dread of sorcery. As a child, Varla had learned much of the Aeon of the Grey Magicians from her father. He had told her the legends of the Grey Waste, how, thirty centuries past, the magicians of Nianga had sought to master the dark sciences and by that mastery to dominate the Earth. In their three cities of Kuth, Shandathar, and grim Sanjan they had learned many of the secrets of creation. They had even dared to tamper with the force which sustains the Earth amid the firmament and with the secrets locked in the fiery heart of the sun itself. Also, so the Scarlet Edda recorded, they mastered a grey magic which gave them control over the human mind; to hold it in thrall in a terrible slavery, or to shatter it to utter madness if that be their whim.

But the Nineteen Gods moved against them and struck them down in their blasphemy, treading their cities into the sand. All the land was laid waste and their people fled in terror.

Again the thought occurred to her that these ruins might well be inhabited. She inspected the floor more closely and, though it was hard to tell in the flickering light, it looked like there was a trail in the rubble. The dust and sand had recently been disturbed by the passing of feet.

What dread secrets lay buried in these ruins?

Varla cursed. The gloomy atmosphere was getting to her. She banished such thoughts from her mind but still fingered the sheathed dagger in her girdle for reassurance as she padded silently through the arched entrance.

She walked deep into the city, passing through countless high galleries and deep pits, all the while following the trail in the dust. All about her to every side lay proof that the ancient magicians had been masters of an incredible science-magic long fallen into decay and ruin. Vast machines of esoteric design and purpose filled chamber after chamber, their ancient cogs, wheels, pulleys, and chains silent and dead as the tomb.

Varla explored these remnants of a past age as quietly as possible. *Who knew what mutated creatures might be dwelling beneath the accursed sands of the Grey Waste? Hideous abominations with cold hearts filled with hatred?* She fancied that shapes slithered and hissed just beyond the glow of her torch; wicked things with glowing eyes, hate-filled and sullen.

Once again she realised she'd been lost in reverie and shook her head to clear the lethargy which had crept up on her.

Then she heard the voice.

It was a faint, wordless mumbling and cursing which seemed to come from all directions at once as it echoed through the cavernous halls, chambers, and corridors.

Padding on silent feet, she followed the trail in the dust. The muttering became louder but no less incoherent. Presently she saw a pale blue luminescence radiating from a doorway ahead. Reaching it, she carefully peered in and saw before her another lofty, circular chamber. But this was unlike the one she had first come upon when entering the city. In the centre of the room there was a wide pit which descended deep into inky blackness. Against the far wall stood a dais of three wide, shallow stairs upon which stood an elaborate black nebium throne carven with uncouth hieroglyphics. All about the wall of the room towered a fantastic machine of curious design and unknown purpose.

This complex device dwarfed all the others she had seen hitherto, and unlike them, this one did not lie dormant and decaying, but hummed with throbbing life. Globes and tubes of glass bubbled and seethed with nameless liquids that glowed with unhealthy hues, sallow and sickly. Cogs and wheels whirred, giving off a low whine that made Varla's teeth ache. Pistons and rods pounded, turning huge belts and chains and wheels. Two thick pylons of bronze stretched upwards terminating in silver spheres covered in countless wire filaments. Between these globes crackled arcs of azure light as if miniature lightning bolts had been torn from the sky and held captive. It was a machine of nightmare. Only the Nineteen Gods knew what unholy experiments the deranged Grey Magicians had carried out with this machine in their meddlings with the forces of nature.

Silently Varla took in the room and, hearing the muttering again, she located its source. Up on a gantry of the machine a figure worked, pulling levers and tapping dials, muttering all the while.

Some sixth sense must have alerted the figure to Varla's presence, for he turned, and their eyes met. To her astonishment Varla recognised him.

«*Xothar Vool!*» she gasped.

«You...you...» Xothar Vool stuttered, almost speechless, spittle flying from his lips. «Varla the Valkarthan!» Slowly he climbed down from the machine and made his way to the nebium throne, ranting all the while. «Destroyed! All my plans destroyed by an uncouth barbarian! Your interference brought down the mighty Dragon Kings in the Temple of the Black Dawn where all my dreams of empire were destroyed!»

Varla entered the chamber and walked towards the magician warily, moving with the grace of a prowling vandar. She skirted the ominous pit, and stopped at the bottom of the dais as the magician seated himself upon the throne and drew his black velvet robes about him.

«We meet again, Xothar Vool.» Varla's voice was sardonic. «So this is where you scuttled off to. Crawling like a sand crab under a stone and cowering in the shadows in fear.» Her voice was calm and her face was a grim, expressionless mask of bronze beneath her mane of wild black hair, but her strange golden eyes blazed with savagery under her scowling brows.

Xothar Vool was more haggard and emaciated than Varla remembered, even though only a few months had passed since he'd made his escape from Dalakh. His features were sallow and unhealthy, his thin lips pale and flecked with spittle. The hot light of madness burnt in his glittering eyes. His pallid flesh was netted with a thousand fine wrinkles, and his eyes glared insanely from the deep shadows of his eye sockets. His cheeks were sunken and cavernous, his skin thin as parchment stretched over his shaven skull. The black robes he wore only accentuated his emaciation and pallid complexion. Upon his head was a strange diadem of twisted nebium within which were set three emerald stones, one at each temple and the third in the centre of his forehead.

With an obvious effort Xothar Vool calmed himself. His eyes feasted on the Valkarthan's astonishing beauty. He felt a hot surge of lust as he devoured the splendour of the woman he once dreamt he would possess but whom he now hated with every fibre of his being.

His febrile eyes gleamed with malignant fires and he spoke with an ominous sibilant hiss, cold and chilling. «Sometimes the Gods are just, barbarian. It seems that Savitar-Negroth, Lord of the Black Dawn, has delivered you to me to witness the hour of my triumph, for my work here is complete. You shall suffer for your crimes and blasphemies against the Dragon Kings.»

«What crimes, sorcerer?» growled Varla. «That I dared foil your madman's plans to return the dreaded Dragon Kings to Lemuria? That I slew their great leader *Ssslithar* and overthrew the temple of The Black Dawn? It is no crime to free a fearful populace from persecution and enslavement.»

The magician fixed his gaze on Varla and gestured to the humming machinery. «The power of the Grey Magicians is finally mine. Soon all the nations of Lemuria will grovel at my feet!»

Varla laughed, a clear bell-like peal of cool mockery. «What foul scheme has that poisoned brain of yours conceived now, conjurer? Whatever it may be, it shall end here on the point of my sword.»

A mocking smile played upon the thin lips of Xothar Vool. «Pup of a Northlander bitch, you are dull-witted barbarian,» he jeered. «I easily escaped you in the Temple of the Black Dawn. You did not know of the hidden door, foolish whelp! The temple is honeycombed with such bolt holes. It was a simple matter to make my way through the tunnels to the edge of the city and escape into the desert, eventually making my way here, for the location of the three cities of the Grey Wastes has always been known to me.» He glared venomously at Varla. «I have scoured the myriad chambers of grim Sanjan and delved deep into its secrets. Much remains obscure to me, but many of the ancient secrets I have learned. Power is mine—the awesome power of the long dead Grey Magicians.

«I alone among the men of this age could have comprehended the dark mysteries hidden within this great city. None other could have grasped the aeon-old secrets hidden within these crumbling ruins.» As he spoke, the magician's shrill voice grew in volume and pitch until he was almost screaming, his eyes wide, his lips wet and his spider-like arms gesticulating wildly.

Again, with effort he calmed himself. «I have toiled these past months working tirelessly on deciphering the secrets of Sanjan, with no sleep or sustenance and no respite, bolstering my vitality with magic powders and potions as I plotted my revenge. I have learned the secret of the grey magic.» Xothar Vool gestured to the huge machine. «This device will amplify the power of my mind a thousand fold. *I shall become a God!*»

Varla shuddered as she gazed upon the awful creation. She knew that the Grey Magicians had harnessed incalculable forces which could shape the very earth itself. What horror was the vile magician planning to unleash upon the lands of Lemuria with this ancient device? Was it true? Was Xothar Vool master of the grey magic?

As if he'd read her mind, as mayhap he had, the magician continued. «With this contrivance I shall be all-powerful. All shall do my bidding. Aye, even the Nine Wizards of Zaar will eventually succumb to my omnipotent mind. Once again Xothar Vool had lost control in his madness and was almost screaming. «I will raise an army; a horde of mindless servitors, all at my beck and call; all eager to fulfil my merest whim. I will rule an empire. *I shall be Lord of Lemuria!*»

Exhausted by his tirade, the magician slumped in his chair for a moment, panting heavily. It seemed comically anticlimactic.

Then he raised his head and glared at Varla. Slowly he sat up, placing a hand to each temple to touch the diadem. His face contorted into a mask of intense concentration. At this, the jewels in the diadem started to glow with a harsh emerald light.

«You doubt me, barbarian? Behold my power!»

Varla watched with astonishment as the humming of the machine grew louder. Somehow Xothar Vool was controlling its workings with his mind!

The engines at the heart of the mechanism began to roar loudly, the noise growing in volume and reverberating around the chamber like thunder. Cogs and wheels began to whirl furiously, turning belts and chains at an alarming rate.

Something was wrong! Varla knew it.

The clamour was now a deafening roar as the machine began to shake itself into ruin. The blue lightning atop the bronze pylons crackled and sizzled with violent energy and began to glow with an incandescent white light that burned Varla's eyes.

Cogs rattled noisily as they sped around, some slipping their gears with a hideous screech of tortured metal. Sparks flew everywhere; wheels shattered and flew from their mountings, and liquids bubbled furiously, boiling dry in great gouts of noxious steam that whistled through pipes and vents. The noise was deafening.

Then the machine died.

For a moment all was quiet save for the hissing of gas and the dripping of escaping liquids. Xothar Vool let out a mighty scream of intense anguish. «*No!* My Mind Machine—destroyed! Once again my dreams of empire have crumbled!» He rose unsteadily from his throne, muttering inanely, his cruel lips beslimed with drool. «*You* did this barbarian!» he spat. «*You!*»

«I played no part in it, magician,» said Varla with contempt. «Mayhap your diseased mind was too corrupted to operate the device.»

Xothar Vool spluttered, almost choking in his fury. «Now you die, Valkarthan whore!» He raised his hands to the diadem once more.

Varla snarled and without warning hurled herself at the emaciated magician…

… only to be stopped in her tracks by a mysterious force.
She couldn't move!
She strained every muscle in an attempt to approach the smirking magician, but it was in vain.

Xothar Vool chuckled dementedly. «No man… or girl… can overcome the will of a God!»

The crystals set in the magician's diadem were glowing once again as Xothar Vool drew on its blasphemous power. It seemingly did not require the now-defunct machine to function.

To Varla, it was as if icy, impalpable fingers pierced the deepest recesses of her mind as she felt the probing tendrils of Xothar Vool's wormy thoughts. Slowly a freezing numbness began to spread over her body. Her limbs became stiff and she could do naught but stand and face the magician. Her sight began to dim and her consciousness became hazy. She felt herself sliding into an abyss of cold darkness. Grimly she fought back. Her sword was no good here; Valkarthan steel could not sever the mental tendrils of Xothar Vool's attack. Intolerable pressure was building. As was Varla's anger. The magician's unclean touch was a violation of her very being. Her anger grew, her mind fought back, her thoughts seething; struggling like a chained and whipped beast that could take no more beatings from a cruel master. Mustering all her mental strength she struck out at the mad magician.

She felt his attack weaken slightly. Again she threw her thoughts at the wizard, and again the onslaught faltered. Varla noted that the emerald light of the crystals dimmed somewhat and their hue began to change to a muddy, unclean olive green.

On she fought, slowly pushing back the invasive feelers of Xothar Vool's onslaught. She was almost at the limits of her formidable endurance when she felt Xothar Vool's attack crumble.

She could move!
Surprised and off-balance, but reacting with instincts that had saved her in countless deadly situations, she moved towards the magician, who was… *smiling!*

He rose from his throne and giggled like an amused child.

Then she heard a faint slithering behind her. She whirled to face the pit.

Something was rising from the dark below. Something big! Varla felt her hackles rise, her neck-skin prickle, and all the superstitious night-fears of the barbarian rose within her. Ignoring the magician, she drew forth her sword with a faint rasp of steel against worn leather and, scowling grimly, her eyes glaring with golden fires, she waited to see what horror would confront her.

Slowly the thing arose from the pit

«*Gorm Almighty!*» Varla exclaimed. She gripped her sword hilt tightly as she gazed upon a vision of insane nightmare.

A creature spawned in the Nethermost Pits was oozing up out of the well.

It was an amorphous, pulsating mass of tentacle-like arms, large watery eyes, and gaping maws. Its coarse hide was befouled with reeking slime and pitted with weeping sores, suppurating wounds, unhealthy growths, and hideous lumps. Several drooling mouths, toothless and leech-like, were opening and closing with a sickening squelching sound, and its eyes, of which there were many, were clouded and diseased, leaking a clear viscous fluid. Myriad arms as thick as Varla's waist, were lashing and twisting violently as if in an invisible wind.

The creature had risen to fill the pit, its shapeless body over-spilling the sides as it sought to reach the barbarian.

Varla fought down a wave of nausea and steeled herself for battle.

Thick tendrils slithered and wriggled towards her. Her sword slashed through a ropy limb which fell flopping to the ground, then another; but the monster suffered no ill effects, and more tentacles advanced upon her.

Varla fought on desperately, her blade a whirlwind of steel, severing limb after limb as they flew towards her, but where one was cut off another replaced it. She swung again and again, her red sword slicing into thick flesh in a welter of gore and slime.

What unnerved Varla most was that the monster made no sound, even when it felt the bite of her Valkarthan steel.

«By Tiandra's teats, die, monster, *die!*» screamed Varla as she renewed her efforts. Limbs fell to her blade, but there were too many. Eventually a slimy coil grasped her sword arm tightly. Instantly she tore her dagger from its scabbard with her left hand. With a war song of the Snow Bear tribe upon her lips she fought on, slashing and hacking as best she could as more coils enveloped her. She fought with the savage courage of the barbarian born, even though she knew there was little hope. Inexorably she was dragged, still fighting like a cornered beast, towards the creature and its gaping maws.

Then, momentarily, it seemed to shimmer, like a desert mirage and briefly Varla could see the chamber walls through it. The tentacles that held her became insubstantial and lost their grip upon her. She fell back a pace and glanced at Xothar Vool. His hands were still touching the diadem. The crystals had momentarily faded but were now glowing a brightly again.

Then she realised. *The magician was still controlling her thoughts!*

With all her barbarian instincts she knew the abomination she was facing was a phantom creature of science and sorcery, not flesh and blood.

«It's an illusion, sorcerer,» she snarled, «nothing but an illusion.»

All she had to do was *believe* it!

The creature again became solid and several tentacles lashed out to regain their hold. But this time Varla did nothing.

As they reached her, she willed herself to believe and cried out again. *«It is nothing but an illusion of the mind.»*

As she shouted these words the tentacles began to evaporate like desert mist and slowly the monster faded into nothingness.

Varla breathed a huge sigh of relief. *She had been right!*

She turned to face Xothar Vool.

He rose from his throne, staggering weakly. The effort of sustaining the mind-creature against the Valkarthan's attack had drained him terribly.

Varla grinned. «Now, *unza*, it is time for you to die.»

But Xothar Vool wasn't finished yet. The mad magician, in one last desperate act, threw everything his damaged mind could muster at the barbarian. An invisible blow smashed into Varla. She gasped with the impact, fighting for breath.

But it wasn't enough.

With one mighty mental surge Varla cast the greasy, questing thoughts of Xothar Vool from her head, and the jewels in the magician's diadem turned black and crumbled into dust with astonishing speed.

«It can't be possible!» the magician screamed, throwing the diadem to the floor. Surprise and horror were writ large upon his skeletal face. *«I am a God!»* He staggered, his mind shattered by the power of Varla's attack. «I… am… a… *God!*»

Varla stared up at the pathetic gibbering wreck upon the throne. «This is how a Valkarthan fights, Xothar Vool. Now let's see how a magician dies.»

Swiftly Varla sped up the stairs and struck the mad magician's head from his shoulders. The last thing he saw was her blade swinging at his neck. His head flew from his body, rolled heavily down the steps of the dais and bumped to the stone floor. His torso staggered, swayed, and fell in a steaming fountain of blood. It too tumbled down the stairs sending a torrent of gore coursing onto the paved floor.

Varla looked down at the decapitated corpse. «A promise is a promise, sorcerer.» She'd vowed revenge on the vile magician when he'd escaped the Temple of the Black Dawn back in Dalakh, and now that revenge was complete.

Varla conjectured that mayhap her path to the ruins of grim Sanjan had been guided by Abramax, Lord of Fate.

Or was it just chance?

She shrugged. Either way, the deed was done. She turned her back on the sorcerer's remains and headed back to the surface.

Varla made the long return journey through the ruins without incident, eventually reaching her kroter by ascending another staircase to the balcony where her mount awaited her, hungry and irritable. The sandstorm had long passed so she led her mount out onto the sand, realising, as she shielded her eyes with her free hand from the fiery blaze of the rising sun, that she had spent the whole night within the cursed city.

Then she heard a pounding on the desert sand.

A civilised person would have paused, wondering what was causing the sound, but Varla was a barbarian born, and instinctively she released her hold on her kroter and ducked. As she did so, a blade whistled above her head, narrowly missing her. She felt something rush past her and turned to see one of the Ebon Acolytes astride his kroter, readying his beast for another attack. Robed in black astride his dark beast with his eyes in shadow, it seemed to Varla that she was beset by a demon from the pits. She snarled and turned to face her attacker. Her eyes were adjusting quickly to the sunlight and, as the priest moved towards her, his wicked scimitar held high, she drew her sword and, moving away from her mount, planted her feet wide to meet the attack.

«So, one of you survived the sandstorm, then,» she snarled. «Come, demon priest, time to meet your god.»

The priest thundered towards her. When he was almost upon her she lunged, avoiding the dripping jaws of his kroter. With a vicious backswing she sliced open the creature's neck and jumped away, watching as the beast collapsed to the sand in a tangle of limbs.

The priest was thrown roughly from his saddle and landed upon his knees.

Varla waited while he got to his feet.

The black kroter died quickly as its lifeblood stained the sands a darker crimson. The priest looked at his beast, his ever since it had hatched from the egg and his only companion in the Black Brotherhood. His eyes blazed with fury and pain and he turned and ran at Varla screaming in incoherent rage, a wild gleam in his dark eyes. Varla sprang to meet him with blurring speed.

Their blades met with a resounding clash and they fought, both attacking simultaneously, stroke raining on stroke almost too fast for the eye to follow.

Varla realised her opponent was a seasoned fighter and no pampered temple acolyte as she parried a blow that narrowly missed her head. Her sword flashed back fast as a striking snake, but her opponent was equally quick, and her blade slid harmlessly off his scimitar. With flashing swords the pair fought in the morning light, their swift blows and parries weaving a glittering pattern of steel in the sunlight. Neither spoke; only a fool wasted energy on words in a battle to the death.

The priest was taller than Varla and he fought with skill and economy, yet with all the sword craft his masters had taught him he could not defeat this uncouth barbarian who had learned to fight while barely in her teens in grim and merciless battles against the hated Black Hawk tribe.

Varla knew she fought a master swordsman as his scimitar flashed in the sun trying to pierce her defence, but wherever it danced it rang against the heavy steel of her blade. The priest was beginning to tire. He was panting heavily and sweat beaded his brow. The lean muscles in his sword arm began to ache with the effort of blocking Varla's crashing blows. His attacks were becoming more and more desperate, and in his growing frustration and fear he was beginning to realise that perhaps he could not kill this barbarian girl.

Varla fought on.

Then his eyes widened in surprise as she stumbled and momentarily lost her balance. He cried out in triumph and drew back his blade for the killing stroke—and felt Varla's blade pierce his heart. She'd tricked him! He fell to the sand and was dead before he struck the ground.

Varla laughed sardonically as she wiped her sword clean against the robes of the corpse. «Give my greetings to your god, priest.»

Behind her, dawn burned golden and crimson in the sky as she sheathed her sword, mounted her kroter and rode towards the Gulf of Patanga and new adventures.

HERCULES VERSUS THE CYCLOPS
By Santiago del Dardano Turann

I.

The leaves of the kermes oak grove danced on the notes of the phorminx and the aulos flute entwined with the Mediterranean breeze. In patches of sunlight through the branches colorful bee-eaters in flashing gems of red, blue and yellow feathers chirped along with the higher notes of the lyre in a chorus condemning the black larks who skulked about picking at the branches in dark corners where they shouted dishormoniously. The shade of the grove created a pool of cool air along a series of large and flat rocks with naval wort and white gagea flowers growing in the crevices.

The youths Hylas and Admetus sat on the edges of the stones where they were ringed by pale hyacinth and white lace tordylium. With their skin luminous in the sun, they sat on their Doric chitons and carefully played the notes of the song they were composing for the next symposium when they returned to Thebes. Hercules stood in the cool of the shade glistening with olive oil mixed with freshly picked and crushed basil leaves while his squire Ioulas methodically ran the silver *stleggis* along his thick back and shoulders to clean the oil from solid skin. His eyes were closed as he listened to the song.

«Hylas, you're not breathing properly so there's an occasional disharmony with the phorminx. When he tries to slow for you it causes you both to weaken the melody.»

«Yes, *kyrios* Hercules.» He lowered his head in shame and his thick blonde curls tumbled over his eyes as he gazed back at the hero.

«Start again, this time sing the beginning, Ioulas.»

«Yes, *kyrios*.» He answered as the scraper followed the hard curves of Hercules' hairy chest. The music began and the thin youth hummed as he worked the instrument on the iron range of Hercules abdominal muscles until the vocal section of the song,

«Come take the *krater* from my hand
When I have mixed the wine

And drink, proclaim our sacred band,
By which love's blessings shine.

«Come take the wreath from off my head
There on the couch to lay
With words such as Apollo said
When Hyacinth did pray.»

«It seems the lyrics inspire you, Hylas.» Hercules told him laughing, and he blushed. «Very good. You were in perfect harmony with the iambic rhythm of the hymn.»

«Thank you, *kyrios*. The harsh Lacademonian boy Elacatas beat me at the discus and the flute at Sparta. I'm determined to not lose again when he comes to Thebes at the full moon.»

«Is it really personal and civic pride you're competing over, or maybe something else?» Admetus asked him and laughed until Hylas punched his shoulder.

«Now Admetus, in the strife of competition one sharpens one's bronze.» Hercules told him.

«In strength and in love.» He added with a steady gaze at Hylas, who looked off to the left and blushed. Two white swallow-tailed butterflies twirled through the air across the camp.

«Are these the only end of life?» Hercules asked, and Admetus paused a moment to reflect and then answered pensively,

«Virtue, *kyrios*, is the object of life, I say,»

«Love is the object of man's desire and is beyond virtue as all are summarized in love, *kyrios*.» Hylas quickly volunteered his opinion.

«Well, Ioulas?» Hercules asked. Kneeling, he was scraping his outer thigh and lowered his eyes and blushed as he spoke boldly:

«*Kyrios*, Beauty is the ideal and end of all man's strivings. Both virtue and love are beautiful, yet this mystic force is so much more than they. It is the animation of man's civilization.» None of them noticed an eagle had landed on the canopy of the oaks and watched them intently.

«Indeed, all well said and expressions of the hearts of noble youths. What joins them all is that they are all expressions of symmetry. There is a harmony and a balance that is found in all, though in different ways. A beautiful face and a well-formed body are good because they are harmonious. Virtue is the harmony of action among men, both an inner and an outer law. Love is a harmony between two whose souls are bound together in a unique quality of the harmony of desire. That harmony is the Beauty of a transcendent light beyond the material visions of beauty, and it shines into the inner eye of man from the Cosmic Order in the stars.

«We all desire this higher realm that is our true home as souls, and when we see some imperfect shadow of its perfect harmony we are drawn to it much like a moth to the flame. The more clearly one sees this higher Beauty in the simulations of the world we know, the higher one's soul rises through the celestial spheres when it passes through the constellation of Sagittarius upon death.»

«*Kyrios*, so we admire the beauty of a youth or the wisdom of the wise man not for what they are themselves, but as if they were a memory of something better that is lost of which they remind us, as, say, the memory of wine to a man who thirsts. But in ignorance we mistake this desire and drink of hemlock rather than fine Tharcian wine?»

«Yes, that is man's true journey and struggle in life. But such long discussions are for a symposium and not a rest on the road of a long journey after an exhausting battle. Pack the horses, we've had enough rest and discussion.» Hercules commanded. Suddenly the youths were in a flurry of activity dressing in their chitons, adjusting sashes, then checking the saddlebags and the horses as he slapped his hands and told them to move faster. Hylas always took longer as he was careful to properly fold and pin his garments with the rare ivory *peronai* Hercules had given him. Since they were gifts from him, he did not complain about them but would grumble watching the youth fussing with the pins.

«Quickly and sharply! If you move around like old ladies like this on the battlefield you'll be dead! In all things be quick and precise!» Hercules commanded them as he wrapped himself in his linen chlamys with a purple border. Because of the heat, the skin of the Nemean Lion was wrapped and draped over a horse. When all was done, Admetus pulled his long, chestnut brown hair behind his head to bind it, and Hercules announced they should hunt hares for dinner tonight as it would be good practice with the bow.

«Hare is greasy and awful and Hercules won't allow us to pick herbs for it.» Admetus mumbled in a low protest.

«That's right, so you learn to live a life that's not overly spoiled by fine things. That's part of the virtue you praised.» Hercules smiled and smacked him on the rear. Hylas laughed at him and he blushed.

2.

«Mercy! Mercy on a wandering old man!» The arthritic voice seized their attention in a net of sound as they prepared to leave the grove.

The crier was an old man holding a long oaken staff. He was wrapped almost completely in a heavily chalked white robe that was so bright in the hot sun that it was difficult to look at directly, much less find some detail of his face in the shadows of the layered folds beyond the hint of white beard. Hylas noticed that the staff was covered with carvings of old letters, and the presence of this archaic alphabet made him wonder if this was not a necromancer. He whispered to Admetus, and after a quick glance the two walked behind the nervously snorting mare.

«Perhaps he's a sphynx.» Admetus whispered.

«Grandfather,» Ioulas instinctively ran to him and asked, «will you please take some kykeon and goat cheese?»

«May those who hold Olympus bless you, child!» Then stretching his arm as if proclaiming in an assembly, he said with oratory boldness, «I crave not barley from the earth that's grown, but an ear into which I may pour out my sorrows!»

«Speak, ancient sir.» Hercules said, striving toward him.

«Ah! From your frame and stride I see you are a noble and a warrior, sir. I was once a warrior too, many years ago, with such youths as now accompany you, as I rode out in battle in my flashing golden chariot with polished spear and antelope horn bows to challenge with my weapons a lawless brood who sought to take from me my inheritance.»

«Did you win?» Hylas and Admetus came running from behind the horse at the prospect of an exciting account of a battle.

«Yes, I did, sweet youths. I locked my foes in a dungeon. But now I am a homeless wanderer who has been deprived of what I once could defend. First, Time robbed me of my youth, then the lawless such as I could once suppress robbed me of all else.» He raised both his hands dramatically and proclaimed, «How cruel is the wheel of fate as it turns, indifferent to our cries, through the realms of the stars! Indeed, all is suffering! Is this not all vanity?»

«Grandfather, what happened?» Ioulas asked sorrowfully.

«Hear me, kind strangers! I come from the town of Kephaliolofos.»

«I know that place.» Hercules said, listening intently. He was clearly remembering someone. «They have beautiful fruit trees in their courtyards and I ate my fill of their fruit there.» The old man continued.

«In better times it was known for chariot makers for the Basileus and for the brewing of a combination of herbs that revive the spirits, sold across the wine dark sea. Recently the town was thrown into an uproar and conquered by a terrible Cyclops named Phaulos who has created an autonomous zone, declaring the town no longer the territory of our Basileus, Sandarakinos, a good man who honors the gods with drops of wine, holy hecatombs of bulls and dispenses justice to the people, though many deem him a braggart.

«By some Egyptian magic this Phaulos cast a spell over much of the population and they rose up to burn the megaron and smashed all the jars they made there, tore all the weaving on the looms in the workshops and broke the oil press! In their madness, they profaned the Sacred Fire of the hearth! He has a hatred for the Shining Gods, they who live on Ambrosia alone and eat not the barley of earth and whom men must revere, and this rebel against Truth and Reason seeks to turn the world upside down into madness with himself as the king of fools.»

«How so?» Hylas asked.

«How to say this? The very words have no meaning when heard and confound the heart to grasp them! He has a mania against the Good and the Beautiful. He declared the ugly and the criminal to be the good of society, and he had all the beautiful youths of the city arrested, confined in his quarters and beaten before binding them to posts in the assembly field before the megaron as objects of mockery. No warrior could remain in the city unless he donned the clothing of a woman. His terrible strength and the powerful hold he has on the broken minds of his followers have terrorized the whole town and all bend the knee to his strange whims arising from his grossly disordered humors. My gray hairs could not save me from the cultists. They who respect nothing but power drove me from my own home.»

«A terrible tale.»

«Phrix is from this town.» Hercules told them with concern. Ioulas looked crestfallen and the old man asked quickly in a whisper,

«Is this a youth you know?»

«Yes, he's a runner and archer of a noble family.»

«Woe! Please make me not speak further! Oh, the memory of that vision disturbs my soul and drags me to the dark heart of Tartarus where lawless Titans mourn. I beg you, noble company, please release this old man to wander on his way. I must speak no more.»

«May the Giant-Killing Hermes, Wayfarer, preserve you on your journey, ancient sir,» Hercules said politely, but clearly absorbed in his own thoughts. They watched as he moved down the trail occasionally proclaiming his woe and did not notice when they turned away to mount their horses that he was transformed into a cloud and vanished.

«We will be going to Kephaliolofos to save Phrix?» Iouslas asked anxiously, stroking the mane of Hercules' white horse before he mounted to ride seated before him. The other two were excited over the prospect of a fight.

«Do you even need to ask? Come now, let's hurry.»

3.

The trail left the small green valley and turned in circles as it descended through increasingly large rocks erupting from barren soil. The last plants they saw formed a wide spread of yellow saffron crocus flowers on both sides of the trail. Hylas noticed they were also growing directly from the rocks and were not natural. Hercules told them this was an omen from Hermes and related the story of Crocus as they rode. He was a youthful companion of Hermes who was killed and transformed into this flower by the God, to whom it was sacred. It made him concerned that a youthful companion of his own, Phrix, was certainly in danger. They rode on and, passing through sheer cliffs of shattered dark stone, they heard high-pitched wailing echoing through the shadows from the crevices above.

«It's a strix!»

«That would be odd. The striges generally are active only at night and it's still the early afternoon before even the heat of the day.» Hercules informed them.

«For them to be active at this hour must be an ill omen.» Ioulas said sternly. «Far-Shooting Apollo, Lord of Tenedos, protect us,» he prayed and leaned back against Hercules' chest.

«Hylas, with your baby face you should beware the strix doesn't try and squirt its foul milk on your lips.»

«That's not funny, Admetus.»

«I have some garlic if you would like, to be safe.»

«Shut up.» He swung a leather strap, used as a riding whip, at him, and Hercules told them to calm down as rocks rolled from the left cliff and across their path. This made the horses nervous, and Ioulas recited a Doric spell against the tiny, black-winged Keres to calm them. There was a low hiss and Admetus excitedly pointed to a swarm of small black shadows that flooded up along the cliff from which the stones had fallen.

«This has become a polluted land,» Hercules told them in anger. «It must be purified.»

They rode for an hour moving around and down the mountains before the town became visible below them in the distance. The north wind of ill-omen whistled harshly through the boulders as they paused to survey the town. The colorfully painted marble megaron on a hill at the center of the town was mostly broken and scorched black. A section had been replaced by a tall, rough wooden structure surmounted by a mismatched collection of torn cotton and woven sheets for a roof. Many of the buildings were damaged, and those around the empty space below the megaron had been removed. Tall sticks could be seen around the emptied field. Admetus pointed out the extensive damage to the walls of the town visible even at this distance as Hercules frowned. A number of people, dark and shadowy, skulked about picking at the long wooden planks that had been affixed over the breaches and holes in the stone walls. Occasionally they could hear long and disturbing deep roars echoing in the valley.

«The Gods have abandoned this land.» Hylas said in awe, but was corrected by Hercules,

«No, a monster is trying to drive them out. Don't give up; the Gods, Reason and Truth will win: we'll see to that with Justice. Let's go do it.»

4.

Rough, large stones were piled about the square gate. Above it a simple pillar, carved from a single large stone, displayed simple, abstract wolves on either side. But the wolf heads had been clumsily chiseled in an effort to remove them. A bedraggled rabble milled about outside the gate behind a long table they had erected to block free access to the main ramp that was the thoroughfare of the town. There were a number of poorly lashed-together wooden placards laid against the wall. As Hercules and his compatriots approached, they could read the awkwardly drawn Linear B letters, and the youths began to laugh. They did not notice, as Hercules did, the broken and scattered *hermai* that had once marked the sacred border of the town.

«Who wrote these? They make no sense.» Hylas blurted out in frustration.

«They keep confusing the dative and the accusative cases.» Admetus said, laughing.

«It's sad,» Ioulas commented. Hercules was the first to approach the table on his white horse and called out to the men politely,

«Good afternoon, citizens. We have come to visit our friend Phrix who dwells in this city. We respectfully request to pass the city gate.»

«Oh you do, do you?» A loud, balding man with a crooked nose responded to him cynically.

«You can't just walk in here like you want! You have to dress as a woman if you want to come in here because you rotten warrior-types have to be put in your place!» A thin man with his head wrapped in rags screamed hysterically; then another hideous man told him proudly,

«And these boys have to cover their faces. The way they look is offensive to us. Beauty is the mark of pollution. This is the beginning of the reign of the Aschimoi! You had better get used to doing things our way because soon we will rule the whole of Helles!» The crowd cheered and repeated, ‹the Reign of the Aschimoi› enthusiastically as the youths on the horses all looked at each other, confused.

«The Lord of the Silver Bow, Apollo, has spread madness here.» Admetus quipped.

«I approached you politely and you tell me you want to ‹put me in my place›…» Hercules began patiently as his horse was becoming agitated from the noise, but they cut him off,

«Politeness is just a way to trick people!»

«Put on the dress, or get out!»

«Obey the Aschimoi! You're the peasant now!»

«Take the whip to him! Teach him his place in our new world!» The others all began chanting with the endless resolve of their resentment, and Hercules realized there was no discussion with them. The mob had gathered united before him screaming clashing slogans with raised fists while several of them pushed the table back against the gate in an attempt to ensure they could not pass. Hercules turned his horse and told the others to prepare.

«Should we not have weapons at the ready, *kyrios*?»

«Yes, *kyrios*, what if the mob attacks us?»

«The ignoble are cowardly and do not attack so directly on equal terms. They burn buildings, strike with arrows from a distance or gather as a violent gang against one who is unarmed. This is only so much noise. Let's go! Hold on, Ioulas!»

The horses charged. The mob scattered in a din of panic as the white horse trampled the table that collapsed as if it had been a structure of autumn leaves. Hercules and the others began to gallop up the stone ramp towards the ruins of the megaron. Twisted voices cursed them from the shadows. They saw faces that were bloated or distorted with rage leering from dark windows and doorways as they rode. Occasionally someone weakly threw a small household object at them, but theirs were mostly impotent cries drowned in their own incoherence. Hylas thought this was the hideous vision of lost ghosts in a cavern of nightmares.

When they reached the top of the hill, a large open space where the assemblies of citizens were once held, the hero and his companions suddenly stopped their advance when faced with the scene before them. Ioulas covered his eyes and buried his face in Hercules' shoulder while the other two youths sat pale and gasping. Hercules trembled with fury and ground his teeth.

5.

The field was ringed with tall and roughly cut poles of black poplar wood. Tied to the poles with knotted ropes were young men who had been beaten and were covered with blood and horse feces. Several were clearly dead from their injuries and exposure to the elements while the others barely clung to life. They rode into the middle of the field and Hercules leapt from his horse and began walking the circle of terror calling for Phrix.

«Here! Here!» Ioulas yelled out, pointing and wiping tears from his eyes with his other hand. Hercules squatted down and wrapped the pole in his arms despite the large splinters that jabbed his arms and chest. His muscles flexed as he stood, pulling it from the ground and lowering it slowly as the other ran to catch the end. Hiding in the shadows, a number of the townsmen stood cursing Hercules and warning him to stay out of their business.

«Phrix! Phrix!» Ioulas called as the other youths ran for knives to cut the ropes. Hercules ran over and pulled them off. The youth's face was swollen and bruised, with large chunks of his long blonde hair torn out and his lips heavily chapped from the heat.

«Hylas! Bring water! Admetus, bring two sheets, one to clean him and one to wrap him!» Hercules gently took the head and turned it to look into Phrix's bloodshot, glassy eyes. «Phrix, you'll be fine now. I'm here.» A thin stream of tears ran from his eyes as he tried to speak, but his voice was squeaking.

«Hercules, please save my friends.»

«Yes,» he answered him simply as they brought him water. «Give him water to drink then clean his face and his body. Ioulas, help me with the others. I'll pull out the poles and you catch them.»

«Yes, *kyrios*.»

Hercules began removing the other poles, and before long they had freed the youths who were still alive, tending to them to the best of their abilities. The rescued scarecrows moaned there in the middle of the field. Hylas angrily told Admetus,

«I can't believe that this is such a barbarian town that they would do this and no one will help us. All they do is stand back and yell.» Then he stood up and shouted, «You're all such cowards!» A resonant deep voice responded to him in an echo that rolled into the field like the stench of an opened grave:

«That's brave talk for one so little. I'll use you like the others, beat you to take that beauty from you and then tie you to a pole to roast slowly in the heat of the solar wheel!»

6.

«Phaulos! Phaulos! Phaulos!» The crowd began chanting and slinked from the cover of the shadows as the Cyclops descended the stairs from the blackened pillars of the megaron to the field. At the sight of him they began to convulse and gesticulate, some rolling on the earth, emitting hollow sounds that reminded Ioulas of the bands of monkeys he had seen with Hercules in Ethiopia.

At seven-and-a-half foot tall the young Cyclops was taller even than the six-foot Hercules and broader in both his smooth chest and shoulders. He bore the additional weight and girth of his stomach from feasting on the fatty human meat of those who resisted him. He wore only a stained chitron with frayed edges. The head was disproportionately large for the body with small ears flattened and sticking out from the side. Long and wiry strands of hair grew from the top of the skull and fell about the head randomly at different lengths. The square and protruding jaw seemed double the length of normal human proportions due to its second row of teeth.

The single eye was set in a bulging forehead with several knobs of bone spanning the broad plane and above a small nose that was more of a snout. The eye was larger than a man's fist and was covered by a second membrane that gave it a wet and glossy appearance. The disc of the green pupil with its serpentine slit appeared positively luminous. Any human transfixed by that gaze was mesmerized and would walk limply towards the phosphorescence.

«Phaulos the Cyclops, your tyranny ends today!»

«Do I hear the squeaking of a mouse? Who are you, mouse?»

«Who am I? I'll tell you who I am: I am Hercules the son of Zeus!»

«Zeus?» He laughed in a rolling, broken manner, joined by the crowd who cackled wildly. The Cyclops spat. «I fear not aegis-bearing Zeus, for I am stronger than that tottering old fool! The son of a tyrant calls me a tyrant, such folly! I bring liberation, granting the desire of these outcasts to destroy all who have denied them what they deserve, crushing it to its very root! The Reign of the Aschimoi will overthrow the rule of the fading Gods who founded Helles! I shall break all that is Beautiful, elevating the ugly and the lowly to the new ideal of personkind.»

«Blasphemy!» Admetus found the strength to break through his fear and cry out horrified.

«You turn the world upside down with the rhetoric of madness you do not believe.» Hercules pointed at him and told him boldly, «You lie to those whom you intend to abuse and to rule worse than Zeus has ever done! You speak of pity for the lowly against the powerful, but all you do is to replace one tyrant with another! You and naught but a fraud!»

«When I have killed you and silenced your pathetic squeaking, I will have deprived that gruel-eating gaffer Zeus of his main tool to resist my rise to power across Hellas.» The strangely wide mouth grinned as, with wide eye, the titan rushed Hercules, yelling, «Die!»

Hercules stood calm with his feet at right angles, his knees slightly bent and his right hand open and extended before his chest as the creature charged him head first, arms flailing. Confident that his greater size and weight must give him victory, Phaulos left himself completely open. Hercules stepped in and thrust his right hand into his foe's underarm, his left hand grasping his neck. Co-opting the force of his charge, Hercules pivoted in a circle, then lifted and spun the Cyclops.

The crowd screamed and the youths cheered as Phaulos was flung in the air and hit the ground hard on his shoulder. He screamed in pain and struggled up as Hercules ran towards him. On one knee, and not fully able to control his left arm from the damage, Phaulos was drooling in fury and punched towards the hero when he was within range. With a slight curving step, Hercules stepped in front of the Cyclops to dodge the punch, simultaneously laying his left hand across the wide chest and seizing his right wrist in an unbreakable lock, forcing the arm up toward his face. He released his grip when his hand hit the Cyclops's neck. With both hands open and in control of his enemy's neck and torso, the hero spun on his hips and with all his strength threw him back and down with a loud thud against the ground, shaking the field. His left shoulder cracked loudly. The stunned Cyclops spit blood and rolled away howling.

When Phaulos struggled to sit up with blood trickling from his mouth and small nose, Hercules ran to him, leapt up, and kicked him on the side of the head, knocking him back down to the ground. Blood spattered from the nose and the left ear. The crowd was now kneeling and crying for him to save them from Hercules. They crawled on the ground, throwing dirt on their heads and biting their hands. Phaulos took a deep breath and emitted a long, deep roar, attempting to work up new courage. He could not use his left arm, but he stood and leaning forward stumbled towards Hercules, cursing him.

«Illegitimate spawn of adultery! Chimera of god and man defying nature! Who are you to judge when you're a misbegotten freak—who should be following me!»

Hercules shifted his stance and, breathing slowly, peered directly into the great single eye of the Cyclops with determination. No man had ever dared confront the serpent gaze, and it drove the monster's blood into a boiling fury. He thought he saw victory ahead with his foe standing motionless. Just as he reached the Son of Zeus, muscle-gnarled arms extended wide to grasp and crush him, Hercules seized his foe's ratty tunic with both hands and, putting his right foot on the other's upper thigh, he fell back on his rounded shoulders. Drenched in sweat, Hercules cried out and flung the toppling Cyclops with all his strength. Completely out of control, the Cyclops flipped into the air with a shriek and landed on the back of his head, shattering his neck. He was dead immediately as darkness closed his eyes. Hercules stood, breathing heavily as the youths ran to him cheering. Phrix lay next to his friends and tried his best to smile though it was painful for him to move his lips.

«I'm not done yet.» The hero told them in a slow burn. His eyes still flashing with rage, he commanded them gravely, «All of you, seize the horse whips. These wretched creatures do not deserve to live in a city built by civilized men. Drive them out to the fields to live like the animals they are!» Then, turning to the cowering mob, «Out with you! Out of these sacred borders you defiled!»

Hercules strode across the field with his glare driving the bewildered herd, cracking his whip with a flick of his wrist. Their screams reached a peak as they pushed and trampled each other in their panicked efforts to flee through narrow alleys. The youths followed Hercules and ran down the thoroughfare yelling and driving the frantic townsmen before them like a flock of bleating sheep. When the town fell silent Hercules and his young friends returned to the field beneath the megaron to attend to the injured.

7.

Wrapped in white woolen blankets, Phrix sat on a bench and leaned against the wall. The firelight fell upon a chromatic wall painting of Zeus in the form of a giant eagle descending towards Ganymede as he rode on a herd of high-spirited Trojan horses. Phrix slowly drank the hot wine mixed with sideritis, fennel and licorice. He passed the clay cup decorated with satyrs to his friend next to him as Hylas asked him if he would like more bread.

«No, thank you, Hylas, my friend.»

The circular hearth was ablaze with a large fire in the center of the low chamber. The dancing light was reflected on mirror stones in the mosaic of the floor, illuminating the geometric patterns. In his bare feet Hylas walked across the floor and sat on the bench with his companions. Outside in the peach trees of the courtyard immediately beyond the blue tile window sills, four nightingales began to sing their love songs to each other in the cool night air.

«I'm impressed with everyone's recovery,» Hercules told them.

«I didn't know you had such a knowledge of medicine. We owe it to you, *kyrios*.» One of Phrinx's friends who sat on the bench with him told the hero.

«Yes, *kyrios*. Thank you.»

«Excellent. You're well enough for us to leave and return to Thebes tomorrow. But tonight, Iouslas, Hylas and Admetus will entertain you with the new song for a symposium.»

TONGA OF LEMURIA
FREEDOM FIGHT
UOHH!!
THING'S HIDE IS LIKE IRON!
EVEN A ZULPH'S GOT A WEAK SPOT!
AAUGH!! YOU BASTARD!
BLUGNUG NOT WANT ROAST PIG THIS BAD!
TONGA OF LEMURIA CREATED BY CLAYTON L. HINKLE
THE ARENA... UNDER THE BLAZING SUN OF OLD LEMURIA, IN THE ANCIENT, WICKED CITY OF TSAR GOL, A THOUSAND AGES AGO--HERE, FOR THE ENTERTAINMENT OF THE RULING ELITE AND THE UN-WASHED MOB ALIKE, SUPER-STAR GLADIATRIX TONGA AND HER FELLOW BATTLERS ARE ONCE AGAIN FIGHTING FOR THEIR LIVES, THIS TIME AGAINST A RAMPAGING ZULPHAR, THE SAVAGE LEMURIAN HELL-PIG!
FREELY AND LOOSELY BASED ON LIN CARTER'S LEMURIA AS CREATED FOR "THONGOR OF LEMURIA", WITH KIND PERMISSION FROM THE ESTATE OF LIN CARTER.
©2019 C.L.H.

THE TRICK IS...
OW! BRISTLY! ...GETTING WITHIN REACH OF IT!
CHOK
ONE ZULPHAR, READY FOR THE ROASTING PIT!
BUT EVEN AS SHE SPEAKS, TONGA KNOWS THAT A SINGLE ZULPHAR IS NOT TO BE THEIR ONLY ANTAGONIST ON THIS DAY...
WOOMF

BROBDINA! GOTHRID! ON YOUR FLANK! A PACK OF KROTERS!
THOSE ARE NOT NICE, TAME, RIDING KROTERS!
SCREEEEE
NO, THOSE ARE ANGRY, WILD, HUNGRY KROTERS!!
ARAAHH!!!
REEAARRGH
YOUR PARDON WHILE I SAVE YOUR ASS, BROBBIE! AND WHAT AN--
THANKS, BUT I WOULDN'T GO THERE IF I WERE YOU, GOTHIE!
KROTERS? NOW BLUG-NUG MAD!
SO AM I, BLUG! BUT STAY ALERT--BY YAMATH'S FLAMING BUNGHOLE!!
VANDARS* NOW?! WHAT'S GOTTEN INTO ZHU ZHARVIS?! UH OH, BLUG, I THINK THAT ONE LIKES YOU!!
*THE 12FT LEMURIAN LION

GO 'WAY VANDAR! FEELING NOT MUTUAL!!
GOT TO ACT FAST, BLUG WON'T LAST LONG!
THAT'S IT BLUG, HOLD 'IM OFF!
THUS THE BATTLE RAGES, AS VARIOUS SAVAGE, PRIMEVAL KILLERS OF LOST LEMURIA FALL BEFORE THE FIGHTING FURY OF TONGA AND HER COMRADES...
...THEMSELVES EVEN GREATER KILLERS, WITH THEIR DEADLY PROWESS AND STEEL-TRAP REFLEXES—WHO BUT THEY COULD WREAK SUCH A SLAUGHTER AND RE-MAIN, IF NOT UN-SCATHED, THEN AT LEAST UN-INJURED?
ANYMORE OF ZHU'S PETS? OR HAVE THEY LOST THEIR APPETITES?
WHAT ARE WE, WARRIORS, OR COM-MON CONDEMNED CRIMINALS?
NO, WE ARE ZHU'S PROPERTY, OF WHICH HE REMINDS US FROM TIME TO TIME!

I SEE THE MOB APPROVES OF THE ENTERTAINMENT ZHU ZHARVIS PROVIDES!
OH AYE, THE MOB TRULY LOVES US, I THINK, AND THEY LOVE TONGA ESPECIALLY!
THEY MAY LOVE US, BUT THEY LOVE BLOOD MORE! WHETHER IT'S THESE MONSTER'S OR OURS, IT'S BLOOD THEY LOVE!
SEEM LIKE MOB MORE BESTIAL THAN BLUGNUG!
IT SEEMS FAT BASTARD ZHU IS TRYING HIS HARDEST TO GET US MAIMED OR KILLED - NOT TOO SURPRIZING BUT WHY ALL OF A SUDDEN?
WE ARE ELITE WARRIORS, HIGHLY SKILLED AND VERY VALUABLE!
IS ZHU ZHARVIS THAT WASTEFUL OF OUR LIVES, OR IS IT THAT HE SEEKS TO WRING EVERY LAST BIT OF VALUE FROM OUR HIDES?
THAT'S IT, I'LL VOW! BECAUSE OUR TONGA'S THE GREATEST THING TO COME ALONG IN YEARS! LOOK HOW POPULAR SHE IS TO THEM - IT'S NO SECRET THE MOB'S JABBERING, DEMANDING THE TRADITIONAL FREEDOM FIGHT!
TONGA FIGHT FOR HER FREEDOM? THAT BE EASY FIGHT FOR TONGA! THEN TONGA FIGHT FOR ZHU NO MORE! AND ZHU CRY LIKE BABY LONG-PIG!
BLUGGIE'S RIGHT! ZHU ZHARVIS WON'T LIKE THAT ONE BIT! UH, HEY BLUGGIE, WHAT'S 'LONG-PIG'?
HUH? OH, IT JUST, UH, SPECIAL DELICACY BACK HOME!
I HAD NOT THOUGHT OF IT, BUT I KNOW ACCORDING TO TRADITION I CAN REQUEST A FIGHT, FOR MY FREEDOM, AS LONG AS THE PEOPLE CALL FOR IT, WHICH I SUPPOSE THEY ALREADY ARE...
BUT, WHAT THEN? I'VE BEEN A FIGHTER, A GLADIATOR, FOR ALL MY ADULT LIFE! WHAT DO I DO, THEN, WITH FREEDOM?
OOH, YEAH 'ADULT LIFE'? YOU MEAN THE PAST FEW YEARS? TONGA GIRL, YOU THINK ON THAT - YOU'VE NEVER DREAMT OF YOUR FREEDOM?
YOU DO WHAT YOU'VE ALWAYS DREAMED OF DOING, OF COURSE!

YOU'LL BE FREE! FREEDOM IS ALL THAT MATTERS— WHA-?!
BY THE — DID YOU JUST DO AND SAY WHAT I HEARD YOU DO AND SAY?!
THERE!! BY THE GODS, MY BATTLE WITH THAT GIRDLE AT LEAST EQUALS THAT WITH THOSE BEASTS OF YOURS! EASE UP AT THE TRAINING TABLE, GIRL!
BY GORM'S IRON PRICK, YOU ARE A CHEEKY LITTLE BASTARD OF AN ATTENDANT, AREN'T YOU?!
YOU KNOW, OF COURSE, THAT WHILE WE ARE BOTH SLAVES, YOU AND I, YOU, IN FACT, ARE MY SLAVE? IS THAT A YES?
GLAK!
GLIK!
AND I BROOK NO INSOLENCE FROM MY SLAVES! AS MY PERSONAL BODY SLAVE YOU WILL ATTEND TO MY NEEDS IN A MANNER BEFITTING MY DESERVEDLY SUPERIOR STATUS—UNDERSTOOD?
A-AYE, MISTRESS! AND W-WHAT ARE YOUR NEEDS?
WELL, YOU'RE NOT BAD LOOKING FOR A DWARF—WE'LL SEE...
HA HA HA! HOW STRANGE WOULD LIFE BE AS A FREEDWOMAN! I THINK I'D MISS LIFE AROUND HERE, WERE I TO FIGHT FOR MY FREEDOM!
IF I, A MERE SLAVE OF SLAVES, MAY BE SO BOLD?
OH, YOU'VE BEEN DEMOTED, BORTHUS? CHIEF TRAINER AND OVERSEER, ARE YOU NOT?
WELL, TRUE... AHEM IF I WAS YOU, TONGA, I'D EVEN FIGHT... YOU! I'D FIGHT THAT BIG, BLUE-SKINNED MONSTER WOMAN, THAT BLOODY FURRY CANNIBAL, THAT BIG NORTHERN OAF, ALL AT ONCE, EVEN, IF I HAD YOUR CHANCE FOR FREEDOM—NOT MINE, THOUGH...
...IF I ONLY HAD MY CHANCE, NOW, OH, I'D LIKELY JUST STAY ON HERE—I AIN'T STARVIN' AND THE WORK CAN BE PLEASANT—HOT BATH? RUBDOWN?
HA HA—OH, BORTHUS! I ALWAYS BATHE MYSELF, BUT THANKS ANYWAY! BUT I THINK OL' BLUGGIE NEEDS HIS TOE-NAILS TRIMMED! HA HA HA
BUT NO MATTER THE "PERKS" OF BEING A SUPER-STAR GLADIATOR, A SLAVE CRAVES FREEDOM ABOVE ALL THINGS! THUS, WHEN BUSINESS BRINGS ZHU ZHARVIS TO THE PRACTICE YARD ONE DAY...
HAIL ZHU ZHARVIS!
AS IS THE CUSTOM, I, TONGA, BY LEAVE OF THE PEOPLE OF TSARGOL, REQUEST THE CHANCE TO FIGHT FOR MY FREEDOM!
OH, HO HO! I WONDERED WHEN YOU WOULD SPEAK! YES, I'VE HEARD THE CLAMOR OF YOUR LOVING FANS, TONGA MY DEAR! I'LL MISS YOU SORELY, BUT OF COURSE I'LL GRANT YOUR REQUEST! YOU SURELY DESERVE YOUR SHOT AT FREEDOM!
OH! WELL, ER, THANK YOU, ZHU ZHARVIS! I SHALL DO YOU HONOR OR DIE IN THE ATTEMPT!
HMMM... THAT WAS A BIT TOO EASY—WHAT ARE YOU UP TO, ZHU ZHARVIS?

"ZHU ZHARVIS, YOU NEVER ACT OUT OF KINDNESS, NEVER... I REMEMBER..."

...TONGA REMEMBERS, WHEN PIRATES OF TARAKUS HAD RIPPED HER FROM HER HOME IN THE RED FOREST, RAPING AND KILLING HER STEP-MOTHER IN THE PROCESS...

...SHE WAS FIFTEEN...

THE PIRATES HAD TRIED, OFTEN ENOUGH, TO RAPE HER, BUT SUCH WAS HER STRENGTH, FEROCITY, AND FIGHTING ABILITY THAT THEY NEVER TRULY SUCCEEDED!

THEY TRIED KNOCKING HER UNCONSCIOUS, AN EXTREME MEASURE TO BE SURE, BUT THEN HER BEAUTY WAS EXTREME — AS WAS HER TIGERISH VITALITY, AND WHEN SHE QUICKLY CAME TO, THINGS DID NOT END HAPPILY FOR THE PIRATES!

WITH NOTHING FOR IT OTHER THAN WASTEFULLY KILLING HER OUT-RIGHT, THEY FINALLY JUST CHAINED HER UP LIKE A DEADLY, BUT BEAUTIFUL, BEAST!

THERE, HER HATRED FOR THE PIRATES OF TARAKUS GREW INTO A SOLID KNOT THAT HAS NEVER LOOSENED!

~ TONGA SMILES WITH SOME SATISFACTION AT HAVING DEALT A BIT OF PAIN AND SUFFERING TO THE BASTARDS — THOUGH SHE RUEFULLY GIVES THEM CREDIT FOR SELLING HER TO ZHU ZHARVIS, THE FAMOUS GLADIATOR TRAINER...

...AND THAT EVENT SET HER ON THE PATH TO BECOMING THE DEADLIEST FIGHTER OF THE AGE!

THOSE PIRATE DOGS WARNED THAT SHE IS A VERITABLE SHE-VANDAR— BAH! BY THE NINETEEN!! THAT BODY! THAT FACE! NOW SHE WILL LEARN, SHE IS THE PROPERTY OF ZHU ZHARVIS!
...THOUGH AT THAT TIME, THE ONLY PATH SHE TROD WAS THAT OF A SLAVE, JUST TORN FROM HER HOME, AND NOW TO BE "BROKEN IN"—
HAH! I KNEW OL' ZHU ZHARVIS WOULDN'T LISTEN TO THOSE UNZAS!* A WENCH THAT LUCSIOUS? STRAIGHT TO THE "ORIENTATION" ROOM!
CRASH
HEAR THAT? HEH HEH HEH THINGS 'R' GETTIN' FIESTY IN THERE! MAYBE SHE DON'T WANNA GET "ORIENTED"!
*UNZA—THE GIANT HAIRLESS LEMURIAN RAT
—THAT WAS WHEN TONGA TOOK IT UPON HERSELF TO—RENEGOTIATE, —SO TO SPEAK—
THOK
HNNNGH
—THE TERMS OF HER SLAVERY 'CONTRACT'!
HRRLGH
UUUH! UUUH! UUUUH!
WHUD
WHUD
YOU CAN SCREAM FOR YOUR GUARDS TO COME IN AND SLAY ME, AND THEY WILL, BUT YOU WILL LIVE THE REST OF YOUR LIFE WITHOUT THESE PALTRY MAN-PARTS I'VE GOT HERE IN MY FIST— YOU DON'T DOUBT THAT I CAN RIP 'EM RIGHT OFF, DO YOU? SO—
—WE CAN DO THAT, OR, YOU CAN HELP ME TO BECOME THE GREATEST KILLER YOU'VE EVER TRAINED, AND BRING YOU RICHES ENOUGH TO CHOKE A DWARK!*
...SO FORGET THIS SILLY NOTION OF YOURS— NO ONE ELSE NEED KNOW WHAT PASSED BETWEEN US HERE— WHAT SAY YOU, ZHU ZHARVIS?
GROAN! KOFF! GASP! ...I-IT- IT WILL B-BE AS YOU SAY... GASP! I D-DO KNOW T-T-TALENT WHEN I SEE IT! MY KOFF-GASP WORD ON IT!
...I KNOW YOU, ZHU ZHARVIS— YOU ARE FAR TOO PRIDEFUL TO EVER FORGIVE ME THAT AFFRONT! WHY ARE YOU SO AGREEABLE NOW? HMMM... WELL, THERE'S NAUGHT TO DO BUT CARRY ON AS IS NORMAL, BUT BY GORM I'LL KEEP MY EYES OPEN, MY WORD ON IT!
*DWARK—A TYRANOSAUR LIKE BEAST, ONLY LARGER.

FREEDOM FIGHT II

TONGA LEARNS IT WILL BE IN THE UPCOMING GAMES OF TIANDRA THAT SHE WILL FIGHT FOR HER FREEDOM, FITTING, PERHAPS, AS TIANDRA IS THE GODDESS OF LUCK!

AS PER THE RULES AND TRADITIONS OF THE ANCIENT GLADIATORIAL GAMES IN OLD TSARGOL, TONGA ALSO LEARNS OF HER OPPONENT TO BE —

SHE IS SKREAXA, FROM THE RIVAL SCHOOL OF ARD THORUS, AND ONE OF VERY FEW FEMALE BATTLERS WHO MIGHT STAND UP TO TONGA —

— ONE WHO, LIKE TONGA, VERY OFTEN FIGHTS AND WINS AGAINST TOP MALE OPPONENTS!

LIKE TONGA, SKREAXA HAS FOUGHT HER WAY OUT OF THE RANKS OF THE 'MEATS', WHERE DEATH IS A SURETY IF YOU DON'T WIN YOUR FIGHTS, TO THIS POINT, ON THE VERGE OF SUPER-STARDOM...

...WHICH SHE CAN NOW ACHIEVE...

...IF SHE CAN KILL TONGA! SO, SHE HOPES TO CONTINUE THE CYCLE, JUST AS TONGA DID WHEN SHE BURST ONTO THE SCENE AS A SUPER-STAR AND EMBARKED ONTO HER WHIRLWIND CAREER!

FOR IN THE ARCANE WORLD OF BARGOLIAN GLADITORIAL COMBAT, ONE RULE IS THAT TOP FIGHTERS DON'T ALWAYS FIGHT TO THE DEATH, BEING THAT THEY ARE VERY VALUABLE — THAT IS NOT TO SAY THAT DEATH IS NOT A FOREVER LURKING POSSIBILITY, FOR IT VERY MUCH IS...

...AS FOR TONGA, SHE HAS SEEN SKREAXA AT PREVIOUS GAMES AND MARKED HER AS AN EXCEPTIONALLY GOOD FIGHTER — AND THOUGH SUPREMELY CONFIDENT AS ALWAYS, SHE NEVER TAKES AN OPPONENT FOR GRANTED, AND PREPARES HERSELF ACCORDINGLY —

— FOR TONGA WAS NOT ABOUT TO LET SKREAXA BECOME A SUPER-STAR OVER HER BLOODY CORPSE!

FOR GOOD REASON IS **TONGA** A **SUPER-STAR** — HER SKILLS, STRENGTH AND ABILITIES COMBINED WITH HER BEAUTY AND FIERY PERSONALITY TO MAKE HER, BY FAR...

... FANS RANGING FROM THE ROYALLY, **FILTHY RICH** TO THE **DESTITUTE**, **RICHLY FILTHY** BEGGARS IN THE STREETS!

... THE MOST **POPULAR** GLADIATOR IN MEMORY! IN A REALM WHERE GLAD- ITORIAL **COMBAT** WAS THE ULTIMATE CROWD-PLEASER, **TONGA** RULED AS A VIRTUAL SLAVE-QUEEN OVER A LEGION OF FANS...

POSSIBLY HER MOST **ARDENT** FAN WAS **TALOS TSAR** — A WEALTHY, HANDSOME YOUNG LORD OF ANCIENT AND PEDIGREED LINEAGE, RELATED TO **THE SARK HIMSELF**, SEEMINGLY UNTOUCHED BY THE DARK RUMORS OF DEC- ADENCE AND DEMON-WORSHIP ATTACHED TO HIS FAMILY...

... HE IS KNOWN AS A **DEVIL-MAY-CARE** PLAYBOY AND **RECKLESS** GAMBLER, WITH ASSORTED FRIENDS AND CRONIES IN HIGH, AND LOW, PLACES! HE IS, OF COURSE, A **FERVENT GLADIATOR FAN** AND IN **TONGA** HE HAS FOUND A VERITABLE GODDESS TO WORSHIP! LATELY, HE HAS TAKEN TO OPENLY PRO- CLAIMING HIS LOVE FOR HER AND TRYING TO GIVE HER GIFTS...

~TONGA IS FIRST EMBARRASSED, THEN INTRIGUED AND AMUSED! TALOS TSAR IS A HANDSOME ENOUGH YOUNG MAN, IF NOT ESPECIALLY PHYSICAL—AND SHE FINDS HIS ATTENTIONS NOT UNPLEASANT, THOUGH SHE REMAINS TOUCHY ON THE SUBJECT!

"BORTHUS! AND I THOUGHT YOU A MARRIED MAN! WHAT POSSESSES YOU TO GIFT ME WITH TIRALONS?*"

"OH, NOT ME, TONGA DEAR! THESE'R FROM YER LITTLE BOY-PAL, THAT RICH LITTLE CATAMITE, TALOS TSAR!"

"YA KNOW, MANY A GLADIATOR HAS HISSELF, OR HERSELF, A SECRET HONEY-LORD, SOME RICH LORD 'R LADY WITH A TASTE FER ROUGH BOYS 'N' GIRLS—YOU COULD DO WORSE'N TALOS TSAR, TONGIE—AIN'T NO SHAME IN IT..."

"YOU MIND YOUR OWN BUSINESS, BORTHUS! SLAVE OR NO, I'M NO DESPERATE LITTLE WAIF, LOOKING FOR A 'HONEY-LORD' TO TAKE CARE OF ME— NOW, GIVE ME THOSE FLOWERS!"

*THE FABLED GREEN ROSE OF LEMURIA

THE TIME FINALLY ARRIVES FOR THE GAMES OF TIANDRA TO BEGIN— AS TONGA GEARS UP, HER THOUGHTS FLUTTER LIKE BIRDS...

"CAN IT BE THAT ZHU ZHARVIS IS SINCERE IN HIS PROTESTATIONS? PERHAPS, AFTER ALL THESE YEARS... ARE MY SUSPICIONS UNFOUNDED? AND HIS WORDS YESTERDAY..."

"...REST ASSURED, TONGA, MY DEAR, I MYSELF COULDN'T BE MORE SURE THAT YOU'VE EARNED YOUR CHANCE AT FREEDOM—AND WHEN YOU WIN, I'LL PRESENT YOU A GENEROUS PURSE, TO BOOT!"

TALOS TSAR ATTENDS THE GAMES OF COURSE, AND IS GRANTED 'THE HONOR OF VIEWING THEM FROM THE SARK'S SUMPTUOUS ROYAL PAVILION...

...IN AN ACKNOWLEDGEMENT OF THEIR FAMILIAL CONNECTION! THOUGH LAVISH WITH FOOD, DRINK, SLAVE-GIRLS AND OTHER REFRESHMENTS, TALOS CAN THINK OF NO OTHER THAN TONGA!

THE GAMES COMMENCE, AND FOR THE DENIZENS OF OLD TSARGOL, ALL IS AS IT SHOULD BE...

AFTER A WARM-UP OF VARIOUS SPORTS AND CONTESTS, THE BLOODY PRELIMINARY FIGHTS FROM THE RANKS OF THE 'MEATS' TAKE PLACE, ALWAYS A CROWD-PLEASER...

...THEN COME THE BEAST-FIGHTS, INTERSPERSED AND INTER-MIXED WITH BIG-NAME MATCHES...

...TONGA'S COMRADES WIN THEIR FIGHTS— GOTHRID AND BLUGNUG AGAINST A CAPTURED SQUAD OF ZANGABALI MERCENARIES, ARMED WITH SPEARS...

...AND BROBDINA IN HER BATTLE WITH A JUVENILE, BUT STILL GIGANTICALLY FEARSOME, ZEME DAR...

... FINALLY, THE BATTLE EVERYONE HAS BEEN WAITING FOR, TONGA'S FIGHT FOR FREEDOM AGAINST SKREAXA, IS TO TAKE PLACE - THE OPPONENTS FACE ONE ANOTHER, AND AT LEAST BY APPEARANCE, THE ADVANTAGE GOES TO THE MUCH LARGER AND AGGRESSIVELY MUSCULAR SKREAXA!
YOU KNOW, YOU DON'T LOOK LIKE MUCH TO ME - PRETTY ENOUGH, BUT SLOW, AND SOFT...
EH? DID YOU SAY I WAS SLOW AND SOFT?
AYE! SLOW...
HUUNH!
AND SOFT!!
KOFF HEH HEH HEH... OOOOAAH AH, GODS! I'M SORRY, I WASN'T PAYING ATTENTION - WELL, THAT WAS A SWEET LITTLE LOVE PAT, SKREAXA!
YOU LAUGH?! I WILL KILL YOU, PRETTY GIRL!
AH, THAT'S THE SPIRIT! LET'S MAKE THIS FUN!!

...SUDDENLY...

UURRGGH

THUS AFTER A FEROCIOUS BATTLE IN WHICH TONGA MUST CALL UPON ALL HER STRENGTH AND SKILL TO WIN, SHE VANQUISHES THE FIERCE SKREAXA! THOUGH SHE WOULD HAVE PREFFERED TO MERELY DISABLE THE BRAVE WARRIOR, SHE WAS FORCED TO KILL HER- AND AS SHE RAISES HER BLOODY SWORD IN VICTORY, AN INDESCRIBABLE FEELING RUSHES THROUGHOUT HER MAGNIFICENT BODY...

...I-I WAS WR-WRONG, Y-YOU ARE NEITHER S-S-SOFT, NOR- S-S-SL-AAHH

WOULD THAT WE HAD MET AS FRIENDS SKREAXA - FOR YOU ARE A TRUE WARRIOR... SHE GOES, NOW TO THE **SHADOWLANDS**!

...AND THUS TONGA, ONCE OF **KADONGA** IN THE RED FOREST, NOW OF **TSARGOL**, WINS HER FREEDOM, SHE TRULY BELIEVES...

14

~A BRIEF CEREMONY TAKES PLACE THERE ON THE BLOODY SANDS OF THE ARENA, IN WHICH **THE SARK**, THE MIGHTY EUKIBOS KHOR HIMSELF, PLACES THE **WREATH OF FREEDOM** ON TONGA'S BROW...

OH HO! I CAN SEE FROM YOUR FACE THIS IS ALL A BIT OVERWHELMING, TONGA DEAR — BUT HAVE NO FEAR, BEING YOUNG AND STRONG, YOU WILL ADJUST!

...AND THE REST IS BUT A **BLUR** TO HER, HER MIND RACING, HER HEART A WELTER OF EMOTIONS...

NOW, YOU MUST READY YOURSELF FOR THE **FREEDOM PARTY** AT THE VILLA, EH?

AND AT THIS PARTY ANOTHER, MUCH MORE **WINE-FUELED**, CEREMONY TAKES PLACE, AS IN FRONT OF THE **HIGH LORDS**, LADIES AND OTHER SUCH NOTABLES, ATTENDING...

...TONGA SHEDS HER PLAIN **SLAVES KIRTLE** FOR THE FILMY ROBES OF A **FREE WOMAN** OF TSARGOL, MUCH TO THE DELIGHT OF THE PARTY-GOERS, INCLUDING TALOS TSAR, MOST ESPECIALLY!

NOW YOU ARE **FREE**, MY LOVE! NOW, WE CAN — AH!! YOUR BEASTLY FORMER MASTER COMES...

TONGA MY LASS! PRAY SPARE OLD **ZHU** ANOTHER MOMENT OF YOUR TIME, EH? YOUR PARDON, YOUNG LORD TSAR?

HAD A BIT OF WINE, HAVE YOU? WELL, HERE — LET'S **TOAST** YOUR FREEDOM WITH THIS LOVELY **SARN-WINE** FROM MY OWN CELLARS...

S-SARN-WINE? WHY, MASTER ZH — THAT IS, AH-SIR ZHU *HIC* THANK YOU! OH, I *HIC*

... THERE, ISN'T THAT A LOVELY VINTANGE? NOW THEN, I HAVEN'T FORGOTTEN MY PROMISE TO YOU, MY DEAR, SO COME ALONG WITH ME...
EH? PROMISE? HIC
WELL, LEAD ON ZHU ZHARVIS! HIC OH! THIS WINE IS GETTING TO ME...
HAHHA, YES, IT IS A HEADY VINTAGE, IS IT NOT? BUT COME IN HERE, I'VE SOMETHING OF GREAT INTEREST FOR YOU...
... TONGA TIPSILY FOLLOWS ZHU ZHARVIS, INTO A DOORWAY...
... THEY MOVE THROUGH A HALL OF INTER-CONNECTED ROOMS, AND BY THE TIME THEY ARRIVE AT THE FINAL ROOM, HER HEAD IS REELING!
YOU REMEMBER, DEAR, I PROMISED YOU A GENEROUS PURSE, WHEN YOU WON YOUR BATTLE, AS I KNEW YOU WOULD?
... IS THIS NOT A GENEROUS PURSE? MY DEAR?
GULP HMMM... ... MMYESHMF?
... W-WHAS' HHAP-P-PEN-N-NING... I D-DON' FF-FEE...
I THINK YOU'VE HAD TOO MUCH WINE, TONGA MY DEAR... THERE NOW, EASE DOWN ONTO THAT DIVAN... THERE, NOW...
... YOU JUST LAY BACK, RELAX AND REMEMBER, YOU'RE YOUNG, STRONG AND BEAUTIFUL - NO DOUBT YOU'LL ADJUST TO YOUR NEW LIFE... HEH, HEH, HEHHEH HA HA HA HA!!
~CONT.~

FREEDOM FIGHT III

≥AAH≤ OH, BY YAMATH'S EVER FLAMING BUNG-HOLE! WHAT— WHY, I'M IN ZHU ZHARVIS' GODS-DETESTED GAOL-HOUSE!! WHAT IN THE SEVEN HELLS AM I...

ARRGH!! THAT CRAWLING UNZA MUST HAVE DRUGGED MY WINE — HE'S BETRAYED ME! THAT BASTARD! WAIT— DID HE... DID HE... MY GARMENTS, TORN, DISHEVELLED... NO. NO! NO, NO, NO!! ARRGH!!

TONGA AWAKENS, CONSCIOUSNESS RETURNING ONLY SLOWLY — GROGGILY, SHE ASSEMBLES HER WITS, TRYING TO DISCERN WHAT HER SENSES ARE TELLING HER... AS SHE MOVES HER LIMBS SHE REALIZES SHE IS CHAINED TO A WALL, AND HER PRESENT LOCATION IS ALL TOO FAMILIAR!

THOUGH MANY EMOTIONS FLOOD TONGA'S MIND, SHAME IS THE LEAST OF THEM — IN BARBARIC LEMURIA, IN THAT BRUTAL AGE, THE RAPE OF A WOMAN IS OF NO MORE CONSEQUENCE THAN THE THEFT OF A LOAF OF BREAD. AND, THOUGH, EVEN AS A SLAVE, SHE HOLDS HERSELF TO A HIGHER STANDARD, INDEED, A WARRIOR'S STANDARD, STILL SHE HAS NO ROOM FOR SHAME...

ZHU ZHAAARVIS!! I'M GOING TO RIP YOUR GUTS OUT!! I'M GOING TO RIP YOUR PALTRY MAN-PARTS OFF AND STUFF THEM DOWN YOUR FAT NECK!!

SKRAKK

...NO, THE EMOTIONS WHIRLING ABOUT HER MIND CONGEAL INTO ONLY ONE — PURE RAGE!!

BUT EVEN HER SUPER-HUMAN STRENGTH CANNOT BREAK THESE CHAINS, AS SHE WELL KNOWS — SUDDEN NOISES FROM OUTSIDE WHIP TONGA'S EYES AROUND...!

CLANK JINGLE KRAK KRAK

TONGA, MY LOVE! THANK THE NINETEEN GODS — I HEARD YOUR SHOUTS, AND I CAME, I-I

—I'VE COME TO RESCUE YOU!!

JINGLE

I'VE THE KEYS TO YOUR FETTERS, MY LOVE - BUT WE MUST HASTEN - I BRIBED A GUARD, BUT I DON'T KNOW...
BY TIANDRA'S TITTIES, I AM GLAD TO SEE YOU, TALOS! BUT, HOW...?
AFTER ZHU GAVE YOU THAT WINE - I SUPPOSE IT WAS DRUGGED, EH? - AND TOOK YOU OFF, I DECIDED TO FOLLOW AT A DISCREET DISTANCE, FOR I TRUSTED HIM NOT, AND MY HEART BURNS FOR YOU, MY GODDESS! ...AH, THIS IS THE KEY! THERE... SO! I FOLLOWED YOU THROUGH A MUCKLE OF ROOMS...
...AND WHEN I CAUGHT UP HE WAS EASING YOU DOWN ONTO A DIVAN, FOR YOU WERE IN A FAINT FROM THE DRUGGED WINE! I WAS ABOUT TO DRAW BLADE AND ACCOST THE VILLAIN WHEN I HEARD A NOISE - THE TRAMP OF MARCHING FEET! BARE-LY IN TIME DID I SLIP BE-HIND A DRAPERY...
"...FOR A SQUAD OF ZHU'S MERCENARY GUARDSMEN HAD ARRIVED FROM SOME OTHER PASSAGE - ZHU'S VILLA RIVALS THE VERY PALACE OF THE SARK, BY GORM! - AND I HEARD ZHU ORDER THEM TO TAKE YOU TO THE COMPOUND, AND THERE CHAIN YOU IN THE GAOL-HOUSE..."
I HEARD HIM ADJURE THEM THAT THEY SHOULD NOT MOLEST YOU IN ANY WAY, UNDER PENALTIES MOST SEVERE - THEN I NOTICED AMONG THEM A YOUNG OFFICER OF MY ACQUAINTANCE, A GAMBLING AND DRINKING COMRADE... THERE! THAT ONE'S OFF...!
HMMM...
...WELL, I MANAGED TO FOLLOW THEM HERE TO THE COMPOUND AND THE GAOL-HOUSE, EVADING DISCOVERY - HERE, I SPOKE TO MY FRIEND, WHO, BEING DEEPLY IN DEBT TO THE GAMB-LING HOUSES, WAS EASY TO BRIBE...
...SO, I GOT THE KEYS FROM HIM! NO DOUBT HE IS SADDLING A KROTER RIGHT THIS MOM- MMMF!
?
NOW, WHERE'S ZHU ZHARVIS? WAIT!! THOSE KEYS!! I KNOW THOSE KEYS!! THEY BELONG TO BORTHUS! QUICK, WE MUST UNLOCK THE ARMORY! COME!!

THE ARMORY? BUT WAIT, MY SWEET! WHY MUST WE GO TO THE ARMORY? LET US, JUST YOU AND I...
HUSH TALOS! FIRST I MUST STOP HERE AT THE SLAVE BARRACKS AND SEE MY COMRADES - HSSST! IT'S ME, TONGA - AWAKEN!!
TONGA!! WE THOUGHT YOU GONE FOR GOOD!
TONGA, THINKING TO WAKE HER SLEEPING COMRADES, IS SOMEWHAT SURPRISED TO FIND THEM ALL FULLY AWAKE AND ON THEIR FEET...!
BORTHUS CAME TO US TONIGHT, STAGGERING DRUNK AND ENRAGED AS A BULL-ZAMPH IN RUT! HE SAID HE LEARNED ZHU'S PLAN - HE LEARNED THAT ZHU PLOTTED ALL ALONG TO SELL YOU TO THE PIRATE KING OF TARAKUS, FOR A SACK OF GEMS WORTH A SARK'S RANSOM!
AYE, BORTHUS SAY PIRATE KING THINK HE CAN TAME TONGA- BLUG-NUG LAUGH!
WELL, ZHU ZHARVIS WON'T BE LAUGHING - I VOW THIS TO YOU, MY FRIENDS, ZHU ZHARVIS SHALL END HIS LIFE ON MY BLADE TONIGHT! I GO NOW TO THE ARMORY!
TONGA, YOU HAVE BORTHUS'S KEYS! FREE US!! WHEN ZHU BETRAYED YOU, HE BETRAYED ALL OF US! DON'T DO THIS ALONE - DON'T THROW YOUR LIFE AWAY! LET US AID YOU IN YOUR VENGEANCE!
AYE!
AYE!! FREE US TONGA!!
AYE!!
AYE!
AYE!
NO, MY FRIENDS! I AM FREE NOW - YOU ARE NOT! THINK OF THE TERRIBLE PUNISHMENTS FOR SLAVES WHO REVOLT!
THE NINETEEN HELP ME - I'VE STARTED A SLAVE REVOLT!
HA! NONE OF THAT TALK NOW - LET US INTO THE ARMORY AND LET THEM METE OUT THEIR PUNISHMENTS THEN!!
TONGA, I, THE MIGHTY GOTHRID, WOULD FOLLOW YOU THROUGH THE VERY GATES OF THE SEVEN HELLS! THIS YOU KNOW! NOW FREE US!!
AYE!!
AYE!!
BLUG-NUG WANNA KILL SOMEBODY FOR TONGA! BLUG-NUG KILL EVERYBODY FOR TONGA! TONGA JUST SAY SO, BLUG-NUG KILL!!
BOWING TO THE INEVITABLE, TONGA FREES THE GLADIATORS, AND THEY STALK THROUGH THE NIGHTED COMPOUND TO THE ARMORY, HER COMRADES FOREMOST...
AH, BY IORGAZON AND BY THAMUNGAZOTH!! THIS IS NOT WHAT I WANTED! THIS COULD RUIN EVERYTHING!!
...FOLLOWED BY A DISTRESSED TALOS TSAR AND THE BULK OF ZHU ZHARVIS' COMPANY OF FIGHTERS - NOTWITHSTANDING A FEW HANGERS-BACK, FOR THIS WAS INDEED A DESPERATE VENTURE!

INSIDE THE WELL AND FULLY STOCKED ARMORY THE WARRIORS ARM THEMSELVES, FOR ONCE FREE TO PICK AND CHOOSE THEIR GEAR AS THEY SEE FIT...
NOT GOING WITH JUST A SHORT SWORD AND BUCKLER, EH TONGA?
DON'T WORRY, WHAT EVER WEAPON TONGA PUTS HER HAND TO WILL SPILL BLOOD BY THE GALLON!
OOH! OOH! OOH! OOH! OOH! OOH!
WHY LIMIT MYSELF TO JUST ONE SWORD, BROBDINA? AS I SEE IT, THE RULES HAVE CHANGED!
AS THEY EXIT THE ARMORY THEY COME UPON A GROUP OF ZHU ZHARVIS' GUARDSMEN-APPARENTLY ENJOYING TONGA'S CELEBRATION!
THEY'VE BEEN HAVING A GOOD CAROUSE AT YOUR PARTY - TIME TO WAKE UP AND DIE, BOYS!
HAH! HAVE AT 'EM COMRADES!!
OH GODS! FORM UP! FORM UP!!
GULP
GORM'S BALLS! IT'S THE GLADIATORS- ARMED TO THE TEETH!!
THE GUARDS MAKE SHORT, IF BLOODY, WORK FOR THE GLADIATORS...
NOW TO THE VILLA, AND THAT SLIMY UNZA, ZHU ZHARVIS!!
HOWEVER, THE CLASH OF ARMS HAS ALERTED MORE OF THE MERCENARY GUARDS, AND STEEL RINGS OUT AGAIN AS THE WARRIORS CLOSE WITH THIS MUCH MORE SOBER SQUAD- THEN, LIKE A THUNDER-BOLT, A MADLY HACKING AND HEWING FIGURE CRASHES INTO THEIR RANKS - BORTHUS!
TONGA!!
ZHU GOES TO HIS SPECIAL CHAMBER - YOU KNOW THE ONE
BORTHUS!!
AAARRGGGH!
GO FIND ZHU ZHARVIS! THESE SCUM WILL PAY FOR BORTHUS' LIFE!
AYE, TONGA, AND GIVE HIM ONE FOR OLD GOTHRID!
THANK YOU, MY FRIENDS!

ZHU ZHARVIS!!
CHRNK
I'M COMING, ZHU ZHARVIS!
DRAW YOUR BLADE, ZHU ZHARVIS!
DAMN YOU, YOU SLUT!! I'LL KILL YOU!!
EEEYAARRGH!!
EARRGKK
COME, TALOS - THERE'S NOUGHT HERE BUT WORTHLESS CARRION...
UNNOTICED BY THE BROODING TONGA, THE YOUNG NOBLE MAN HAS QUICKLY REMOVED AN OBJECT FROM THE GHASTLY CORPSE, NEARLY LOSING HIS GORGE IN THE PROCESS - BEFORE SCAMPERING AFTER HER...!

REALIZING THEIR ONLY CHANCE FOR SURVIVAL IS TO GET AS FAR AWAY FROM TSARGOL AS POSSIBLE, THE NOW FUGITIVE GLADIATORS RAID ZHU ZHARVIS' EXCELLENT STABLES FOR MOUNTS AND PROVISIONS...

...THEY THEN UTILIZE A LITTLE KNOWN GATE IN THE CITY WALL, WHICH ABUTS THE COMPOUND, TO FLEE THE CITY AND HEAD OUT TO THE COUNTRYSIDE, AS DAWN BREAKS OVER OLD LEMURIA...

...THOUGH ALL ARE WARRIORS OF SPECTACULAR ABILITIES, A FIGHTING UNIT THEY ARE NOT, AND DISAGREEMENTS ABOUT THEIR FUTURE PLANS SOON ARISE...!

...FINALLY THEY SCATTER—SOME TO SEEK THEIR FAR-OFF HOMELANDS, SOME TO JOIN, OR BECOME, BANDITS, WHO HAUNT THESE HINTERLANDS... TONGA AND HER COMRADES, ALONG WITH TALOS TSAR, ARE LEFT TO THEIR OWN DEVICES!

AS THEY REST AND HOLD COUNCIL, TALOS TSAR SEEKS TO CONVINCE TONGA TO ABIDE AT HIS COUNTRY ESTATE A WHILE, WHERE SHE'D BE SAFE— BUT TONGA WANTS TO BRING ALONG HER COMRADES, AT WHICH TALOS BALKS, SHOWING GREAT RELUCTANCE, AND STARTS TO STAMMER EXCUSES UNTIL BROBDINA SPEAKS UP...

HOW'S THIS? WE'LL REST A BIT HERE, THEN SCOUT BACK A WAYS, WATCHING FOR PURSUIT, LAY A FALSE TRAIL, SET A TRAP...

OH, IT'S DISGUSTING, IS IT? THAT'S NOT WHAT YOU SAID WHEN FIRST WE MET, GOTHRID! WHEN I SPANKED YOU ALL ABOUT THE ARENA?~HAHAHA~ ALRIGHT MY FRIENDS, FOR A DAY OR TWO!

QUIT YOUR SPUTTERING, TALOS TSAR! WE ARE GRATEFUL FOR YOUR HELP, AND WE CAN TAKE A HINT, EH BLUG?

HELP? WHAT HEL—OOOF—

AYE, THEN WE CAN RETURN TO TALOS TSAR'S VILLA IN A DAY OR TWO, SHOUTING A WARNING SO AS NOT TO SEE ANYTHING DISGUSTING!

THOUGH TALOS IS SURELY HANDSOME ENOUGH, HE'S A BIT OF A WEAKLING! HOPE I DON'T HURT THE POOR BOY! ~SIGH~

TALOS TSAR IS SOMEWHAT MOLLIFIED, THOUGH THERE IS A PECULIAR GLEAM IN HIS EYE, WHICH GOES UNNOTICED BY THE SPIRITED WARRIOR BAND...!

22

Panel 1:
AFTER DETERMINING THEIR BEARINGS AND DIRECTIONS THE GROUP SPLITS UP, WITH **TONGA AND TALOS TSAR** TRAVELING BACK COUNTRY TRAILS TO AVOID ANY PURSUIT...

AYE, SADLY THERE ARE FEW OF US TSARS LEFT, SO WE DON'T REQUIRE THE ENTIRE COMPLEX OF BUILDINGS IN WHICH TO LIVE...

...BUT WE **LIVE WELL** HERE, TONGA! I'LL MAKE BOOK THAT ONCE YOU'VE SAMPLED LIFE HERE AT **HOUSE TSAR**, WHY, YOU WON'T BE **ABLE TO LEAVE**! AH, OUR EVER-VIGILANT SERVANTS HAVE NOTED OUR ARRIVAL!

BY THE NINETEEN GODS, TALOS! IT'S LIKE A GREAT OLD PALACE! BUT THE JUNGLE SEEKS TO RECLAIM IT!

...THEY ARRIVE AT A **MASSIVE** STONE BUILT COMPLEX, SPRAWLING IN HALF RUINED GRANDEUR...

Panel 2:
WELCOME HOME LORD TALOS! WE HAD HOPED YOUR **TRIP** TO THE CITY WOULD END SATISFACTORILY--

YES, WELCOME LORD TALOS - WE SEE YOU HAVE BROUGHT HOME THE ER--, GUEST--IS SHE...?

Panel 3:
SHE IS THE **LADY TONGA**, OUR GUEST, AND WE WILL SPARE **NO EFFORTS** IN SEEING TO HER COMFORTS, NOR TO MINE, FOR WE HAVE ENDURED A MOST TRYING TIME!

Panel 4:
OF COURSE MY LORD, HOWSOEVER, MIGHT I REMIND MY LORD OF THE **UPCOMING** RITES?

HAVE NO FEAR ON **THAT SCORE**—ALL IS IN ORDER! NOW, YOUR TASKS ARE TO **DRAW HOT BATHS**, SET ASIDE **SUITABLE RAIMENT**, AND PREPARE **FOOD AND REFRESHMENTS**!

Panel 5:
VERY WELL, MY LORD, AND WE WILL **SEE TO THE BEASTS** AS WELL—WE ONLY WISH TO AVOID ANY UNWONTED--DIFFICULTIES--

Panel 6:
THERE'LL BE NO DIFFICULTIES! NOW GET ABOUT YOUR DUTIES! WE ARE VERY TIRED AND HUNGRY--DO NOT DALLY!!

23

DESPITE THEIR STRANGE RECEPTION, TONGA LETS HERSELF RELAX INTO THE UNACCUSTOMED, AND UNEXPECTED FROM THE OUTSIDE, LUXURIOUS SURROUNDINGS, AS SHE BATHES, EATS, DRINKS WINE, RESTS, EATS MORE AND DRINKS MORE, UNTIL THE DAY PASSES INTO NIGHT, AND NIGHT INTO DAY, AND ANY MEMORY OF STRANGE SERVANTS AND "UPCOMING RITES" IS WASHED AWAY — THOUGH THE SERVANTS ARE THERE, WATCHING...

...SHE ALLOWS TALOS TSAR HIS REWARD FOR HER RESCUE, AND FINDS HIM AN ENTHUSIASTIC LOVER, THOUGH SOMEWHAT OVERLY DRAMATIC, AS THOUGH ALWAYS AWARE OF THE FIGURE HE CUT..!

BUT SHE ENJOYS HERSELF, AND HIM, AND SHE PARTIES! THEY DRINK MORE WINE, AND OTHER INTOXICATING NECTARS, THEY INHALE THE SMOKE OF THE GREEN LOTUS BUDS...

...AND TONGA FURTHER RELAXES INTO A STATE OF DELICIOUSLY VOLUPTUOUS LANGUOR...

...AND SO PROFOUND IS THIS LANGUID STATE THAT IT FEELS AS IF MORE THAN MERE SEX, DRINK, AND DRUGS MUST BE AT IT'S ROOT — AND SO IT MAY TRULY BE, FOR TONGA FAILS TO NOTICE THE SERVANTS OF TALOS TSAR, GLARING MALEVOLENTLY AT HER FROM HIDDEN CORNERS AND ALCOVES, THEIR FINGERS WEAVING COMPLEX FIGURES, THEIR LIPS CEASELESSLY MUTTERING, AS IF SPEAKING SPELLS, OR CURSES... BUT UNSEEING, TONGA FINALLY DRIFTS INTO A DEEP SLUMBER....!

...IT SEEMS TO TONGA THAT SHE IS SLUGGISHLY FLOATING- FLOATING TOWARDS AWARENESS...
...OPENING HER EYES, HER MIND FAILS TO GRASP WHAT IT IS SHE SEES...
...NOW STRANGE SENSATIONS, HARD STONE PRESSING INTO HER, ROUGH IRON RESTRAINING HER, MAKE THEMSELVES FELT...
WHA- YAMATH'S FLAMING BUNGHOLE! WHAT IS THIS?! WHO THE FUTTERING HELL... ...GORM'S BLOOD!
...AND CONCSIOUSNESS RETURNS...!
SHE IS ENTIRELY TOO SPIRITED- THE SPELLS WE CAST SHOULD HAVE TURNED HER INTO A QUIVERING MASS OF FEAR, BUT THERE IS A FORCE ABOUT HER THAT TRANSCENDS THE MERE MORTAL...
YES, THIS YOUNG FOOL, BEING INFATUATED WITH THIS BELLOWING WARRIOR WENCH, HAS PUT INTO JEOPARDY THE CALLING FORTH OF OGZUTHU! BUT THERE IS NAUGHT TO DO BUT GO FORWARD!
AND I TELL YOU, I CAN HANDLE HER!
YES, YOU DO... BUT LET US PERFORM A FINAL MIND BLAST, TO WEAKEN HER BODY, AND THUS SOFTEN HER SPIRIT!
YES, THAT MAY BRING HER CLOSER TO DESPAIR- WENCH! LOOK YOU INTO OUR EYES! YOU CANNOT ESCAPE YOUR FATE! YOU WILL GIVE IN TO PAIN AND DESPAIR!
NO! NO! N-- AAARRGH
OOAH OGZUTHU, NA KANU MEK! OOAH OGZUTHU, NA KANU MEK! OOAH OGZUTHU, NA KANU MEK!
AN INDETERMINABLE TIME LATER, TONGA AGAIN FIGHTS HER WAY TO CONCSIOUSNESS...
AYE, WE TSARS ARE FEW, BUT WE LIVE WELL BECAUSE WE SERVE OUR GODS FAITHFULLY, DO YOU SEE?
OH!
OOAH OGZUTHU, NA KANU MEK!
OOAH OGZUTHU, NA KANU MEK!
WELL, YOU MIGHT CALL THEM DEMONS- BUT WHATEVER YOU CALL THEM, THEY REQUIRE THE OCCASIONAL SACRIFICE! HA HA HA HA HA
WH-WHAT? N-NO!
TO BE CONTINUED...

FREEDOM FIGHT V

Though **Talos Tsar** feels he may **easily dominate Tonga**, neither he nor his "**servants**" have reckoned the full extent of her **super-human vitality** — nor her outrage at being used in this manner! Before ever Talos's **lance hits home**, the golden warrior maid erupts in a paroxysm of **writhing fury**...

"AH, BY **THAMUNGAZOTH**, YOUR MAGNIFICENT B—OW! HEY, HOLD STILL— UGH! YOU **BITCH**! I—CAN'T— AAH!"

"**FUTTER YOU**, YOU PERVERTED LITTLE **DEMON LOVING CATAMITE**!! YOU'LL NEVER GET YOUR PATHETIC LITTLE **PRONG** INTO ME AGAIN!!"

"OOAH OGZUTHU, NA KANU MEK! OOAH OGZUTHU, NA KANU MEK! OOAH OGZUTHU, NA KANU MEK!"

...AND TALOS IS LIKE A MAN WHO, FOR SOME REASON, IS TRYING TO **RAPE AN INFURIATED SHE-VANDAR**, THE 12-FOOT LONG BLACK LEMURIAN LIONESS, ONLY **PARTIALLY HELD IN CHECK** BY HER CHAINS!

"...OOAH OGZUTHU,...**LOOK**! POOR **OGZUTHU** MATERIALIZES ONLY **FAINTLY**! THE YOUNG FOOL HAS **FAILED IN HIS TASK**! THIS WARRIOR WENCH CANNOT BE DOMINATED BY SUCH AS TALOS TSAR! **SHE DOES NOT DESPAIR! SHE DOES NOT FEAR!** AND OGZUTHU **NEEDS** DESPAIR! HE **NEEDS** FEAR!"

"HALOO THE HOUSE! IS ANYBODY **NAKED** IN THERE?"

"YES, I SENSE EVEN NOW THE CALLOW YOUTH APPROACHES HIS CLIMAX, AND HAS YET TO ACHIEVE **PENETRATION**! DAMN THE **WEAKLING**! WHY DID HE NOT BRING BACK SOME TREMBLING SERVING MAID, NOT THIS— EH?"

"AH, GODS! OH NO! OH NO!" "YOU BASTARD!"

"WHAT IS THAT?!"

Panel 1: QUICKLY! WE MUST DESTROY THESE INTRUDERS! OGZUTHU MUST COMPLETE HIS MATERIALIZATION!

Panel 2: SKREEEEK!

Panel 3:
- GORM'S IRON YARD! WHAT MANNER OF HELLSPAWN BE THESE?
- NO MATTER, IF THEY STAND BETWEEN US AND TONGA, THEN THEY DIE BY OUR STEEL! AT THEM, BROTHERS!
- AAK! NO ONE CALL BLUG-NUG UGLY FROM NOW ON!

Panel 4: MEANWHILE, BACK AT THE SACRIFICIAL CHAMBER...
- AH... OW! OH WAIT OH WAIT— OH GODS! OH... UUUUUHHH! YOU'RE CRUSHING MEEEEEEE!! GASP!
- HAH! YOU LIMP PRONGED LITTLE UNZA! YOU'LL NEVER GET THERE, YOU WEAK BELLIED ROPE PUSHER!!

YOU SLIMY, SLIPPERY BASTARD! YOU STILL CAN'T FIND IT! ≷GASP≶ DAMN THESE CHAINS! ARRAAAGH!!
AH GODS!! HERE IT COMES— O-OH-OHHH! ≷GASP≶PUFF-PUFF≶ OH, T-TONGA, YOU BITCH!! ≷GASP≶
THERE!! I FELT A LINK GIVE WAY! I'VE GOT TO PUT ALL I'VE GOT INTO IT NOW!!
HUH?
AAAAAAAAAAHHHHHH!!!
AS TONGA SCREAMS IN AN ALL-OUT EFFORT TO BREAK HER CHAINS, A STUPEFIED TALOS TSAR WONDERS AT HOW HIS CLUMSY, LESS THAN STELLAR PERFORMANCE HAS DRIVEN HER TO SUCH A VIOLENT CLIMAX...
≷GASP≶ O, ≷GASP≶ ≷PUFF≶ MIGHTY OGZUTHU, ≷PUFF PUFF≶ HERE IS YOUR OFFERING, ≷WHEW≶ SOFTENED UP AS YOU ≷PUFF≶ P-PREFER... EH?
HAAAHH!!
...BUT HE BLITHELY ACCEPTS THAT SUCH IS THE CASE, AND HE HAS DONE HIS PART FOR OGZUTHU— BUT THEN...
GACK!!
THE ONLY THING SOFTENED UP AROUND HERE IS YOU, TALOS TSAR! YOUR PET WILL HAVE TO GO THROUGH YOU TO GET ME, YOU UNZA-BASTARD!!
GORM, MY HEAD REELS— MY STRENGTH FADES! BUT I'LL KILL THIS LITTLE BASTARD IF IT'S THE LAST THING I DO!

AT THIS MOMENT TONGA'S COMRADES COME RUSHING DOWN THE STEPS, BEARING BLOODY WEAPONS AND MINOR WOUNDS THEMSELVES...
BY GORM, ANOTHER DEMON- TONGA!! WHAT IS IT DOING TO TONGA?!
AVANGRA'S TESTICLES! WHAT EVER THAT THING IS, IT'S GOING TO DIE!!
TONGA FALL BACK! TONGA HURT! BLUG-NUG KILL DEMON-THING!!
=GASP= HER GRIP, IT- =GASP= IT LOOSENS..!
NO-USE... CAN'T-HOLD-ON... =UUHH=
...THE ENRAGED BATTLERS CHARGE THE DEMON, NOT REALIZING TALOS TSAR'S PART IN THE DRAMA- AND HE SCUTTLES PAST THEM, RUNNING UP THE STEPS IN FRANTIC FLIGHT..!

BY GORM, I THOUGHT DEMONS TO BE NEAR IRON HARD!
WELL, THIS ONE'S ABOUT AS HARD AS A TSARGOLIAN CHEESE SITTING IN THE SUN!
HEY! SAVE SOME CHEESE FOR BLUG-NUG!
UNBEKNOWNST TO THE THREE HEROES, OGZUTHU'S SOFTNESS IS THE RESULT OF TALOS TSAR'S FAILURE TO CONSUMATE HIS ATTEMPTED RAPE OF TONGA, THUS THE DEMON NEVER QUITE FULLY MATERIALIZED!
ENOUGH OF THE MONSTER- TONGA REGAINS HER SENSES! BROBDINA, COME CHOP OFF THESE CHAINS!
OOOHH- MY FRIENDS, YOU'RE HERE! YOU SLEW THE DEMON! MY THANKS!
AFTER THEY LITERALLY HACK AND SMASH THE MONSTROUS THING INTO PIECES, EACH PIECE AND BIT TURNS INTO SMOKE AND SINKS INTO CREVICES IN FLOOR AND WALLS - NOT TRULY DEAD, BUT RETURNING TO SOME REGION OF THE SEVEN HELLS ...!
30

A MOMENT OF CAREFUL AX WORK AND TONGA IS FREE OF HER BONDS...
GODS!! TALOS TSAR!!
LEND ME YOUR KNIFE, GOTHRID!
TALOS TSAR!! I'M COMING FOR YOU!
DAMN YOU, YOU BITCH! YOU'VE RUINED EVERYTHING!
I'M NO MEAN SWORDS-MAN, DESPITE WHAT YOU MAY THINK- AND YOU ARE A NAKED WENCH ARMED WITH BUT A KNIFE...
...SO I'M GOING TO KILL YOU, YOU FUTTERING BITCH!!
AAAHH!!
NO!!

UUUHH
OOHHH... OOOoFF
AAAIIIIEEEMMFFFGGRGL
SO, TALOS TSAR MUST OF BEEN ENMESHED IN DEMON WORSHIP AFTER ALL, JUST AS THE GOSS-IPS ALWAYS INSISTED...
AYE, HE WAS THAT...
... BUT HE'S PAID IN FULL FOR WHAT HE TRIED TO DO TO ME, AND FOR WHAT HE DID TO ALL THE OTHER POOR GIRLS HE LURED OUT HERE...
OH, THAT WAS TALOS TSAR PAYING IN FULL WHAT BUG-NUG HEARD!
THANKS FOR THE LOAN OF YOUR KNIFE GOTHRID, IT CAME IN HANDY!
HA HA I DON'T BLAME YOU- BY GORM'S IRONSHAFT I FEEL REALLY GOOD RIGHT NOW, LIKE A WIEGHT'S BEEN LIFTED FROM MY SHOULDERS! LET'S SEE WHAT WE CAN LOOT FROM THIS PLACE!
TSARGOL IS WAY TOOHOT FOR US NOW, SO WE'LL NEED TO HIT THE TRAIL SOON...
... BUT FIRST, I NEED TO BATHE AGAIN, AND RID MY-SELF OF TALOS TSAR'S FOULNESS AND FILTH! DO YOU KNOW THIS PLACE HAS HOT, AND COLD, WATER THAT COMES WITH THE TURN OF A HANDLE? DOUBT-LESS MORE MAGIC!
AH WELL, IF THAT KNIFE'S BEEN WHERE I THINK IT'S BEEN, THEN YOU CAN KEEP IT!

DAWN FINDS THE WARRIORS RESTED, PROVISIONED AND ON THE TRAIL— **TONGA** VOICES HER IDEAS FOR THE FUTURE...

MY COMRADES, IT SEEMS TO ME THAT THE **PIRATE KING OF TARAKUS** IS THE CAUSE OF ALL THE TROUBLE WE'VE ENDURED...

...SO I SUGGEST WE GO TO SEA, WITH A FAST BOAT AND A TRUSTY CREW AND RAID THE RAIDERS!

RELIEVE 'EM OF THEIR ILL GOTTEN GAINS, AND STING THAT BASTARD LIKE A WASP IN HIS TUNIC!

WELL, TO DO ALL THAT WOULD BE FINE, BUT IT WOULD TAKE **CONSIDERABLE WEALTH** TO FIT OUT AND CREW A SHIP— WE'RE PROVISIONED, BUT THERE WERE PRETTY SLIM PICKINGS AT THE VILLA OTHERWISE...

HEH

HEH HEH HEH HA HA HA

HA HA HA HA HA HA HA HA HA

33

HERE GOTHRID, CATCH! BUT DON'T SPILL ANYTHING!
AND MAKE SURE YOU THROW IT BACK, YOU BASTARD!
HOLY TIANDRA'S TITTIES! THIS IS A FORTUNE IN GEMSTONES! IT'S A SARK'S RANSOM!
THAT WAS TO BE MY BRIDE PRICE! PAID TO ZHU ZHARVIS BY THAT BASTARD PIRATE KING OF TARAKUS- BUT ZHU WAS TREACHEROUS, FOR I WAS NO LONGER HIS TO SELL, WAS I?
I FIGURED OUT THAT TALOS TSAR LOOTED ZHU'S CORPSE FOR THAT BAG OF JEWELS, THINKING TO KEEP IT FOR HIMSELF! WELL, AS IT TURNED OUT, HE LOST THAT ONE, AND ANOTHER ONE WHICH HE WAS VERY ATTACHED TO, AS WELL!
NOW, TOSS IT BACK, YOU BASTARD!
THE END

TIMAIOS PRESS

We publish thought-provoking, modern and classic literature for those who are interested in speculative fiction and fantasy, in the history of science, philosophy and ideas—books for the general public, as well as students and teachers.

www.timaiospress.com

BOOKS BY AND ABOUT:

S.T. Joshi — G.K. Chesterton — Lady Cavendish — Epicure — Lucretius — Atomism — Francis Bacon — H.P. Lovecraft — Camille Flammarion — Diogenes Laërtius — Emanuel Swedenborg — Erasmus Darwin — E.T.A. Hoffmann — Plato — Andrew Crosse — Edgar Allan Poe — And others.